Astonished, she looked up at him. A mistake, that. The gaze that met hers belonged to the dangerous man he warned of. She stared, captivated by that face. His vague smile stirred her.

Was he going to kiss her? Was he that bold? It appeared so. The very notion had her pulse quickening.

What to do? She must not allow it, yet—she could not bring herself to move away, or utter some arch reply. She just waited, and the waiting itself affected the air and the garden and the space between them. She experienced a most shocking excitement.

It seemed a long time they stood there, gazes locked, until the waiting turned almost painful. An outrageous idea entered her mind—to stretch up and kiss him first.

HIS WICKED REPUTATION

MADELINE HUNTER

JOVE BOOKS, NEW YORK

THE BERKLEY PUBLISHING GROUP
Published by the Penguin Group
Penguin Group (USA) LLC
375 Hudson Street, New York, New York 10014

USA • Canada • UK • Ireland • Australia • New Zealand • India • South Africa • China

penguin.com

A Penguin Random House Company

HIS WICKED REPUTATION

A Jove Book / published by arrangement with the author

Jove Books are published by The Berkley Publishing Group.
JOVE® is a registered trademark of Penguin Group (USA) LLC.
The "J" design is a trademark of Penguin Group (USA) LLC.

For information, address: The Berkley Publishing Group,
a division of Penguin Group (USA) LLC,
375 Hudson Street, New York, New York 10014.

ISBN: 978-0-515-15516-7

PUBLISHING HISTORY
Jove mass-market edition / March 2015

PRINTED IN THE UNITED STATES OF AMERICA

10   9   8   7   6   5   4   3   2   1

Text design by Kelly Lipovich.

HIS WICKED
REPUTATION

CHAPTER 1

It was well past noon when the maid delivered the breakfast tray to Hendrika's opulent bedroom. Gareth Fitzallen finished reading the final drafts of a complicated business contract while the servant threw back the curtains and opened the window.

Hendrika purred, stretched, and rubbed her eyes. Gareth collected the vellum sheets he had spread over her body, the better to keep them organized. The maid plumped up an assortment of pillows. Hendrika sat up and rested her back against them, exposing her lush, naked body to the maid, to Gareth, and possibly to the family who owned the tall, narrow house across the canal.

"Do you require anything else?" the maid asked. Her downcast eyes still allowed a gaze that rested on

Gareth's bare chest. She glanced up into his eyes for a second through her lashes. Her nostrils flared. The maid was becoming a problem. He did nothing to encourage her, but inevitably Hendrika would see one of the sly smiles or hot looks sent his way.

Hendrika shooed the woman away, then poured coffee into the two cups. "What are all these documents?"

"The shipment to England from Honfleur. We have finalized the terms of the sale. The count's factor and I need only sign. And you, too, of course."

Although fair like many of the residents of Amsterdam, Hendrika's eyes could grow very dark when she became thoughtful. They turned black now. "You are sure your brother the duke will guarantee your payment? Elbert would turn over in his grave if he knew I took this cargo from one foreign port to another on credit alone."

He set down his coffee on the tray, gently brushed a long lock of her curly blond hair aside, and bent to plant a distracting kiss on the full globe of her breast. "Of all that we have shared this last month, I suspect your late husband would find our partnership in this shipment the least of it."

Strong fingers stretched through his hair, then held his head in place, encouraging him to distress Elbert's ghost all the more. She squirmed, almost upsetting the tray, and giggled in the guttural way she had. Then she pushed him away and returned to her breakfast, her breasts now heavy and hard and their tips protuberant. She buttered some bread. "Which jam do you want?"

"Cherry."

Two newspapers had come up with the tray. She took the Dutch one and gave him the one out of Paris. He munched his bread while reading the French political news.

Suddenly a grip closed on his arm. Hendrika exclaimed something in Dutch.

"Gareth, my love," she whispered after taking a deep breath. "Look at this here. Can you read it? Should I translate?"

He took the paper. She stroked his arm while he read the short notice she indicated. Five words in he barely noticed her there.

"Zeus." His own breath caught and held before he exhaled.

His half brother Percival, the fourth Duke of Aylesbury, was dead. He had died more than a week earlier. Suddenly. Abruptly. Unexpectedly.

"This is shocking. He was not a sickly man. Far from it. Young still, too. Only thirty-three."

"What is meant, the inquiry is open?" she asked softly.

"It is just a formality. I must go back, of course. Immediately. I need to help the others, and—"

"Of course. Of course," she cooed sympathetically.

He turned the paper's sheets until he found the schedule of packets from Amsterdam to London. Cutlery and china clinked while Hendrika returned to her meal. He set the paper aside on top of the stack of vellum.

"We will need to sign these contracts today, now."

He gestured to them. "I will send a message to the lawyers and arrange a meeting."

She examined her bread while she slathered jam on it. "With your brother dead, is that wise? His name swayed the count to extend credit to you. It swayed me too. That and other things."

He stretched out beside her and helped himself to a bite from her bread. "There is now another half brother who is the duke, one who loves me even more. God forbid he drops dead as well; there is yet another in line. We never run out of them. Nothing has changed." He gave her a reassuring kiss.

She made the kiss a long one, then looked into his eyes. "But you will leave now, and I do not think you will be back. So I must ensure I am paid one way or another."

She dipped her short, blunt knife into one of the little blue and white pots, then smeared the garnet jam around her breast. "Cherry, I think you said you prefer this morning." She took the pot in one hand, and the knife in the other, and gestured for him to remove the tray. Carefully, slowly, she drew circles of jam around her other breast, dabbed two large globs on her nipples, then painted streaks down her body.

"Here, too, I think." She spread her plump thighs, and painted lower yet. "Oh, yes, and here. You must be your wicked best this morning, so I do not worry about your credit today."

He let her finish as she wanted. Then he braced himself above her and began licking the jam, so she would think about nothing at all for a very long time.

CHAPTER 2

Eva hitched her clumsy bundle higher under her arm. A snapping breeze threatened to unveil the object shrouded in old burlap. She stopped to tuck the coarse fabric closer all around the heavily sculpted plaster frame. When she had chosen this painting, she had failed to consider how hard it would be to hide and carry it.

While she fussed with her burden, she kept one eye on a figure moving on the road. Another stranger. With nearby Birmingham's growth, and with all the people displaced by the failed harvests, strangers moving through the countryside hardly merited note. Yet this one raised a tiny alarm, for reasons she could not name. Maybe he moved too slowly for a man with someplace to go. In fact, it looked as if he had actually slowed so he would not pass the house's drive before she reached its end.

This was not the first time she found herself wondering about a stranger. Last week there had been another one, this time in town. Only she was sure she also saw him later, on the lane near her house.

She scolded herself for inventing ghosts. Her current mission made her nervous, that was all. She should not have this painting, and guilt made her overcautious.

She walked on. She glanced back at the house she had just left as she approached the point where its drive met the road. Years ago, before half the trees lining this private lane died, most likely one could not see much besides chimneys from this spot. Now the derelict condition of the building was visible to all. More a large hunting lodge than a proper manor house, it consisted of stone wings attached to a rustic Tudor core. Thirty years ago it might have been considered haphazard in design. Now the tastemakers would think it charming.

Each time she visited, more damage could be seen. Today a whole section of garden wall had vanished, its stones no doubt pilfered to build some outbuilding on one of the nicer properties of Langdon's End. She expected to round the bend in the road one day and discover nothing more than a heap of rock.

She turned onto the road, fussing with the stupid frame, trying not to keep looking back at the man now walking behind her. Suddenly she heard something that froze her fingers. A horse approached. From the sound of its hooves, it was galloping toward her and nearing the bend in the road ahead that would bring her into view.

She quickly examined her burden to make sure nothing showed, then walked forward with long strides, hoping she appeared to be a woman going about her day's perfectly honest, completely legal, not the least untoward business. In seconds a huge black horse, its head strained against its reins and its teeth bared like a stallion out of hell, bore down on her. Hooves clamoring, breath snorting, that devil head grew larger fast.

It passed that point where its rider should have slowed upon seeing someone on the road. It just kept coming. Alarmed, she jumped aside to make way, damning the rogue who had carelessly risked her life to his whim. At that the horse reared up. Its front hooves pawed the air, and the beast let out a long, furious whinny.

Cool moisture gathered around her feet and ankles. She looked down to see she had stepped right into a deep puddle. She cursed again. Her shoes would probably be ruined.

"My sincere apologies." The voice came from on high while she lifted one foot to determine the damage. Soaked. Ruined for sure.

"It is a little late for courtesy," she snapped. She concentrated on placing her feet in such a way as to exit the puddle without stepping in it yet again. The burden she carried did not make it any easier. She could barely see over it. Perhaps if she lifted it above her head . . .

"The house distracted me. I know coming upon you so fast was inexcusable, but it appeared no one was about."

"If you had been watching the road, you would know it appeared no such way." She looked behind her to point to the other person on the road. Only he was gone. Perhaps he took a shortcut through the woods.

Her skirt proved too narrow for the long strides she needed. She had no choice except to slosh through the puddle to its edge.

A hand jutted in front of her face, grabbing for the painting. "Allow me to relieve you of this so you do not drop it."

She smacked the hand away and made her way to dry grass.

The horse panted and quivered, probably deciding whether to take a bite out of her. She looked up its considerable flank and the long legs and handsome boots that gripped it. She looked higher, up the dashing garnet riding coat to the casually tied cravat. Finally her gaze rose to the face of the man who had addressed her.

Her fury momentarily left her. It lasted no longer than a three-count, she was sure, but in that tiny pause, not only her anger ceased. Her breath did, too, and the movement of the leaves in the breeze, and perhaps even the revolution of the earth.

The rider was beautiful. No other word would do. Handsome would be too vague a description. Attractive would be inadequate. Thick black hair, dark eyes, and eyebrows that arched perfectly, all graced features both regular and precise. The only flaw, a rather wide mouth, could hardly be called a disadvantage, seeing as how it gave the man both expressive possibilities and an undeniable sensual quality.

Then again, he did not need the mouth for that. His air and manner, the very way he sat on that horse, announced he would be nothing but trouble for a woman. Of course, most women would find him too delicious to resist. She suspected he knew that. How could he not when fools like she stared gape-mouthed upon seeing him?

Those dark eyes scrutinized her as surely as she did him, only with much more amusement than she experienced in her own study. He had probably noticed that three count. She doubted he found it a novel reaction to himself.

"I have ruined your shoes. I insist that I pay for another pair."

It had been his fault and he should pay, but she reacted badly to the offer. She resented that he noticed she could ill afford the loss of the shoes. She hated that he sought to subject her to his charity.

"The only payment I ask is that you not gallop that horse on this road while you are admiring architecture. You are too easily impressed by the latter, if that house distracted you."

He turned to look at the house. "I think it handsome."

She rearranged her bundle in her arms. "On the

outside, perhaps it would appeal to those who favor sentimentality over sophistication. Inside it is derelict, however. No one has lived there in my memory, and its owner does not maintain it. It is a haven for vagrants and thieves, and the people of the local town would be glad if it burned down. Perhaps one day it will." She hoped not. That house had been very useful to her the last five years.

Hitching up her painting again, she began walking down the road. She heard the horse move. Then she felt its breath on her shoulder. She started, and almost jumped aside again.

"Won't you allow me to help you carry that? Or better yet, give you a ride to where you are going? It looks to be a heavy package, and those shoes must be uncomfortable now."

She looked back over her shoulder, up at the stunning face now marked by a winning smile. No, that mouth was no flaw. Masculine and firm, it turned him from merely beautiful to seductive. He gazed down at her warmly. Perhaps a little too warmly. That should have alarmed her anew. Instead little flutters beat inside her. It was all she could do not to blush and mew.

"No, thank you. I will manage."

"You do not have to be afraid. I promise to behave myself. I am utterly harmless."

His expression, most amused by his own words, put the lie to his reassurance. *Come with me and I will show you the most wicked delights,* those teasing eyes promised.

"I am not afraid of you, sir. Your horse, however, terrifies me. Could you keep back a bit more?"

He held back, but still followed. "Are you going to the town? It is some distance. At least a mile."

"I would not accept a ride with you, even if I had five miles to walk. Please, be on your way, and I will be on mine."

A nod of acquiescence. He turned the black beast, trotted down the lane, then halfway up the drive to the house. He then sat there looking at it. He had given up the game because something interested him more than dallying with her.

Eva looked back one more time before the bend in the road took the rider out of her view. He appeared magnificent, with the breeze blowing back his hair so his fine profile cut the sky, his gaze absorbed and pensive. If she were a good artist and not just a middling copyist, she would feature him in a grand composition full of dashing action. Instead, she painted his image on her memory.

Her ruined shoes did not bother her on the half mile to her family home. Nor did the clumsy weight of the painting. She smiled all the way. How bad can a poor spinster's day be when the most beautiful man she had ever seen in her life flirts with her?

How like Percy to let the property go to ruin. Percy had known he would never win in Chancery, so while his lawyers kept the case languishing in court, he had simply let time devalue the object of the contest.

Gareth rode out his frustration, galloping hard. By the time he handed the stallion over to a groom at an inn, the worst of his anger was gone.

The next day he rode into Coventry much recovered. He had a lot of practice at swallowing disappointment, and had learned early that if he allowed Percy to ruin his mood for days on end, he handed Percy a victory.

Besides, Percy was dead. That thought alone made the day sunnier.

He dismounted in front of an elegant house of more than average size. No ruin this, but then Percy had never been able to touch what their father had given to Mrs. Johnson. Gareth hoped that Percy's last thought had been one of fury over how neatly Father had worked that out.

Mrs. Johnson received him in her delicate drawing room. He strode over, bent, and kissed her. Her arm encircled his shoulders so the kiss became an embrace.

"It is so good to see you, Gareth. I assume you have heard the news."

He settled into a chair. "I returned as soon as I read about it, Mother. Terrible news. Just terrible."

His mother maintained a sober face, but her eyes sparkled at his ironic tone. "Yes, terrible. He was still so young. Why, what, thirty-three? So sudden and unexpected too."

"A tragedy."

"Have you been back to Merrywood yet?"

"I thought I would see you first. I will head there in the morning."

She reached over and patted his arm affectionately. He rarely had to explain much to his mother. They were of like minds, just as surely as they were of like visage. His eyes, his nose, even his mouth came from her. Had Allen Hemingford, the third Duke of Aylesbury, been less sure of her he might have suspected Gareth was not his bastard at all. Instead, he had accepted his mistress's claim, and fulfilled his contract to her.

That contract, worked out when she was eighteen, had not only provided this house, a carriage, servants, and an income for life. Being shrewd, she had also insisted her children by the duke be provided for, and be allowed to have the surname Fitzallen in the ancient way—bastard of Allen. Percy had never been able to interfere with the income Gareth received, either. The house near Langdon's End was a different matter. Aylesbury had left that to him in a codicil to his will. Percy had contested the legacy before his father was cold.

Not that the income came close to his mother's. On it, he could live as a gentleman bachelor with a decent degree of fashion. As it was, however, almost all of it went to the lawyers pleading his case in Chancery.

So he had found ways to augment it. Fortunately, he inherited his mother's shrewdness, and doing so had not been too difficult after finishing the education also provided in that contract. An eye for art had helped.

Other gentlemen might not invite him to their parties and would never introduce their sisters and daughters to him, but his blood meant they might trust him to find a buyer when they had a collection to sell. With the economy in shambles these days, a great deal of art was changing hands. It was the sort of occupation that did not reek of trade, since he did it all as a favor for everyone involved.

"You just returned, you said." Mrs. Johnson spoke while she served the coffee one of her servants had brought. She was entitled to four of them. There had been a Mr. Johnson for a short while. Perhaps as long as a week, Gareth guessed, before the man took the healthy payment made to him and sailed to America.

When the duke had met Amanda Albany, she was unmarried. An innocent. What the duke wanted was not done with unmarried girls. So he arranged a marriage for her, with an army captain by the name of Johnson. Only it was not Johnson's nuptial bed to which young Amanda Albany had gone that wedding night.

"I disembarked less than a week ago. Why? Does it matter?"

"It may. I have been in correspondence with old Stuart. You remember, the footman with the limp. He and I have remained friends since Allan died. He says there is some question about Percival's death. The coroner has left the entire matter open, and investigations are being made by the magistrate."

"Has anyone laid down information that would imply something untoward happened?"

"No, but eyebrows are up. A sudden digestive infirmity with extreme pain and quick death—well, my eyebrows would be up too."

Hence the notice in the paper in Amsterdam, that inquiries were under way. "You worried that they would look to me, didn't you?"

"The enmity between the two of you has been long, and the business over that legacy might encourage them to wonder."

"Have no fear. I was out of the country. I can prove it."

Her expression lightened. She suddenly looked younger than her forty-eight years. Also intelligent and formidable. She would have made the duke a splendid duchess had he not already married Percy's mother, and had Amanda Albany not been a butler's daughter.

Her change in mood implied she had worried a bit about his doings recently. It is a hell of a thing when your own mother thinks you capable of murder. Then again, given the right circumstances, she probably was also.

"I expect Lancelot and Ives will be at Merrywood," she said. "What with the title's transition to Lance and the settling of the estate."

"I hope so. I want to see them." Since Lance now became duke, presumably he would be involved in the inquiries. Ives would take a hand in the estate settling, being a lawyer.

He did not lie in saying he wanted to see his half brothers. Unlike the relationship he had with Percy, Gareth had gotten on well enough with them over the years. And, of course, Lance would now decide about that case in Chancery.

"There is to be a reinterment next week," his mother said. "A mausoleum was quickly built, to Percival's deathbed orders. Now that it is ready, they are digging him up to put him in it. It is a monstrosity, according to Mr. Stuart. I have a drawing here somewhere. I shall find it, so you can prepare yourself. It is so hideous that one wonders if he was determined to be remembered for something, even if it was being the duke who was buried in the ugliest pile in the family graveyard."

"He never had any taste. Father always said so, which drove him mad." He spoke absently, his mind on other things. If magistrates were sniffing around a duke's death, the new duke was not likely to turn his mind to minor matters, like a small property tied up in the courts. Damnation, even in death Percy was going to be an ass.

"I rode up near Langdon's End," he said, "before coming here."

His mother's expression of forbearance chastised him. She thought he should let it go. The daughter of a butler and the mistress of a duke, she did not have a sense of property, even if she had a life interest in this house.

"He has let it go to ruin. There is no caretaker. It is derelict and turning into a shell. I doubt any furniture remains worth using. I was told thieves have been busy."

"Did you enter it?"

"I am forbidden to, remember? I walked around the outside, however, and looked in a few windows. He knew contesting the will would not hold, so he made sure when I finally got it, the house would be almost worthless."

"Perhaps fate has intervened before that happened. Lance has no reason to continue the fight."

"Perhaps." He stood. "If you don't mind, I will go above. I have been on the road too many days."

He took his leave, but her voice stopped him at the door.

"Lady Chester wrote to me. Her niece still sighs over you, and wonders when you will return to London."

Lady Chester's niece was an attractive woman in an unhappy marriage to a boorish viscount. "When I do, I will call on her, but she will be disappointed if she expects anything more."

"You love and leave too quickly, Gareth. No wonder your reputation is not the best."

"I would have stayed longer in the lady's bed if she had not started to try to buy me. A man does not allow his lover to keep him if he has any pride. I did us both a favor in ending it."

"You were not so particular with Lady Dalmouth."

"I was much younger then, and Lady Dalmouth had much to recommend her besides her gifts." Most notably, Lady Dalmouth possessed sexual experience such as few men are honored to enjoy. Randy, resentful, and ready to take on the world, he had been a willing student, and had barely noticed how he had become the lady's whore until the morning she ordered him to change his coat because she did not favor its color that day.

"Women are kept all the time. I managed to hold on to my pride well enough. I do not see why it should be any different for men if two people share affection."

He had hurt her. He had not meant to, but one hour in his mother's presence and he was fifteen again, and she was trying to plan his life.

"You were not merely the duke's kept woman. You were his true wife and the law be damned. Write to Lady Chester and tell her that I am enthralled with a widow in Amsterdam, so her niece does not expect me to dance attendance if I go up to town."

CHAPTER 3

"They look dry to me," Rebecca said. She gingerly tapped the surface of the painting with her fingertips, then peered to see if any paint had come off on them.

"That one needs another week," Eva muttered, her attention mostly on the painting she had carried home three days earlier, at the cost of a pair of shoes.

"The others don't."

"I cannot go to Birmingham every time a painting is ready. We can ill afford that. I will wait until all of those are dry, then transport them all at once."

Rebecca sighed loudly and threw herself on the divan. Eva felt bad for her sister. Compared to the excitements in Birmingham, their home on the outskirts of Langdon's End and the town of Langdon's

End itself held little of interest. The place where one was born and raised never did if one had an adventurous spirit. Rebecca itched for novelties, travel, and the worlds her reading revealed to her.

For a year now, Rebecca had been petitioning to go to London. Eva appeased her by letting her go along on the periodic visits to Birmingham when Eva took her paintings to Mr. Stevenson, a stationer who put them in his window for sale.

Her sister lounged on the divan, one of the few substantial pieces of furniture that had not been sold. She pouted prettily, but then all of Rebecca's expressions looked adorable. Her hair poured down her shoulders, making a thick stream of shiny curls so luxurious no one would notice that the dress she wore had been mended in four places.

Eva envied Rebecca sometimes, which was not fair. Rebecca could not help being beautiful. Only it felt unjust that Rebecca had gotten the better version of everything they had in common. Rebecca's blue eyes possessed the color and depth of a clear, perfect sea, while Eva's could only be called really blue on the sunniest days. The looking glass reflected back some nondescript color too pale to be notable, no matter what it might be. And Rebecca's hair had the rich, deep color of mahogany, while Eva's own appeared the flat, dull brown of a tree trunk. If that were not bad enough, Rebecca was also smarter. If she demonstrated none of the wiliness required for survival, it was only because Eva sheltered her from the experiences that called forth such shrewdness.

A girl as lovely as Rebecca deserved better than what she now knew. So far, however, other than those day trips to Birmingham, Eva had not been able to give Rebecca the chance for better. She had a plan, however, and this painting she now started was part of it.

Eva turned her attention back to her task and debated whether to remove the heavy plaster frame before proceeding. She would have to put it back on if she did, but she worried she might get paint on it if she did not. It dwarfed the oil canvas it decorated. She had never understood how owners of art could not see as clear as day when a frame detracted from the treasure it held.

Deciding to leave the frame on, she set her canvas panel on her easel next to the chair. Her canvas was larger than the painting by almost three inches in height, but she could not afford another. She would just have to dab in more up there, extending the trees and sky.

"Why did you choose that picture this time?" Rebecca asked, now standing by her shoulder. "I can't imagine who will buy your copy. The subject is not grand at all."

The painting showed three little boys playing near a fountain. Rosy-cheeked and bedecked in their best garments, they formed an informal group portrait most likely, but might have been done merely to indulge the artist's whimsy.

"It is by Gainsborough, Rebecca. Someone will buy it for that reason alone since his style is still popular. And the boys will appeal to mothers and grandmothers in ways Greek gods will not."

"Only if the gods are clothed. Paint them naked and those mothers will like them well enough."

"Rebecca!"

"Please do not act shocked. If the sisters Neville have books of engravings of naked statues in their library, I think it is safe to say that women do not mind viewing such things."

The sisters Neville were two spinsters of considerable income who lived in Langdon's End. They saw in Rebecca a potential fellow bluestocking and made their library available to her—including, it appeared, engravings of ancient statues of naked men.

"I am sure the sisters have those books only because they are educational about the ancient Greeks."

"Oh, yes, they are educational." Rebecca smiled slyly. "I have learned a lot. Come with me sometime and I'll show you the best ones."

"If I come with you, it will be for better things than that." Eva opened her paint box and began smearing paints she had mixed yesterday onto her palette. "Now go away. I must concentrate on this."

Rebecca pouted again. "But I wanted to talk to you about something very important. I have been thinking about our lives here, and believe we should make a change. I have a plan . . ."

Eva stopped hearing what Rebecca said. The words became a sound in the background of her consciousness, much like a running brook will flow without one hearing every bubble. She barely noticed when Rebecca left.

Four hours later, while she cleaned her brushes and

admired the day's progress, a few of her sister's words poked through the fog of her memory. They nibbled and jabbed until she paid them some mind and tried to reconstruct the content.

When she thought she had, she laughed. Surely Rebecca had not said that. Her sister would never propose in all seriousness that they sell the house, take the money, and go to London to become courtesans.

Merrywood Manor, five miles outside Cheltenham in the Gloucester hills, had not changed one bit during Percival's time as duke. He was leaving the renovation of its dated Palladian-derived design for his future duchess, he liked to say. Gareth assumed Percy was too miserly to ever renovate, or even take a wife, although the latter probably would have eventually occurred, a duke's duties being what they were. Percy's unwillingness to invest in the estate's properties had been obvious as Gareth rode in. A tenant cottage that had burned down at least five years ago still remained a pile of charred wood, and even Merrywood itself displayed evidence of needing some maintenance.

Gareth presented himself at the door of the manor house the way he always did, as a visitor. A bastard did not treat the family estate as home. The first time he came after his father died, Percy made the limitations clear by refusing to receive him. His father always had, and even the servants gave him entry during his father's life, even if his father was not at home.

He had watched his father's burial from the saddle of his horse on an overlooking hill. As the cream of the peerage carried the casket to the simple grave, a carriage rolled up and his mother stepped out. Head high, wearing an expression that dared Percy or anyone else to interfere, she had walked through the gathering of nobles to stand by the graveside while her lover was laid to rest. The duchess had been dead a good dozen years by then, but Gareth suspected his mother would have done it even if the duchess, too, had stood by the grave.

Today the door of Merrywood Manor bore a huge wreath draped in black bombazine. He wondered if Percy, with his last breaths, had ordered this gargantuan wreath along with the mausoleum.

He waited in the reception hall while his card was carried away, and followed the butler to the library after his reception had been given the nod. In the library he found Ives, the youngest of the legitimate brothers, and at thirty, two years older than Gareth. Officially named Ywain, which he hated, Ives was tall like all of the third duke's progeny. He now stood by a window that showed off his classical features. Its light caught the golden streaks in his dark brown hair. Upon hearing the door open he turned. A black armband wrapped the sleeve of his dark coat.

They waited for the butler to leave. Ives fought a battle with a grin that wanted to break out on his face. Devilish delight showed in his green eyes. He bit back the expression, coughed, and assumed a somber demeanor appropriate to the reunion. "Good of you to come, Gareth. I know Percy would be touched."

Gareth kept his expression blank with difficulty. "I read about it in Amsterdam and was on a packet by morning. So unexpected. So shocking."

"Yes, yes. As you can imagine, we are beside ourselves."

Oh, he could imagine. Around the time he turned fifteen, Gareth had realized Lance and Ives were his comrades in arms against Percy. They knew why he hated the duke's heir, but he still did not know what had happened in this family to set full-blooded brother against full-blooded brother.

"Amsterdam, you say?" Ives asked.

"Yes."

"I am glad to hear it. I assume your journey was both pleasurable and profitable."

Someone else who had wondered whether Percy had been done in by his bastard half brother. Gareth could hardly mind. He must have threatened to kill Percy half a dozen times in Ives's hearing.

"I am brokering a French count's collection. I found an industrialist here who has the money, and who desires an instant gallery to grace his newly built grand house. The paintings should arrive in a fortnight."

Ives gestured to a tray with a brandy decanter and raised his eyebrows quizzically. When Gareth nodded, Ives proceeded to pour. "Lance will want you to find such a buyer for some pictures from here. The ones Percy bought are not to his taste."

Gareth took the glass and sipped. "Are they to anyone's? I cannot sell what no one will buy."

"Perhaps you can locate a rich industrialist with bad eyesight. Or you can lie and claim they are the finest paintings dabbed in the last two decades."

"Only if we speak of works done by Spanish nuns. All those pastel fat cherubs and heaven-gazing saints with their palms of martyrdom— Do you think Percy was a secret dissenter?"

"That would require him to have had principles of some kind, would it not?"

Gareth almost choked. Ives sucked in his cheeks.

"Oh, hell," Ives sighed. "It won't do to be speaking ill of the dead. Not now. We would not want the servants to see us as anything but suitably mournful. Reports of raucous glee might be misunderstood. God forgive me, Gareth, he was my brother—but when I got the news in London, it was all I could do not to throw open the window and shoot a few pistol balls into the sky to celebrate."

"I'll wager you didn't only because the sound would have frightened your actress friend. How is she?"

"Expensive."

Gareth assumed that affair would end soon. "Why would reports of our mood be misunderstood? I assume no one believes he was well loved."

Ives turned very sober indeed. "It was possibly murder, Gareth. You surely heard. Even the papers allude to it."

"Were you hoping I was in England that day and eyes would turn to me?"

He got a sharp look for that. "Eyes had already turned. Inquiries are afoot in London to learn your whereabouts. So it is a damned good thing you were out of the country. I am truly relieved to have one fewer brother to protect with my lawyer's eloquence."

They stood there, glasses in hand, drinking the brandy.

"Where were you that day?" Gareth asked.

"In London. In court during the day and at a dinner party at night. I am of no interest to the magistrate."

They each took another swallow.

"And Lance?"

Ives let out a deep, long breath. "He was here. He was right in this damned house."

"Indeed I was," a voice said.

Gareth looked over his shoulder. Lance had just entered the library, appearing his formidable, unconventional self. Dark-haired, dark-eyed, dressed in arrogance and sharp intelligence as surely as black coats and boots, he flashed a smile that stupid men misunderstood as friendly. He had not shaved today, and the rough growth on his face emphasized rather than hid the long, thin scar on his right cheek.

He strode over, clapped a welcoming grasp on Gareth's shoulder, then helped himself to some brandy. He faced them cup in hand.

"Pity I did not have the courage to do it. I think we

are all in agreement, gentlemen, that Percy was a terrible excuse for a human being who sowed sorrow wherever he went. Let us toast him in death for the years of misery he will never now create."

"You must stop saying things like that," Ives snapped, slamming down his own glass. "A modicum of discretion is in order at least."

"He is worried they will hang me," Lance said to Gareth. His tone contained indifference to Ives's concerns, or anyone's opinion.

"I am not worried they will— Damn it, do you want people to wonder your whole life, should no culprit be found?"

"Hell if I care. As Duke of Aylesbury I expect I could survive a few cuts."

"Listen to me. I do not expect you to weep over his grave, just try not to dance on it. Damnation, a man has died, and it is incumbent on his closest relatives to at least show some seriousness, lest eyebrows rise."

"He is right," Gareth said, working his face into an expression suitably glum. "A man has died, as he said."

"Of course I am right," Ives intoned.

Lance lowered his eyelids and smoothed away the smile. Feature by feature he created a mask. "More like this?"

"Yes, much better," Ives said.

"Hellishly uncomfortable. It will take too much thought to keep it up."

"Yet you must. Think of me inheriting everything after you swing. That should keep that grin in check."

"Don't they have to prove there was a murder before accusing someone of murder?" Gareth asked.

"The damned physician wrote up that he was possibly poisoned," Lance said. "Hell, wouldn't you think that if the man paying you is dead, you would be currying favor with the man who will pay you next, and not create drama by putting in writing there may have been a murder? That scribble was enough to stir the pot, and to support the accusation should other facts become known."

"Which will not happen," Ives said. "There are no other facts. There was no murder. Percy ate something that was tainted, or succumbed to a long-festering malady of the gut. That is our story, gentlemen. The magistrates are on a fool's errand, and the coroner is making much ado about nothing."

Still wearing his sobriety, Lance threw himself into a chair, lounging in the bored, languid pose that so clearly communicated both his arrogance and ennui with life. Gareth thought he appeared thinner, and somewhat haggard. He could not tell if current events caused that, or if it only reflected a long period of hedonistic excess prior to Percy's death. They none of them had reputations as saints, but Lance also could not be bothered with discretion or restraint.

For a few minutes Lance's vision turned inward, but then he focused attention on Gareth. "Perhaps you should give the eulogy, Mordred. You were the first to see all he could be."

"Do not be perverse," Ives scolded. "And I trust you are not going to pick up using that nickname for Gareth."

"If you want, I will do it," Gareth said. "As for how he addressed me, Ives, he is only reminding me of how eloquent my eulogy could be if I am given a free hand."

Mordred had been Percy's name for him. Resentful that their father had graced a bastard with the name of one of King Arthur's knights, just like his legal children, Percy had decided a more appropriate one was in order. The conceit of those names had been the duchess's idea. The duke's using it on his bastard, too, had been an insult to her that just kept cutting.

"I am joking of course. You can be a pallbearer at the interment if you like. If you prefer to decline that is understandable."

"I will watch it the way I watched my father's funeral, from afar, if you do not mind."

Lance threw back the rest of his brandy. "Hell, no, I don't mind. I think I will ride. Waiting for something to happen is driving me mad. I would suggest we all visit a brothel, but Ives here has insisted we must pretend to be too sad for pleasure."

He strode from the library. Ives watched him go, then turned and aimed for the garden doors. "Come walk with me, Gareth. I need to speak to you on another matter."

"He laughs at the danger, but he is no fool. It is unlikely that he will ever be formally accused—he is now a duke, after all—but the shadow can follow him forever." Ives spoke between puffs on a cigar. Ives smoked only when agitated. That he had resumed the habit said he was concerned about recent events and not assuming it would all turn out well.

"I expect his reputation does not help." Lance had been a hell-raiser as a young man. Being the spare had made him more reckless than Ives, or even Gareth. A darkness lived in Lance, too, its origins unknown to Gareth. Not a criminal darkness, however. The notion Lance would poison anyone, let alone his own brother, could not be taken seriously.

"What truly does not help is that he cuckolded one of the magistrates," Ives said. "The man knows it and will not let this chance pass, duke or no duke."

Gareth had to laugh. "Remind me, should I be tempted, never to bed the wife of a man who can give me legal trouble."

"As if you would listen any more than he would. I must remain here with Lance and play the lawyer to his incorrigible client. I do not want him doing or saying something while in his cups that only makes it worse, and I want to keep informed of the thinking of those who are looking to make trouble."

"That sounds wise."

"Wise, but inconvenient. I was supposed to go north to investigate something, and now I cannot. I thought perhaps you might indulge me and take my place."

Gareth hesitated. Ives often served as the Crown's

prosecutor in serious crimes. The something he needed to do up north might involve confronting dangerous men. While Gareth acquitted himself well enough in such situations, he was not inclined to seek them out, let alone for third parties unnamed.

Besides, he had his own mission now.

"I had thought to remain here for a few days at least, after the reinterment. I hope to speak with Lance."

"That property is on your mind, of course. How could it not be. If you do this for me, I will plead your case for you, and convince him to drop the matter entirely. I do not believe it will take more than a few minutes and a few words, once I bring his attention to it."

Ives had tried that with Percy, to no avail. Gareth thought Ives a brilliant lawyer, but property had a way of bringing out the worst in men.

"Furthermore," Ives said. "This business I speak of is in the region of that lodge. I will get Lance to agree to allow you to use the house while you are there. You can begin settling in."

Suddenly Ives's proposal had appeal. "What is the matter you need me for?"

"A collection of art has gone missing."

Not only appeal now, but real interest. "Whose collection?"

"It was not owned by one person. Rather, it comprised works owned by a number of people."

"Which people?"

"No one important. Only half of the members of the House of Lords."

"I t was during the war," Ives said. He and Gareth now sat on a bench beneath a tree. "Right around 1800. Everyone worried about invasion. You probably remember how it was then, even though we were boys. Napoleon already had the reputation for cultural rape. He picked out the best art and sent it back through the lines, to France. A number of very prominent lords took to worrying about the art in their manor homes. Their wives and daughters might suffer the worst, but, by George, their paintings would not end up in some French palace."

"You say it like a joke, but a lot of art was looted by the French."

"As it has been by every army down through time. Napoleon's methodical looting distressed these lords, however. The Corsican brought experts with him who knew what they wanted. It was assumed he knew which families here owned what, and had a list ready. Any house gallery between the coast and London was considered vulnerable. So they hit on a solution to foil him."

"Move the art," Gareth guessed.

Ives nodded. "The best of the best got crated up and moved north, to the center of England, to await the end of the war. Only when that day came, and those who organized this went to retrieve it, it was not there."

"Stolen?"

"It is not being called theft yet."

"Where was it stored?"

"That is where it gets delicate. The repository was a property owned by the Duke of Devonshire."

"*Delicate* puts a fine point to it. No wonder there has been no rumor or gossip about this. To say it was stolen insults a very powerful man."

"There has been mild criticism about his vigilance. Nothing more. No one has dared to suggest he or the current duke in any way decided to divert any of the paintings to his own collection."

"That family owns one of the best collections in the realm. They do not need anyone else's."

"Yet the paintings sent north are gone. The government has preached patience because the Regent had his hand in the original idea, but tempers are wearing thin. I was charged with learning what I could."

Learning what he could might mean all kinds of things with Ives.

"Do you intend to question Devonshire?" Gareth asked.

"Do I look mad? He is coming for the interment, however."

"I would not have thought Percy would have found any favor with Devonshire."

"He didn't. At all. The last duke once called him a miserable little demon. At best it is a matter of rank respecting itself. A duke dies and other dukes attend his funeral. At worst, the current Duke of Devonshire is coming to drive a stake into Percy's heart."

"Perhaps Lance will broach the topic for you. *I say there, Devvie, what do you think became of all that art your father agreed to store in your attics?* He would do it if you asked."

"The danger is he will do it even if I don't ask. Do not remind him of the matter. He knows of it, of course. All the lords do. Those who lost have not been silent among their peers. Since none of ours went missing, our brother is unlikely to think of it unless prodded."

"How will you explain my little mission to him, then?"

"I was not intending to explain anything. We have never expected an accounting of your comings or goings."

In other words, the new Duke of Aylesbury would not give a damn why Gareth was going north.

"If you arrange for me to have use of the lodge, we have ourselves a bargain."

Ives stood. "I promise to see that legacy wholly resolved, once this other business is behind us. Until then, Lance will agree it is only right that you should use it as your own."

It was all the assurance Gareth needed. Lance could be willful, even whimsical, but he was fair. A clean deed would be forthcoming sooner rather than later now. That derelict pile would be his, and he could start improving it. He followed Ives back to the house, making plans.

CHAPTER 4

"The big house has been let, I hear." Rebecca mentioned the news while she sat on a burlap sack, watching Eva pluck weeds. The plantings behind their home had been laid out for flowers and shrubbery, but Eva had started tucking vegetables amid the blooms three years ago. It saved them a few pounds a year on food, all for little effort.

Growing vegetables had been the last of a long string of economies, and the one Eva least minded. Her father had sold off most of the land, and what was left brought in minimal rents. Her late brother's five years of infirmity meant he had not been able to supplement their income with any kind of employment, not that Nigel would have taken up a trade even if he had had the health to do so. He had been a gentleman's son and intended to die a gentleman himself, even if it meant his older sister had to sell the household furnishings to ensure they all had enough to eat.

"Who has taken it? I cannot imagine anyone wanting to live there," Eva said.

"No one knows, but some boys saw a light through the lower windows two nights ago, and there are reports of a horse in the stable."

"If not for the horse, I would say it was all nonsense and some of Langdon End's young men had decided to get drunk there one night."

"Whoever it is, I expect they will make themselves known in town soon. They are sure to be quality people. Even in its present state, the rent would be high for such a large house and property."

"I expect so." Eva hoped the rumors were wrong, and that at worst the house's owner had sent a servant to stay a brief while. Perhaps some traveler had simply made use of an empty house and would soon be on his way. She had come to think of that house as abandoned and rather counted on it remaining so.

"I think you should call on them," Rebecca said. "Perhaps they have a daughter who would be my friend."

"I will do that if you promise not to complain that our house is not suitable for guests, since they are bound to then call on us in turn."

Rebecca flushed. "Maybe if they have a daughter I will meet her in town."

"Maybe you should allow her to know your circumstances when you meet her. There is no shame in our situation, and if this imaginary new friend is worthy of the name, she will not care."

Rebecca stood abruptly, her brow knitted from her pique. "I do not mind our situation, but I do resent your acceptance of it. Instead of improving, it gets worse and now I cannot even have friends, because we do not have enough chairs since you sold them all."

"I sold them so you would not go hungry. And, of course, our situation is improving, even if you do not see the fruits of that yet. Our year of mourning is now over, and we can participate in society again. You can attend assemblies and meet other girls in town, and if you can restrain yourself from talking about philosophy in the first few conversations, you will find friends who will change everything."

"I am not speaking of social matters."

"Financial ones, then? My paintings are selling well enough so our circumstances are not so dire as they were, even with the bad harvest and unpaid rents. I think I am doing splendidly." She smiled and gave her sister a wink. "You are uncommonly out of sorts, Rebecca. It is not like you to complain with such vehemence."

Her attempt at lightening the conversation was to no avail. "What happens if no one wants your paintings someday?" Rebecca asked.

"I will find another way to improve our lot, should that happen. You are not to worry."

"I do worry. You may see improvement, but I see more of the same for years on end. I say we make big changes, not your little ones. Let us make the best of our breeding and youth and blaze another trail while we still can."

Eva looked up at her sister. Rebecca's face flushed and her posture stiffened, but she met Eva's gaze boldly.

"You refer to your improper proposal from the other day, I fear." She should have paid more attention at the time, and pulled that particular weed at once. "You cannot be serious, Rebecca."

"Why not? The sisters Neville say such a life can bring a woman security and even riches."

Eva laughed and stood. "Darling, you do not even comprehend what such a life entails. I wonder if the sisters Neville really do either. I cannot imagine why they would speak of such things to you."

"I asked them, and they answered frankly. Not everyone thinks women should remain ignorant."

"You are not a woman. You are a child."

"Oh, tosh! Look at me, Eva. Really look at me. Do not let the memories obscure what you see." Tears sparkled in Rebecca's eyes. Her defiant expression turned into one of pitiable unhappiness. "I am no child. I will be nineteen soon. Not one man has proposed. Not one. I have not even had a tragic love, like you did. And look at yourself. You used to have dreams of being an artist, but you have only done copies for years now. And I cannot remember the last time I saw you sketch."

Turning on her heel, Rebecca ran to the house.

Eva gazed over the garden she had known all her life. A memory came to her of playing with a much younger Rebecca amid the shrubbery. Then others flowed, of comforting her little sister when their father passed away.

She dropped to her knees and continued pulling weeds. As her gloved hands yanked the tiny intruders out, her heart accommodated the words with which Rebecca had slapped her, hard.

Her sister did not really want to become a fallen woman. Rebecca just wanted to know she would have some kind of life besides this one. The lack of suitors would weigh on any young woman Rebecca's age, and cause a restlessness that made her vulnerable.

Her thoughts turned to Charles, the "tragic love" Rebecca had thrown in her face. Not really tragic. Rebecca had been too dramatic. After all, Charles had not died. He had not forsaken her. He had merely gone away as he had planned, only without her because she could not—no, *would* not—marry him and go too. To do so would mean leaving her brother alone and sick, weak from that pistol wound that forever after affected his health.

That duty had cost her dearly. Marriage, her youth, her art—

She avoided thinking about all of it, because when she did her heart turned angry and frightened.

She almost never thought about Charles anymore. She rarely grew wistful with thoughts of what might have been. She hated that she did now.

She shut the memories away and thought about her plans for the future, plans she did not confide to Rebecca lest they not come to pass. With her sister's unhappiness, it might be time to embark on that path sooner than intended.

She returned to the house, washed her hands, and mounted the stairs to her bedchamber. She pried up a loose floorboard in the corner, and fished out a little sack hanging on a nail she had pounded into a joist. She sat on her bed and emptied its contents in her lap. The shillings clinked as they fell into a little mound.

Coins entered this sack, but never left. She saved them for a purpose other than security, although they provided that too. With this money, she intended to give Rebecca the better she deserved. She had planned to have more before taking the first step, but now she decided more boldness was in order.

Surely if a decent, established man met Rebecca, he would fall in love and offer marriage despite her lack of fortune. She merely had to find a way for worthy prospects to see Rebecca. She also needed Rebecca to look very, very lovely when they did.

And once Rebecca was settled, Eva would be free to make her own future different as well.

Gareth surveyed the shelves holding bolts of fabric in Duran's Cloths, a draper's store in Langdon's End. He had already waited half an hour for the proprietor to serve him. From the look of things it would be quite a while longer. The woman commanding Mr. Duran's attention must have examined every bolt of fabric in the place, and showed no indication of knowing her mind yet.

While he practiced patience, he mentally made a list of the items he needed if he were to spend even one more day in Albany Lodge. That was not the historic name of the property. It actually had none that he knew of. In the will, it had only been called the Warwickshire hunting lodge. On his ride here he had sorted through names until he found one he liked. Considering how he had come to own it, naming it after his mother seemed fitting.

As he anticipated, Albany Lodge had been emptied of almost everything that could be moved and much that should never be. Most critically he needed bedclothes. He had only had serviceable linens the past few nights because he had stopped in Coventry again and, expecting what he would find, begged some off his mother. He should have hired a wagon and cajoled her out of much more.

He needed to purchase pots, soap, flints, kitchenware—everything. Tools, too, he reminded himself. He would hire craftsmen to do the skilled work, but he could manage a few repairs himself. Expensive, all of it. The count's collection had better make it to Honfleur in time for Hendrika's ship.

Gareth glanced over to see Mr. Duran, the proprietor, fold some muslin. Thin feminine fingers plucked coins out of a reticule and set them down. He could

not see the woman's face, but something about her
feathered at his memory. Then he recognized the
pelisse and bonnet. It was the woman he had forced
off the road near Albany Lodge. His mind saw her
again, her eyes throwing daggers of fire while she
upbraided him for carelessness.

She wore the same bonnet and pelisse today. Both
had seen current style some years ago. Their brown
hues proved unfortunate to her coloring. They turned
her into a winter palette that begged for red or bright
blue. There were birds whose feathers helped them
hide on tree trunks, and these garments had done the
same on a road flanked by woods.

He doubted that camouflage was her goal. Most likely
she wore this because she possessed little else that was
presentable. If so, ruining those shoes had been no small
matter to her. No wonder she had cursed him.

Still, even in her dull browns, she was a prime arti-
cle. All that spirit, and with a woman's look to her, not
that of a young girl. He had looked for a ring that day,
and did so now again. Not a wife or a widow, it appeared.
A pretty spinster then, with a charming upturned nose
and clear, intelligent eyes.

Mr. Duran mumbled something. The woman softly
replied. Gareth could not hear either one, but he recognized deference in the shopkeeper's expression.
The man even made a vague bow as the woman took
the muslin and turned.

She strode out, her expression determined and her
gaze not seeing much in the shop. Definitely not him

lounging near the wall. As the door closed behind her, he approached the counter.

Mr. Duran blatantly assessed his garments. The analysis resulted in a toothy smile. "Good day, sir. In need of something for your journey?"

Gareth looked over his shoulder. He could still see the brown bonnet through the shop window. A feather bobbed beside it. She had stopped to speak to someone.

"Do you have something I can write with?" he asked Mr. Duran. "I must visit other shops, and can list what I need and come for it later."

Mr. Duran produced a piece of paper and pencil. Gareth hurriedly jotted down a list. He handed it to Duran and headed to the door just as the brown bonnet moved away.

E va thanked Mr. Duran and turned to leave the shop. As she did, she spotted a blue cape passing the shop window. She hastened out to the lane, lest that cape be too far gone when she emerged.

"Miss Neville and Miss Ophelia Neville, good day to you both." She blurted the greeting as soon as the door opened.

The two women, one tall and one short, turned and greeted her in turn. They looked much alike with their very fair, long faces that might have graced a Tudor court painting. They also both had extremely fair hair. It possessed tight curls that resisted taming.

Ophelia Neville, the shorter, younger sister, tried nonetheless to dress her hair fashionably, even if it, at best, appeared a pale yellow haze around her crown.

Jasmine Neville, the older, taller one, had surrendered to nature's whim. She let her frizz fly free down her shoulders and back. By adopting an artistic wardrobe of exotic wraps, turbans, and capes, her stylishly eccentric appearance served as a foil to her sister's conventional one.

"It was fortunate that I met you today," Eva said. "There is a matter which I need to address with you."

Jasmine's lids lowered. "Pray tell what that is, Miss Russell."

"It is about my sister."

"She is well, I hope."

"Very well, thank you. However, she visits you too often, I fear."

"Your fear is misplaced," Ophelia said. "We are delighted when she visits. She has been given free use of our library, and we love to see her engrossed in the books."

"You misunderstand. My fear is that her visits are exposing her to ideas unsuitable to her."

Jasmine seemed to grow even taller. Her head angled back dramatically and her eyes narrowed. "There are no such things as *unsuitable* ideas to a thinking person. If an idea is ill considered or bad, our intelligence will tell us so when we deliberate it."

"Some ideas are better saved until a thinking person is an adult, don't you agree?"

"Rebecca *is* an adult," Ophelia said gently. "She is almost nineteen. Would you have her be like so many women, ignorant of the variety of philosophies in the world?"

Eva's jaw tightened. "I do not speak of philosophies. I am not objecting to your introducing her to tracts by dissenters and radicals, alongside the great classical thinkers. She is sensible enough to make of those what they are worth."

"I think Miss Russell is referring to more worldly things, Ophelia," Jasmine said dryly. "Worldly with a capital *W*."

"Indeed I am. I must object when you encourage my sister to look favorably upon a vocation as a—as a"—she groped, too vexed to think straight—"as a professional mistress!"

Ophelia's eyes widened. Jasmine's narrowed even more. Jasmine took one step closer and became very tall indeed. "We do not corrupt young women, Miss Russell. The insinuation that we do is not to be borne."

"We really do not," Ophelia hastened to add. "Rebecca was reading a history in which vague reference was made to a courtesan, and she looked the word up in the library while visiting. The definition surprised her enough that she asked us to explain. We neither of us believe in lying, so, of course, we did explain. Most discreetly and objectively, I assure you."

"We certainly did not encourage her to look favorably on the profession or life." Jasmine's voice rose with each word, until they rang like a sermon spoken from a high pulpit. A man passing by slowed a bit, to hear more. "My sister and I are the last people to want a rare jewel like Rebecca to become some lout's sexual slave, no matter how great the compensations or how silken the bonds."

Eva caught her breath. She was sure those last words had been heard for a quarter mile. People across the lane actually stopped and stared.

"Please lower your voice," she hissed. "I applaud your views regarding women becoming se—se—" She could not say it. "Of becoming *slaves* of any kind. We are of like mind, but some circumspection in speech is called for. If you talk that frankly to Rebecca, I must prevent her from continuing her friendship with you."

"Oh, dear. Jasmine, you have shocked nice Miss Russell. You must learn to control your words when you are in high dudgeon."

"I did not initiate this conversation. I am an efficient speaker, even if Miss Russell is not. As for Rebecca, our door is open to her. If you want to keep her away, find something more interesting for her to do." With a self-satisfied sniff that expressed her view of that likelihood, Miss Neville turned and walked away. Her sister hurried to catch up.

Face burning, Eva collected herself. Well, that had hardly ended as she intended.

Across the street two women still stared. The poor things had probably never heard the word *sexual* spoken before. Eva was sure she hadn't, let alone heard it shouted on a main road in full hearing of passersby.

The whole town would probably feed off the story for a week.

She tucked her new muslin against her body and walked on. She hoped Rebecca liked the pattern. This visit to town had cost more than the coin paid for it.

She forced her mind to practical matters. Should she make Rebecca the new dress, or hire a dressmaker?

"We meet again," a voice said as boots fell into step beside her shoes. "How kind of fate to arrange that."

She started so badly that she jumped aside, much as she had hopped into a big puddle two weeks ago. The same face looked down at her as had that day.

The careless horseman had returned, looking as handsome and dangerous as ever.

Seeing him up close hardly dimmed his attraction. She took in the details in a daze that created slow motion. The mildest cleft in his chin. The high bones of his cheeks that together with well-formed eyebrows brought attention to his dark, devilishly wicked eyes. The waves of disheveled hair that flattered him more than carefully brushed hair ever could.

He wore a blue coat today and a cravat indifferently tied. He still looked expensive. A gentleman, that was obvious.

"I did not intend to startle you," he said. "I apologize if my greeting took you unaware."

His vague smile communicated more than friendliness. He could see how impressed she was. Of course he could, when she gawked at him like a schoolgirl.

"If I am surprised, it is because I am not accustomed to being greeted by men I do not know."

"Ah, a *stickler*." He said it like it was a disease. "Wait here, please. Promise you will not move." After she nodded, he strode back into the shop, and soon emerged with Mr. Duran. Mr. Duran listened to words muttered into his ear as the two of them approached her.

Mr. Duran cleared his throat. "Miss Russell, may I introduce you to Mr. Gareth Fitzallen. He is new to the region and eager to make the acquaintance of its leading citizens and families."

Mr. Fitzallen bowed. Eva had no choice but to make a quick curtsy. Mr. Duran returned to his shop.

Eva tried to figure out how to shed the beautiful man who had gone to some trouble to obtain an introduction. Not that an introduction by a tradesman really qualified as a proper introduction. Clearly Mr. Fitzallen was not the kind of *stickler* to care about that.

"I am pleased to make your acquaintance, sir, but I am hardly a leading citizen. If you have settled in the region, I am sure our paths will cross again, however, and I look forward to greeting you next time with more courtesy." Trusting he would hear the dismissal barely hiding in the farewell, she began walking down the lane again.

Those boots once more fell into step beside hers.

"Do you live here in town?" he asked.

"My home is a half mile or so into the country."

"What a coincidence. So is mine. I am living in the ruin where we first met."

That was not good news. "Surely there were better houses to let in the county than that one. I would not think it was even inhabitable."

"It is barely livable. I came to town today to purchase a few items to help make it more so."

"I would think a gentleman like yourself would require more than barely livable."

"I desire much more, but in truth require very little. I will make do with livable for now. I am hoping you will take pity on me and direct me to the shops and craftsmen that can be trusted." He flashed a disarming smile, one designed to make a woman swoon. "See, there was a reason I accosted you so rudely. I know no one else to ask."

This man knew how to exploit his natural gifts to full effect. Knowing his game did not save her from succumbing. Her heart danced a jig. A joyful, naughty one. *Get hold of yourself, you goose.*

"I fear if I help you, it will only encourage you further in what is a bad bargain. I warned you the house was derelict inside, yet you let it anyway. If you did not trust my judgment on that, why should you do so when it comes to shops and craftsmen?"

"I did not let it, as such. It belongs to me, crumbling walls and all. So either I leave it to vagrants and fires, the fate you predicted, or I take possession and attempt to save it. I chose the latter."

She halted her steps and turned to him. "Yours?"

"Mine."

She dragged up what little she knew of that house. "Years ago it belonged to the Duke of Aylesbury, although it is said he last visited fifteen years ago. Has the current owner finally sold?"

"It was left to me upon the third duke's death. I have not been able to take residence until now."

Why not? She bit back the question in favor of one less intrusive. "Are you a relative? Expect to be called on mercilessly by every hostess in Langdon's End if you are."

"Perhaps you will let it be known that the house will not be suitable for me to receive callers for some time. Except you, of course, since we are friends."

Friends now. What charming nonsense. As if she would ever call on a bachelor at his house. She assumed he was a bachelor, if he was the person buying drapes and such.

It seemed a prudent moment to continue walking. She paced along with her escort until they came to a red door. "This shop is owned by Mrs. Fleming. She sells sundries and general wares. I need to take my leave now, so I can purchase some thread." She held up the muslin by way of explanation.

"Is that for a dress? The pattern favors you. It makes your eyes appear very blue."

More silly flattery. No one had ever commented on her eyes.

He peered through the window. "I will join you. I see some pots in there."

Pots. She looked in the window and recognized the ones he now spied. "They even stole your pots? How terrible," she murmured.

"I am grateful they left the pieces of one bed, so I did not have to sleep on the floor. And one chair and a small table."

One chair.

Mrs. Fleming, a small, frail woman with graying hair, favored simple dresses, big aprons, and severely bound hair. She did not hide her surprise at seeing Eva walk in with a man. Her eyes grew wide as the dashing appearance of that man became obvious. She flushed to her hairline and pretended to sort through the jars on the counter in front of her.

"Good day, Mrs. Fleming. I need some white thread, if you would be so kind."

Mrs. Fleming opened a drawer and produced the thread. "Three pence."

Eva handed her the pennies. "Allow me to introduce Mr. Fitzallen. He owns the old ruin on Thatchers Road. He has taken residence there and needs to replace the items stolen from the house over time. Pots and such."

She gave Mrs. Fleming a meaningful look, then sent a sharp glance to the pots that had attracted Mr. Fitzallen's attention. They had appeared in the shop the morning after a day she crossed paths with Mrs. Fleming's son on the road near the ruined house. He had been carrying a bulky sack on his back.

Mrs. Fleming bit her lower lip. "I've pots, sir, but only small ones, and they be used and old. You probably want better."

"I think they will do for now."

Glancing at Eva, Mrs. Fleming took them off the shelf and placed them on her counter. "For pots for stews and soups, you'll be wanting the ironmonger at the edge of town. The whitesmith is out there, too, if you be wanting tin to store flour and such."

"I will be sure to visit them. Thank you." He added some knives and eating implements to the pots. He moved on to the lamps and candles, then to the shelves on the other side of the shop that held crockery.

Eva took the opportunity to whisper. "You just sold that man pots that are already his, I think."

"What was I to do? Bits of that house are all over town. Who expected the owner to turn up after all these years of neglect?" She smiled at Mr. Fitzallen while he filled his arms. "What is a few pots, anyway. It isn't as if I helped myself to *chairs*, now is it?" She lowered her head and looked up at Eva.

Eva preferred not to dwell on the chairs. At the time, it seemed to her they would be happier carted off than used for firewood by vagrants. "We must spread the word that those who borrowed from that house must return the items."

"Unless they *sold them*, of course. Can't then, can they?"

No, they couldn't. She could not return the chairs.

But if a line of townsmen brought back borrowed items, she might be able to return that which she had borrowed, too, without it attracting notice.

"I will spread the word, as you must also," she whispered. "He may be related to a duke, but I think he will turn a blind eye to anyone bringing back his belongings, as long as they do find their way back."

"Related to a duke! What is he wanting with you? Nothing good, I'll warrant."

Eva had no idea what he wanted with her, or if he wanted anything at all.

Mr. Fitzallen set the last of his items on the counter. "That will be all for now. I am sure as soon as I am not distracted by two lovely ladies, other essentials will occur to me, though."

Eva all but rolled her eyes at the flattery. Mrs. Fleming glowed and, for an instant, she appeared twenty years younger.

"We can bring all of this to the house," she offered. "My son will carry it."

"How good of you. You have my appreciation."

Mrs. Fleming *giggled.* "It is nothing, sir. Nothing."

Eva took her leave while Mr. Fitzgerald paid. He caught up outside and strolled along as if he intended to spend the day in her shadow. To be polite she pointed out the lane to the church, although he showed more interest in two taverns they passed.

"It is an attractive town," he said. "It appears prosperous."

"Although there are old families in the area, out on

land beyond, many who live here moved from Birmingham after they made their fortunes. In the early morning hours, you can see the men going to Birmingham on horse or in carriages. There are many new homes if you stroll the lanes, usually of good size. The assemblies are full of fine garments and jewels."

"Industrialists? I doubt I will be well received. My experience has been that the newly prosperous are more critical than most about a person's birth. My own is a mixed blessing. I am indeed related to dukes. In fact, I am a duke's son. However, my mother was not his wife."

He was a bastard.

An awkward lull passed while she sought some response. "Your birth will not signify, I believe," she said. "I hope people will be enlightened enough to know better than to judge a person by things he does not control."

"I am glad to know that there are some free thinkers in Langdon's End, and feminine ones at that," he said, then added, "I could not help but overhear your conversation with those other ladies outside Mr. Duran's shop."

Her face heated as the exchange with the sisters Neville repeated in her mind. "Perhaps I was wrong, and you are not a gentleman after all, if you eavesdrop on private conversations."

"Hardly private. It rang through the town more clearly than a church bell."

"I am sure you misunderstood what you heard."

"Perhaps. However, so that you know me to be

enlightened, too, I assure you that I also do not believe women should be sexual slaves. Unless they enjoy the role, of course."

"While there are unfortunates who find themselves in that role, I am sure none of them enjoy it."

He appeared about to debate the matter. She gave him a withering look. He retreated from the topic, but not from her company.

"My apologies," he finally said. "I fear I have shocked you."

"I suspect it amuses you to shock people, Mr. Fitz-allen. If so, you will find my friendship quite lacking, since nothing shocks *me*."

"Nothing? You are indeed enlightened."

She hastened her steps. She heard a low laugh as his strides kept up.

She abruptly crossed the lane and led him to the door to Mr. Trevor's office. "Mr. Trevor is an archi-tect," she explained as she pressed down on the latch. "He can advise you on workers, and help you far more than I ever can."

Mr. Trevor, a young man with blond hair, spectacles, and an obsequious manner that Eva found irritating, jumped up from his chair when he saw her. She marched over to his massive desk strewn with drawings, and pointed to her companion. "Good day, Mr. Trevor. This is Mr. Fitzallen. He owns the old ruin and intends to rehabilitate it. He will need much advice and many references."

The men greeted each other. Mr. Trevor turned his

attention back to her. "I am grateful for the introduction, Miss Russell. I confess, however, that I had hoped you came about your own property."

"I have already given my answer on that. Now, I will leave the two of you together and be about my business. Oh, and Mr. Trevor, could you let it be known that anyone who chances upon items removed from Mr. Fitzallen's home should return them? There were many who thought it an abandoned house. In error, it appears."

With that she strode out, before Mr. Fitzallen could find a way to take his leave as well.

M r. Trevor watched the lady depart. A man's appreciation showed in Trevor's pale eyes.

"Miss Russell is quite self-possessed, is she not?" Gareth said. "I am fortunate she agreed to aid me as a newcomer."

"She is also a formidable opponent, sometimes. Her weakness is she allows sentiment to at times govern what is a natural intelligence." Trevor sank back into his chair. "I have a family that wants to purchase her property for a handsome sum. She will not sell. She will starve first, I fear."

"She is from one of the old landed families, is she not? They are usually loathe to sell."

"Oh, it is understandable. The Russells once owned five hundred acres, an unentailed freehold. But times being what they are . . . Her father sold much of the land, and her brother's illness sent their situation into a steep decline, of course." He spoke like Gareth knew all this. Gareth did nothing to indicate he did not. "She will sell eventually. She will have to. It will be for the best. She will do far better in a small house here in town."

"I would not count on that happening soon, if it has not already. Once that legacy is gone, it is unlikely to be regained. Property is not easily or cheaply obtained in England. It is why your client wants hers."

Trevor nodded absently, then focused his attention. "Just how bad is that house you have? Is the roof sound at least?"

They spent the next half hour discussing Albany Lodge's condition. Gareth left the office with an agreement that Trevor would visit in two days to assess the damage.

He paid a visit to the ironmonger, then walked back to the main lane and entered one of the taverns, the White Horse.

His appearance stopped conversation. Ten men stared at him in the silence. None of them were gentlemen. This, then, was the tavern favored by the longtime workers and tradesmen of Langdon's End. The new residents, those industrialists building new homes, drank somewhere else.

He sat and called for an ale. The buzz of talk resumed. He took in the dark wood, timbered ceiling, and uneven plastered walls while he drank.

A young man of about twenty-five years, wearing a

brown coat, loose pantaloons, and old-fashioned shoes, sidled over to his table and smiled so amiably all his teeth showed. "Are you the fellow who has taken the old lodge?"

"I am. How did you know?"

"All the talk, it is. How some gentleman from London is going to live there now. Mrs. Fleming told Harold there what you look like, so we figured it was you." He laughed. "Funny, you don't *look* mad."

Gareth called for another ale for his interrogator. "I must be, though, to take on such a pile of stone, right?"

"Probably. Not that I'm one to judge. Best if someone takes it on, is how I see it."

"And others don't?"

The man shrugged.

Gareth gestured for the man to sit when the ale came. "What is your name?"

"Erasmus. Don't laugh. My father had some odd notions. He sent me to school to learn my letters and numbers, another odd notion, so I guess I can live with the name."

"My name is Gareth Fitzallen."

Erasmus took a long drink of ale. "I know. Mrs. Fleming told Harold that too. Also that Miss Russell said anything taken from that house was to be returned."

"Is anyone likely to listen to that?"

"Could be. Miss Russell is liked, in a respectful kind of way. She's quality, but doesn't talk down, like some can. And she has no bother with the new ones much."

"The new residents are not liked as she is?"

"Nah. Noses higher than the queen's, but their grand-fathers were no better than me." He drank again, then leaned over the table with a conspiratorial grin. "Few months ago, some of the new ones were in Mrs. Flem-ing's shop and got very critical of the wares. This wasn't good enough and that wasn't of quality. Miss Russell was there and she told 'em to leave if they were so poorly bred as to not know when to speak and what to say." He chuckled. "Word is their mouths fell open so far you could've seen their lungs." He nodded. "She is true quality. Like you be. Maybe not so high as you, but a gentleman's daughter."

"What is your trade, Erasmus?"

Embarrassed, Erasmus raked his roughly cropped brown hair with his fingers. "My family were tenant farmers. Our place bordered the lake. Real nice land, that. The owner sold, though, and we were put out. Four generations we were there. Now there's no crops but roses, and big houses full of the new ones. So my trade now is whatever comes along." He smiled as a thought came to him. "I guess I'm a this-and-that monger."

"As it happens, I need someone to do this and that."

"Do ya now? Well, I'm your man. There's not much this or that I can't do."

"Come to the house tomorrow. We will start with the this." Gareth stood to go.

Erasmus looked across the tavern to the table where his fair-haired friend still sat. "Say, do you need others?

Harold there was in the army during the war. Served an officer, he claims."

"Tell him to come, too, if he is interested."

After leaving the tavern, Gareth stopped by Mrs. Fleming's shop to purchase one more item, then retrieved his horse from the stable and headed home.

Home. He had to smile at the word. In a manner of speaking, he had not had one since he was sent off to school as a boy. He rather liked that he did now, even if it was a derelict pile of rock.

Erasmus and Harold would be useful in many ways. They knew the town well, and its people. For example, they would know where Miss Russell lived.

CHAPTER 5

Rebecca carefully stitched together a sleeve by the light of the front window. Eva worked on the bodice so that she might fit it today.

"Have you heard from Sarah yet?" Rebecca asked without raising her head from her work.

"I only wrote two days ago. I do not expect an answer right away."

"Do you think she will allow us to stay with her? I would so love to spend several days in Birmingham, and not just the odd day."

"I think that she will."

Sarah was the daughter of her mother's sister, and older than Eva. That side of the family had never been close, probably because her father's family had not approved of his marrying the daughter of a merchant. A wealthy merchant, to hear it, who could have bought and sold Papa three times over even in the best of times.

She kept up a sporadic exchange of letters with Sarah, so that all connection would not be lost. That did not mean Sarah would look kindly on her cousins asking to impose on her hospitality.

If Sarah begged off as expected, the rest of that stash of coins would have to be badly depleted to pay for an inn or a hotel, and they could only stay one night instead of two or three.

Eva shook out the bodice and admired the fabric. She had chosen well. It appeared fresh, but not too girlish. Rebecca would have objected if she were made to appear a schoolgirl in this new dress.

. "Who is *that*?" Rebecca said.

Eva looked over to see her sister staring out the window. Rebecca stood and opened it so she could see clearly.

"Is it another of those strangers who have been about too much the last month?" Eva had seen another one crossing the field beyond their garden four days ago. He could have been a neighbor's friend, of course. He was far enough away that perhaps he was not a stranger at all. Yet unease had prickled through her, much as it did with some of the unknown faces and figures dotting her world these days.

"He looks to be a gentleman, or a very wealthy man, and he is riding a big black horse and is quite dashing. Goodness, he is coming right to our door, I think!"

Eva walked over and peered out. She drew back

quickly and shut the window, then looked around the library. "He is a new acquaintance of mine. I never expected him to call, however. Clear the fabric and notions off the divan. *Quickly.*"

Rebecca hurriedly scooped up her work and dumped it into the sewing basket. Eva tried to make the table where she sat more presentable, then turned the one chair to face the divan. She was thanking God that protective cloths draped the borrowed painting and her work in progress when the rap on the door echoed through the house.

She pointed to the divan. "Sit. We will give him the chair."

"Who is *he*? How did you meet him? Why did you not tell me you had a new friend?" The questions tumbled out in a low voice.

Eva had no time to explain. She went to the door and opened it.

Mr. Fitzallen stood there in all his compelling splendor. She had convinced herself that she exaggerated his appearance in her mind, but no, she had not. At least she did not gawk or fluster this time.

"Mr. Fitzallen, how kind of you to visit. Please join us, and tell me what I can do for you."

He entered and followed her into the library. "I have not come to impose on your helpfulness, Miss Russell. I was riding by and thought I would pay a social call." He made a bow to her, then one to Rebecca, but he did not give her sister any special attention.

The same could not be said of Rebecca. Eyes wide

and face slack, Rebecca appeared struck dumb. *Just as I did several times now,* Eva reminded herself.

"How generous of you, sir." She introduced Rebecca, took a place on the divan, and invited Mr. Fitzallen to use the chair.

"Do your efforts progress well at the lodge?" she asked.

"Ever well, thank you. I hired two of the townsmen. One is proving skilled at repairs. The other was a batman in the army, and has begun organizing the household and serving as valet."

"That must be Harold. He is an honest man."

"As are many of Langdon End's residents, I am learning. I now have three more chairs and two tables. They appeared outside the door yesterday morning, along with a basket of cutlery and several copper pails. I have you to thank for that, I believe."

"I am relieved to hear some of the borrowed items were returned. I think more will be. Then you will not have to furnish the house completely."

Rebecca's big eyes turned on her at mention of borrowed items. Eva ignored her.

"I welcome that. Mr. Trevor visited and drew up a list of major repairs. Today I rode the property, to see what was what there."

"If you have been riding long, you must need refreshment. I can only offer water, but it is from a good spring." She stood. "I will go and bring some for you."

He was on his feet as soon as she. "Allow me. The day is fair. Do you have a garden?"

"Yes, a very nice one."

As he turned to walk around the table, Mr. Fitz-allen saw the paint box. His gaze went to the walls, and two of her paintings that decorated them. He paced over to one, casting a distressingly interested glance at the shrouded canvas on the easel. He squinted at the landscape on the wall.

"Which of you is the artist?"

"I dabble," Eva said. "They are just an amateur's whimsy." No one ever bought her own paintings. Several had been in Mr. Stevenson's shop for years.

"A very good amateur," he said.

"How kind. Thank you." Eva led the way toward the back of the house. "Come along, Rebecca."

"Do you mind if I do not?" Rebecca responded. "I will read my book here, if it will not be thought rude."

"You have been reading for hours," Eva said point-edly, locking her gaze on her sister's. "The day is fair and fresh air will do you good."

"Too fair, I fear," Rebecca said, all innocence. Her big eyes kept shifting subtly to Gareth, and she barely kept a smile from breaking. "This wool I am wearing will be uncomfortable."

"For your health's sake, I must insist that you—" Eva broke off. Rebecca had looked in Gareth's direc-tion with something akin to alarm.

Eva looked over to see Gareth's fingers reaching toward the edge of the cloth covering the borrowed painting.

"Mr. Fitzallen, let us leave and enjoy the garden even if my sister will not," Eva hastened to say.

The fingers halted their path. Mr. Fitzallen agreeably followed her toward the back of the house.

She brought her guest out to the garden, then returned to the kitchen to fetch a crockery tumbler. By the time she returned, Mr. Fitzallen was carrying a pail of water up the path from the springhouse.

There were only benches back here. She sat on one with him, and he dipped the tumbler into the cold water. The breeze blew cool but the sun shone warmly. Tiny leaves speckled the branches of trees and shrubbery, and the tips of plants poked up from the earth.

"It is a very nice garden. Your gardener maintains it very well."

"I am the gardener. I have found that I enjoy growing things, and moving plants and such. Rather like painting, since it is all about color and light and forms."

"Have you been the gardener since your brother became ill?"

"You were told about him? I suppose there is little privacy in a town like ours. I was ignorant of my family's finances until he came home with that pistol ball in his side. His infirmity meant I became aware of how dire our situation had become. I let the servants go at once. So, yes, I have been the gardener since then."

"Yet you discovered a new joy, so you triumphed over adversity."

"Yes. I am proud of this garden. It is my creation now. I like that."

She also liked saying that out loud. There were those who pitied her and Rebecca, as if all that mattered were money. Mr. Fitzallen did not seem to, and that impressed her. She experienced a companionable intimacy with the man listening.

He sat two handsbreadths away from her, so close that her side felt his warmth. His masculine presence affected her in confusing ways. Both comforting and enlivening, his aura promised novelty, fascination, and care.

Perhaps he had not been teasing about being friends. It would be nice to have one.

"It is a nice property." He held up his tumbler, gesturing to the land within the walls, and beyond. "That spring alone makes it valuable, and it is well situated. You could sell, and have an easier future than what you have known recently."

They stood and began strolling on the garden path. "This house and spot of land are all we have. When Rebecca marries, I will give my share to her, so she is not without some sort of fortune. But . . ." She gazed around the garden, then back at the house. "It is also who we are. If I sell, who will we be?" She laughed lightly at her own words. "That sounds stupid. Of course, we will be the same people, just . . ."

"I understand completely."

She could see it in his eyes that he did.

"It was a tragedy that your brother became ill," he

said. "I do not think you have enjoyed life much these past years, while holding things together, for all your pleasure in creating this garden."

"Yes, a tragedy, in several ways." *Your tragic love.* "But. . . had I not been required to hold it all together, I fear we would have lost everything. He expected a gentleman's life that we could not afford."

He stopped walking and turned to her. They stood in the little orchard at the back of the garden, beneath branches dotted with first growth. "I understand that completely too. We will have to make sure you have some fun now, however. I will make it my mission."

"It will be an easy one. I intend to have a good deal of fun in the future. I have spent the last months during our period of mourning planning just how to do it."

He laughed. "Is Langdon's End prepared for Miss Russell determined to have fun? Is the world?"

"Possibly not. The world will have to adapt. You are still welcome to join me, even if it need not be your mission to help."

"Perhaps it is I who will need help. I am a stranger here, remember? Unfortunately, I fear you will be well on your way before I return from a journey I must make."

"I think you have no trouble catching up on fun, when you want to."

He smiled nicely. His stance altered in the subtle ways that spoke of someone preparing to leave. Something stopped him. "Ah, I almost forgot. I brought you this." He reached into his coat.

The gift was a long length of ribbon. She recognized it from Mrs. Fleming's shop. An elegant strip of satin, its deep lavender color spoke of spring.

The gesture touched her. "Thank you. It is beautiful."

"It will look pretty with that muslin you bought. The purple will bring out the primrose in the fabric, and also the blue in your eyes when you wear it."

She carefully wound the ribbon around her hand. "The muslin is not for me. I am making a new dress for my sister."

"Ah. Of course, you are. Well, you can use some of it for the dress, but promise me you will keep enough to wear in your hair."

He left her speechless for a long count, while she gazed down at the ribbon. "You are too kind. I am ashamed that I misjudged you initially. You are not dangerous, as you appear to be."

"Call me Gareth, please. In turn, I would like to address you in private as Eva, if you will permit it."

"Gareth," she said lowly, trying out the informality. "Yes, Eva will do when no one is about."

"I am honored. Now, since we are friends, I am obligated to say something. I must warn that your judgment is actually very sound, Eva. I am indeed dangerous. Especially to lovely, mature women like yourself."

Astonished, she looked up at him. A mistake, that. The gaze that met hers belonged to the dangerous man he warned of. She stared, captivated by that face. His vague smile stirred her.

Was he going to kiss her? Was he that bold? It appeared so. The very notion had her pulse quickening.

What to do? She must not allow it, yet—she could not bring herself to move away, or utter some arch reply. She just waited, and the waiting itself affected the air and the garden and the space between them. She experienced a most shocking excitement.

It seemed a long time they stood there, gazes locked, until the waiting turned almost painful. An outrageous idea entered her mind—to stretch up and kiss him first.

He stepped back. His gaze shifted to the garden, away from her. When he looked at her again he was just the charming new friend once more, although the smallest thoughtful frown creased his brow.

He bowed. "I must take my leave now. I will be back within the month. Perhaps as early as a fortnight. I will call on you when I return."

Then he was gone, striding through the garden to the side portal.

CHAPTER 6

"I see my letter found you," Ives said as Gareth walked into the library of Langley House in London.

"I hired a man for Albany Lodge who had enough sense to forward it on. What are you doing here?" The letter had arrived that morning, catching Gareth as he planned to leave town. The count's paintings had arrived, their purchase completed, and transport to their new home arranged. Hendrika's fee had already made its way to Amsterdam, and his own purse bulged happily with his commission.

If he did not face the return to Langdon's End with total contentment, the reason had to do with Eva Russell. A pleasant friendship had become complicated in the span of one minute during his visit to her.

He had almost kissed her. He could not deny it, although it made no sense. Eva Russell was not the kind of woman he pursued. Unmarried, gentry, country—she was the opposite of the ladies with whom he had affairs. Nor did he kiss, or do anything else with women, impetuously. Yet in that garden the joyful simmer of arousal that he knew so well had almost defeated his better sense.

He had warned her off while the battle with his inclinations raged, but it had done no good. It still amazed him that he had managed to walk away from her breathless anticipation. His own astonishment with his own impulses had probably saved the day.

Ives set aside a book he had been reading. "Lance insisted on coming. He was going mad. I could not stop him, so I had to accompany him to keep an eye on things."

"Any change in the inquiry?"

Ives shook his head. "It is stalled, but they won't give it up yet. The magistrates visited to chat with Lance. None dared accuse him, but the questions turned pointed."

"And his answers?"

"He regaled them with explanations of the many far better ways to kill a man than poison. Some were quite creative."

Gareth laughed. Ives did not. He leveled a curious look at Gareth instead. "Albany Lodge?"

"It needed a name."

"I wish Percy were alive to hear the one you gave it."

"Once the property is mine free and clear, I will go to his grave and tell him all about it."

"That will ensure he does not rest peacefully for a long while."

Gareth walked around the library. "I have not been in this house in years. Nothing has changed much. I am glad."

"I hope the memories you are pacing through are good ones," Ives said.

"Better ones than the memories bound to Albany Lodge. Percy tainted those, deliberately, while the time in this library with the duke had nothing to do with Percy, or anyone else."

He circled through the vast space, impressed by the warm familiarity it produced. Dukes by nature and position were not given to easy intimacy, but there had been a few times here when he had felt like a son.

Let me hear you read this here, so I know that school is not neglecting you. A gentleman is known by his mind and education, Gareth, as well as his blood. The boys at school are hard on you because you are a bastard, but remember why you are there, and whose son you are.

"You are free to stay here when in town," Ives said. "Lance said as much. Or at Merrywood, when you are near there. He told the servants you would use the family properties as our father's son."

Gareth kept pacing and peering at details, mostly to hide his reaction to this astonishing offer. With one small gesture of generosity, Lance had wiped away a lifetime of never belonging in any of the houses, or anywhere at all. It moved Gareth, and would take some time to accommodate.

"Have you made any progress on that investigation?" Ives asked.

"A little. I traced the likely path of the wagons. I rode the same route when I came to town, taking note of my surroundings and the properties I passed or crossed."

"I have taken the opportunity while here to gather some information for you. Names of servants and teamsters, such as can be remembered. Also letters of introduction to the families who live near the final resting place of the paintings. I am sure you can find an excuse to visit them."

"That will be helpful." Hell if he knew how he would find an excuse to visit them. Ives sometimes forgot that he and Lance could turn up at the door of any aristocrat and expect the easy hospitality those families shared without question. Gareth could not. "Do you have a list of the paintings that went missing? Without it, I will not know what I have found, should I find anything at all."

"That will be forthcoming in a week. I will have it sent to you. Here? Or . . . Albany Lodge?"

"I should be back there by then. In fact, I should be leaving in the morning, so I will take my leave now."

"I would prefer you did not." Ives objected mildly, with some chagrin. "Our brother desires to go out tonight. I cannot prevent it. However, I would like some help with him, if you do not mind."

Right now he would probably throw himself in the way of a musket ball for Lance. He immediately recalculated his schedule to allow for sleeping in tomorrow. "I don't mind. A night on the town with Lance is never boring."

"Yes, well, I regret to say our goal is to make it very boring indeed."

Boring meant gambling in halls favored by the well-born, instead of one of the democratic halls Lance preferred. Ives put his foot down when it came time to choose, because Lance's favorite venues almost always featured one or two bouts of fisticuffs among their denizens, which Lance had a weakness for joining.

At midnight, Ives and Gareth found themselves watching Lance bid higher and higher at the faro table. Patrons who had already lost too much watched too. A thick crowd had formed.

"He is being deliberately reckless," Ives muttered.

"He can afford it now, I assume."

"No one can afford it unless they win most of the time," Ives said.

Lance did win this time. He did not notice the buzz of talk that created. Behind him, Gareth heard one comment most clearly. "He looks calm for a man who probably did a murder. Of course, so did the French on their way to the guillotine. Blood will show, no matter what, eh?"

A few masculine chuckles responded.

Gareth glanced sideways to see if Ives had heard. Regrettably, he had, if his hard jawline meant anything. He looked down to see Ives's fist clenching.

That was the problem with Ives. He talked like a lawyer and thought like a lawyer, and he appeared eminently sensible and even-tempered—but when angered, he often threw the first punch.

"They are in their cups. Ignore them," Gareth muttered.

"Can't do that. Can't let such talk stand. One more word and—"

"Poison it is said," that man's voice said. "A woman's weapon. I always said he was all talk."

Ives pivoted and pushed through the knot of bodies to the voice.

Gareth followed. He found himself facing Lord Kniveton. He knew the viscount well, although they had never been introduced.

"Speak ill of my brother, and you will answer to me," Ives said.

Kniveton thought that very funny. "What are you going to do? Thrash me with a stack of briefs?"

"I am more inclined to meet you on the field of honor than in a court of law."

Kniveton paused just enough to show he was worried he had started down a bad path. Then he sneered. "It would be a shame to kill you when it is your brother I'd like to see dead."

Ives moved so fast Gareth almost did not grab him in time. He clung to Ives's arm so he could not follow through with his fist. "Do not let him goad you, Ives. Kniveton is only slandering Lance because he mistakenly thinks Lance fucked his wife. He extracts a coward's revenge, nothing more."

"Who in hell are you?" Kniveton bellowed, drawing attention from the closest in the crowd.

"I'm the bastard brother."

"Ah, yes, I have heard about *you*. Well, bastard, I don't think he made free with my wife, I *know*, and I'll be the first to vote his conviction when the lords try him."

"Your desire to harm his name and person is misplaced. He did not cuckold you."

"I know he did."

"You are wrong."

"The hell I am. I found a letter she wrote to him. Hemingford, she addressed him."

"That would not be him." Ives, his temper under control, turned back into the lawyer examining evidence logically, methodically. Gareth would have preferred angry, but silent. "He is never called Hemingford by his lovers."

Kniveton frowned. "If not him, who? Not Percival."

"Percy was too much a miser to get entangled with a woman who expects the gifts your wife is reputed to demand."

"Reput— What the— That only leaves—" He glared at Ives.

"Sorry, not me. I insist my lovers address me in another way. Calling me Hemingford lacks the appropriate sentiment."

Gareth looked over with curiosity. "You never struck me as one for all the darlings and pet names women use."

"I can't abide them. I much prefer being addressed My Lord and Master, actually."

"Hell, if it wasn't one of the two of them, who was it? We've run out of Hemingfords, so someone is lying."

An odd silence fell. Gareth tried to appear as perplexed as the others.

Ives cast him a sidelong, questioning look.

Kniveton gazed sharply at Lance, who had won again, then suspiciously at Ives. Then, quizzically at Gareth. One could all but hear his befuddled brain sorting through it all.

"You."

"Under the circumstances, so you do not disparage my brothers in ways that will lead to a duel, I will admit it. She was addressing that letter to me. It is I with whom she still does wicked things in her dreams."

"The hell you say. You are not a Hemingford."

"Not officially. She liked to call me that anyway. Perhaps she found it more erotic to suck the cock of a duke's son if she pretended he were legitimate."

Kniveton appeared confused for a three count, as if he needed a moment to believe he had heard correctly. His two friends bit back grins.

"How dare— She never— I should call you out!"

"If you must, then do. However, I would rather not kill you over a pleasure so long ago enjoyed, fond though the memory might be."

Kniveton lunged. Gareth ducked. Kniveton's fist

landed on the jaw of a man in the crowd who had turned to watch the show.

Ives grabbed Kniveton, set him back, and gestured to his friends. "He is foxed, and will be grateful tomorrow if you remove him now. He does not want to duel with this one. Bastard he may be, but he can shoot a button off a man's coat without ripping the wool it decorates."

The two of them restrained Kniveton, and pulled him away.

Ives's mouth and forehead frowned, but his eyes twinkled. "You did have to describe the lady's finest talent."

"If she were my wife, I would want to know so I got my fair share."

The crowd dispersed. Lance walked to them. "What did Kniveton want?"

"To see you swing," Ives said.

"I can't blame him. I did fuck his wife. She really likes to s—"

"Yes, we know," Ives said.

Lance wandered away, toward the hazard table.

Ives looked at Gareth. "Damn, all this talk of the lady's predilections has me hard as an iron rod. Did you lie to draw the fire, or am I the only brother who did not get his fair share, as you put it?"

Gareth shrugged, and followed Lance.

E va handed her shopping basket to the footman, who set it aside. Then she followed him into a pretty drawing room decorated in the incongruous styles of the two women who lived in this fine house. Jeweled tones mixed with pastels, and paisleys with florals. Pretty landscapes decorated the walls, right next to somewhat odd images reminiscent of Mr. Blake's illustrations.

The sisters Neville received her from their respective perches. Ophelia sat in a diminutive upholstered rose-hued chair. Light from the window turned her blond hair into a haze, making it look like the pale ethereal seed head of a dandelion waiting for a strong breeze or breath. Jasmine lounged on a divan, her long curls following the same hills and valleys as her shapeless silk robe.

They had sent a letter yesterday, inviting her to call on them. They never had before. She assumed they wanted to discuss the same topic she had broached outside Mr. Duran's shop, only in the privacy of their home.

Tea was served. Eva sipped slowly, enjoying the luxury. She never drank tea. Good tea was far too expensive, and cheap tea tasted like the adulterated bad bargain it was.

"We are so happy you have called," Ophelia said. "We would have called on you, but your sister said you prefer if people do not."

"As if we care how many chairs there are," Jasmine intoned. "Life is what it is. There is no shame in a woman's poverty, especially since it is almost never that woman's fault."

"How understanding of you," Eva said. "All the same, Rebecca thinks it would prove awkward to ask guests to stand the whole time."

"She is correct on that, Jasmine. You must admit it."
Jasmine nodded, grudgingly.

"As for why we would have called," Ophelia continued. "One reason would be to know you better. We have often commented that it was too bad you never came with Rebecca, so we could make your better acquaintance. While your brother was ill, it was understandable, of course, but since then—"

"You should be out and about more, and not only to shop," Jasmine interrupted. "You never attend assemblies or stroll along the lake. You took on some habits while you cared for him that you should endeavor to break now that your year of mourning is over."

"I do not think Miss Russell needs our advice, sister." Ophelia subtly rolled her eyes in Eva's direction. "Even if she may understand it is only your good heart that causes you to offer it."

Eva just smiled.

"We also wanted to speak to you about something else," Ophelia said.

"Since you spoke so frankly with us the other day on the lane, we assumed you would not mind our doing the same in turn," Jasmine inserted.

"I can hardly object, as you so neatly point out. Pray tell, what do you feel obligated to say?"

"I hope you know that we speak and act as friends," Ophelia said.

"Of course. With good hearts, as you said."

Jasmine righted herself on the divan. Her exotic robe made her appear like some foreign oracle. "We have friends in London. Old friends. Good friends. We wrote to them, to learn what we could about him."

"Him?"

"Mr. Fitzallen. Gareth Fizallen," Ophelia said. "Did you know he is the bastard of the Duke of Aylesbury? The third duke, of course."

"His mother was the butler's daughter. Aylesbury made her his mistress. Kept her for years. Decades. Until he died," Jasmine said.

"Such arrangements are not uncommon among the nobility," Eva said, lest the sisters think she was so provincial as to be shocked by the revelations. "Nor is a man responsible for his own birth, I think you will agree."

Jasmine looked at her sister meaningfully. Ophelia appeared chagrined.

"I told you," Jasmine said. "See how she defends him."

"Only because I, too, strive to have a good heart," Eva said.

Jasmine speared her with a knowing glare. "See here. Your sister said he called at your house. Brought a little gift. Erasmus says he has asked about your brother's illness and other things related to your family's history."

"Other things," Ophelia echoed quietly.

"So we wrote to our friends to see what he was."

"And learned he was a bastard. I already knew that. He told me at once. It should not matter to anyone, but perhaps my heart is too good if I think so."

Jasmine threw up her hands. "Tell her, Ophelia. Perhaps she will hear it better if it comes from you."

"Tell me what?"

Ophelia looked pained. "We do not expect you to care that he is a bastard. However, it is his character that gave us pause. It is not the best. He has a reputation that we thought you should know about, lest you . . . that is, so he does not . . ."

"Seduce and abandon," Jasmine boomed. "Tell lies, take advantage, and bring shame upon your family."

Her voice rang through the drawing room. Eva looked to be sure the windows were closed.

"He is reputed to be very wicked," Ophelia said. "Most skilled in his seductions. Wives, widows, women of maturity like yourself—"

"Mostly wives," Jasmine said. "But our friends say he considers any female over twenty-three fair game, and some suspect he has even deflowered innocent girls." She lowered her voice, as if confiding a secret. "We are told that he employs certain *exotic* techniques that leave women enthralled, even addled, and unable to give him up. Some of the highest-born ladies, names you would know, have sought to keep him closer than is wise. As a young man right out of university he had a long affair with one lady, who herself has a reputation for romantic excess. The relationship became notorious. She kept him like a pet and spent a small fortune on him."

"Perhaps she corrupted him," Ophelia offered. "His current character would not be his fault, then. Not entirely."

"Oh, sister, sister, sister. You will always look for excuses for the wicked. It does you no credit."

"That is not true. You always see the worst and I do not, that is all."

Eva cleared her throat to draw their attention, before she witnessed a long exchange of bickering. "I am grateful, of course, that you chose to share this with me. I need to reassure you that Mr. Fitzallen has no such interest in me. I am the last woman to turn such a man's head, even for a few hours. I think we can all agree that while he may someday be wicked with a lady in Langdon's End, it will not be me."

They both looked at her in a peculiar way. Then at each other. Then at her.

"It goes without saying that we are not concerned about *you*," Jasmine said.

"It is Rebecca whom we fear will attract his wickedness."

Of course. They worried for beautiful Rebecca. *It was me he almost kissed. He gave that little gift to me. I am the one he might seduce and abandon.* She came close to saying it. Shouting it. Except she knew the sisters were correct. She was in no danger. None at all.

On reflection—much reflection—she had concluded she had been mistaken and he had not almost kissed her. For one thing, from the sound of things, Gareth did not *almost* kiss women. Far from it.

"You are so good to be concerned for my sister. I am truly touched. If it gives you any peace, let me say that he barely looked at her when he visited."

"That is a common strategy of such men. The question is whether she looked at *him*," Jasmine said.

"How could she not? Of course she was impressed. He is very handsome. However, after he left, I asked her what she thought of him. Her response will amuse you. She said he was beautiful, but old."

"He can't be more than thirty years," Ophelia said. "Perhaps even a few years younger."

"To a girl her age, thirty is ancient. It was when I was eighteen." Rebecca's dismissal of Gareth as too old had been a mixed blessing. While she was glad Rebecca would not form a tendre for him, finding her sister a husband would be much harder if she persisted in thinking thirty years was old.

Ophelia looked relieved. Jasmine appeared half-appeased.

"You must keep an eye on her, all the same," Jasmine said. "Who knows what wily plans he might have. He has no fortune, so if the worst happens she will hardly be better off if he does the right thing, which his reputation suggests he will not. Other than a modest income from the duke, and that pile of stone he now calls Albany Lodge, he has nothing. As a bastard, he never will."

Eva stood. "I will be very cautious and make sure Rebecca does not get enthralled or addled, I promise. Now, I must return to her. I have been gone overlong."

She stepped out of the house, not knowing whether to be insulted or amused. The sisters Neville had not told her anything she had not already surmised about Gareth. Of far more interest had been the reference to *exotic techniques*. She wondered what in the world that meant, and why they apparently left women begging for more.

On her way home, she remembered the errands that had sent her to town in the first place. She fished into her basket for a letter that had come. She had picked it up while posting one of her own.

Sarah had written. She opened the letter, hoping she could give Rebecca good news. She made a little jump of joy after she read the first sentence.

Sarah had invited them to visit for a few days when next they went to Birmingham.

E va tapped her fingertips against the gray-blue of the fountain, checking to see how tacky the oil paint remained. If she packed it carefully, perhaps it could make the trip to Birmingham along with the others. She would have to tell Mr. Stevenson to hang it immediately, however.

She had spent the last ten days finishing this painting, and the dress, and attempting to create miracles of improvements on other garments. Right now Rebecca sewed by the light of the big window, attaching some new trimmings to an old pelisse. The goal—the hope—was to appear not nearly as out of date as the age of those garments might indicate.

She lifted the painting she had copied. Wrapped again in its burlap, she rested its weight on her hip. "I am going now. I should be back in an hour or so."

Rebecca looked up. "Can it not wait until we return

from our journey? I had hoped to have your help with this."

"He is gone now and may have returned by then. Best if this resides in its attic when we leave town."

"I doubt he will miss it if it is never returned. You said that attic is hard to find. And should he discover it and somehow know something is missing, he is not likely to think you took it what with so much else missing too."

"It is a painting of some value, Rebecca. A few chairs that would probably end up as a vagrant's firewood are one thing. A Gainsborough painting is another. Honesty decrees I return it."

"Go then. I will begin to warm the soup if you are not back soon."

Eva let herself out of the house and strode down the drive to the lane. Albany Lodge sat no more than fifteen minutes north of their house. She reached the road that connected the two properties, and soon passed the crossroads with the other road that took one to Langdon's End.

She rounded the bend and Albany Lodge jumped into view. It appeared no different from the past. Nothing indicated someone now inhabited it and that repairs were under way.

He would be gone at least a fortnight, Gareth had said. Erasmus and Harold had not been working at the property during its master's absence. She trusted no one would be about this afternoon and see her complete her mission.

Tacking for horses, a jumble of cutlery, and an assortment of jars and crockery bowls decorated the lodge's portico floor when she arrived at the lodge. The citizens of Langdon's End had done as she now did, and taken advantage of Gareth's absence to return more of the items borrowed over the years. This batch had perhaps been lured out of its temporary lodgings by the vicar's sermon on Sunday, in which he preached on the commandment not to steal.

Gareth's habitation proved more obvious inside than out. Refuse and dust had disappeared. A few items of furniture gave the reception hall a spare but lived-in appearance. Someone had even cleaned the fireplace and scrubbed the hearthstones. She looked in the library and saw similar improvements.

The painting grew heavy in her arms. Carrying it up the stairs proved a chore. She soldiered on, up to the servant quarters then down to a small door tucked to the side at the end of the corridor. She had missed this access to the upper attics her first few times exploring the empty house. When she finally found it and ventured above, the contents had amazed her.

She clutched the painting firmly and maneuvered the narrow stairs into the dusty, warm space right under the roof of one of the stone wings to the house. Little light penetrated because it had only one window, which was small and obscured by the deep eaves of the roof. It would be easy to miss the forms against the walls, covered by blankets. She almost had.

She set down her painting, carefully positioning it

so it stood in front of a large, flat surface hidden by a blanket. She slid the blanket up. A bit of light caught the bright colors of tulips and glass on the canvas surface, rendered with such realism as to invite one to touch the different textures. The painting was Dutch, she was sure, and probably from the seventeenth century. She had been tempted to try and copy it, but it was just large enough to be impossible to carry home.

She let the blanket drop so that it covered the three little boys and the fountain, now returned to their stack of paintings. She looked down the wall at other small canvases that she would not be able to borrow now that Gareth had moved into the house.

He had not found this attic yet, but eventually he would. Then he would most likely move the paintings back to the walls below, from where they had no doubt been taken when the house was closed up after the last time the duke visited.

Even if he never found them, she could hardly cart one out right under his nose, or return it the same way.

Could she?

She walked to the final stack of paintings and lifted the blanket. She had intended to borrow the ones here. Without them, she was not sure how she and Rebecca would live once the money from the current group was spent. It might be impossible to build new lives, too, let alone have the fun she so proudly informed Gareth she intended to have.

If Gareth made journeys like this one with any kind of frequency, and if she did not tell him about the attic, might she on occasion still ply her copyist trade and earn a few shillings?

She lifted the front painting, a small landscape with peasants in front and a ruined castle in the background. She thought the subject would appeal to many of Mr. Stevenson's patrons.

Her conscience debated with her practicality over the temptation to leave with a bundle just as she had arrived. While she concentrated on her conflicting inclinations, an intuitive awareness crept into her mind.

She froze and listened. Nothing. And yet—she sensed she was no longer alone in the house.

Perhaps Erasmus had come by, or Harold. Should they see her leaving, she expected she could come up with a passable excuse. All the same her heart thudded and alarm sharpened her senses. She set down the painting, tiptoed to the attic's top stair, and listened again. More silence.

She tried to tell herself she was being a goose, but she still felt someone's presence. Not up on the servant's level, but below somewhere. She felt more than heard footsteps.

What if it was not Erasmus or Harold, or even someone from the town? What if a thief who knew the house had returned, unaware that it now was inhabited? What if one of those strangers who seemed to always be around had entered? She did not want to come face-to-face with such a man.

She also did not want to get trapped up in this attic.

Listening hard, sure she was wrong but knowing

she was right, she descended the stairs as quietly as possible. She pulled the door closed behind her, and aimed for the servants' stairs to the lower levels.

By the time she reached the first storey, she convinced herself she had conjured up ghosts out of thin air. All the same she slipped quickly past the doors to the main staircase, making as little noise as possible.

Light poured over the threshold of the door closest to the stairs. She tried to recall the house's arrangement. That door led to a bedchamber, like most of the rooms up here, but it had not been a big one or very grand, as she remembered. It had been emptied of everything years ago.

All the same she attempted silence while she approached. She cautiously peered around the doorjamb.

Her memory had failed her. This was not a minor bedchamber. It was the entrance to a large dressing room. Worse, the owner of the house now occupied it.

And he was naked.

Gareth stood with his back to her, without a stitch of clothing on. He appeared to be preparing to dress. Garments waited on a chair nearby, and he worked at unfolding a shirt. Water pools glistened on the floor near the washstand.

Every inch of her body tensed and demanded she leave, fast, and make her escape. Her mind refused to listen. She just stared with breathless fascination.

She had seen her brother naked, of course. Even as an adult, since she had taken care of him. But by then he was wasted and thin and nothing like this. This man was in his prime, with tense, broad shoulders and tight skin and muscles and hard, round swells for his bottom. She found that part especially compelling, although she looked hard at his legs.

He set aside the shirt, and reached for trousers. Suddenly his hand froze a few inches above the garments. Awareness flexed through him like a ripple. His profile hardened into dangerous planes and his mouth into an uncompromising line. His other hand stretched toward the dressing table.

Alarmed, she turned and scurried back the way she had come, to the servant stairs. She prayed the garden door below would be unlocked.

*D*amnation. Gareth acknowledged the prickle in his blood for what it was. A warning. Someone else was in the house, and not far away.

He reached toward the dressing table. Upon arriving back, he had set his dagger there when he undressed. He never traveled without one, after being the victim of a highwayman when he was at university.

His hand closed on it, and he turned. He saw no one in the chamber, or at the door. Someone had been there, however. He had all but felt the thief's breath.

He threw the dagger down, pulled on his trousers, grabbed the weapon again, and strode out of the dressing room. He'd be damned before he allowed trespassers to make free with the lodge, especially while he was inside it. One confrontation, one capture and strong warning, and word would spread that the situation had changed.

Faint sounds came to him, from the back of the house. Whoever had intruded now descended the servant stairs, and not even stealthily. He did not pursue in that direction. Rather he ran down the main stairs, outside, and around the house.

More sounds back here, in the basement kitchen. The low windows proved too dirty to peer through. He walked down the stairs to the submerged door, and positioned himself to its side. With luck the thief had not availed himself of a kitchen knife.

The thud of the door's bar shoved aside. His thief pushed against a door whose hinges needed oil. On the third attempt the door flew open.

Gareth grabbed at the figure flying out, swung it around, and slammed it against the stone wall. Even as he did, he knew he had made a mistake.

CHAPTER 7

Eva landed hard against the stones. A cry escaped her and her eyes clenched against the pain. When she opened them again, an astonished, furious Gareth held her shoulder against the wall. Her gaze locked on the dagger aimed at her chest. His own chest, still naked, framed the view.

"Eva! What in hell—" His gaze shifted from her to the dagger. He threw the weapon down and lessened his grip on her shoulder. He did not release her, however. "What are you doing here?"

She thought fast. "I went for a walk and thought I would see if Erasmus was here. I had a question for him."

Gareth's lids lowered. "Things are not so improved that they require a caretaker when I leave. If you have been to town even once during my absence, you would know he was not coming here while I was gone."

Thinking fast had not helped her. Nor did thinking slowly. She could not drum up another good reason for being here.

"Did you come here to see whether I had returned?" His gaze darkened. Deepened.

"Of course not." There was nothing else for it. "You said you would be gone at least a fortnight, and I thought perhaps while you were gone I could see the improvements you had made."

"Do you often enter other homes when their owners are gone?"

Such an unfortunate question. "I am sorry. I should have never entered."

"Do not apologize. I am glad you came." His hand fell from her shoulder. Finally. "Come inside. I will show you the improvements." A slow smile formed, but he looked no friendlier. "Several chambers still require new fabrics and such. You can advise me."

"I . . . really cannot . . . That is, it would not be . . . appropriate for me to . . ."

Her words died in her throat. He had stepped closer. That put her nose at most six inches from his chest.

"Come now, Eva. If it was appropriate for you to enter the house, and appropriate for you to watch me wash—"

"I did not watch you wash!"

"Correction. Watch me dress. Even so, after that

you can hardly quibble about your setting foot inside to advise on drapery."

She was mortified that he realized she had seen him before he dressed, incomplete though the dressing had been. She should pretend she had not, and react with anger. Only at the moment, try as she might to summon shock and indignation, she instead found herself making heroic efforts not to stare at his naked chest which, it seemed to her, all but begged for very close study indeed.

She forced her gaze over his right shoulder, then his left, then to the ground—anywhere except the handsome face and the knowing half smile of private amusement. That chest kept looming in her view, however, drawing her glances like a magnet draws iron shavings. She noted how taut the skin looked and how hard, and the tight lines as it tapered to his trousers. She wondered what it felt like . . .

She sneaked a glance at his face. He was watching her watch. His expression appeared intense, serious, and as wicked as the sisters Neville had warned.

She looked down, feeling her face heat. "I should go . . . I must go."

A hand on her chin turned her face. "Do not be embarrassed. It is normal to be curious. The only shame is if all the *musts* and *shoulds* drown out the *wants* that we hear inside ourselves."

She smelled the soap he had just washed with. She pictured him standing in the dressing room not long ago. Her mind filled with that image, and the sensation of his hand on her face and the shocking way she yearned to press her fingertips against his body, to discover more and to perhaps feel if his blood thrummed like hers was doing now.

He tipped up her chin so she looked in his eyes. Dark eyes, endlessly deep and full of life and experience and thoughts of only her.

His thumb caressed her lips. They trembled and pulsed from the connection, and the sensation entered her blood. That felt so good. Terribly, wonderfully good.

He angled his head and kissed her mouth. Gently at first, but almost immediately it became a ravishment. It was as if one small breach meant the whole wall fell.

Oh, what a kiss it was. She let herself enjoy it while she inhaled the scent of him. She allowed the *wants* to have their way, and to respond to his wants in kind. She did nothing to end the kiss because she did not want it to end. Five years of duty disappeared, and she was a girl again, rediscovering the taste of forbidden fruit.

She did not object when he embraced her. She felt no shock at finding her body pressed against him so that she felt his skin through her garments and his warmth all around her. He deepened the kiss, calling forth chaotic wonderment and daring. Pleasures cascaded through her body until she lost all sense of propriety.

She ventured her own embrace. The sensation of his skin beneath her palms entranced her. She pressed her fingertips against the hard muscles beneath the soft skin. That very small aggression emboldened him. He tightened his embrace in return and seduced her lips apart so his kiss could become invasive.

More astonishment, at how she reveled in the way his size and strength dominated her. Her sensuality, dormant for so long, too long, raged now, as if this physical contact fanned its flames.

His forehead pressed hers. He gazed down at his hand while his fingers trailed over her neck and along the top of her dress. "You surprise me, Eva."

"Do you want me to push you away and storm off indignant?"

"Hell, no. Not unless you want me to die. Come here." He drew her to a bench set against the house's bricks and pulled her onto his lap. His finger splayed over her crown to hold her head to a fevered, demanding kiss. The pleasure began again, as if there had been no pause.

His head bent and he kissed her neck, and the skin exposed by her bodice. Thrills started shooting deep and low until she wanted to squirm. Caresses, firm and knowing, made it worse. A touch on her breast, light as a feather, made her gasp. Others, less light, had her head swimming.

That felt too good. Wickedly so. Much better than the vague arousals caused by the few embraces with Charles, when her breasts pressed his chest enough to stir her. Gareth's caresses proved deliberately provocative. She knew, even as she succumbed, that his goal was to master her will.

She did not care. Did *not care*. All the *shoulds* lined

up, and her desire kicked them away. She wanted this, her body did as did her soul, but mostly the part of her that controlled all of her senses demanded it.

He unbuttoned her pelisse and slid it off so masterfully she barely noticed. The fastenings on her dress loosened under his caress on her back. That same hand gently eased the fabric off her shoulders and down her arms while his other hand continued distracting her by fondling her breasts.

When the fabric of her chemise moved, however, she started in shock. Reality forced itself into her awareness. The most gentle kiss on her cheek urged her to be calm.

"I want to see how lovely you are, Eva. And I want you to know the best pleasure. You will allow it now."

She did not agree, nor did she object. She did allow it, as he commanded. Aghast at how the promise of pleasure swayed her, she watched him push the chemise off her shoulders until her breasts rose high and bare above the garments bunched at her waist.

"Perfect," he muttered, dipping his head to kiss one, then the other. "You are beautiful, Eva."

The flattery poked at her better sense. A poignant ache shot through her, as she acknowledged that just perhaps, maybe, she was being a fool. But then his fingertips started playing at her bare nipples, and she thought about nothing at all.

Heavenly. Luscious. She did squirm now, to try and relieve the pulsing need torturing her more and more. His head lowered to kiss her again, then he used his tongue and teeth to make her arousal unbearable. She held on to his bare shoulder while wave after wave of incredible sensation crested in her body.

"Are you a virgin?" His question feathered into her ear while his touch continued tantalizing her.

She barely heard. Barely answered. Finally she nodded.

Fingertips rolled over her two nipples until she was breathless and immobile. His mouth began its devastating arousals again, while his caresses claimed all of her. Her hips and thighs, her bottom and back. All of her. A sensual stupor engulfed her. The need pulsed more and more, aching and wanting. A frantic yearning entered her euphoria. It grew until it absorbed the pleasure within itself.

Then, unmistakably, he stilled. His hands did, and his whole body. Her body screamed in frustration, but beneath her silent chaos she heard what he heard. Noises came through the quiet day, from around the other side of the house.

Horrified, she looked at herself, and at him. Reality forced itself into her stupor. More sounds now. Gareth stood with her in his arms, carried her over to the door of the house, and set her on her feet. "Come with me."

He led her into the kitchen, then up to the first level. "No one will come inside, I promise you. I will see what is happening. Go upstairs and wait for me."

He strode toward the front of the house. She ran up to the public rooms, fighting to get her chemise and dress back on as she did. She ran to the front room and looked out the window. Down below the sounds came again. She opened the window a crack.

"You are back, sir. That is a surprise. Did not expect you so soon." It was Erasmus speaking. "I seem to have disturbed your rest. I apologize. I just came to bring that stone in the wagon there for the wall, and saw these things here. More must've heard of Miss Russell's instructions that things taken be returned. I thought I would bring them inside."

"That is not necessary. I will do it," Gareth said. "Just bring the stone to the garden."

"I'll take the wagon to the back garden portal, and unload it there. Are you home for a time now, sir? Should Harold and I come tomorrow?"

"I may leave again for short journeys, but you can both come tomorrow morning. I will come along and help with the stone."

Eva stared down at her haphazard dressing. Her close call stunned her. What if Gareth had not heard Erasmus, and they had been discovered like that, both half-naked? What if Erasmus had not come at all?

She finished fixing her garments. She fastened her dress with trembling fingers. When the wagon wheels outside faded away, she slipped out of the chamber and down the stairs.

Gareth tried to give a damn about the stone wall while Erasmus explained what must be done. He had found similar stones at a mason's farm a bit to the south, he explained, and had taken it upon himself to procure it.

All the while Gareth's mind was on that bench, with Eva on his lap. Her astonished cries of pleasure formed a melody behind Erasmus's drone.

Had they not been interrupted . . . His mind's eye saw Eva totally naked, straddling his legs, her eyes glistening with her abandoned joy.

He glanced to the bench near the garden door. A brown smudge caught his eye. Eva's pelisse. The fantasy vanished. Erasmus's voice seemed to boom. The last hour presented itself with ruthless objectivity.

What in hell had he been thinking? Nothing sensible, that was clear, if there had been any thought at all. He could not remember. A lie, that. He had thought plenty, and would have taken her except for the interruption. Even when he sent her above to dress, he fully intended to join her and unfasten that dress again.

That brown pelisse loomed on the bench, visible out of the corner of his eye. If Erasmus saw it, there could be hell to pay. For Eva. Always for the woman. His own reputation had long ago become famous for such things, but he hardly suffered for it.

He pictured her above stairs, worried about that pelisse, perhaps watching from a window. The way she had accepted pleasure had charmed him. Incited him. Still, he prided himself on control. He did not act impulsively. He did not put women at such risk. He did not even trifle with women like Eva Russell.

"It should only take one or two days," Erasmus explained, summing up what had been a lengthy lesson in wall building. "Less time with help from Harold."

Gareth pulled half his mind out of his crotch. "It will be good to have the garden secure again."

Erasmus nodded. "I'll be taking the wagon back now, unless you want me to put all those things from the portico away."

"No need to do that now. Be on your way."

Erasmus walked toward the garden's back portal. Gareth strode to the house, grabbed the pelisse, and entered.

He formed his apology on the way upstairs. He went to his dressing room and pulled on a shirt, then went looking for Eva. He looked forward to correcting his inexplicable error in judgment.

He could not find her. He threw open the door of the final room he searched. It was empty too.

He strode to the window. In the distance, he could see a small brown form moving quickly along the road to where it bent out of sight.

CHAPTER 8

Eva peered into her looking glass. Besides her face, its reflection showed the chaos in her chamber. Most of her garments lay on her bed, waiting for her to choose the ones she would take to Birmingham. She had been too agitated the past two days to complete the task, and now she would be up half the night getting prepared.

She opened the drawer of her dressing table a crack and eyed the crisp white letter within. It had arrived this morning, delivered by Erasmus. Before she read it, she took the opportunity to ask Erasmus to keep an eye on the house while she and Rebecca were gone. Not that there was anything to steal. She felt better knowing someone would check on occasion, however.

With Erasmus working for Mr. Fitzallen, stopping by here would not be inconvenient.

Mr. Fitzallen. She had forced herself to think of him that way ever since she ran from his house. It had been a mistake to allow the informality of first names. One of many mistakes.

He also had retreated into formalities in that letter.

Dear Miss Russell,

Business affairs take me away again for several days. When I return, I will call on you, to speak words that our last meeting demands.

Your servant,
Gareth Fitzallen

She assumed he would call on her to apologize. If that notion produced a foolish pang of disappointment, she could not be blamed. He had disrobed more than her body. He had uncovered yearnings and needs she did not even know existed in her. She rather wished he had not, so she would know some peace again.

She had only to think of that hour with him to shock herself anew. Yet, the long, strict scold she gave herself as she hurried home needed repeating over and over. Left to her own mind's memories, the wonders and pleasures would have their way and send her into a most inappropriate reverie.

"What are you staring at?" Rebecca now loomed in the reflection, too, right behind her.

"My eyes." His flatteries needed to be remembered. She must force herself to keep the evidence that he was a lying seducer fresh in her thoughts. Humiliation lay buried in the truth beneath those lies. Was it enough to keep her from believing him in order to be swayed?

Rebecca pulled pins out of Eva's hair, so her locks fell free. Rebecca picked up the brush. "They are unusual. Changeable. Sometimes green, sometimes blue, other times almost gray. I think it depends on the lighting. And your mood, of course. When you are angry they are definitely green, with golden sparks all but flying out of them." She worked the brush down Eva's back. "I have always envied you your eyes."

"That is ridiculous. You could never want to trade these for yours."

"A lot you know. Mine are blue in an ordinary way. When yours are blue, they are the color of a perfectly clear pale jewel. But it is the way they change that I envy."

Eva looked again. Right now in the candlelight, she could not tell what color they were. All she saw were the tiny reflections of the candle's flames.

"You have not packed," Rebecca said, while still tending to her hair. "That means you can make room for my gift."

"Gift? What gift?"

Rebecca set down the brush. "I will be right back."

A few minutes later Rebecca's steps sounded on the floorboards. She entered Eva's room, only nothing of Rebecca could be seen except her feet. The rest of her hid behind a dress that she held high by the shoulders.

A woman would wear such a dress to a dinner party or the theater. Constructed of satin more silver than gray, it bore embellishments of tiny white beads and lace on the neckline and sleeves. A tasteful band of lace decorated the lower skirt.

"Where did you get this?" Eva cried. "It must have cost a fortune."

"It cost nothing but time." Rebecca laid it down on the bed. "I used one of Mother's old dresses and redid it, took another dress for the underskirt, then took the lace off yet another garment. We must fit it once we are in town, but I think it will be close enough."

"The laces and fabric in that trunk were for your wardrobe, not mine. You were supposed to—"

"I have not slighted myself, Eva. I just used some of what was left for this. If we have a chance to attend an assembly, you cannot go otherwise."

Eva had not intended to attend such events at all. Rebecca would do better with their cousin at her side, anyway.

She fondled the satin. She embraced Rebecca and gave her a kiss. "It is a wonderful gift."

"I am glad you like it." Rebecca smiled impishly.

"You will turn every head when you wear it. Why, we will probably find you a suitor before we come home."

Eva watched her sister leave, then turned to her packing, shaking her head. Sweet Rebecca had it all backward.

G*o to Chatsworth. The steward Montley will speak with you.*

That had been all Ives's letter had said. It needed no further explanation. If such an introduction had been obtained, the chance should not be lost. So Gareth had ridden up to Derbyshire, and the main estate of the Duke of Devonshire.

Gareth approached Chatsworth's manor house in late morning. He had already ridden through extensive grounds almost as large as some counties. One of the most famous houses in the world now beckoned beyond the river. He stopped his horse on a rise of land to admire the building and its placement, and the evidence of improvements being showered on the estate by the current duke.

He could not guess what his reception would be. Presumably this steward would not pretend a higher station. The man would have had some experience dealing with bastard children of dukes, as the last Duke of Devonshire had sired two.

Grooms took his horse at the house. The butler took his card. Shortly he was escorted to a back office where the steward, Mr. Montley, sat at a high secretaire of incalculable value. A library table beside the desk carried stacks of account books.

Greetings completed, they moved to two chairs that looked out over the back garden.

"I should explain that I am not actually the steward," Montley said. "My position can best be described as a special secretary. With all of the properties, His Grace felt the need for someone to watch and coordinate all the estate stewards."

"If you are the man who knows something about these pictures that have gone missing, then you are the man I need to speak with."

Thinning dark hair and spectacles made Montley look older than his years, which Gareth estimated to be the late thirties. Perhaps he had been a friend of the duke, and thus more trustworthy than those stewards. He bore the air of gentility and education. A younger son of some peer, most likely, for whom this position had more appeal than the church or the army.

"I know what little there is to know. I regret that the actual events that led to the misplacement of the pictures remain unknown."

"*Misplacement*. That is a word not used before in the matter."

"It is our belief that when the last duke died nine years ago, and the estate was in transition, that these pictures were inadvertently removed from their resting place and sent elsewhere due to some misunderstanding on the part of the household that held them."

In other words, *it was not our fault.*

"Will you share with me the reason you believe this?" Gareth used all the charm he could muster to say it. There was no profit in challenging Montley.

"It is the only logical explanation, of course. In addition, the caretaker remembers the inventory made at that time, and a good many objects removed. The other properties have been searched in an attempt to see where the pictures were sent. During the last few years I have personally traveled to each one, because there is no point in sending a list of paintings to butlers who would not know a Raphael from a Rubens."

Gareth pictured the many properties of Devonshire, all stuffed with art. He could believe it had taken years to go through it all. The duke owned eight major estates and many smaller ones.

"You visited each and every one? I envy you. You probably know more about the duke's collections than he does."

Montley gestured to the table. "I took the opportunity to make a complete catalogue. The inventory made at the last duke's death, while lengthy, had some ambiguities and omissions. Lest you wonder if those were not omissions, but instead the inadvertent incorporation of the missing paintings into the duke's own collection, let me assure you that I do know Raphael from Rubens. Unfortunately, none of the pictures belonging to his fellow peers could be located in those houses."

"Do you have a list of those paintings? My brother

has sought to obtain one, but is meeting some resistance."

"Perhaps someone fears the list will be published, to the embarrassment of all if it is released." A meaningful gaze all but said that Devonshire did not want that list circulating.

"Without such a list, I can hardly help. You will be on your own in this mission."

"That might be for the best."

"The Prince Regent does not agree. He charged my brother with investigating. I am here instead, due to the death of my half brother. If Devonshire wants no one except you involved, he should tell the Crown that, and I can go about my other business." He leaned forward companionably. "No one thinks there has been negligence on your part. Yet after, what, four years, the mystery remains. A new pair of eyes and less fastidious methods might yield new facts."

Montley laughed. "Less fastidious methods? What, do you intend to beat information out of the servants?"

Gareth just looked at him.

Montley frowned. "I am sure your brother would not approve."

"You do not know my brother well, do you?"

Montley flustered. "I see."

"Those paintings did not grow legs and walk out of storage."

"No. Of course not."

"Someone knows something about this. That person has not confided in you. Perhaps he will confide in me."

Montley gazed out the window a long while. Finally he stood.

"I am authorized by the duke to take you to the house where the pictures were stored. It is not far from here."

Most families would be proud to have Dunbar Green as their main estate. For the Duke of Devonshire, however, it was an uncelebrated property far down on the list of his holdings. It suffered from Chatsworth's proximity a mere hour's ride away, no doubt, although Gareth considered that it had probably been a convenient secret refuge from the big house for lovers over the centuries.

Not as big, not as handsome, not as lucky in its designer, Dunbar Green also showed some signs of neglect. Montley noticed Gareth eyeing the eaves as they approached on horseback.

"There is work to do in the attics," he mentioned. "We will get to it soon. At the moment, His Grace is distracted by plans for a new wing at Chatsworth."

His Grace probably had not visited this property in years, if ever. "Does anyone live here?"

Montley shook his head. "He may sell it. The estate came to him unentailed, if you can believe it. The flexibility it has given him to alter the family's investments from land to more current profits could be an argument against tying the land up that way."

"If every heir were wise, that argument might stand.

Too many would gamble it all away if given a free hand. Or so I am told."

"Or their wives would," Montley said dryly. Gareth assumed he referred in part to the last Duke of Devonshire's first duchess, whose gambling debts would have been ruinous to all but a handful of peers.

As an uninhabited house, Dunbar Green had few servants. The white-haired man who took their hats upon entry looked old enough to have been there many years. Bent and filmy-eyed, and barely alert to their presence, he studied the floor while shuffling to his duties.

"We will be going up to the attics," Montley said to the man, even as he led the way to the stairs. "Have the horses fed and watered."

The attics were above the servant quarters, with small windows in dormers over the eaves. The usual remnants of a house's long history filled it. Montley gestured around. "As you can see, most of the furniture and such was moved to this end, to make room to store the pictures over here."

Gareth walked over and examined the space. He judged it large enough to hold at least one hundred framed paintings if they were boxed and lined up front-to-back in long stacks against the wall. The center of the space, under the roof beam, would be high enough to accommodate the largest canvases, those of palatial size.

"I imagine they were shocked to find it empty," Gareth said.

"That is putting a fine point to it. The arrangements were made twenty years ago, of course, and with the last duke's permission. The current duke was not even aware of them, until he received a letter from the Prince Regent informing him that men were coming to retrieve the goods."

"Are any of the Prince's treasures involved?"

"He does have a home on the coast. A few choice works from Brighton were included, I am told."

They left the upper reaches of the house and went outside.

Gareth took in the lay of the land around the house. "Are there any external buildings that I cannot see? Could they have been moved somewhere right on this estate?"

Montley shook his head. "A few servant cottages and a vicar's house. All have been searched." He stepped down as the horses were brought around.

"I think I will ride a bit, all the same," Gareth said.

"What are you looking for?"

Damned if he knew. Still, there was nothing more to learn from Montley.

"Well, return when you are done with it. We will put you up, and you can spend the evening with the collection, if you like. But I doubt you will get through even a tenth of that which is out for public view."

"I will be there."

Montley trotted his horse down the lane. Gareth began to mount when he noticed the servant who worked the door looking out a window. Rather suddenly the man did not appear so old and filmy-eyed. Leaving his horse, Gareth returned to the house.

The man held the door wide and stood aside, asking no questions.

"A word with you," Gareth said.

"Me, sir?" He squinted up, confused.

"Yes. You have served here a long time, I assume."

"Fifteen years. Was at Chiswick House until I began to slow. This is where they put those of us getting on in years. I'm to be pensioned off next year."

Fifteen years. That meant he came after the pictures were hidden in the attics. "When the last duke died, were there any big changes here?"

"Changes?"

"Movement of household goods. Visitors wanting to go through the attics or peek under the floorboards."

He laughed. "Getting what they could before any inventory, you mean."

"That is what I mean."

"A lady came by. She took a pillow from one of the bedchambers. A relic of fond memories, she said. Perhaps she had enjoyed a particularly pleasant house party."

"Nothing else? In all that time during the transition?"

He set his face into a placid mask and shook his head.

"Come now. You will not be criticized for telling

me. No one will challenge that pension. Devonshire needs to know this. I ask in his name."

"One day the second duchess arrived. A wagon accompanied her. She explained that the late duke had given her permission to take what she wanted for her own house, from any of his properties. I expect she chose this one because there would be no one to gainsay her."

"What did she take?"

"Chairs and tables, I suppose."

"You don't know?"

"I discovered the obligation to be occupied elsewhere during most of her residence."

Wise man. No wonder he had lasted so long in a duke's service. He could not report what he had not seen, nor answer questions should they be asked.

"Were there any other such visits during your tenure here?"

"A few overnights while journeying elsewhere, on the part of relatives or nobility who did not want to impose on the main estate. There was one house party before the late duke passed. Mr. Clifford brought some of his naval officer friends here for a long hunting weekend."

Clifford was old Devonshire's bastard, by the same woman who later became his second duchess. The same duchess who had raided the place after her husband died. "Did you discover the need to be occupied elsewhere that time too?"

"Why, yes, sir. How did you know? My old aunt

was feeling poorly, and since Mr. Clifford had brought his own servants, I took a short journey to visit her."

"Were there any other times you discovered the need to be elsewhere?"

"Due to my aunt's condition, I took the opportunity to visit her whenever visitors came with their own people."

Gareth took his leave, mounted his horse, and set out to ride the property looking for who knew what.

He did not like that two of the people who now had to be questioned were the last duke's wife and bastard son. If Ives had suspected where this would turn and had thrown him into the fire, he intended to thrash him soundly.

CHAPTER 9

Going to Birmingham proved a complicated matter. Since she needed to also transport the paintings, Eva hired a wagon to take them to town. She and Rebecca sat in the back hoping it would not rain and ruin their bonnets.

The first stop upon reaching Birmingham was Mr. Stevenson's stationery store. A short, bald man with bulbous eyes, he greeted Eva with a bigger smile than normal. She assumed that was because beautiful Rebecca stood at her side this time.

"I have brought ten paintings," she explained. "I hope you can take them."

Mr. Stevenson beamed with delight. "Of course. In fact—" He gestured to the walls of his shop.

Eva looked around. Only three of her paintings decorated the walls, and they were all landscapes she had painted with no more inspiration than her own eyes and middling talent.

"The rest were all bought last month," Mr. Stevenson said, enjoying her surprise. "A buyer from London took every one. He expressed interest in more. I think, Miss Russell, that we have found a most lucrative patron."

"Why would anyone want so many paintings? I am grateful and relieved, of course. I feared we were close to your having no more room for new ones."

"I think, but may be wrong, that this patron has his own picture shop, and is reselling them there."

"Truly? What is his name?"

"He did not say. I did not press him. I was too happy to care overmuch."

"How will you let him know we have more, then?"

"I will find a way. Now, come, come. I have your money and a handsome amount it is indeed."

Eva gestured for the waggoneer to bring in the paintings, then followed Mr. Stevenson to his back office. There, with some ceremony, he opened a strongbox and counted out pounds.

She stared at the banknotes as the stack grew. There had been ten paintings here. The final stack contained twenty pounds. She had seen two pounds per painting, far more than in the past when ten shillings would make her dance.

"You can see why I am excited by this development," Mr. Stevenson said. "You will be bringing more, I trust."

Her own excitement cracked and crashed. She had no idea if she could ever bring more. Her source of paintings to copy had been closed. "Had this buyer no interest in the landscapes?"

"I fear not, Miss Russell. He did admire them, but they were not what he sought."

She tucked the banknotes into her reticule. "I understand. Thank you, Mr. Stevenson. It appears our alliance has finally born the best fruit. I will write and alert you to when I am coming with another group."

"Please do, please do." He fawned pleasantries on her while he escorted Rebecca and her out to the street.

"He was lying," Rebecca said as soon as the shop's door closed behind them. "He knows the name of that patron, and is writing to him already to say he has more. Only you will not see the money until you bring him additional paintings, which you will not be able to do."

"I am embarrassed that my little sister's shrewdness surpasses my own," Eva admitted. "I was so mesmerized by all that money that my wits deserted me."

"What will you do?"

"Regarding Mr. Stevenson, I do not know yet. However, there is one thing I most definitely intend to do immediately." She gestured for the waggoneer. "Sir, please go and procure for us a hackney cab. Once it comes, you can commence your journey back to Langdon's End."

With twenty pounds in her reticule, she would be damned before they arrived at their cousin's house in the back of this wagon.

Cousin Sarah, red-haired, plump, and vivacious, extended both warmth and the best hospitality. She and her husband, Wesley, lived on a fine street of newer houses, all of them tall and elegant and white. The less savory elements of Birmingham, bred of its industries, did not touch their neighborhood. Five servants tended to their needs inside, and two more took care of their carriage and horses at the back of the large garden.

The family had adopted a high degree of gentility in its workings. Mr. Rockport might leave the house each day to tend to trade, and late nights on the town might be a rarity, but Eva grew nostalgic for her youth beginning the first day. She might have been sent back in time, to before the deprivations and frugalities. From breakfasts in the morning room to evenings of card play in the library, she found so much of her visit painfully familiar.

"I have the day all planned," Sarah announced the first morning, after pressing more tea on Eva when Eva offered halfhearted resistance. "We must go shopping, of course, so I can show you how we lack nothing to be had in London here. We will return early and have a light supper, because tonight we will attend a musical performance."

Rebecca clapped her hands with excitement, to

Sarah's joy. Sarah had taken to Rebecca immediately, and already confided to Eva that such a jewel should not be left to languish in Langdon's End. With a five-minute conversation the evening before, her cousin became her conspirator in finding Rebecca a good match.

Normally a visit to the shops would make Eva get busy lining up reasons not to buy, preparing excuses that did not reveal how precarious life had become. With twenty pounds tucked away, however, she did not feel so poor and vulnerable. She might not spend a penny, but she also would not experience the undeserved shame attached to impoverishment.

"You will have to wear the silver silk tonight," Rebecca said.

Sarah pouted. "I was so looking forward to loaning some of my own dresses. You will borrow one, won't you, Rebecca? Some are appropriate for a girl your age."

"We will see," Eva said, before Rebecca could clap her hands again.

"In the least, I hope you will avail yourselves of the headdresses and wraps in my wardrobe."

Rebecca looked over, pleading with her eyes.

"We can hardly decline such generosity," Eva said. Sarah meant well, and her cousin's desire not to be seen with unfashionable country cousins probably had very little to do with the offer.

She told herself that again several times as the day unfolded. In particular, when they passed a milliner's shop and Sarah insisted on going in and having

Rebecca and her try on new bonnets with the latest brims, she repeated it to herself.

"You must have them," Sarah exclaimed. "They will be perfect for tomorrow's excursion to the park."

Eva calculated their likely cost, and the wisdom of depleting the twenty pounds by that amount. Her bonnet, with its high crown and deep brim, brought a lot of attention to her eyes. She was starting to like her eyes. They appeared quite impressive looking out from this bonnet.

Rebecca removed her own and set it down. "We cannot afford new bonnets right now, Sarah. I do not mind wearing the ones I brought, if you do not mind my wearing them."

"Of course! That is to say, I did not mean to— I had hoped to make it a gift to you, Rebecca. And you too, Eva."

Eva smiled at Sarah. "You may make a gift to Rebecca if you like. I see no harm in that." She untied the ribbons beneath her chin. "As for this one, I will think about purchasing it before I leave town."

They left the shop a half hour later, with Rebecca giggling the way a girl should about her new bonnet. All the way home Sarah and Rebecca discussed the fashions they had seen on the streets and in the shops and on the fashion plates. Just talking about such finery had Rebecca alive and bright and more beautiful than ever.

"I regret that we do not have a box," Sarah said that evening as her carriage carried them to the theater. "You look so lovely, Rebecca, that it is a shame you won't be displayed in one."

Rebecca did look lovely. Adorned in one of Sarah's evening dresses—innocent white and with a neckline not too daring, and decorated most discreetly with fine cream embroidery—she would be the most lovely female in the theater, Eva was sure. Her sister's beauty did not dim her approval of her own appearance. She wore the silver silk and a feathered headdress from Sarah's collection, along with high kid gloves taken from the chest of her mother's old finery.

They took seats in the orchestra, but in front rows reserved for the privileged. The rowdier elements of society could be heard behind them, priming their voices to shout approval or not of the entertainment to come. Young men of all stations roamed in little packs, admiring the women up in the boxes and staring more boldly at the ones in the chairs below. Rebecca, seated between Sarah and Eva, attracted a great deal of attention. From her serene expression, she appeared not to notice.

They attended without Sarah's husband, who had a business dinner that night, and in their excitement had arrived early. The seat beside Eva's remained unclaimed as the time for the performance neared. Suddenly, however, a man's form stood in front of it. Eva was talking to Sarah and merely noticed someone there out of the corner of her eye.

"Mr. Fitzallen!" Rebecca's head popped up from their tête-a-tête and her gaze aimed to her left. "Look who is here, Eva."

Eva did not look right away. First she saw Sarah do

so, with widening eyes. She also waited while her own face flushed so hotly she feared it would be visible to all, despite the cool gaslight in the theater.

Finally she turned her attention to the man who had last seen her half-naked.

"Miss Russell." He bowed. "Miss Rebecca Russell. What a surprise to chance upon you here."

"Yes, a big surprise," Eva managed. "Your journey is completed then?"

"I arrived back this morning and decided to come to town for the evening. The opportunity for good music drew me."

Eva introduced Sarah and explained she and Rebecca were visiting her cousin for a few days.

"Are you with friends, Mr. Fitzallen?" Sarah asked. "Please join us if you are not."

"Thank you. That is a generous offer. I think I shall."

And with that Eva found him in the chair next to hers, just as the musicians came out.

The theater hardly hushed, but the din decreased. Gareth chatted with Sarah, his body angling in that direction so that it almost touched Eva's. Rebecca squinted at the stage, waiting for the performance to begin. Sarah told Gareth about her husband's business.

Finally the music began, and the singer came out to warble her operatic program. Gareth straightened and looked forward. Sarah's head met Eva's in front of Rebecca's chest.

"Who is this gentleman?"

Eva knew Sarah meant what is this gentleman, as

in what was his pedigree and wealth. "He is the bastard son of Aylesbury."

"No!"

"Yes, and of little fortune, so do not start making plans about my sister."

"I am more interested in making plans about myself. He may have little fortune, but he has the best connections, unless that family has forsaken him entirely. You must ask him to dinner tomorrow, so he can meet Wesley. I will invite some other young men to meet Rebecca."

"For Rebecca's sake I will try, but do not expect much success." She truly did not want to be successful. Gareth would probably think she pursued him if she posed the invitation.

She gave her attention to the performance then, at least until she heard a low masculine voice in her ear.

"You ran away, Eva. Did you fear being found in my house?"

"Yes." *No, I gazed down at my own naked body and my behavior shocked me silly.*

"I told you I would not allow that to happen."

She found some spine. "Even so, I had to go. My behavior cannot be excused. I needed to leave, to reclaim some dignity."

That voice again, closer. Quieter. "Are you saying you regret it?"

If I regretted it, I would not relive it every night before I sleep, and touch my own breasts to know something of that pleasure again.

"Yes."

"You did not enjoy it?"

"No. I am sorry. I am not one of your London sophisticates, I fear."

"I am aware of that. Your hasty departure prevented me from apologizing. The blame is entirely mine. You were overwhelmed, and did not know your own mind. I should have never kissed you, or let things get as far as they did."

It was the apology she expected, and probably deserved. Yet she rebelled at the way it described her.

"You are too kind in taking all the blame. I may regret my recklessness, but I was not so overwhelmed that I lost all ability to reason. I think that perhaps you have begun to believe the gossip that says you are irresistible."

"Convenient gossip, for your purposes. I am impressed you do not embrace it. Although your honesty leaves me confused."

"How so?"

"You were not overwhelmed, and you did know your own mind, yet you allowed me liberties that you now regret. One would conclude that although I am not irresistible, perhaps pleasure was. Yet you claim you did not enjoy it."

"I was curious. At my age, that is not uncommon."

"Ah. Of course."

Nothing. No more words for what seemed a long spell. He watched the performance. His hands fell to the chair beside his legs.

A touch on her left thigh's side almost made her

jump up. His hidden hand's finger meandered up toward her hip, pressing through the silver silk. She stared at the singer, wondering what to do.

"You are lying," he whispered. "Even now you tremble. Or perhaps you merely shake with curiosity."

She did tremble, so much that Rebecca glanced over quizzically. That finger's caress continued, raising scandalous thoughts and yearnings as she imagined it on her bare skin.

"I insist you stop that," she hissed.

He took mercy on her and did stop.

The singer's performance ended, and she left the stage. The noise in the theater multiplied as numerous fists thumped approval on chair backs and arms.

"I think Eva is chilled," Rebecca said to Sarah. "She has been shivering. Although I would be sorry to miss the rest of the program, I think we should go."

"Oh, dear. Are you ill, Eva?" Sarah peered over, and reached to feel her neck. "You do seem too warm. Perhaps we should do as Rebecca suggests."

"Really, I am fine. We do not—"

"It would be a pity for you ladies to miss the rest of the evening. I will be happy to escort Miss Russell back to your house," Gareth said.

Sarah only hesitated a few seconds. "It would be nice to stay, and I have seen some friends I would like to introduce to Rebecca."

"I can stay," Eva objected. "I am not chilled at all. Truly, I am fine."

Sarah felt her face again. "We dare not risk it, what

with all the spring fevers. Your face is very flushed, too, Eva. You must accept Mr. Fitzallen's escort, or Rebecca and I must take you."

Rebecca tried to appear willing to go, but the option to stay, once presented, had her pleading with her eyes for that choice.

Eva stood. "This is ridiculous. I am not sick."

"I fear you will be very sick by morning, unless you rest now," Sarah said. "Get to bed as soon as you arrive back. And tell the cook to fix you some broth for supper." She leaned closer. "Do not forget that little request I made about tomorrow, please."

Gareth helped her to the aisle, his face a picture of solicitous concern. One would think she needed salts from the way he hovered and guided her out of the theater.

The night air felt wonderful. The theater had made her a bit warm, she admitted to herself. Or rather the man sitting beside her had.

She stopped and faced Gareth under a lamp attached to the theater's façade. "You wicked, wicked man."

"Delightfully wicked, I hope."

"Annoyingly wicked tonight. You will not take me back to Sarah's house. You will hire a carriage for me, and send me on my way."

He sent one of the theater's footmen to bring a hired cab. She looked out into the night and tried to ignore his presence while they waited.

When the carriage arrived, he held the door for her. To her dismay, however, he climbed in behind her.

"I will not have it," she said. "Get out."

"I promised to deliver you safely to your cousin's house. As a gentleman, I will be good to my word." He settled across from her. "See, you have nothing to fear from me. I do not importune women, least of all those who are ill."

"How thoughtful."

"Your cousin summed up my character quickly enough. She entrusted you to me, after all."

"My cousin knows nothing about you. She merely did not want to leave herself." Sarah's willingness to hand her over to a stranger actually had another explanation. Much like the sisters Neville, Sarah assumed someone like Gareth would never have an interest in such as she. Not even for the basest reasons.

She supposed Sarah also assumed she would have more sense than to allow a man like Gareth to misbehave. That alternate explanation salved her pride a little.

"You *are* ill, correct? The warmth and shivering had no other particular cause, did it?"

"Not only am I ill, I am sure I am contagious." She gave him Sarah's address. He opened the window and called it to the driver.

Through the dark they rolled. She refused to look at him. She stared at the window beside her and hoped she appeared annoyed and unassailable.

He would probably try to kiss her soon. Who knew what scandalous things this man could do in a dark carriage? If she were not careful, she might find herself half-naked again. That would be a fine thing, arriving at Sarah's house in such a state.

Her whole body waited for him to move. A touch on her knee would probably come first. Then he would sit beside her. Another half a block and the rogue would embrace her and force a kiss on her. In minutes, she would be fighting for her virtue.

She tingled as she imagined each step he would take. Anticipation filled the carriage. His presence seemed to grow until it invisibly pressed her. Her breasts swelled, betraying her resolve with their sensitivity.

Any moment now, she was sure. If he had teased her in the theater, he would be ruthless now that they were alone. She almost could not breathe from the suspense, and her mind lined up the words to put him in his place.

She sneaked a glance at him. Then she turned and stared at him through the dark. She squinted hard, to be sure she saw correctly.

He had fallen asleep.

She wanted to hit him with her reticule.

The carriage stopped, jolting him awake. He reached for the door's latch. "My apologies, Eva. My only excuse is I was in a saddle most of the day."

"There is no need to apologize."

He stepped out and handed her down. She had walked three steps to the door when she remembered Sarah's request. Considering Sarah's generosity, it would be ungrateful to pretend it had slipped her mind when it had not.

"My cousin asked me to invite you to dinner

tomorrow night. It will be a small gathering, and I am sure you will find it very dull. It is also a long way to ride from Albany Lodge just for a meal. I will explain that you are tired from your travels and—"

"I would be happy to attend."

"It is not necessary."

"I will stay in town tonight at the Kings Arms. Tell her to send word of the time if it is other than nine o'clock."

She stood there helplessly, trying to find a good reason why he should change his mind.

He stepped closer and she jumped back. She hurried to the door so he could not kiss her, if that was his plan. His low laugh followed. That made her furious. He turned back to the carriage.

"Go and sleep, Eva, so you may recover from the malady that infected you tonight."

She ran up to her chamber. She called for broth, so Sarah would not think her instructions had been ignored. After she ate it, she went to bed. She did not sleep easily, however.

An image occupied her mind and would not give her peace. In it she was naked in the carriage, while Gareth sucked her breasts until she was delirious from pleasure.

Gareth lounged on his bed at the Kings Arms, debating whether his friendship with Eva Russell were making him a fool. He sipped at some port. The more he imbibed, the more an ass he felt.

He had intended to return to Albany Lodge tonight, yet here he was at an inn, with no purpose other than dallying away the time until he could attend the same dinner as she. It was the sort of fawning strategy to be in a woman's company that he had not employed since he was twenty, and then the lady had promised unimaginable erotic lessons should he find favor with her. The ultimate prize had been well worth the inconveniences.

That was not the situation now. The problem might not be that he was a fool, but that Eva was not one.

Perhaps that was her attraction. It was a hell of a thing when the quality that made a woman interesting to a man was also the quality that ensured he should never have her.

She looked lovely tonight in that silvery satin. A mature woman, not some girl like her sister, and self-possessed. She had brought Rebecca to the city to try and find her a match, it appeared. More likely Eva would be the one to receive a quick proposal.

He got up, stripped off his clothes, and washed. Yes, she had looked lovely in that silver dress. Only he had not seen it much. He spent most of the time at the theater seeing her naked, bending this way and that to his command, while passion set her free.

A pointless fantasy, and he would not indulge it in the future. He had apologized, and she had uttered the appropriate discouraging words. He would not succumb to the temptation to tease her, or even flirt. They would both retreat, with dignity, and all would return to how it was a week ago.

CHAPTER 10

Sarah was good to her word about the next night's dinner. Eva produced Mr. Fitzallen with his aristocratic connections, and Sarah produced three young men who might be suitable matches for Rebecca. Two elderly female friends rounded out the table. The last two performed their social duties quietly, politely, and unobtrusively.

Eva had allowed Sarah to press one of her dinner dresses on her to wear. Eva did not resist very long, and enjoyed slipping into the primrose silk. Her decision to appear better than she might had nothing to do with Gareth Fitzallen's acceptance of the invitation to join them. Nothing at all.

The meal proved a much better one than Eva had enjoyed in her own home for many years. Sarah spared no expense, and even served turtle soup. Servants hovered and offered and poured nice wines. Wesley, Sarah's husband, showed impressive social grace in presiding over it all.

The three gentlemen invited for Rebecca's sake were all youthful members of Wesley's industry—the casting of small objects in a variety of metals. For the first twenty minutes, they all seemed more intent on talking to one another than to any of the ladies at the table. Then Sarah took matters in hand. All but tapping the table for attention, she exerted her hostess's prerogative to address each one and to pose questions, always including Rebecca in the conversation that ensued.

Eva watched carefully, to see the reactions to her sister. That all three gentlemen were impressed went without saying. Only a fool would not recognize her beauty. Rebecca, on the other hand, seemed to favor the quietest of the three, Mr. Trenton. Eva hoped that was not because Mr. Trenton, with his large dark eyes and longish dark hair and somewhat careless dress, appeared to be impersonating a French poet.

Concentrating on the table's conversation allowed her to ignore as much as possible the man sitting beside her, placed there by Sarah in her ignorance. Also seated next to Wesley, Gareth appeared more than content to converse with his host, however. It went without saying that Wesley proved more than happy to gain better acquaintance with a man with Gareth's connections.

"You have an admirer."

The low comment entered her right ear. Gareth had taken advantage of his host's distraction, caused by his wife's insistence he give an opinion on the state of the banks.

"If you speak of yourself, now is not the time—"

"What conceit. I am referring to Mr. Bellows across the table. He pretends to watch his hostess, but his gaze drifts to you."

Did it? She had not noticed.

"He is too short for you," Gareth said.

"While of middling height, he appears tall enough."

"You can do better."

"He is here to meet Rebecca, not me."

"In either case, you should know he is new to his position, and his income cannot be more than three hundred pounds a year. Of course, that fellow over there who has attracted your sister's eye probably has even less."

"If Sarah invited them, I am sure they have great expectations, and their futures hold promise."

"She invited them as a cover for her real candidate. Mr. Mansfield down there is worth at least two thousand a year. He owns his own company. He has been watching your sister with great interest, rather like a man inspects a gelding at auction."

That was not good news. Of the three of them, Mr. Mansfield was the oldest. At least as old as Gareth, whom Rebecca had decreed to be "too old." Also of the three, he had the least polish, even if his coats looked expensive and his cravat had no doubt seen the hands of a valet. A bit rough-boned in his face, not at all middling in height, and by nature intimidating in his manner, he would never have as much appeal to Rebecca as the French poet, who, fortunately, had not noticed how interesting Rebecca found him.

"I called on you when I returned, as I promised." Gareth's voice came very low now. Eva gazed straight ahead, pretending to listen to the conversations crossing the table. "Then Erasmus explained you had bolted."

"Is that why you came to Birmingham? To make that apology? It could have waited. You did not need to inconvenience yourself." The implication of his words sank in. "And I did not *bolt*. This visit had been planned long before—a long time."

A lengthy pause, extended enough that she almost deciphered the context of an exchange between Rebecca and Mr. Mansfield, one in which Rebecca seemed to be disagreeing with the gentleman about something. Mr. Mansfield took Rebecca's earnest rejection of his views calmly and with vague amusement.

"You are a confusing woman, Eva. Almost vexing," Gareth said. "I expected my efforts to behave as a gentleman to be met with grace if not relief. Instead, you are so snappish I wonder if I regret the indiscretion more than you do."

She felt herself flushing, furiously, mostly because he touched on the embarrassing truth that she had not regretted it nearly as much as she should. Worse, she resented a little that he had proven so predictable in his own reaction. Guilt, apologies, total retreat—one did not expect a man with his reputation to be so ordinary after an indiscretion. He was supposed to delight in such things.

She tried to compose a good retort, but just then Wesley turned his attention back, and Gareth's own moved to his host.

Down the table, she heard Rebecca say, "I doubt that there is anything for which you and I have common sympathy, Mr. Mansfield."

Across the table, Sarah sighed.

Wesley Rockport was a man of business. Gareth knew such men well. Successful ones like Rockport took on the veneer of gentility bit by bit. His host had been doing that for some years now, so the distinctions between him and a gentleman remained only those of birth and occupation. Which were the only two things that gentlemen said mattered.

Really successful men like this eventually set their sights on the modes and trappings of the aristocracy. When that happened, after they had built or bought their estates and big houses and furnished it all as decreed by a professional decorator, they turned their attention to the long, empty gallery. Gareth was more than happy to find them art to fill those walls.

Rockport did not want to talk about art though. He wanted to discuss shipping and insurance and probe at Gareth's connections to businessmen and markets on the continents. Gareth spoke freely about it all. He had nothing to lose in doing so. He hardly gave away secrets. Anyone who traveled, paid attention, welcomed new friendships, and asked questions would know as much as he.

When called upon by Rockport, he gave the man the better half of his attention. Most of the rest remained on the woman by his side. A sliver of his mind, however, noticed the rest of the party and heard their own conversations. That sliver eventually heard fair-haired Mr. Bellows address Eva.

"You are very quiet tonight, Miss Russell. I hope that all our talk is not overwhelming you."

"I much prefer listening to my sister, Mr. Bellows. She is far more informed of the world's events than I."

"Admirably so. However, if I may say, there is much to be said for a quiet woman, Miss Russell, such as yourself."

"I do not think anyone would describe me as quiet, Mr. Bellows. The role of observer that I take tonight is not a common one for me."

"I think Mr. Bellows is saying that women should restrain themselves from voicing opinions as freely as your sister," Gareth could not resist inserting himself. "That is a rather outmoded way of viewing things, sir. Even the Iron Duke has ladies with whom he discusses politics."

Bellows appeared flummoxed for a moment, but regained his footing soon enough. "Well, I am a simple man with simple notions, not a duke, so a duke's predilections do not count much for me."

"All the more reason to admire a woman who is not simple. One like the young lady holding her own with Mr. Mansfield, for example. With her blood and her intelligence, imagine the sons she will give a man. That does not even factor in that she is as beautiful as an angel, and the sort of woman to make men of the highest station envious of her husband, whoever he will be."

Eva abruptly rearranged her position in her chair. In doing so her elbow jabbed Gareth sharply in his side. "My sister has many fine qualities, of course. Far be it from me to list them all, lest I be thought too proud of her. It is generous of you to do it instead, Mr. Fitzallen. However, I am sure Mr. Bellows does not require your tutoring on the matter. You have a charming tendency to think no one knows his own mind as well as you might know it for him."

"Have I crossed a line? My apologies, Bellows. Forgive me."

Bellows barely heard him. The lesson had been heard and swallowed. Bellows turned his attention to Rebecca quite thoroughly, and jumped into the breach once her little argument with Mansfield drew to a friendly end.

Gareth returned his attention to his host. So much for Mr. Bellows.

"Mr. Mansfield is worth at least two thousand a year," Sarah explained to Rebecca once she, Eva, and Rebecca were alone after the men had withdrawn. She led them all to her drawing room upstairs while she talked.

"I would not care if he were worth ten thousand," Rebecca said.

"Oh, yes, you would, my dear. Yes, you would."

"He has the most antiquated notions. He does not think women should be educated."

"And who does, I ask you?"

"Forward-thinking men and women. *Me*."

Eva followed them and the conversation into the drawing room. The elderly ladies retreated to a corner to chat. Sarah dropped onto a divan and patted the cushion next to her, beckoning Rebecca.

"Now, dear, allow this old married woman to explain. Men never think the way they ought when we meet them. No one has yet presented them with better views. It is our duty to broaden their minds on matters to which they have never applied themselves. It is part of what wives do, you see. It is our great mission."

She looked to Eva for agreement.

"Cousin Sarah is the voice of experience, Rebecca. You would be wise to listen to her."

Rebecca pouted and picked at her skirt absently. "I thought Mr. Trenton more attractive."

Sarah sighed. "My dear, Mr. Trenton is a clerk in my husband's office, and is unlikely to ever be more. He does not have a head for business. I only invited him and Mr. Bellows because it would be too obvious if I only invited Mr. Mansfield."

"I still like Mr. Trenton better. He is quite soulful. He writes poetry. Did you know that?"

"Oh, good heavens." Sarah turned to Eva, desperately.

"Rebecca, other than his views on women's education—and please let me remind you that our father had the same views, as did our brother, so hence, neither of us had much schooling beyond the norm given to women today—besides that, why does Mr. Mansfield not find favor with you?"

Rebecca thought about it. "He is too big."

"Too big?" Sarah exclaimed. "He is certainly bigger than that skinny Mr. Trenton, but he is not monstrous." •

"Still—he is big and I suspect he is gruff and rough. I should always be afraid of him. Even the way he looks at me makes me uncomfortable. Even Mr. Bellows is better, although he is boring."

Sarah's gaze slid sideways to Rebecca. Her expression no longer revealed exasperation, but comprehension. She took Rebecca's hand. "There is no reason to be afraid of Mr. Mansfield, my dear cousin. Beneath all that masculine bravado, he is very kind. Should he call on you here, I want you to agree to see him. I will be with you, so you have no reason to object. You should not discard a man worth two thousand a year and likely to be worth much more in the future on the basis of one argument over women's education. Don't you agree, Eva?"

"I do agree."

Rebecca nodded, but sighed mightily while she did. When the gentlemen soon joined them, Rebecca did manage to engage the poetic Mr. Trenton in private conversation. If Mr. Mansfield cared, or even noticed, he did not show it. Instead he drew Eva into conversation about her family.

"The two of you are alone, Wesley said."

"Yes. We lost my brother a year ago."

"Have you no other family nearby, where you could live?" As soon as he asked he realized his error. He glanced at Sarah and flushed.

"I chose not to impose on Mr. and Mrs. Rockport. I was of age, and able to manage things. I did not even seek to move here. I am fond of Langdon's End. It is my home."

Gareth had disengaged from continued discussions with Wesley and now sidled over to sit with them. "It is a charming town, with a fine lake on its east. But if the city keeps growing, it will probably be absorbed by Birmingham."

"I know it well. I have visited often. Some friends of mine live there. Mr. and Mrs. Siddles. Perhaps you know them," Mr. Mansfield said.

"I have not had the pleasure," Eva said. "And Mr. Fitzallen is new to the region."

"No doubt you both move in different circles from the Siddles," Mr. Mansfield said, as if he had made another error.

"I have not been moving in any circles for some

time. My brother was ill for years before he passed, and his care occupied most of my time."

Mr. Mansfield frowned sympathetically. "Consumption?"

"Pistol ball."

"I trust the hand that held that pistol saw justice."

"My brother refused to lay down information, to my consternation."

"It is a tragic story," Mr. Mansfield said. "Not only that he perished while still young, but that he left two sisters to fend for themselves, with no protection." His gaze drifted to Rebecca. Her conversation with her poet had lagged. Mr. Mansfield excused himself and wandered in her direction.

"So what really happened to your brother?" Gareth asked.

"As I said, he never explained. Not even to me."

"Yet you must have an idea. If my brother came home with a pistol ball inside him, I would at least learn what I could."

"You are too inquisitive about my family's affairs, I think."

"Come now. I am not Mr. Mansfield, whom you want thinking well of your family. I am your friend Gareth, who has seen you half-naked. So, was it a duel, do you think?"

She really wished he would not talk about the naked part so casually, as if it were nothing to keep a secret. "I do not think it was a duel, although I allowed the doctor to believe that."

"It would explain your brother's refusal to speak of it. He could not make accusations without implicating himself in a crime."

"Exactly. Only, I do not see Nigel dueling. I may do his memory a disservice, but I suspect that a night riding between taverns and getting drunk with some friends somehow took a bad turn. He was often gone from home at night in those days."

"The Langdon's End version of a young blood, you mean."

"Yes. I think one of those friends lost his head over something and shot Nigel."

"It was probably over a woman."

She turned on him. "Not every man spends all of his time pursuing women. Not every man's misfortune starts with one."

"How true. I should not have jumped to that conclusion. Did he have strong political views that might lead to a deadly argument? Convictions for which he would risk his life rather than back down?"

His steady gaze said he had already guessed the answer. Nigel had no particular views that she knew about. His only goal had been to enjoy his youth while he had it. The truth was Nigel was more interested in carousing with friends than tending to the family's already limited estate.

She had long ago stopped trying to explain away that wound. Everyone in Langdon's End had concluded the same as she quickly enough anyway— That her brother's refusal to speak of it only confirmed the likelihood that the story would not put him in a good light.

"Are you remaining in Birmingham much longer?" she asked, to change the subject. Thinking about Nigel did not make her happy or even nostalgic. An unforgivable bitterness colored many of the memories—expressed in his vocal hostility, born of his infirmity, and her silent resentments.

"I was going to stay another day, but have decided to return to Albany Lodge tomorrow. And you?"

She looked to where Rebecca, sitting stiffly on the edge of a settee, tolerated the conversation of Mr. Mansfield who sat on a chair in front of her. "I do not know yet. At least another day. Perhaps more."

Wesley approached them then. Gareth's expression welcomed their host.

"I will call on you when you return home, unless you forbid it. We are still friends, I trust," Gareth whispered just before Wesley sat in the chair on his other side.

"I do not think you should," she whispered back. "You must not."

But he had already turned toward Wesley by then, and she did not know if he had heard her.

That night while Eva prepared for bed, Sarah slipped into her bedchamber. "If Rebecca ruins this chance with Mr. Mansfield, I will be very vexed, Eva. I chose him with great thought and care."

"We are both so grateful to you that I am sure neither of us wants you vexed. However, you speak of a chance when there is no indication at all that the man favors her any more than she favors him. I do not think he will call."

"Nonsense. He will be here tomorrow. He knows you are both supposed to leave in two days. If he comes as I expect, you must leave Rebecca here with me at least a week longer. You can stay, too, of course."

"I should return home. There are things I must do there. If Rebecca wants to stay, however, I will permit it."

Content with her plans, Sarah turned to the door.

"I still think you are being too optimistic about Mr. Mansfield," Eva said.

"He makes her uncomfortable, Eva. Those were her words. When he looks at her, she is *uncomfortable*. She is too young to know what she is really feeling. Oh, you do not know either, do you? Trust me that her discomfort is not the normal kind, but speaks well of the prospects."

"I understand what you refer to, Sarah. However, it is Mr. Mansfield whose interest I doubt. Among other things, he probably will care when he learns she has almost no fortune. For another, he made it clear tonight that he does not approve of clever women, and Rebecca is very well-read and quite opinionated."

"Oh, Eva, you are adorable. She has rare beauty, and she has gentle blood. He would want her even if she were a confirmed radical and bluestocking and owned one dress. Tonight all he is thinking is how he can claim the prize before the serious competition understands a contest is at hand." She opened the door.

"If you anticipate callers, what time do you think it will be? I want to buy some canvases and brushes to take home with me tomorrow morning."

"He will be early, but not too early. Two o'clock I would think. Why do you want painting materials? Do you dab?"

"It is my favorite pastime. I want to start some views very soon."

"Take the carriage, then. I will have no use for it tomorrow."

After Sarah left, Eva got into bed and gazed up at the canopy. She had not even tried to paint a view for over a year, after it became obvious that Mr. Stevenson's patrons had no interest in them. Her last visit to his shop hardly encouraged her to take them up again.

All the same, she itched to paint one, even though it made no sense financially. It would be her own creation, not a copy of someone else's. She experienced much more drama when doing her own work. Copying produced pleasant melodies in her heart. Her own compositions played like symphonies. She missed that, and since she had enough money to buy an extra bit of canvas, she could afford to indulge herself.

Mr. Stevenson's glee about the recent big sale entered her mind. So did the sight of him counting out twenty pounds. She needed to continue the copies, too, of course. Which meant she needed a new source

of paintings, now that Gareth lived at Albany Lodge.
She thought she knew where she might find some oth-
ers to borrow. As soon as she returned to Langdon's
End, she would take steps to arrange that.

Thinking about the paintings led her to thinking
about the ones she had already borrowed, which in
turn led her to thinking about the day she had returned
the last one. She cursed as her body came alive in the
night, reliving too well the sensations Gareth had
called forth. She dared not close her eyes, because if
she did, she saw him standing there, his chest bare,
then wearing nothing at all as she peered around a
doorjamb. Her body's sensitivity grew while fantasy
hands caressed her most indecently.

He had taunted her at the music performance after
she said she had not enjoyed his kisses. Even as he
apologized, he made sure her body admitted the lie.
Damn him and his conceit. He did not only guess
what she suffered if she allowed the memories to have
their way. He *knew*.

CHAPTER 11

Mr. Mansfield indeed called at Sarah's house at two o'clock. Eva received him along with her cousin and Rebecca. What followed could kindly be described as a mildly awkward half hour.

His interest in Rebecca could not be mistaken. He addressed most of his conversation to her. She thus had no choice except to respond. By the end of his visit, the exchanges turned less formal and stilted. Rebecca even laughed at a bit of wit he tried inserting. Unfortunately, Rebecca had prepared herself for the meeting, and just when things were getting friendly, she launched into a lecture on what Voltaire and Rousseau had written about education. For twenty minutes everyone in the room except Rebecca listened to a philosophical comparative analysis with frozen smiles on their faces.

When Sarah finally interrupted—"You must feed me such elevated thinking in small pieces, dear, and allow me to digest this latest morsel now"—Mr. Mansfield even thanked Rebecca, and promised to give the question some thought. Despite his patience, by Rebecca's later accounting it had all been a waste of time.

That evening Sarah posed her idea that Rebecca stay on as her guest. Rebecca quickly accepted, but only, Eva suspected, because she hoped the poet would also call, and because anything would be better than returning to the boredom of Langdon's End.

"Leave her to me, Eva," Sarah said quietly while they kissed good-bye the next morning. "We may not have a proposal in hand when I send her back to you, but we will be very close, I think."

Rebecca loitered in the doorway, watching her leave. Eva waved through the carriage window. Her small trunk, rolls of canvas, and new boxes of pigments and brushes rode atop the vehicle.

She had hired this carriage so that Sarah could use hers to take Rebecca around town to show her off. Eva suspected Sarah intended to chance upon Mr. Mansfield.

Four blocks from Sarah's house, she directed the carriage to the closest coaching inn. There she had all her property removed and transferred to an oxen-led wagon that she learned was making a delivery in Langdon's End. She left Birmingham as she entered it, ensconced in the back of that wagon, thus saving three-fourths of the cost of the carriage hire.

It was twilight by the time the wagon lumbered up

the lane to her house. The waggoneer quickly unloaded her belongings, dumping them without ceremony on her doorstep. He rolled away seconds after she paid him.

Throwing open the door, she bent and pushed the boxes and canvas over the threshold. She stood while her eyes adjusted to the shadows deepening in the house.

An ugly thrill of alarm shot up her back to her head. Squinting, she advanced on the stairs and felt a large shadow. Her hand just kept going. The sixth step was gone, removed, revealing the space beneath the stairs like a gaping mouth.

Her gaze darted around the library on her left. What she saw left her shaking. She made her way to a lamp and tried to light it. Her hands trembled so much that she barely managed it.

Light spread through the chamber, revealing horrible destruction. The divan had been upturned and its upholstery slashed. Wallboards were peeled off. Even a section of the floor was destroyed, the boards thrown haphazardly around.

Then she saw the paintings.

Two of her views decorated this chamber. Only now they lay on the floor. She ran over to them and looked down in horror. Someone had taken the turpentine from her paint box and smeared it all over them, ruining them forever. As if that were not cruel enough, the remnants of mixed paints had been smeared all over one of them, as if the criminals who had done this thought that amusing.

She feared what she would find in the other

chambers. Fighting a shock that threatened to paralyze her, she ventured to the rest of them.

The same chaos greeted her everywhere. Her mind jumped to her own bedchamber, and the nail in the joist below the floorboards, holding her bag of money. She rushed back to the stairs to go and see if she had been the victim of theft as well as vandalism.

She stopped cold there, with one foot on the first step. A floorboard had creaked above. Terror did a little dance on her skin. She could not breathe. She listened hard, waiting. Then she heard it again. A footfall, as if someone shifted his weight.

She turned on her heel and bolted from the house and ran as fast as she could down the lane.

Skirt hitched high, Eva ran so hard her side hurt and her breath came in gasps. Her bonnet fell off, lost in the night. She dared not look back to see if anyone followed, but she thought she heard someone else on the road.

At the crossroads with the road to Langdon's End, she paused a moment, heaving deeply to catch her breath. She peered down the road, flanked by trees and woods. How fast could she run that mile? Would she even be able to without fainting dead away?

The road ahead beckoned. Another minute she would be at the bend, and Albany Lodge would be in sight.

A horse whinnied in the distance behind her, terrifying her. Not debating her choice, not thinking at all, she ran again.

Rounding that bend gave her some heart. Albany Lodge could be seen in the gathering night, and she thought she spied some light in a window. No one would hear if she were accosted this far away, but she found comfort in that light and ran harder, no longer so afraid and witless.

She did not worry about going up the lane. Instead she ran cross-country feeling safer with each step. Finally the house loomed in front of her. Only then did she stop, her breaths heaving so hard she feared she would be sick.

A horse passed on the road. She instinctively dodged behind one of the trees. Was it the intruder in her house, following her? There was no way to know. He could still be in her home.

She calmed slowly and pressed that tree for support so she would not drop to the ground. As sense returned, she realized her predicament. Had Gareth remained only a friend, she would not hesitate to pound on his door and pour out her fear. That he had become something more made her hesitate, and shy about intruding.

She only needed to be near him to be safe, she reasoned. She could stay by this tree, although the spring damp would become unpleasant during the night. If she were very quiet, she could sit on the stone steps, however. Dawn would wake her, and she could then walk to Langdon's End and find help.

Moving soundlessly, she walked to the steps and

sat on the top one. She rested her back against the wall, and pulled her pelisse close for warmth. Now that panic had receded, the chill of the night entered her bones.

Suddenly light flooded her. She looked up. Gareth stood in the threshold, candelabra in hand, his shirt blazing from the flames' reflections.

"Who is out there?" The light from the candles made a slow arc, finally finding her. "Eva? What the hell are you doing sitting out here?"

Eva just stared at him. Her eyes appeared extremely large, and her face unhealthily pale. She huddled with her knees drawn up to her chest. She looked small and young and terrified.

He turned and put the candelabra on a table near the door, then returned. He reached down and lifted her to her feet. "What is wrong?"

She leaned into him as if her legs had no strength. He embraced her. The tremors in her body had nothing to do with him.

"You are shivering." It was not that cold tonight. "Where is Rebecca?"

With a deep inhale, she collected herself. She stepped back, out of his arms. "She is still in Birmingham. I returned today, and—someone was at my house while we were gone. I saw the evidence of that, and"—she covered her cheeks with her hands—"I lost my head. There are no other words for it."

He embraced her shoulders with one arm and encouraged her to move. "Of course you did. Come inside."

She let him guide her to a chair in the library. Since she still shook, he lit a low fire. Then he poured a finger of brandy and handed her the glass.

"I do not imbibe strong spirits."

"You do tonight. Drink it."

He stood over her until she did.

She made a face after it went down, but some color returned to her skin. She looked around the library's bare shelves and few chairs and one table.

"I thought he was still in the house," she said. "Whoever had entered it, that is. I thought I heard him above, so I ran and"—she gestured helplessly at herself—"you were the closest. I thought he followed me. I may have imagined that part. I don't know."

She was more herself now. Much more, if she felt obligated to excuse her arrival in the middle of the night. She had chosen to sit on cold stones all night lest he misunderstand.

"How did you know there had been a housebreaking? Was something missing?" He could not imagine what thieves would want to take. So little remained in that house.

"He—they destroyed things. Threw items all around and poured turpentine on my paintings. They tore up floorboards and pulled off panels. They must have been very angry that there was nothing of value to take. I expect they laughed and thought it all great fun, ruining the home of someone else."

"They were probably men who used to make free with this house, and when they saw they could no longer, they went looking for another. Since yours was close and empty, it was vulnerable."

"Perhaps." She frowned over the possibility. "The region is changing. The city grows closer all the time. I see strangers moving about the country, on the roads and lanes and crossing fields. I have been foolish to think my life would remain the same. I do not think I will ever again feel as safe as I used to."

The thought had her huddling in on herself again. Her brow furrowed over sad eyes. Left on her own she would ponder the invasion all night, and emerge at dawn afraid of her own shadow.

"You are very safe now, Eva. Tomorrow we will go to your house and see how bad it is in the light of day. Until then you are not to think about it." He held out his hand. "Come with me. I was about to find some supper. You can help."

She let him lead her down to the kitchen. He lit some lamps and peered at the shelves. Warmth hovered near his shoulder. She stood close and peered up too. Her proximity started his blood simmering. *Not now, you ass.*

"The ham would be good," she said. "I have not eaten all day, and would accept some if you offered it."

He brought down the ham, cheese, and some bread that wasn't too stale. He filled thick glasses with beer from the small keg against the wall. "Harold has taken to making sure there are basic provisions here."

She found dishes and knives. "I expect he and Erasmus hope to work here all the time someday. When you staff your household, they want to be first in line."

"That will not happen until some legalities regarding the property are settled. I have explained that to them so they do not pass up other opportunities should any arrive."

She sat at the rough-surfaced worktable. He sat across from her so he would not be tempted to touch her.

She carved at the ham. "I am surprised you do not already have whatever servants you may need. You appear the sort of man who would."

When he had thought to distract her with a meal, he had not expected to end up talking about himself. "I have never felt the need for them. I am alone and move around a lot."

She made a display of concentrating on how she cut up her ham. Curiosity poured off her as clearly as fear had less than a half hour ago.

"Ask if you want," he said.

Her knife went to work cutting her cheese into mouth-sized morsels. "That would be rude."

"You are wondering how the bastard son of a duke lives, if he has no obvious living."

Slice. Slice. Slice.

"My father left me a respectable income. I also serve as a go-between on some business affairs, Eva. A broker. Normally one side is in England, and one side is on the Continent. I travel there often."

"Is that why you never married? Because you move about so much?"

Thus, inevitably, did a woman's curiosity lead.

He laughed. "The question assumes that marriage is a good idea, and a state to aspire to."

"You do not think it is?"

"I suppose as a financial arrangement it has much to recommend it, with the right person. Since I am not such a person, it never came up with a woman who might be the right one in turn for me. The truth is I have never once thought about getting married."

"Never? Not once? Even if it were hopeless, not even one thought in passing while you were with someone you loved?"

Her earnest tone charmed him. How to explain? She need only think about it from a different direction to understand. It meant leaving behind her old notions of how the world expects one to view such things.

"No, not once, Eva. As for love— Love is really desire, prettied up to justify physical needs. Some call it love, because calling it what it really is sounds too base, and because it promises longevity after desire inevitably fades."

A flush rose from her neck to color her face. Not from embarrassment with the subject, as it would be with most women. Anger brightened her eyes. "You are very cynical."

"I am honest, when so few people are about these things."

"What about your mother and father? Was that mere desire?"

"It was most definitely desire, and little else. The duke hardly knew her when he struck that arrangement."

"But he stayed, you said. He remained after it should have faded, by your telling."

"He stayed because she became a friend, and a confidante, and the only person he trusted without question. He stayed because she made it very easy for him to stay. He also stayed to spite his duchess whom he came to loathe. If he loved my mother at the end, it was like any kind of familial love, not special and different the way the poetry and romances lead one to think."

She rose and started clearing the table with abrupt, jerking motions. Plates clattered into the sink. "I think you are wrong." She pushed the ham platter back on its shelf. "I think your experiences have badly affected your way of looking at these things."

"My experience was better than most. I saw a better relationship between the duke and my mother than my brothers saw between him and their mother."

"I am not talking about that experience." She pulled up the pail. "If you get some water I will wash these plates."

He stood and took the pail. He set it down. "What experiences do you refer to?"

She angled back, leaning against the sink. "I expect you have had many experiences that might badly affect you. That is all I meant."

"You sounded like you spoke of particulars."

With a display of annoyance, she picked up the pail and tried to pass. He did not allow it.

"I will only say this, since I would never insult my host after I sought sanctuary in his home. Your reputation has followed you to Langdon's End. That is all."

"What reputation is that?"

"It was said that you leave women so enthralled by pleasure that they lose all sense and will do anything to keep you nearby." She blushed hotly, but also looked him right in the eyes.

"The gossip both flatters me and insults me," he said. "I do not know whether to get angry or to preen like a plumed bird. There are not many men reputed to make a woman lose all sense due to pleasure, after all."

"I do not know how you can make light of it. Reputations matter in this world."

"Mine is wicked, that is true, but in the best of ways. I would rather be known for this than as someone who is cruel, or ruthless, or unprincipled."

Her brow puckered. "Yes, I see what you mean. As character flaws go, yours involve the least of sins. Still, to indulge one's mere desires without restraint— to lure others to do the same . . . "

"There is nothing mere about it sometimes. It can be a maddening force. An internal tempest. A compelling necessity." He bent until his eyes were inches from hers. "But you already know that, Eva." He touched her lips with his fingertips. "Don't you?"

CHAPTER 12

She should turn her head, so he could not touch her like this. Only that tiny caress on her lips almost mesmerized her, and his closeness created a horrible tease to her body. Not dangerous, however. Her bedazzlement felt wonderfully normal. Almost comforting, after the way the evening had begun. The remnants of the fear that sent her running down the road vanished as she enjoyed his attention and allure.

"I did not come here for that." She breathed the words more than spoke them.

"I know."

He did not sound sincere, or even much interested. Perhaps he did not believe her. Maybe he assumed she really had come there for that, then lost her nerve and sat on the steps to decide what to do.

"My house really was broken into. Truly."

"I do not doubt it."

"Then why—"

His lips brushed hers. "I am not sure. Perhaps because you are curious, and I am badly tempted to enlighten you." She felt a faint smile against her cheek while his breath on her skin made happy shivers dance down her spine. "Perhaps because a woman who speaks her mind without hesitation challenges me. Maybe because your spirit hints at all kinds of passions."

She sought refuge in society's rules, but half-heartedly. "It would be ignoble of you to seduce me after I came here for help."

His head angled so he spoke in her ear. None of him actually touched her anymore. Not one spot. Yet he might have been embracing her naked body from the breathlessness that possessed her.

"I am not going to seduce you."

"You aren't?"

He shook his head slightly. His soft hair feathered against her face because he had dipped his head so his phantom kisses warmed her neck. She fought the urge to squirm in reaction to his sensual taunts.

"I will enjoy the sweet torture of wanting you, however. Temptation is its own pleasure." Again his breath feathered her ear and neck. "You feel what I mean. Right now, you do."

She certainly did. He had her aroused worse than when they had embraced in the garden. So little space separated them that she need only exhale for her breasts to touch his shirt. The small gap begged for closure.

"I would expect a man like you to press your advantage," she murmured. "Not settle for sweet torture."

He looked down at his fingertips. They slowly drew a line at the neckline of her dress. The proximity of his hands to her breasts seemed designed to drive her mad. She waged a losing battle against her inclinations because she had been caressed by that hand before, and she had been naked, and it had been wonderful.

"As I said, I may be called wicked, but I am not unprincipled. There are many reasons why I cannot have you, tonight of all nights. A long list. You are ignorant. You came here for safety. You have drunk strong spirits. Since you are an innocent, you would expect I do the right thing afterward. I do not seduce women who do not know their own minds and will wake up with regrets, Eva, even when I badly want them."

That tracing line connected with her skin briefly, in a small caress. The sensation streamed through her body.

Surely he would step away now, after that fine speech. She could not bear this any longer. Her body ached with anticipation. She understood what he meant when he spoke of the pleasure of temptation. In the garden she had briefly tasted the fulfillment of that promise, and now the temptation swept away caution and reserve and what little remained of propriety.

"What if—what if there would be no regrets?" she

asked. "What if I am tired of being ignorant, and more than passing curious?"

He just looked down at her upturned face.

"What if I know my own mind very well, and there will be no expectations at all?"

"Eva—"

"What if being held by you sounds very safe to me tonight, and very right, in ways nothing else would?"

His expression hardened. His lids lowered. Sensuality became a palpable energy between them. Her anticipation sang in a higher key. She did not think it possible to want a man to embrace her more than she did right now.

Only he didn't embrace her. Looking in his eyes, lost in them, she knew, just knew, the instant when temptation lost the war.

She could not believe it. She had just offered herself and he was going to *turn her down*. He was supposed to be wicked, damn it.

To make it worse, he smiled like she was a sweet child and kissed her *on the forehead*.

Furious, she threw her arms around his neck to hold his head down and kissed him on the mouth. Her breasts pressed against his chest and her whole body cheered with relief.

Surprise. The smallest hesitation. Then his inconvenient decency blew away on the winds of raging desire. His embrace enclosed her so tightly that her body melded against his. Strong fingers held her crown so his kisses could ravish her mouth, her neck, her chest. Her own hands and arms pressed and grasped and learned and knew. *Yes,* she thought, *Yes, yes*, as his hands moved over her and the force of his want dominated her.

A low sound in her ear. "Not here." Here, anywhere, she did not care. They moved, she did not know how. Still entwined, still sharing fevered holds and hard, deep kisses, like a whirlwind they spun upstairs, slamming against walls, fumbling with garments, blind with impatience.

Joy when her dress loosened halfway up the second flight of stairs. Euphoria when he pressed her to the stairwell wall and pulled down dress, chemise, and stays until his warm hand could touch her breasts again. *Yes,* as she knew that pleasure once more, so much better than in her memory. *Yes*, when his head lowered and his tongue flicked.

She could no longer walk with the dress sagging low. He lifted her in his arms and carried her the rest of the way, to a bedchamber white and brown and spare.

He sat on the edge of the bed and set her on her feet in front of him. She found herself looking down into dark eyes and a face transformed by passion. Hard. Hot. A spiral of need spun through her, down to her vulva.

He pushed her garments down her hips and made quick work of her stays' lacing. Her dress and chemise fell down her legs, and the stays flew through the air, leaving her naked in front of him.

His hands and gaze moved down her body, from her shoulders to her knees. "You are beautiful, Eva." He pulled her closer, between his thighs, one hand on her bottom and the other on her back, and kissed her so passionately that her knees almost buckled. Then his mouth moved to her breasts. Tongue and teeth began devastating arousals, while his caresses claimed her hips and thighs, her bottom and back. All of her. A sensual stupor engulfed her. The need pulsed more and more, aching and wanting. A frantic yearning entered her euphoria. It grew until it absorbed the pleasure within itself.

His hand slid between her thighs. He touched her at the center of her desire, where all the sensations collected and pulsed. She cried out from the intensity, and almost pulled away. He held her so she could not, while he touched her again with a long stroke.

A compelling union of pleasure and excruciating need maddened her. He lifted her and set her on his knees facing him, her legs straddling his. She looked down as his hand again stroked her, only now she was open to him. Shockingly so. Before she closed her eyes to contain the delirium, she saw he was looking down there too.

She almost wept. She begged with a series of pleas, for mercy, for something. "Soon. Very soon," he said.

His hand moved again. A caress sent her reeling. "You will know this now, because I cannot be sure you will when I take you."

He pressed her forward, against his chest. He embraced her there while he deliberately made her madness worse and worse, until she thought she would scream.

Then she did scream, right into his shoulder, as all

the need burst apart and exquisite sensations flowed out of it. She lost all other sense in that moment, and only reclaimed herself slowly while she sagged, naked and astonished, in his arms.

She did not know how long they sat like that, with her limp in his arms while that glory echoed in her. Finally he stood, turned, and put her on the bed.

Gareth stripped off his clothes and joined Eva in bed. She still lulled in a stupor, but not so much that she had not watched him undress.

"Come here." He reached for her. "Here, like this." He positioned her on her back, on top of him, her head against his shoulder and her body exposed to the air, his gaze, and his hands.

She flailed a little, surprised at being propped like this. He nuzzled her head and caressed down her sides until she allowed herself to sink against him. That caused her bottom to press his erection. Up her hips went, abruptly. Down they came again, carefully testing, as shock gave way to curiosity. She shifted so she nestled him between her thighs. He moved her slightly again so the tip of his cock pressed her mound.

She squirmed just enough to make a spike of feral craving obliterate his thoughts. "You really are wicked," she said. She arched sensuously against him.

He kissed her shoulder and face. Her breasts rose higher, round and firm, their dark tips tight again. He lightly skimmed them with his thumbs, and she all but levitated. He feathered caresses on the tips again. She grasped the sheet on either side of his hips and twisted the fabric in her fists.

He continued teasing her while desire re-inflamed her. She rocked against him, her thighs caressing his cock and her mound pressing its head. He hardened and swelled even more. His hunger took on a ferocious edge.

He found enough control to avoid ravishing her at once. *Carefully. Slowly.* A few threads of sanity chanted his better intentions, but erotic images entered his head, goading him.

He rolled her off, onto the bed, on her stomach. He rose up on an arm so he could look at her while he caressed her back and bottom. He imagined her rising to her knees—

Her head lifted, as if she saw his mind. He kissed her in reassurance and smoothed his hand over her curves. "Allow yourself to accept the pleasure, Eva. Think of nothing else."

She returned to hugging the mattress. Slow kisses down her spine had her breath quickening again. A small moan of delight sounded when his caress traced the cleft of her bottom, then lower and deeper between her legs. He stroked her still swollen, soft folds and she moaned again and again, descending once more into abandon.

His own pleasure sharpened, taking power from how he controlled her now. He touched very specifically and she cried out. Her hand instantly covered her mouth. He touched again, deliberately, and that hand barely muffled her next cry.

"No one can hear you except me, Eva. Do not try to deny what you are experiencing."

Eyes closed and face softened from passion's command of her, she half shook her head. "It is so wonderful it is frightening. Shocking. Outrageous that you watch me while once more I—while I—"

He stroked deeply and her bottom rose up to allow him better reach. "While you give yourself over to pleasure, and to me?"

She nodded.

"Do you want me to stop?"

She bit her lower lip and shook her head.

"Then move your hand from your mouth and give yourself totally. I want you to accept just how shockingly wonderful it can be."

Her hand fell away. He caressed her slowly, watching how passion made her more beautiful and radiant. Her breathing turned staccato when he stroked her vulva. He inserted one finger, then two, into her tight velvet passage. Her lips parted for two sharp intakes of air. He stroked deeper. She grasped the sheet she hugged and moaned.

"Oh," she breathed. "Oh, yes."

She was wet and open and more than ready. He was far gone himself, pushed to the limits of his restraint. His head and body urged completion.

He rolled her over. They shared one long, deep, unbearably erotic kiss while he sought to fight back the storm. Only the kiss did the opposite, and his mind darkened to everything except thrusting into her. He

licked and sucked her breasts until her soft cries grew
louder, more insistent. She grasped at his shoulders
frantically, helplessly. When he added caresses to her
vulva again, her cries became a long series of exclamations of both affirmation and frustration.

It was time. Now. Except—

He did not ask. He did not think. He moved his
kisses lower, down her body, not caring if he shocked
her, not considering anything except the primal drive
directing him. Lower yet, until he kissed her mound.
Lower yet, while he pushed her legs apart.

She screamed. Not happily. He looked up her body
to where she watched him, eyes wide.

He kept his hand on her, letting pleasure make his
argument for him.

"I've never— I did not know that—" She could
hardly speak in her frenzy. "That seems truly wicked,
not in an average way."

He settled down between her thighs. "I will wait
until you ask me. I will only caress you until you ask
for more."

"I do not think I will— I would never— *Oh*." The
plaintive *oh* came when he carefully pressed her clitoris.

He knew how to keep a woman on the brink. He left
her on the edge until she writhed in glorious agony. He
experienced more than the usual torture himself, and
only kept control because he focused on her reactions.

"I— I— Please— I—" Her words emerged as short,
gasping breaths.

"Do you want more, Eva?"

She looked down through heavily lidded eyes. A special madness showed in them. Her nod was tentative, but that was enough.

He kissed her thigh while he leashed his mind to what was left of his sanity and physical restraint. Then he turned his head and gave her the most intimate of kisses.

O*h.* The sensations were unbearable. Shocking. Incredible.

She tensed, as her body recoiled from such intimacy. Pleasure quickly defeated the retreat. She dwelled in a place not of this world, and her whole body and mind begged for more, for relief, for an eternity of such unworldly arousal.

She glanced down at him, at what he was doing, at what he must be seeing. Shocking. Scandalous. Within the intense need on which her entire being focused, odd, disparate thoughts drifted. What her mother would have said if she knew. How Charles had never wanted her like this. How surprised the people of Langdon's End would be.

Shouting them down, dominating any other voice, was the one that had brought her to this bed. *Know it all. Take it all. It may have to last you a lifetime.*

Something changed. Subtly, but undeniably, Gareth became more demanding, as if he heard those voices and sought to silence them. The pleasure became demanding, too, as it had the last time, only many times worse. It pushed all thoughts out of her head, and obliterated all control.

She no longer owned herself. He did, with what he did to her. He pushed her deeper and deeper into an insanity of need until nothing else existed. Deeper still he sent her. Groans and cries sounded in her head. Then it all constricted and her consciousness screamed and begged and reached for another wonderful end.

It did not come. Instead Gareth came up over her, into her arms, his body lining hers, dominating it. He pressed into her slowly. She clutched at him as a new awe and a new shock took hold. She could not resist him even if she had wanted to. She did not control her body enough to do so yet.

He pressed deeper. She felt him distinctly against flesh still sensitive and swollen from his kisses, and inside her as her body stretched to accommodate him. She sneaked a look at him. His fiery eyes and tense expression stunned her. She realized, just knew, that this was not how it normally would be for him, and that he was forcing a restraint for her sake.

She closed her eyes and gave no voice to the discomfort he now caused. She let herself feel it fully, as she had the rest.

He stopped finally, filling her. He did not move. She looked again. His eyes were closed and he appeared less harsh. She wrapped her arms around his neck and brought him down so she could kiss his shoulder, then his lips.

"You have survived it?" he asked quietly.

She nodded, and opened her eyes. She looked right into his. A mistake, perhaps. In that instant she understood the real dangers of what she did. The wickedness might not haunt her life, but the intimacy would. Letting him strip her of reserve left her vulnerable and exposed in other ways. She knew the power of that now.

He moved, carefully. A renewed tension spread through him. She understood despite her ignorance. After a while she moved too, encouraging him to find his own pleasure without so much care. He responded with harder thrusts. Masculine need engulfed her Even so, to the very end when she saw and felt his own shattering, she could tell that he held something back so he would not hurt her too much. She felt him withdraw an instant before the tension broke apart.

He came down on her then, covering her, his face pressed to hers and his hair feathering her face. She did not mind his weight. She held him to her body, taking in his warmth. Her fingertips skimmed his skin while she branded her mind with the sensation of touching his body. She savored the intimacy that she had discovered tonight—invasive, even frightening, but wonderful too.

Her fingers caressed his back. Tentative. Careful, as if she feared disturbing him. He let her, and enjoyed the soft touch, while their tight embrace caused the bliss to stretch longer than normal.

His mind slowly found itself, and saw the new

colors in his contentment. Surprise, and relief. The latter that he had avoided brutalizing her. Surprise that he had come so close to doing so. Few women in the past had inspired that possessive hunger, and none of them had been the least bit like Eva Russell.

He rose up so his weight rested on his forearms, not her, and he did not continue crushing her. He looked down into eyes that glistened with—what? Tears?

Hell, he had hurt her more than he thought. She was a virgin, after all. A virgin. What had he been thinking? He should be horsewhipped.

The truth was, try as he might, he could not summon any shame or regret. The only concern was whether she would. She had said she would not, but what did she know?

He caressed her face and kissed her. Her expression lightened, then turned rueful. "Afterward, like now, what does one do?" she asked.

"Normally I like to run through the garden naked and play satyr chasing nymph."

For an instant she believed him, then she laughed. "More naughty games, you mean."

"Yes, but not in gardens. However, I do not think you would want more tonight, no matter how mildly wicked." He rolled off her and onto his back. "Not only due to being ravished for the first time. You traveled all day. Sleep is in order."

He reached for the sheet. In doing so he saw the one on which they lay. No blood from the looks of things, even though he had felt the hymen give way.

He pulled her into an embrace, covered them with the sheet, and got comfortable with her head on his shoulder and her hand on his chest.

"This will be very boring if you normally play wicked games all night," she said.

"Are you saying you are disappointed that I am not going to impose on you again?"

"No. You are quite right about that. I am somewhat tired and . . . sore. I think that you must find me very dull compared to the women you have known. That is all I meant."

He looked down on her crown, tucked under his chin. Reassurances were in order, but the last ones he had expected her to need. *What are you talking about? Hell, fucking you was incredible.* No, that would never do. He formed a response carefully. It took some time to pick through the potential ramifications of each word.

"I am not your tenth lover, but your first, Eva. It is a privilege to be so honored, especially by a woman who could have a choice from among many men."

No reaction from her. Nothing at all. He realized that she had stilled totally. She had fallen asleep. So much for his well-considered declaration.

He drifted too. When on the brink of sleep, he felt her move. He opened his eyes to find her looking up at him with a soulful expression that contemplated what she saw. Then she planted a kiss on his chest, and nestled closer for the night.

CHAPTER 13

Gareth gazed down at Eva's face and tangled hair. Her expression looked ethereal in the soft northern light. Dawn had broken two hours ago, and he had risen to wash and dress. Fresh water waited for her in the dressing room. He would not have minded staying abed with her until she emerged from her dreams, but he assumed she would be more comfortable being alone in the bright light of day.

He left the chamber and descended the stairs, listing the various matters he had intended to address today. One involved riding back toward Chatsworth, and calling on two local estates near enough to Devonshire's properties to suggest someone at them might have awareness of the history of the paintings once stored there. At best now he could leave in two days.

It might take that long to help Eva put her house back in order and swear information about the intrusion.

The letter to Ives would have to wait as well, but it needed to be sent soon. Ives's own letter had come yesterday, and his queries indicated someone, or rather Someone, had pressed him in turn for information. Ives had never said the Prince Regent had requested this investigation, but Gareth assumed that was the Someone behind it all. Annoyingly absent from that letter had been any news regarding Lance, the investigation, and status of the inquiry into Percy's death.

His concentration on duties not being accomplished kept thoughts of the night at bay until he entered the kitchen and found coffee already made. He strode to the garden door and looked out. Harold had come, on his own and without Erasmus, unbidden. He labored on the wall, hoisting stones into place, finishing the work that Gareth had started himself yesterday.

Gareth's mind snapped to the woman sleeping above. Damn.

He paced the kitchen, thinking fast. Of course, he should have thought it all through last night, fast or slow, so long as he thought at all. He cursed himself soundly, but even as he did, all the old rationalizations for ignoring the rules leapt forward.

Gentlemen did not seduce innocent ladies, even if those innocents threw themselves at said gentlemen—supposedly. That he could name important gentlemen who had did not matter. That he had been taught this by his own father who had bedded a virgin he could not and would not ever marry made the lesson all the more comical. Not to mention he was not, officially, a gentleman. He was a nonperson, and if there was any benefit to being one it should be that he did not have to give a damn about any gentlemen's rules.

Yet here he was, with a lady up in his bed, and her reputation in his hands.

He watched Harold. Big, brawny, and blond, Harold moved methodically with the stones. He would probably finish by noon. Harold was supposed to be serving, when he served at all, as a house servant, as valet and manservant, not doing hard labor. Yet there he was, proving his worth at a most inconvenient moment.

Better Harold than Erasmus. With Erasmus, Eva's name would be on every harpy's lips by tomorrow. Erasmus's tendency to gossip had been handy, but there were times when discretion called. Like right now.

He ran his fingers through his hair, and opened the garden door. He mounted the stairs to the garden, and walked down to where Harold worked.

Harold broke off and took the opportunity to wipe his face and hands with a rag tucked in his shirt.

"I did not expect you today," Gareth said.

Harold nodded. "You said you started to rebuild this yourself. Mentioned it while I served dinner yesterday. I thought it better if I took care of it. No reason for us both to have bad hands."

Gareth all but smoothed his palm over his face, to see just how bad his hands had become that Harold felt obligated to intercede. Had Eva noticed?

"Good of you," Gareth said. "I am glad you are here. There has been a small disaster, and I need your help."

Harold frowned, and set down the stone he had just lifted.

"It requires absolute discretion," Gareth continued. "I am sure that when you were in the army, there were times when you were called upon to keep silent about important matters."

"Many times. Not only military matters. My officer had private things I would learn about, seeing as how I served him. I know how to keep my mouth shut, sir, if that is what you are asking."

"It is. I know you hope to be a valet someday, either mine or another man's. It is much like with your officer. If a valet's discretion cannot be trusted, he is worthless."

"No one will hear of this disaster, sir. Not even Erasmus, who has a loose tongue, if you hear me. He is a good friend, but he does like to talk too much."

Gareth could only hope Harold was good to his word. "Last night near dusk, Miss Russell returned home to find someone had invaded her home, destroying much of it. The intruder may have still been there. She thought he was. She ran here for protection."

Harold's eyes widened. "Miss Russell? Was she harmed? If one hair on her head was touched, I'll kill the man if I find him. The world has gone to hell, if I may say so, sir, if a woman cannot feel safe in her own home. I am undone, sir, undone by this news. Not a small disaster at all, but a very big and shocking one."

"Yes, well, it being night, and there being no

alternative, she stayed here so she would be safe. She is upstairs in the chamber that has the new bed I just bought. You can see the problem we face, I am sure."

Of course Harold could see it. Other than one sharp, suspicious glance, he spent the next few minutes ruminating, scratching his head, and staring at the wall.

"I am not one for strategy, sir. No one made me an officer, after all. But I think it best if when she speaks to the magistrate, it not be mentioned that she stayed here. My silence will count for nothing if the magistrate starts talking, and if he does, she can be ruined for nothing more than refusing to risk herself to the criminals among us these days."

"My thoughts exactly. She took the sensible course, but she will have to pretend she took the stupid one and did not come and inform me of this until this morning."

"I can go and alert the magistrate. He most likely will not get to her house for a couple of hours, since he lives on the other side of town. If you escort Miss Russell back—"

"That is a fine strategy. Perhaps you should start off now, and Miss Russell will wait for the magistrate at her home."

Harold's expression assumed a military solidity. "Just one thing that might complicate the plan, sir. Miss Russell—will she lie? She might refuse to do that, being the sort of woman she is."

"I will try to convince her of the necessity."

Harold headed for the garden portal. Gareth aimed

back to the house. Miss Russell had better not balk at lying. Surely she would see the sense of it.

He returned to the bedchamber. Eva was up and he heard her in the dressing room. He left and walked across the house to the only other bedchamber with an actual bed. He pulled back the coverlet, mussed the sheets, and even gave the mattress a few good thumps with his ass to make it look slept on. He mussed a towel in the dressing room, then threw it on the floor for effect. Deciding the chambers would convince Harold that good Miss Russell had spent all her time there, he went looking for the lady in question.

He found her dressed and tidy in the bedchamber. She sat on a chair, looking calm but perhaps a little confused. All the same he thought she looked adorable. Pretty and pert and alluring in spite of herself. She appeared completely capable of deciding she wanted a man and telling him so, which was not the Eva Russell the world knew. It was probably not the Eva Russell she knew.

Lest the awkwardness grow, he strode over, lifted her into his arms, and gave her a kiss. She blushed.

"I trust that is not embarrassment," he said, caressing her pink cheek. "If so, I'll not have it."

"Of course not. No embarrassment and no regrets, just as I promised. I do feel a little strange, as if I am slowly waking up from a vivid dream." She toed at the carpet. "We were more than a little mad last night, weren't we?"

"Insanely so."

"Utterly mad."

"Yes."

Her arms angled out in a hapless gesture. "I think everyone should allow themselves to be mad at least once, don't you?"

"Absolutely."

She felt at her hair. She straightened her sleeves. "I should return home. I look a fright. I did not even have a brush with me."

He had not noticed. He did not think she looked a fright at all. The morning light made her skin appear flawless, and her changeable eyes showed as blue right now. She appeared ravishing despite her sensible dress. As for her hair, he could not see it without thinking how silken it felt against his skin.

"I should return home," she said again. "I need to—do many things."

"I will take you. I sent Harold for the magistrate. You need to let him see what happened, so he can alert other homeowners to be cautious and try to find the culprit."

"Harold—" Her gaze shot to the bed.

"It is well he was here. I would not want you to wait on the magistrate alone while I went for him. Have no fear that Harold saw you. He did not enter the house. He does know you stayed here, however, but I believe he will be discreet."

That appeased her, mostly. Her growing acknowledgment of her danger could be seen in her eyes, however. "If he is not discreet, it will not matter if I stayed in a locked chamber all night or if I ran from my house with a murderer after me. I can bear the scandal myself, but I fear it will ruin my sister's chances."

"There will be no scandal."

He led her down the stairs and left her while he went out to saddle and bring his horse around. She waited outside the front door for him, her reticule in hand. He led the horse while together they walked to the road.

How odd the day seemed. How strange to be walking beside Gareth in the sunshine, with his monster of a horse plodding behind.

She glanced at him on occasion. Her heart still danced at the sight of him. Perhaps it always would. If she had thought last night's intimacy would dull that girlish excitement, she had been wrong.

Upon wakening, and seeing where she lay, and remembering the night, there had been one moment of panic. It passed, however, as the memories grew clearer and his phantom body pressed hers. The small soreness still throbbing deep inside provoked a smile, not dismay. While she washed, she wondered if she had become as wicked as he, to partake of pleasure so casually with a man she did not love, then know no guilt afterward.

Wicked. An interesting word. Not at all the same as *evil.* Far more damning than *naughty*, though. One could not deny that *wicked* often carried implications of being a sensual rogue. She supposed she was one now too.

He had said last night that she could have had her

choice of many men if she wanted. It had been a gentle kindness that touched her. A generous and thoughtful lie. He, on the other hand, most certainly could have had his choice of many women.

"I am hungry," she said when they rounded the bend that took Albany Lodge out of sight.

"I should have fed you something."

"I will find some cheese when I get home, assuming the intruders did not take it or ruin it. Nor could we dally for a breakfast this morning. It would not do to have the magistrate arrive at my house only to find me gone."

Gareth pushed open the door, which she was sure she had not closed when she ran. Her trunk, canvas, and other things still lay right over the threshold, where she had dragged them. He stepped inside.

"It is worse than you said, Eva."

She followed, and looked around the front chamber at the destruction that greeted her return yesterday. Gareth walked over and picked up one of her paintings. He stared at it with angry eyes, then set it down. He came back to her and took her hands.

"We will see how bad it is in the rest of the house. Before that, you need to consider what you will say to the magistrate about last night. I think you should say you spent the night here and came for help in the early morning. I know you do not want to lie, but—"

"It is a lie, but one that can be excused. Should the truth ever become known, it will be obvious why I obscured it, and I do not think anyone will blame me."

He took her face in his hands. "Since I do not think I will have the chance to do this later—" All of last night lived in the kiss he gave her. Then he led her to the reception hall and handed her up the stairs.

She went to her bedchamber and stared at the corner floorboards. Nothing. No one had pried them up. Her coins still hung on that nail. Even more weighed down her reticule. She would survive this destruction because she had some money. She shuddered at the thought of how she would have managed if she did not.

The boards were fine, but nothing else. All the beds up here had been overturned. Cupboards had been emptied, their contents strewn around the space. A storage area behind a low door in Rebecca's chamber gaped, the door open and the trunks ransacked.

"It looks as if they searched for money or valuables," Gareth said.

"One has only to enter to know there will be none. We do not even have decent furniture."

More of the same waited on the next level. There was no furniture up here, but some trunks that held her mother's clothes and memories lived in one room. Those too had been violated, and on seeing this final assault, she lost her composure.

Weeping, she dropped to her knees and began gathering the old silks and shoes that still held the scents of her childhood from long ago. Even the destruction of her paintings did not hurt as much as this. A murderous rage took hold of her. She held the dresses to her face and cried out her anger and frustration.

Gareth knelt beside her. He took the clothes from her hands, folded them carefully, and placed them back in the trunk. "I do not like the idea of your living here alone."

"It is my home." She wiped her eyes with her hand. "I'll be damned if I will be driven out."

"Still—"

"I will not be made afraid to live in the only home I have known by whoever did this. I *won't*."

He said nothing more. He stood, and offered his hand to help her up.

They went back to the library and waited for the magistrate.

Sir Thomas Pickford appeared to be a competent magistrate. Tall, slender, and still much the officer he had once been in the army, he paced through the house, noting the destruction. He returned to the library and set its one chair close to the divan where Eva waited.

"You did not see them?" he asked her.

She shook her head. "I do not even know if it was one or more."

"Probably more. Two at least. The chambers above show a careful method. This down here—" He gestured around. "A different mind did this."

"It is clear she has nothing to steal," Gareth said.

"True, but they searched just the same, while they had their fun." He ignored Gareth and peered at Eva.

"Is there anyone you have angered? Someone who might want to do this in spite?"

"That is an odd question, Sir Thomas," Gareth said. The notion anyone would want to hurt Eva was preposterous.

"Not so odd, sir. Look around. We do not see the likes of this in this county, I can tell you that. Oh, there are thieves enough, but this—" He shook his head.

"Well, you have seen it now. I trust you will find those responsible."

"I will try, but there is no telling who they are or where they are, is there? I will make inquiries, to find out if anyone saw something, perhaps while passing on the road in the evening. We will do what we can." He turned his attention back to Eva. "It was not wise of you to wait until morning to seek help, Miss Russell. Are you going to be alone here much longer?"

"My sister will return in a few days."

"Well, lock your doors. I do not think they will be back, but better to be careful."

Sir Thomas took his leave, riding off. Gareth began setting the rest of the furniture in order in the house. When he came down from the bedchambers, he found Eva wiping paint off the landscapes.

He had felt a bloody rage on seeing the way those two paintings had been ruined. There could be no point in it other than cruelty. Perhaps Sir Thomas was correct and someone had done this out of spite.

Eva noticed him watching her. "I can use the canvases again," she explained.

"They were lovely, and well done."

"Not really. I know I have a middling talent. I enjoy painting, however. I intend to work at it and get better too."

He went over and took the canvas from her hands and looked at it. The remnants of the landscape could still be discerned. "Middling talents paint like everyone paints, Eva. This had a distinctive look, what with the way you used light on the ground and trees. You do not give yourself enough credit."

"Forgive me, but—do you know what you are talking about?"

"Actually, yes. I do. Art is the one thing I know very well."

She beamed at his compliment, then laughed. "Not the one and *only* thing, I think it is safe to say."

Her bawdy allusion heartened him. She seemed to be recovering from the renewed shock of seeing her house like this.

She set the painting aside and reached for her reticule. "I would like you to do something for me, if you would be kind enough."

"Anything at all."

She plucked some pound notes out of the reticule and thrust them at him. Sparks of determination flashed in her eyes. "Please buy me a pistol, and teach me to use it."

CHAPTER 14

After buying Eva her pistol, Gareth made a little tour of Langdon's End. He stopped at the White Horse. Erasmus was there, as expected, and greeted him with a toothy smile. Gareth gestured him over to a table, ordered two ales, and informed him of the situation with Eva.

Erasmus displayed the same shock Harold had. It appeared genuine, which meant Harold had been good to his word, even when it came to his friend. Better, actually. Not only had Harold not revealed Eva's presence in his home this morning, he had not even spoken of what sent her there.

"It musta happened yesterday," Erasmus said. "I walked by every morning she was gone and saw nothing out of sorts on the property. Didn't go this morning because Harold said she was back when I passed him in town."

"As you can imagine, she is very afraid." Gareth patted the wrapped bundle he had set on the table. "She asked me to buy her a pistol. If it makes her feel safer, that alone is a good reason to do so."

"Has she ever used one?" Erasmus looked incredulous.

"She will know how soon enough. I want you to keep your ears open. Let me know if you come across any indications of who did this. Such types often take to boasting, especially when in their cups."

Erasmus nodded. "I will tell Sir Thomas too."

"Tell me first. The magistrate can have what is left of the scoundrel after I am done with him."

He set a coin for the ale on the table and left the tavern. Considering how Erasmus liked to talk, within hours it would be well known that Miss Russell now kept a pistol in her house, one that she knew how to use. He also assumed that word would spread that Mr. Fitzallen protected the lady and would not wait for a court to mete out justice.

Both bits of information might help if that housebreaking had been the work of men grabbing the opportunity to steal. Another possibility had entered Gareth's mind when he saw the deliberate destruction of Eva's paintings, however. Before he left the town he made one more stop.

Mr. Trevor stood to greet him when he entered the

architect's office. A bit of brandy was offered, and they settled into chairs near the window.

"The materials for the roof should be here this week," Trevor said. "Once work starts, it will not take long."

Gareth allowed a few more minutes of conversation about Albany Lodge's improvements before moving to his real reason for visiting.

"Miss Russell's house was entered while she was gone. You will hear of it soon if you have not already."

"Why that house? She has nothing of value."

"No one seeing that house would assume it contained nothing of value. It is a handsome gentry home. This is no longer an isolated village but a growing town, and all sorts pass through, I expect."

"This is dreadful. Bold. This is not a place where people bolt their doors, or grow suspicious of every face. At least it has not been such a place in the past. I fear this will change that."

"No doubt it will, if the details become known. After finding nothing, the intruders took out their anger by methodically destroying what little was there. Floorboards, walls, furniture, crockery—room by room, her possessions were turned into debris."

"Thank God she was not there, nor her sister. It isn't safe, two women alone, living in the shadow of a city like Birmingham— She must be terrified."

"Not so much terrified as furious. Although, having seen the destruction, I cannot avoid the thought that terrifying her might have been the goal. A few details seemed unnecessarily cruel, and personal."

Trevor stood, flushed from his alarm at the idea. "Surely not. Who could want to harm her? She has no enemies. The townspeople love and respect her."

"The old ones do. The new ones hardly know her." Gareth studied Trevor, who now gazed out the window while he accommodated this new notion. "How badly does your client want that house and land?"

Trevor turned on him, stunned. "What are you implying?"

Gareth just looked at him.

"My client is a respectable businessman, Fitzallen. He is worth seven thousand a year due to hard work and shrewd dealings the last ten years. What you suggest is insulting to him, and uncalled for."

Gareth stood and faced Trevor squarely. "I'll wager you know almost nothing about this man, other than the face he chooses to show you and the size of his income. He is wealthy from trade, which is hardly damning, but ten years is fast success in any business, so he may be the sort to knock over anything and anyone in his way. She won't sell him what he wants, so perhaps he tried to persuade her by making her feel unsafe in her own home."

"Your accusation is outrageous. You do not have any evidence of this, yet you malign a man—"

"Who is he? Tell me and I will find out soon enough if I am correct."

"I'll be damned first. You are no more a gentleman than he. You, too, may be the sort to knock over anyone in his way, for all I know. I'll not have you accusing my client when this was probably a random crime."

Gareth set his brandy glass on a table. "If this was a random crime, there will be nothing more. If there is any further attempt to frighten Miss Russell, however, I will be back. If you do not give me his name then, I will learn it another way so he and I can have a conversation."

He walked to the door.

"You are out of your depth, Fitzallen. He has lawyers, the best that money can buy. They will ruin you financially if you impugn him."

"I have a better one, and since he is family he will not cost me a shilling. He is also the sort to show no restraint with men who threaten women. Tell your client to be glad I am the one suspicious of him, and not my brother."

T he pistol felt less heavy in her hands now. Not nearly as leaden as when she first picked it up and clumsily followed Gareth's direction on how to load the ball and powder. Nor did she find it difficult to hold steady, the way she had the first two times she fired.

She aimed at the thick, large wooden board Gareth had brought and set against the garden wall. "Now?"

"Whenever you are ready."

She fired. The crack assaulted her ears. Smoke rose from the end of the barrel. She did not startle this time, although she did not think she would ever grow accustomed to the noise.

She peered at the board, seeking the ball's destination. Gareth eased the pistol out of her grasp.

"Much better, Eva."

"Really? I do not see where it hit."

"You did not hit the board as such."

Her gaze shifted to the wall. A third black dot now decorated it, near two others. The wall might be stone, but lead balls did not bounce off. Rather they embedded themselves, eternal reminders of her poor marksmanship.

"How can you say *much better* when I still don't come close to a board as big as a barn door?"

"You were closer this time."

"By an inch!" She took the pistol back, sat down, and lifted the bag of powder. "Are you a good shot?"

"You will not meet many who are better."

He did not say that with pride or conceit. He merely answered a question. She tapped powder into the pistol. "Did it take you long to become so good?"

He sat beside her and watched her load. "Every summer I spent a few weeks with my father, right up the road at the lodge. It was the only time I spent with him to speak of. The summer I was twelve, he taught me to shoot. He made me practice every day, for hours. I came to hate that pistol. Here was this precious time, and I was alone in that garden, firing over and over."

"Did he know you hated it?"

"He knew. Finally, when my aim was sure, and I

could reload fast, he told me that with my birth, the day would come when men challenged me, or insulted me and I had to challenge them, but if it were known that I was a crack shot, fewer men would take that step. A man known to always hit his aim is not a man with whom other men want to duel."

She finished loading, then cradled the pistol in her hands. "Was he correct? Did knowing how to shoot well spare you those challenges?"

He took the pistol from her. "Mostly. Not always in the manner he expected." He raised the weapon and sighted the board, then lowered it again. "It probably kept my brother from killing me, though."

She looked at him in surprise. He gazed down at the pistol.

"One of those summers, my oldest brother came to visit. I think our father had begun to suspect what was in Percy by then, but he never guessed the whole of it, and I think he was pleased to see Percy make this gesture of acceptance toward me. One day my father was gone, riding the property, and Percy offered to teach me how duels are done. He explained it all, and we acted it out, the pacing off—all of it. And suddenly I was facing him and we both had loaded pistols in our hands." He looked at her. "I looked at him, and I knew, I just knew, that he intended there to be an unfortunate accident."

"You are sure?" The idea stunned her. "Your own brother?"

"I was sure. He was standing right below the outer branches of a tree, and one of those branches all but touched his head. So I aimed for that branch, hit it, and it snapped and fell on him. It startled him enough that I had time to reload. Percy looked at that branch, then at me, and decided the dueling lesson was over."

He stood and handed her the pistol. "I was fifteen years old. He was twenty. Now, only one more. Light is waning quickly. You will never learn to shoot in the dark."

She wished there were more time today. She needed to learn this right away. She hated how vulnerable she felt now in her own home. While Gareth had gone to town today, she spent the time cleaning the destruction, but all the while she listened for anyone coming up the lane or passing near the garden.

She missed again. Gareth eased the pistol out of her grip, then took the powder bag too. "You do not need to be able to hit anything, Eva, because it is very unlikely you will actually fire. Just wielding a pistol will send intruders running. I am tempted to take the powder with me, so you do not do something rash or hurt someone by mistake."

"Don't you dare take the powder away. I promise not to use it on my own until I am expert with this pistol. However, I'll not be treated like a child who shows no sense, or a woman too stupid to avoid shooting her own foot."

"I said nothing about shooting your own foot." He caressed her shoulder in a soothing rub. He had done that a lot today since arriving with the pistol and that huge board on a wagon with Harold at the reins. It was the kind of comforting touch one used on people who grieved, or who had become undone by emotion.

Side by side they walked through the garden to the house.

Cleaning the house and practicing with the pistol had distracted her from his attraction, but just walking beside him made the pull he exerted tantalize her again. Invisible tethers between him and her body tightened in naughty, teasing tweaks. She had no idea if he did that deliberately, or if it just happened as a result of his mere existence.

"Have you written to your sister about what happened?" he asked.

"I have a letter to post tomorrow, but it does not contain this news. I do not want her to worry, or to shorten her visit with Sarah."

They entered through the kitchen in the cellar. Gareth lit a lamp while she followed her nose to the hearth. A pot simmered there. Harold must have brought it, the way one brings food to invalids.

"Stew," she said. Beef stew, from the smell. That was a treat. Her stomach made happy noises. "Will you have some? There appears to be some fresh bread too."

He responded by taking two plates off the high shelf. A good amount of broken crockery had littered the floor a few hours ago, but not everything had been destroyed.

He went out to the springhouse for water, then they sat down to their meal. She noticed how he watched what she ate.

"Do you approve?" she asked. "Have I eaten enough to keep up my strength and not become sick from a nervous disorder?"

"Do not scold me for worrying about you. You were not physically harmed, but you were still assaulted. It takes a body some time to recover from that."

"I am fine. Did I faint? No. Did I cry like a madwoman? No. Well, I did cry, but not hysterically, and in anger, not sorrow. Nor have I lost my appetite. See?" She scooped more stew into her mouth.

His eyes narrowed on her. "You are sure you are fine?"

"Completely."

"Absolutely fine?"

"Totally."

"I am happy to hear it. I will not worry about it in the least henceforth."

"That suits me."

She took the plates and carried them to the sink to wash. When she was done, they went upstairs. "Will we practice with the pistol again tomorrow?"

"If you like, but not too early."

She led him to the reception hall, and the door. "I promise to wait for whenever you choose to come."

She realized he no longer walked with her. She turned to see him leaning against the wall, arms folded, watching her.

"You will not have to wait on my arrival, Eva, because I am not leaving tonight."

He meant well and it charmed her, but she did not want him hovering like an angel. "I do not need you to be here. I promise I will not stay awake all night, cringing with fear."

"All the same, tonight you will not be alone in this house. Do not argue with me. I will not be gainsaid on this."

"Do you intend to stand guard? Sleep on the divan with your own pistol at the ready?"

"That was my intention. However, since you are completely, absolutely, and totally recovered, I have decided your bed would be more comfortable."

She did not think he believed *she* should sleep on the divan instead. The implications instantly had her imagining the sensations, remembering the ecstasy. Her attempt to summon indignation over his presumptuous announcement saw little success. Desire became a living force in the space separating them.

He came to her, kissed her, then led her to the stairs. Up they climbed.

"I had intended to think a while before we did this again," she said. "I really should."

"Think all you want. Starting tomorrow."

"I cannot have an affair with you. You must know that."

"All I know is I want you and you want me."

"Still, we should—"

He stopped and pulled her into his arms. His kiss ravished her mouth and showed none of the restraint of last night. "No more *shoulds*. Not now, or I will make you wait until you ask again. I will make you beg until you are screaming."

"I had rather counted on your doing that anyway." It just blurted out, leaping over all the *shoulds* trying to get a good foothold in her thoughts.

The look he gave her caused her legs to wobble. With a quick scoop he lifted her into his arms and strode up the stairs.

It was different this time. No desperation. No shocks. Pleasure did not riot through her body. Rather it lapped through her in waves, controlled by Gareth's masterful caresses and kisses.

Nothing especially wicked happened either. He took her carefully, almost sweetly, and they entwined in an embrace that permitted her to hold him close. She knew incredible pleasure, but little delirium. Instead she felt him around her and in her, in a stunning intimacy. Even the power at the end did not obscure that, but rather intensified it. And as she rested in his embrace afterward, she knew this was the more dangerous passion of the two she had experienced, because it was the one that touched her heart.

Eva woke first. She stayed in Gareth's arms for a while, savoring the calm and peace. Then she eased out of his embrace and left the bed.

She donned an undressing gown and slipped downstairs. She quickly walked down the garden path, bucket in hand, to get some water. Upon opening the spring-house door, she froze.

Someone had been here since she last used the spring, and not merely to get water. A big box that held her gardening tools no longer had the hoe and shovel on its top. They had been moved to the floor. Peering into the box, she saw that its contents had been rearranged haphazardly. She looked around the little hut. Nothing had been broken or destroyed, but she suspected her house invaders had come here too.

Gareth must have seen this when he came for water yesterday. He probably had not realized something was not normal. A shiver up her spine spoke the answer. If this springhouse had been searched, someone had been looking for something specific, not merely taking advantage of an empty house to see what could be had.

She carried the bucket back to the kitchen and warmed it by the hearth. Then she carried it upstairs to her dressing room and washed and dressed. Back down in the kitchen she readied a pan to cook some of the eggs Gareth had brought back from town yesterday. She set the table. Ever since she began doing for herself, toting all the food up to the dining room made little sense.

With all prepared for cooking breakfast, she went up to the library. Her new canvas and paints still sat on the floor in a corner. She removed a small hammer from a drawer and began prying one of the ruined paintings out of its simple frame.

She planned to use the new canvas for copies and

reuse these ruined canvases for her own work. The idea of creating a composition of her choice, of allowing the symphony to play, excited her. She would make some sketches at the lake, and perhaps paint a long view that took in the lake's western shore—a sunset view, with purples and oranges streaking the sky and trees casting long shadows on the water. The result would be much improved on the painting that had been destroyed. She just knew it.

She looked down on the roll of fresh canvas. As for that, she needed to find paintings to copy. Good ones, so Mr. Stevenson's new patron would want them.

She set about wiping even more turpentine on the painting, finishing what the intruders had begun. The painting had been well dried, so removing all the paint would not work. She managed to reduce the landscape to a ghost of its former self, however. New paint should obscure it enough.

Sounds above told her Gareth had risen. She wiped her hands and set the canvas on her small easel to dry. Again the new materials arrested her attention. If she told him about those stored paintings, would he let her use some?

She recoiled from broaching the subject. Short of lying to him, she could not avoid a confession if she raised the matter at all. Her behavior could only make him think less of her. He assumed she was a lady, *a good, honest woman*. Not a thief who took chairs to sell and paintings to copy. Not the kind of person who kept neglecting to tell him about those pictures in that attic, because she hoped to find a way to take a few more in the future.

Even admitting to the copies would embarrass her. He had complimented her landscapes. She did not want to tell him she had used her small talents the last two years mostly on slavishly reproducing the art of other painters. That would be like discovering that a great wit only repeated clever observations other, truly interesting people had said first.

"You have made it worse."

She looked up to see Gareth five feet away. He wore a waistcoat over his shirt and no cravat. He looked at the ghostly landscape on her easel.

"It was ruined, and now I can reuse the canvas. I have plans for it." She set the bottle of turpentine back in her paint box and closed its lid.

"Big plans, from the looks of that roll there."

He meant the new supplies. *That canvas is for other things, like copying the paintings in your collection.*

"When do you expect your sister to return home?" he said.

"If you ask because you worry about my being alone—"

"I would prefer you were alone. I could stay every night then. If you allowed it."

Would she? The unspoken question hung there, waiting for an answer. Not the one in her heart. That one shouted its joyful affirmation. The rest of her held back, trying not to be swayed by the sensual power of his presence. *Think. You must think, even if you do not want to.*

"I do not expect her return before next Saturday, unless something changes."

He pointed to her new canvases. "I need to ride to Derbyshire tomorrow, but then I am going to London. You could come with me. You should see the art there, and the other sites. People will have started arriving for the Season, so the parks should be lively."

She had never been to London, but her imagination had constructed it in her head many times. Bigger than Birmingham, and better in every way. Big parks full of fashionable coaches and people. Thousands of shops. Magnificent buildings. And, yes, art everywhere. The finest art made by the very best artists.

"I do not have a wardrobe for London," she pointed out.

"We will find a way to see you do."

His mussed hair framed his incredible face, leaving a few appealing locks skimming his brow. The eyes under that brow captured her attention. They reflected charm and amusement, but also his sensual intensity. They were the eyes of a rogue, but still retained the joyful, devilish lights one sees in the eyes of naughty boys.

Think. You must think before it no longer matters if you do.

"I hope you are not offering to buy me a wardrobe. I could never accept that." She stood and turned toward the stairs. "Nor could I visit London without Rebecca. She has dreamed of going for so long, you see." It killed her to say it. The most delicious food had just passed under her nose, but she could not indulge.

"She can come too. Write to her today. Invite your

cousin as well. She will be your chaperone. No one will raise an eyebrow then."

He astonished her. "Sarah really will be a chaperone if she comes. She would not take her duty lightly."

"It is not my intention to seduce you in London, if that is what you think, Eva. I am only plotting the fun that I promised when we first met."

"You agree, then, that when we go to London this affair will end?"

"If that is what you want, of course. If you have no expectations from me, I can hardly demand any from you."

Very true. Very sensible. She wondered if anyone else in the world had as dispassionate view of the dealings between men and women as Gareth.

"I will write and ask her, but I do not know if her husband—"

"He can come too. Tell her that I will introduce him to some people he will appreciate meeting. Reassure your cousin that there will be no need to find rooms in a hotel. You will all stay at Langley House."

"Langley House?"

"My father's house in London. Now my brother's. The Duke of Aylesbury's residence."

She stared at him.

"So it's settled then." He smiled with beatific contentment, and wandered off.

CHAPTER 15

Gareth rode back to Albany Lodge after breakfast and set about writing a letter to Ives, informing him of the upcoming conversation he intended to hold in Derbyshire. He also mentioned that he had made the presumptuous decision to invite some friends to London for a fortnight, to stay at the family house. Not a week, as Eva assumed.

Out in the garden, Erasmus and Harold worked on the wall. He joined them and rolled up his shirtsleeves.

"Any word from the magistrate, sir?" Erasmus asked.

"Not yet, but it is early to hear anything." He lifted one of the big stones.

"He found nothing to help?"

"Not at the house. Whoever it was left nothing behind to point to him."

"The village is in a state about it. Was all you heard this morning."

"Don't you be stirring the pot more," Harold said. "We don't want every fool for fifty miles knowing that there's women living there on their own, now do we?"

Erasmus paused with a stone halfway raised. "I never thought of that."

"You never think much at all before you go wagging your lips, that's the problem," Harold said.

"If anyone wags back, be sure to let me know," Gareth said. "That is the magistrate's only chance of finding the culprits. If someone who knows something talks."

Following an afternoon of finishing the wall with Erasmus and Harold, he sent them off after having them bring up water for a bath. He spent a half hour in the water, laying out the plan of Langley House's chambers, deciding which ones would provide privacy and discretion.

He rode back to Eva's home in late afternoon. As he neared the property, the unmistakable crack of a pistol split the air. He kicked his horse to a gallop and tore down the lane and up to her door.

No other horses were tied outside. Silence poured out of the house. Cursing himself, he kicked open the door and called for her. More silence.

He strode to the back of the house and looked out the window and cursed again, this time at her. Eva sat on a stone bench, loading the pistol. Even from the window, he could tell she had missed the big board again with that last shot.

Damnation. He had told her not to do this alone, without his supervision.

She stood and took aim. Proud. Straight. Determined. He saw her face. Flushed. Eyes bright. Lids low.

He knew that look. Apparently, using a pistol aroused Miss Russell.

She had no desire to hurt anyone. The very idea terrified her. Yet, as she held the pistol straight out and aimed, she could not deny the visceral satisfaction she took in its deadly potential. The contrast to what she experienced that night as she ran down the road made her heady.

She aimed as true as possible, then pulled the trigger. The sound, familiar now, assaulted her ears. She immediately looked at the big black dots where her prior attempts had hit. No new dot could be seen. Only then did she look at the board and see the hole in it.

Elated with her progress, she sat down and began loading again.

A shadow fell over her lap. A hand came over her own, stopping her. She looked up at Gareth. He did not appear happy. His stern expression caused her insides to tighten in anticipation of the night. Gareth angry looked a lot like Gareth in the candlelight, while he moved in her.

"I hit the board." She pointed to it, very pleased with herself.

"I told you not to use the pistol unless I was here."

"Yes, but you were gone and the pistol was here, so I—"

"You could have hurt yourself."

"Only I did not. I remembered just how to do it, the way you taught me."

"You disobeyed me *and* you broke your promise." He just stood there, arms crossed, eyeing her severely.

"I forgot about the promise. I can't even remember making it. And, look, I *hit the board*."

He glanced to it. "So you did. That does not excuse you, but I suppose I may not turn you over my knee the way I intended."

Turn her— What a notion! The very suggestion was— She squirmed. Goodness, she had never expected such a threat to cause *that* reaction.

He sat beside her on the bench, as if he meant to do it. He took the pistol from her. "You appeared quite confident with it."

"Much more than yesterday. It frightened me then."

"And now?"

"At first it did, but when I held it up to aim— I liked it more than may be wise." He sat close to her, but not close enough. She breathed in the scent of soap. He gazed at the board, and she gazed at his profile. She wished he would turn so she could kiss him.

"How did you like it? What do you mean?"

She tried to articulate the thrill she had experienced, but currently anticipation of what waited in her chamber soon preoccupied her. "I became stronger."

"You felt powerful."

"Yes, in a very exciting manner. Alive and strong and powerful."

He looked at her. "Did that give you pleasure?"

Another startling notion, yet—something akin to pleasure had colored her dizzy reaction. Sensations much like sexual ones accompanied the power.

They returned now, and merged with the purring arousal Gareth incited. Looking in his eyes, she could tell he, too, was aroused. He had been when he came into the garden.

Their gazes locked for a long, thrilling, and silent agreement. She glanced to the house, then looked back at him.

"There is no one about," he said. "You can be alive and strong and powerful right here."

She nodded. She did not want to wait. She already swam in pleasure. She threw her arms around his neck and kissed him hard. She pressed her breasts against him so his chest would tantalize them. The kiss became hard and hungry between them.

He stood and took her arm. "On your knees, Eva."

She did not understand, but she slid off the bench to her knees in front of him.

"Lift up your skirt."

She obeyed, but it took some doing. She got it above her knees, then higher yet.

"Now the chemise too."

She pulled it up into the bunch of cloth now at her waist. The cool evening air flowed around her hips and thighs. She reveled in how bad she was being.

He took a step back. He looked at her nakedness. At her mound and thighs. The heat in his gaze, the firmness of his jaw said desire tortured him as much as it did her.

"Your sensuality is power, too, Eva. Take pleasure in that part of it. Right now I would do anything to have you. *Anything*." He looked in her eyes. "Do you understand?"

She did understand, she thought. Mostly. She knew what he meant about power at least. It thrilled her, having him want her so much. It also aroused her unbearably.

"You do not have to do anything to have me except take me, Gareth."

He stepped around her. She glanced back to see him kneeling behind her. He bent her forward until she rested on arms and knees, and he pushed her skirt and chemise up more so her bottom was totally uncovered.

A pause then. She thought she would scream with impatience. Waiting carried its own erotic torture. Finally he stroked her twice, no more. He entered her in a slow thrust that filled her completely. A barely audible moan of pleasure accompanied the thrust.

Another pause, with him in her, filling her like never before. Caresses smoothed over her bottom. He adjusted the position of her legs, then gently pressed her back down so she hugged the grass. "You must let me know if I hurt you."

She soon understood what he meant. This was different, feral, primitive. He thrust again and again, deeply and hard, until it seemed her womb itself came alive. She knew the pleasure differently too. More powerfully. More confidently. *Yes,* she thought each time he stroked into her. *Yes*, when the pleasure quickened around him, with a profound depth that tantalized her to want more and more. *Yes*, right until the feverish violence of the end, when the release made waves of ecstasy glow through her entire body.

E va tied on her bonnet. She pulled on her gloves. She lifted the leather-bound sketchbook and tucked it under her arm. Deciding she looked as presentable as she ever would, she left her house to pay her first social call in years.

She stopped in Langdon's End to post her letters to Rebecca and Sarah. She should receive a response by tomorrow at the latest. She trusted Sarah would find a way to convince Wesley to allow her to accompany her cousins to London. It was not the sort of treat a wife like Sarah would take well to being denied.

Gareth had left her bed before dawn today. He would be on the road now, on his way north for that meeting he had. One day, probably. Two at most, he had said while he made a very sweet good-bye by driving her mad three times in quick succession, first with his hand, then his mouth, then his rod. She had barely found the strength to see him off. Nostalgia had tinged their actual parting. When he returned they would journey to London. This morning, in the dark before dawn, their affair had ended.

Inevitable, that. Even continuing this long had been risky. Sorrow touched her heart when she thought about it, relieved only by the knowledge that they would continue as friends. Special friends, who had shared an intimacy that few friends ever approach.

She smiled to herself now while she walked the lanes, greeting people who had known her all her life. Could they now see how she had changed? She felt so different that she wondered if she would recognize herself from even a month ago if she met herself in passing.

She presented herself at the home of the sisters Neville. Their servant took her card, one of the five she had left (*have new cards made immediately so they will be ready for London*, she noted on her mental list of things to do). The woman returned and escorted her back to the library.

Jasmine and Ophelia waited for her, sitting in the exact same spots as the last time she had come. Ophelia appeared delighted to see her. Jasmine eyed her with naked curiosity.

"I am impressed to see you out and about," Jasmine said after very brief pleasantries had been dispensed with. "We heard about your ordeal. Most women would have taken to their beds for a week."

Eva swallowed the temptation to make a joke about how much she had enjoyed her bed the last two nights. "It was a shock, of course, but I was not harmed, so all is well."

"It is said Mr. Fitzallen sent for the magistrate."

"He is my closest neighbor, and was kind enough to help me. He has proven to be a good friend."

"How fortunate for you." Jasmine's tone implied raised eyebrows even if her face showed none.

"Indeed," Ophelia agreed. "How fortunate, too, that Rebecca did not come back with you. I hate to think what coming upon such a scene would have done to her. The young are so easily impressed. She might have become fearful of every creak of a floorboard."

"Rebecca is too brave to turn into a mouse suddenly," Jasmine said. "Do not assume everyone has your character, sister. I keep telling you that, regarding the good as well as the failings."

"I am very aware of it. You, for example, do not have much of my character at all, and we are sisters."

"I certainly do not have your tendency toward feminine weaknesses, I am happy to say."

"I do not think being a woman is a failing. If you do, that is one way in which our characters do not align."

"I am hoping Rebecca will not be too alarmed when she hears what happened," Eva said, reminding them of her presence. She enjoyed a good argument as much as anyone, but today's visit had another purpose.

Tea, for example. The servant brought it and they all indulged. Eva considered whether she might use some of the money from Mr. Stevenson to purchase some of her own, if everything today went well.

"What have you there?" Jasmine's eyes narrowed on the leather sketchbook that Eva had set by her feet.

Eva could not believe her luck that Jasmine had turned the topic to art. "It is my old sketchbook. I am going to stroll along the lake and choose a view for a painting, then do some first sketches."

"Rebecca told us you dabbled. Are you any good?"

"I admit I have a middling talent, but I enjoy it."

"I am sure you are very accomplished," Ophelia said soothingly.

Jasmine held out her hand. "Here. Let us see."

Letting Jasmine view the sketchbook had not been part of the plan. Not only did the sketches reveal her life from when she sketched frequently, they also documented how little she had done during the last two years.

"It is not intended for viewing," she said. "A sketchbook is much like a journal, and full of private thoughts."

"It is full of pictures, not words. If you cannot bear the thought of anyone seeing your work, you will never be successful as an artist," Jasmine said.

"Miss Russell does not want you looking in her sketchbook, Jasmine," Ophelia said with exasperation. "Nor did she say she sought success as an artist. She dabbles because she enjoys it."

"She says she does not want success because all women say that and think that. It is bred into us to have no ambition. She may be a brilliant talent, not a middling one, and not even be aware of it. How could she know?"

Rather than open a new argument, Ophelia accepted Jasmine's scold. Chagrined, she looked at Eva. "Do not show it if you do not want it viewed. However, my sister is very knowledgeable about art. She has many artistic friends, some of them famous. If you do have a brilliant talent, she would spot it."

Seeing an opening, Eva pointedly looked around the library's walls. "Did you choose the pictures here, Miss Neville?"

"I did. Some. My father and his father bought many of them."

"I have heard it said that students of art are encouraged to copy their betters. I wonder if that would help me improve."

"That depends on whether you even can improve. There is no point in copying great art if you cannot even draw decently, for example."

Eva looked down on her sketchbook. She had hoped that the sisters Neville would open their home and art to her much as they had opened their library holdings to Rebecca. She had not expected to have to prove herself worthy, as if she were applying for a position as their portrait painter.

She lifted the sketchbook. "I think I draw quite well. You can decide for yourself." She handed it to Jasmine.

Jasmine opened the book on her lap. Ophelia moved to sit beside her. From her chair, Eva could see which pages they viewed.

Jasmine quickly paged past the earliest sketches, the childish ones done many years ago. She stopped right where she should, however, at the first sketch done when Eva was more mature and confident.

Slowly the sheets turned. The views, the flowers, the flurry of horses from the two years when they enthralled her. It had been a long time since she had taken the time to peruse these herself, so she eyed them almost as objectively as the sisters did.

Another pause. A long one. Jasmine and Ophelia looked with great interest at a portrait done in pencil. Eva's heart fell. It was a drawing she had done of Charles one lighthearted summer afternoon in the garden.

He appeared more rakish in her picture than he did in her memories. He never wore his cravat loosely tied like that. His blond hair almost never blew in the breeze.

"I do not recognize him," Jasmine said.

"He left Langdon's End before you arrived. Over five years ago."

"Where did he go?" Ophelia asked.

"America."

"Only after that stupid war ended. Sheer idiocy," Jasmine muttered. "To fight the French and the Americans at the same time. If I could vote, I would never vote Tory again."

Ophelia looked over, right into Eva's eyes. Her gaze communicated a special comprehension, and sympathy. The younger sister had seen more in that drawing than Eva realized was there.

Jasmine paged through the rest—the drawings that became less ambitious, and limited to small views of their own property during the years caring for her brother. Also less frequent, until, one day, the sketch-book had resided in its drawer for an entire year without being touched.

"Goodness, what are these?"

A scattering of buildings covered the two pages open on Jasmine's lap.

Nostalgia gripped Eva's heart. "Those are not mine. My brother, while ill, distracted himself for a few days. Those peculiar views were the result. He soon lost interest."

"Perhaps he assumed if you could do it, he of course could too. The talent did not run in the family, however." She quickly moved on.

"Middling, as you say." Jasmine closed the book when nothing but white pages showed. "Not hopelessly so. Unschooled, however. If you lived here all your life, you have had few opportunities to see really good art, so how could you learn? I think we should invite Miss Russell to make use of our paintings, sister, so she can try her hand at some copies and learn. There are tomes with engravings, too, Miss Russell. They reproduce the very best examples of art. Not the colors, of course, but you will learn much by studying the compositions."

"You are too generous. My sister and I will be making a visit to London very soon, and I will have the chance to see the masters there, but that is not the same as being allowed to take the time to truly study them."

"London! Are you giving Rebecca a Season?" Ophelia asked.

"That is beyond our means. However, we will make a journey with my cousin and her husband. They live in Birmingham. That is where Rebecca has been—visiting their home."

"Better to wait until autumn," Jasmine said. "Soon town will be full of young bloods, and once they see Rebecca, you will be sorry you brought her. Why, the whole group of you will be little better than mice strolling through a field full of feral cats."

Ophelia glanced at her sister, then caught Eva's eye. "I am sure my sister will give you some letters of introduction to artists. Won't you, Jasmine?"

"I suppose I will, so my sister does not sulk," Jasmine said.

"I envy you, Miss Russell," Ophelia said. "I always enjoyed town during the Season."

"You certainly did." Jasmine's voice dripped with innuendo.

Ophelia flushed.

Eva drank her tea.

CHAPTER 16

Most of the investigations that led to Gareth riding to Derbyshire had occurred through the mail. Over dinner at Chatsworth during Gareth's visit there, the duke's special secretary, Mr. Montley, had provided a few details hitherto unknown. The most interesting information had been the name of the transport company hired to bring all those paintings north, Underhill's of Ramsgate.

A query to Underhill's in turn produced the names of the teamsters who drove the wagons. Underhill's kept records in good English fashion, and even had the towns and parishes for those men. A few more letters and Gareth had the locations of two of them.

He rode into the village of Bellestream to pay a call on Mr. Ogden, who had moved north to live at an old family property after an ox kick had broken one of his legs two years earlier, ending his teamster days forever. The property consisted of a small cottage on a spot of land hugging the edge of the village. The ground flanking the walk to the door displayed the first shoots of the reawakening garden.

Mr. Ogden came to the door and eyed Gareth with curiosity and suspicion. Completely bald but with thick eyebrows over small eyes, Ogden appeared a hearty man of considerable girth that his waistcoat struggled to contain. The ox that took him on must have been very brave.

Gareth handed over his card and Ogden spent a long time peering at it before inviting him in. Ogden limped to a nearby room and they settled on chairs in a sitting room full of patterns and frills. Ogden gazed around as if he had never seen the place before and had suddenly realized how out of place he appeared.

"My aunt lived here till she died," he said with a grin. Two of his teeth were missing. Another ox kick perhaps. "My days at the reins were over, so I moved here."

"It is your days at the reins I want to talk about. I have been sent by an agent of Parliament to assist an inquiry by the Lords."

"The House of Lords sent you? Well, now, that explains the oddness of a gentleman showing up at my cottage. Are the lords looking into the sorry state of the roads? I can bend your ear a good while on that."

"I will inform them of your willingness and ability to give information on the roads. Right now, however, the inquiry regards the transportation of a large number of crates by the Underhill company some twenty years ago. They informed me you were one of the teamsters. This journey started near Ramsgate at the estate of one of the lords, and ended in Derbyshire at the property of another. There were five wagons."

Ogden's ham of a hand came down hard on his knee. "I remember it well. Awkward crates, all different sizes. We were warned we would be drawn and quartered if we opened any, as if after sitting on a board all day we would be wanting to pry into the cargo. Lots of threats there were, and admonishments not to dally or detour or leave the wagons. We had to sleep right in with the crates, and take turns going to piss."

"Did anyone inquire about the cargo, either before you set out or along the way?"

"Raised some interest, it did. Bound to when five big wagons lumber down the road in a line. Since we knew nothing, we had nothing to talk about though."

"Come now. Did you not guess? The size and shape of those crates must have inspired some speculations for an experienced man like yourself."

Ogden grinned. "If it's my thinking you want— They reminded me of the time I transported a huge looking glass from the coast to London. The special kind, like kings have in their palaces, not some polished metal or small curved thing. Big and flat it was, and as tall as a ballroom, and crated up much like what I drove that journey. So I said to myself, maybe this is a cargo of looking glasses, all different sizes, that the lord wants for his manor house." His eyebrows rose expectantly, waiting to hear if he were correct.

"You were very clever, and very close." It sounded neat, and almost plausible, except it made no sense. Who would transport five wagons of plate looking glasses under secrecy? It came out too easily, too, as if Ogden had prepared the answer, in anticipation of being asked about it one day.

"I must ask a few pointed questions now. It would help if you answered directly and simply. You will not be in any trouble if an answer is not what may be considered the correct one. Do you understand?"

Ogden nodded.

"Did you in fact stay with the wagons the whole way? Were you at any time away from the others?"

"As I said, when I had to piss."

"Longer than that."

Ogden chuckled. "Well, sometimes I had to do more than piss, sir."

"Of course. Longer yet. Long enough for someone to have in some way affected some scheme regarding that cargo."

He shook his head. "Not possible." He shook it again, vigorously. His hand rubbed his knee.

Gareth waited. Ogden squirmed.

"Well, there was that one night . . ." he muttered.

"I did not leave my post, mind you. One of the others went to a tavern for some ale and returned with a nice little keg, and I enjoyed my cups, as it were. I crawled under my wagon to sleep it off. Dead to the world, I was. We all were, I suppose, until well after dawn."

And there it was, the broken link in the chain of secrecy, subterfuge, and careful plans. A keg of ale had undone it all, and now there was no way to know if the crates that arrived in Derbyshire even had pictures in them.

One of those lords should have gone along with the wagons, or sent a trusted man with these teamsters. Probably all those days on the dusty roads plodding along with oxen did not appeal to any of the gentlemen, so they all convinced themselves it was unnecessary, providing sufficient threats were made.

This little inquiry of Ives had just become harder.

"The other teamsters, Mr. Ogden—were they friends of yours?"

"We got on well enough after a day or so, but I was the odd man out. Underhill employed all the others. I was brought in from Margate because he needed an extra man. He kept me on, so he must have liked the looks of me."

Gareth had nothing else to ask. He rose to take his leave, and Ogden limped along back to the door.

"What was in those crates, if I may ask, sir?"

"Pictures."

Ogden's face fell in surprise. "You don't say. I'll be damned. All that trouble for a bunch of pictures."

"Amazing, isn't it?"

Ogden shook his head in astonishment. Gareth returned to his horse, not believing for a second that Ogden had been ignorant of the contents of the crates.

"This is a surprise," Gareth said when he entered his library at Albany Lodge and found Ives sitting there.

"I had hoped to arrive before you went north to see that teamster, so I could join you. When I found you had already left, I decided to wait here."

Gareth poured them both brandy, then sat and told Ives about his meeting with Ogden. Ives was not pleased to hear about that keg of ale.

"Hell."

"Yes."

Ives contemplated for a moment, his brow clear of furrows but his eyes hooded. "A switch cannot be ruled out, but it would be a most elaborate scheme, planned in advance by someone who knew everything. And dependent on those men getting so drunk they slept through it all. I do not like this possibility being there, but I think it is unlikely."

"I am assuming one or more of them were part of the plan, and that keg was no accident. If Underhill employed them, they may have heard something long before they took up those reins. Not so unlikely then."

"When you come up to town, we will ride out to

Ramsgate and talk to Underhill. Now that you have opened this new front in the war, we need to see what he is made of. When will you be in town?"

"I plan to start out day after tomorrow."

Ives gazed into his brandy. "And when will your guests arrive?"

"The next day, I expect."

Ives looked over with a small, knowing smile. "Which one are you after? The married one? Please do not tell me it is the young innocent. Even we have our standards, and you always said girls bore you."

"Have no fear, I do not intend to launch a scandal from Langley House."

"So, not the young girl. Then——?"

Gareth scowled at him, annoyed. "The truth is I am pursuing the husband. Wesley Rockport has a business that is growing fast. He is at the point where men start buying culture."

"So you plan long strolls through the gallery at Langley House, to impress upon him the need for a collection."

"I don't intend to say a word about it. The gallery will speak for itself."

"Be aware that Lance and I may be in residence some of the time they are there. Lance chafes at being rusticated and may insist on coming up to town again."

"I will keep them all out of your way."

"I insist on meeting them, especially if the ladies are pretty."

"By all means," Gareth said coolly. "They are both

pretty enough, but not your style. Nor do I want the husband calling you out. These industrialists are not like us. They actually love their wives and react badly when someone attempts to seduce them."

Ives took the warning in stride, but curiosity lowered his lids again.

"Devonshire should be coming up to town for the Season, I expect," Ives said, changing the subject. "Certainly his mother will be there, and his bastard brother. I will ask Prinny to smooth the path for us to talk to the latter two."

"If you are there to do it, you do not need me."

"I would like you there. Then we can compare our reactions and perceptions later. I would want to be very sure further inquiries in that direction were called for before I began them." Ives stood and stretched. He looked around the sparsely furnished chamber. "You do have an extra bed here, don't you?"

"One. It is yours if you want it."

"No servants, however. Damn, I should have brought one from Merrywood."

"A manservant comes by day. You will have to get yourself into bed, but he will serve you in the morning. There will be water enough upstairs now. He always brings up extra before he leaves."

Ives rubbed his hand over his face, feeling the rough growth shadowing his jaw. "Can he give shaves without butchering?"

"Yes. Unlike Percy, he does not seek to draw blood whenever he has a sharp weapon in hand."

Ives stilled. His hand fell from his face. "Did Lance tell you about that?"

"Percy's smug satisfaction told me."

Ives picked up his valise and walked to the door. "I'll find that one extra bed now." He looked back, over his shoulder. "You did not miss much for someone who only saw us a few times a year, Gareth."

L *ondon.*
Eva barely contained her excitement as the carriage passed the final toll. Out the window one could see the last of the countryside giving way to the outskirts of town.

Rebecca hugged the door of the carriage, her head to the window so she missed none of it. Wesley and Sarah faced them in the cramped space.

"Do you think the duke will be there? Residing in the house, that is," Sarah asked.

"I do not know."

"I think it safe to say he will not be there when we are." Wesley spoke matter-of-factly, without the least resentment. He might dress like a gentleman and have an income that exceeded that of many of them, but his voice said he knew that dukes did not socialize with such as he, or even acknowledge an acquaintance.

Both he and Sarah looked splendid. Sarah wore a fashionable cream carriage ensemble with Prussian blue trim. Wesley's coats were impeccable. They had arrived in Langdon's End two days ago to take Rebecca and her to London in their fine carriage. Trunks tied to the roof held a good amount of Sarah's wardrobe. "For all of us," Sarah had explained. Sarah's lady's maid rode up there, too, along with Wesley's manservant.

They entered London in style. The carriage slowed to a crawl and descended into streets flanked by tall houses and busy shops. The neighborhoods grew finer and finer until they turned onto one with independent houses of astonishing size that faced a big park. One more turn, and they stopped at a corner house that filled most of its block.

"Oh, Eva, look." Rebecca moved from the window so Eva and Sarah could gape. Curved outer stairs led up to the main door, and four levels rose above that one.

Wesley dipped his head to look also. "You will be spoiled proper when this is done, Sarah. I won't be able to keep you in the style to which you will have become accustomed."

Sarah giggled and planted a kiss on his cheek. "Well, now, Wes, my love, you will make it up to me in other ways."

The look that passed between them hinted at what occurred between them behind closed doors. Eva wondered if she would have noticed that a month ago . . .

A little army of servants marched out the door. Footmen helped them out of the carriage while others brought down the trunks. Men took the ribbons from the coachman. All the soldiers wore livery.

Eva absorbed the activity like a series of fascinating

pictures. She angled her head back to study the house, then the ones near it.

"Welcome, Rockport. I see you survived the journey in a carriage with three ladies."

Her head snapped upright. Gareth stood five feet away, greeting Wesley. He bowed to Sarah and Rebecca, and finally to her. When they all walked to the house, he managed to fall into step beside her.

"I fear we may lose our way in here," she said with a laugh as they mounted the stone steps.

"You may lose your way, but rest assured, I will not."

More servants. More activity. A footman took Wesley away with his valet trailing behind. A housekeeper named Mrs. Summers led the rest of them up the long staircase, then up again to the next level beyond that.

They approached a double set of doors. Masculine voices could be heard nearby. Mrs. Summers opened the doors to reveal an apartment of impressive size. Sarah bit her lower lip and tried to appear unimpressed, but her eyes became large and round.

"Mr. Rockport is beside you," Mrs. Summers said, angling her head toward those voices. She walked through a flanking sitting room, and to a door on its far wall. "This, Miss, is for you," she said to Rebecca, throwing open the door to reveal a bedchamber fit for a princess.

Sarah and Rebecca were beside themselves, all but dancing with barely controlled glee. They whispered to each other while pointing to the drapery, the silk upholstery, the sitting room's magnificent secretaire, and the garden views out the back window.

"Your maid will have a chamber above," Mrs. Summers told Sarah. "Someone will come for her and take her to it, after she has had time to settle you." She turned to Eva. "If you would come with me now, Miss Russell."

Eva left the lovely apartment in Mrs. Summers's wake. Past the stairs they walked. Down a corridor. Through another landing for more stairs. To a door tucked into a corner. Not one of those big double doors, either. A rather small plain one.

Mrs. Summers ushered her in. Eva had been given an apartment like Sarah's. Perhaps not as large, but it had beautiful light and a group of three big windows on one wall from which one could see the park.

"I was told you draw," Mrs. Summers said, "I thought that the northern light in the sitting room would suit you."

"This will do splendidly. Thank you."

"I will send a woman up to help you." With that, Mrs. Summers left.

Eva did not wait on the servant. She unpacked her valise, then meandered her way back to Sarah's chambers. She found all of her travel companions basking in the luxury of their lodgings.

"Where did you go?" Rebecca asked. "You must try my bed. Just lie on it. You will not believe the quality. It will be like sleeping on clouds."

"My own chambers are at the other end of this storey. You can come see them, but we will need a ball of yarn to unwind, so you can find your way back."

"Oh," Sarah said, her enthusiasm dimming. "I hope they are as nice as this. If they are not, I will not be able to enjoy myself as much."

"They are perfectly charming." Lovely, actually. Airy and full of cool light.

"We will use this sitting room to gather," Sarah said. "It will belong to all of us."

"Thank you. That will prove convenient. Otherwise I might never see you. My apartment is quite out of the way."

How kind of Gareth to have Mrs. Summers put Eva in a room with such lovely light.

How kind, and how convenient.

CHAPTER 17

At Gareth's suggestion, they all planned a walk in the park during the fashionable hour. It took Sarah and Rebecca over an hour to prepare.

Eva waited on them in the sitting room while feminine talk and laughs poured out of Rebecca's chamber. Other than having the servant assigned to her fix her hair, and donning her best pelisse of light blue wool, she had made no special efforts. When her sister and cousin emerged from the bedchamber, both eyed her critically, then shared a knowing, meaningful glance.

"Oh, I forgot something," Sarah said, clapping her hand to her forehead. "Let me get it from my chamber." She hurried to the door on the other side of the sitting room, ducked in, and came back holding a bonnet. It was the one Eva had tried at the milliner's that day in Birmingham.

"I liked it so much I purchased it," Sarah explained. "However, it looks far better on you, Eva. Why don't you wear it today? The dark blue ribbon will even set off your pelisse nicely."

"Yes, Eva. Why don't you borrow it?" Rebecca encouraged.

Eva untied her own bonnet, and accepted the one Sarah held. This was all a lot of bother over nothing. Rebecca was the one to be put on display to lure a good husband. Her own plans envisioned a different path devoted to her art, not matrimony. In fact, working seriously as an artist required independence.

When she checked the bonnet in the looking glass, she had to admit it flattered her as much as she remembered. In the reflection she also spied Rebecca's relief being communicated to Sarah with another meaningful look. She realized Sarah had not offered the bonnet to make her more attractive to potential suitors. Rather, her cousin and sister did not want to walk in the park with an Eva turned out poorly.

The door to the sitting room opened and Gareth and Wesley walked in.

"France or the Netherlands?" Wesley was asking. "The French economy still suffers from the war."

"There is money enough there, but the industries have not recovered, so it may actually be the better choice. You must go yourself and see how things lie, however."

Wesley turned his attention to his wife. "Are you quite ready, Sarah?"

"Don't I appear ready?" Sarah made a little turn on her toes.

"Ready and lovely, I would say."

Eva agreed with the compliment. Sarah's ensemble of greens and yellow set off her red hair. She wore a darling hat that angled just so on her carefully clustered curls. Rebecca's muslin dress with the primroses had been transformed by a primrose pelisse. Her bonnet played up her innocence and brought attention to her lovely face.

"I will be the envy of every man in the park," Wesley said, offering one arm to his wife and one to Rebecca.

A different arm presented itself to Eva. "No, I will be," Gareth said in her ear.

"They are all so beautiful," Eva said. She moved her head this way and that to see the ladies in the carriages and along the path.

Gareth paced alongside her, in the wake of Wesley and the others. "They are more wealthy than beautiful," he said. "A bit of silk, a bit of paint, a flattering dress and hat—they go far to create an illusion."

"Perhaps, but some of these women are undeniably beautiful in their own right, and you know it."

"Every woman is, in her own way, Eva."

She smiled ruefully and shook her head. "You are a charmer, Mr. Fitzallen. There is no denying that."

"I am too conceited to deny it. It comes naturally to me. Would that more people endeavored to be charmers. Charm is oil on the machinery of society."

"That sounds philosophical. Take care or I will call Rebecca to join us and she can explain what every sage from Plato on said on the matter."

Up ahead, the young lady in question was turning a lot of heads in the park. "Did she spend enough time with Mr. Mansfield while in Birmingham to numb his interest with her discourses?"

"Sarah fears so. My sister is normally not boring, so I think it was deliberate. I suspect when the poetic Mr. Trenton called on her, she did not mention Plato or Rousseau at all."

"You will marry her off within the year, I am sure, unless she takes a dislike to the notion."

"I hope so. I would not want her and me to become like the sisters Neville." She regaled him with an accounting of the sisters' bickering, mimicking the older sister's booming voice and the younger sister's tiny one, until they both laughed hard enough to make further speech impossible.

"When Rebecca marries the fine man you and Sarah choose, what will you do?" he asked when they could talk again.

Her eyes lit. "I intend to improve my art. You said I had talent, and Jasmine Neville agrees, but I have a lot of work to do, and a lot of catching up. Jasmine even gave me a letter of introduction to Mary Moser. Can you believe it? I wrote to her when I was a girl, and she even responded, so I think she is a kind person, but I will still be nervous making a call on such a famous lady painter."

"One of her pictures hangs in the gallery at Langley House. You can study it and ask her about it."

"Do you think I can study the others too?"

"Spend as much time there as you like. Sketch if you want. I will tell the housekeeper to unlock the doors if you ask. It isn't as if you are going to steal any of them."

She gave him a peculiar look, then laughed. "Oh, goodness, of course not. I may be committed to *disegno*, but I would never have designs on Aylesbury's old masters."

"Since you promise to be good, I will see about obtaining entrance to some other private collections."

Another odd look.

Suddenly, up ahead, Rebecca froze in her tracks. She pivoted and hurried back to Eva. "Hide me."

Eva took her sister's hand. "Whatever—?"

"He is here. Of all the bad luck."

Gareth saw the source of Rebecca's distress. He nudged Eva, and drew her attention to Sarah and Wesley. A man had just greeted them, and they now chatted with him. Mr. Mansfield. Gareth doubted Mansfield's arrival in London had been a coincidence.

"You cannot be rude," Eva said. "I am sure he will be on his way in a minute."

Their steps brought them to Sarah, who beamed. "Look who is in town, too, Rebecca."

Eyes downcast, Rebecca greeted him and made a small curtsy.

"It was very bad of Sarah to make him come," Eva whispered. "Rebecca is quite vexed, and I do not blame her."

"Your cousin is tenacious, that is certain."

Not only tenacious. Sarah proceeded to prove she could best most mothers of the ton when it came to throwing a girl and a man together. Somehow, and Gareth missed just how, Sarah and her husband walked on a few steps ahead of Rebecca and Mansfield, with Eva and he in turn following a few steps behind. Which left Rebecca alone to chat with Mansfield.

Which in her pique she did not do.

"Oh dear, she is very, very vexed," Eva whispered.

"The park is a rustic pleasure in town, is it not?" Mansfield said.

"For those who live in town I suppose it is a pleasure," Rebecca said. "Since I live in the country, I do not appreciate the respite as much."

"Surely nature is always a refreshing and welcomed experience," Mansfield said. "I am told there are poets and philosophers who believe its contemplation can lead to a transcendent experience."

Eva grasped Gareth's arm. *Transcendent?* she mouthed.

"He has been reading up," he murmured.

"There are indeed," Rebecca said, sounding like a governess. "It is an old idea born anew recently. It has had several periods of popularity, and derives from

Neoplatonist philosophers who first wrote soon after Rome's fall. One of its proponents was Dionysius the Areopagite, whose works survived to kindle a revival during the twelfth century—"

Eva rolled her eyes. Gareth pantomimed sliding a noose over his neck and jerking up the rope. Eva bit back a laugh until her eyes teared. She then made the motions of loading a pistol with a ball and powder and turning it on herself.

Enjoying the park far more than poor Mr. Mansfield, they trailed in Rebecca's wake while Rebecca droned on, giving Mansfield a most detailed lesson on Neoplatonism down through the ages.

E va read a book after she prepared for bed. She anticipated enjoying the sleep of the righteous. She deserved some benefit from being good today.

Walking with Gareth in the park had been much harder than she had expected it to be. She had known their affair could only be temporary, that each day it continued increased untold risks for her. She had not known, however, that ending it would be so hard. The more they laughed and joked like friends today, the less she saw him as a friend.

If he had taken her hand and dragged her away to have his way with her, she was not sure she would have found the strength to resist.

Not that he had done anything close to that, or even shown much inclination to do so. Oh, there had been a

few mildly flirtatious smiles and looks, and a few innuendos about their past passion, but on the whole, Gareth
seemed to have swallowed his promise and their
renewed "friendship" without any indigestion at all.

Despite being tired, she tried to focus her thoughts
on her book. She feared that when she slipped into
bed, a phantom Gareth would be there too. That ghost
might invade her mind and arouse her body, and
seduce her into thinking any risk was worth embracing the real man again.

A quiet knock on her door made her start. She stared
at it, and all the anticipation she had known with
Gareth poured out of the past. She must upbraid him,
of course, for breaking his promise. She must send him
away. Yet her heart urged that door to open, and for
him to stride over and pull her into his arms and obliterate her arguments and good intentions with a kiss.

The door did open an inch. Then another, until it
was ajar. She gripped the book so hard it hurt her
hand.

A head poked in and looked around. "Eva?"

Her heart sank. Not Gareth. Rebecca had come.

Rebecca saw her sitting in the chair and came in.
"I almost got lost, but remembered the way after all. I
wanted to see you alone, without Sarah about."

Eva patted the bed beside her chair. Rebecca sat,
and pushed her long hair back over her shoulders. She
wore a nightdress but no robe or wrap. She appeared
lithe and innocent.

"I hope you are not going to complain about Mr.

Mansfield, Rebecca. Sarah insists she did not arrange for him to be in London at the same time as us."

Rebecca cocked her head. Her brow puckered. "I never thought Sarah had arranged it, or that he came to London following me. To do that would mean he was at least somewhat romantic, and I do not think he has a romantic ounce in him."

Eva almost defended Mr. Mansfield, but let it be. It astonished her that Rebecca really thought the afternoon a total coincidence. Her sister could be very stupid for someone with such a smart brain.

"What do you have there?" Eva asked. Rebecca had carried in a little pouch much like the one hanging from a nail at home, under the floorboard.

Rebecca opened the pouch and poured out a pile of shillings. "There are sixty. He owes you more. Mr. Stevenson, that is. I visited his shop the day before we left, and your paintings were not there. He said some were sold, but the others were in patrons' homes, being considered for purchase. I think he lied, and that he hoped giving me this for you would allow him to wait a long time before giving you the rest."

Eva reached over and stacked the coins. "Did you tell Sarah about the paintings?"

Rebecca shook her head. "We were visiting a shop on that street, and I said I needed some air. I took the opportunity to run into Mr. Stevenson's."

"To whom did he sell the ones he admits were sold?" Three, if he intended to pay her the same as before. She had brought him nine.

"They were taken by that picture seller from London. That is why I think Mr. Stevenson lied. He said that man would take all you could make. Mr. Stevenson must have written him at once to say he had more available."

They admired the shillings. Eva felt almost rich.

"Such good fortune, Rebecca."

"It is a pity it cannot continue. Perhaps you should tell Mr. Fitzallen that you borrowed those pictures and copied them. You are friends now, and he might not mind too much and permit you to borrow more."

"I did not borrow them. That requires the owner's permission. I stole them. That I returned them halves the sin, perhaps, but it was still theft. And do I confess to the chairs too? That was outright theft, for all the excuses I found to call it something else."

"You should probably leave out the chairs."

"It is all of one sum, with respect to my character. If I say I took some pictures, why should he believe I returned all of them when so much else disappeared from that house? I could not blame him for wondering. A person who helps herself to that which is not hers, even temporarily, cannot be trusted not to forget to return what she takes."

Rebecca poked at the shillings. "I suppose if we are frugal, what you have now will last many months. Eventually it will all be spent, however. Then what?"

Eva hoped that by then Rebecca would have married well and have a husband's support. Presumably that husband would not allow his wife's sister to live in poverty, although Eva did not relish the idea of becoming the dependent sister. Nor did she intend to, since Mr. Stevenson had now found her a way to support herself so well.

"You are not to worry. I may have found an alternative," she said. "Miss Neville has said I can copy some of their paintings. Several look quite good. I think Mr. Stevenson's London buyer would like them."

Rebecca's expression cleared. "That is wonderful. I am so glad that you are becoming the sisters' friend too. I knew you would like them once you knew them better." She stood and went to the door. "I am going to spy into every picture shop we pass while we are here. I think Mr. Stevenson is getting much more than he pretends for those paintings. You would, too, if you could offer them to that man directly."

Eva guessed she would as well, which was why Mr. Stevenson would never allow her to know that picture seller's name. As for Rebecca finding him during their visit London was very big, with many streets and lanes and many picture sellers. They would probably return to Langdon's End as ignorant of that buyer's name as when they left.

G areth took his guests to the British Museum the next day. The excursion proved both educational and tiring for all. Only Rebecca remained enthralled to the end, and he suspected she would have petitioned to remain longer if Sarah had not complained about her sore feet.

Eva gave most of her attention to the art, especially the Greek marbles. Sarah joked none too subtly about how *very* educational those nude male sculpted figures must be for innocents like her cousins. Eva smiled serenely at being the source of Sarah's amusement, and studied the reliefs and statues all the closer, only once sliding Gareth a glance that communicated their private reason for finding Sarah's innuendos very funny.

The butler eased Gareth aside as soon as he and his guests returned to the house.

"It would be best if I take your guests to the drawing room or morning room, sir," he said. "The duke and Lord Ywain arrived while you were out and are now in the library. The Earl of Whitmere is with them."

"The drawing room, then. Please take them up and see about refreshment. I will join them after I see my brothers."

He found Lance and Ives lounging on divans in the library, still wearing riding coats. Lord Whitmere, one of Lance's old friends, also appeared to have been riding.

"Imagine my surprise to find these two on the road," Whitmere said, after their greetings. "An odd bit of fate."

Blond, robust, and athletic, Whitmere initially appeared to be the light foil to Lance's dark presence. Unfortunately, he was not. He and Lance normally found each other during spells of recklessness. If fate had brought them together, it was not a good omen.

"I told you he would probably ride down, Gareth."

Ives flourished a gesture toward Lance. "Here he is, in all his ducal magnificence."

"Indeed I am," Lance drawled lazily. "Explain to Ives how I must participate in the Season, Gareth, so it is not said I hide at Merrywood due to guilt."

"He has a good point, Ives."

"We are in mourning. Deep mourning. Am I the only one who remembers that?"

"I'll wear an armband, and not dance much," Lance said.

Ives shook his head. "I would feel better about this if the last time he went out on the town we did not come within an inch of dueling to protect his good name, Gareth."

Lance shrugged. "Should that happen again, point the man toward me. I'll not have either of you fighting for me, when I will happily do it myself."

"Too happily," Ives said to Gareth, pointedly.

Gareth did not need to be alerted. The truth was Lance looked like hell. If they rode here, they had not brought their valets, and unless his valet shaved Lance, he could not be bothered shaving at all. A rough growth shadowed his lower face, making the scar appear a thin river snaking through a forest. His heavy lids might be due to drinking, or worse.

Ives's concern said he voted for the "or worse." Lance sometimes suffered from spells of brooding. *Melancholies*, their father had called them, although the word was inaccurate in many ways. Lance did not turn sad or anxious during his spells. Rather he became blissfully indifferent to almost everything and everyone around him. He also exuded a fearless indifference to life itself. He *would* happily duel when in such a state.

Whitmere watched Lance, forming his own conclusions. No doubt he anticipated a wonderful few weeks dwelling in hell with his old friend.

"Ives said he told you about the guests I have imposed on the household," Gareth said.

Lance barely nodded. "A Birmingham tradesman and his wife, along with the wife's two cousins," he said."

"Do not worry that they will be a nuisance. You will hardly ever see them or know they are here. They are staying on the third storey, away from the public rooms and your apartments."

"I do not care if I see them. In fact, if they are here, I should greet them. It is my home." He sat up. "Where are they?"

"It can wait until you are presentable," Ives said. "You look like a highwayman."

"I choose to do it now." He stood and peered at Gareth expectantly.

"They are in the drawing room," Gareth said.

Up they went, with Whitmere in tow. Lance came alive with each step. That was unfortunate. Gareth had been prepared to explain later that he was ill.

One could not unexpectedly present a duke, an earl, and a lord to anyone except other peers without it garnering strong reactions. Gareth's introductions to the disheveled, unshaved Aylesbury fell on the ears of three people who faced Lance gape-mouthed. Wesley mumbled something incoherent. Sarah and Rebecca fumbled vague curtsies. Only Eva acquitted herself well.

To make it worse, Lance decided to play the host, for reasons only he could know. He invited the ladies to sit, then he did as well. Wesley perched his ass too. Gareth remained standing, as did Ives. Ives kept sending Gareth sharp glances that said no one found this situation stranger than Lance's own full blood brother.

Other than eliciting from Wesley the general nature of his business, Lance led them through ten minutes of the smallest of small talk. Then he stood, excused himself, and walked out. As he passed, he asked Gareth to join him again in the library. Whitmere tagged along. Ives dallied to make his own greetings before exiting.

Down below, Lance sought out the decanters and poured three whiskies. He handed one each to Gareth and Whitmere and tossed back the third.

"The young one is very lovely. A perfect gem, but also painfully innocent and far too young. She will never do."

"No. Never," Whitmere agreed.

"Do for what?" Ives asked, coming toward them from the door.

Lance shrugged. He returned to his divan, slouched low and stretched out his legs.

Gareth glared at him. "Do for *what*?"

Lance yawned. "It would be better if I escorted a lady to the DeVere ball next week, so I make it clear how indifferent I am to the stories about me. I thought one of your guests might do, since I am not in the mood to suffer the company of the women I normally would use. But as I said, the girl is too young. Rumors would start, and I might find myself under obligations I did not intend."

"Allow me to repeat, once again. You are not going to any balls," Ives said. "You are in deep mourning."

"And if you do go anyway, you are not escorting any of those women up there," Gareth said firmly. "None of them will do. They are not for you."

"A fine friend you are, Fitzallen," Whitmere said. "Denying those nice ladies a ball. They will not thank you for it."

Lance seemed to lose interest. He closed his eyes.

Ives gestured to Gareth. "Let him sleep. We will go to the garden and set the times for our meetings."

"There is the other one, of course." Lance's voice, not loud at all, arrested Gareth's attention.

"You mean Mrs. Rockport?" he asked.

"No, the other sister. Eliza—Edith—"

"Eva. Miss Russell to you."

"Lovely name. She is pretty, too, in her own way. Poised. Nice eyes." He sat up. "I say, Whitmere, why don't you escort the girl, and I'll escort her sister."

"That sounds splendid. Only you must allow me my time with the elder one. She looks to be a sassy wench, and I'll be wanting companionship this Season."

An insinuating inflection of *companionship* had Gareth thinking murder. He walked over to where Whitmere sat and hovered over him. "If those ladies are not for my brother, they are certainly not for you. The path to their company is through me, and I forbid it. I have not thrashed an earl in several years, but am prepared to do it, so do not doubt my resolve on this matter." He looked over his shoulder. "Ives, who was the last earl I thrashed? His name escapes my memory."

Ives scratched his head and pondered dramatically. "Let me see. Not the viscount or the baron, but the last earl . . . Ah, I have it. It was the Earl of Whitmere, wasn't it? Early one summer morning alongside the Serpentine."

Whitmere rearranged his limbs on the chair, sucked in his cheeks, and looked anywhere except up at Gareth.

"Don't let him threaten you, Whitmere," Lance said. "He only did that because you tried to take liberties with his mistress. These ladies are only friends of a friend. He'll never go through with it."

Whitmere looked at Lance dolefully.

"As for you," Gareth said to Lance. "If you are determined to set tongues wagging by attending the ball, you may dance one time with each lady, but only if you are shaved and sober."

Lance laughed heartily. "You sound like a tutor. Doesn't he sound like a tutor, Whitmere?"

"Or a vicar. Are you going to take this? By Zeus, I've half a mind to— Half a—" Both sides of his mind chose to seek solace in the brandy instead.

"I'm not going to fight him over country women I barely know and that he has chosen to protect, on some inexplicable impulse. You and I will find better things to do than go to that ball, anyway."

Whitmere blinked. "How did it go from my escorting a rare gem and her fetching older sister to the ball, to my now not attending at all?"

Lance began to ponder aloud the better things to do. Ives caught Gareth's eye, turned, and walked to the doors to the terrace. Gareth followed, pretending he did not hear Lance speculating on a prank that involved another duke's carriage and a large amount of horse dung.

"What was that about?" Ives asked once they were in the garden. "While you did not sound too much like a tutor, you became very pointed very quickly."

Gareth had no idea what that had been about. He only knew that hearing Lance and Whitmere discuss Eva made him see red. Even now it was all he could do not to punch something.

"I did not like the implications of all that *she will do* talk. You know those two when they get together and Lance is in one of his moods. I have some responsibility for the ladies, after all."

"Of course."

"Nor do they need Lance and Whitmere in order to attend the ball. Lady DeVere is sending an invitation directly to Miss Russell, for example."

"You arranged that, did you? That will be a treat,

although the thought of arriving alone might put her off the idea."

"I will escort her. Unlike you and Lance, I do not have to pretend I am in mourning."

"Whitmere may still go, for all of Lance's hoping they will play at being naughty schoolboys instead. I trust you will not make a scene if he asks Miss Russell to dance. She has caught his eye, that is clear."

"I may warn her that his intentions are not honorable, but I will not make a scene."

Ives laughed. "Hell, you do sound like a vicar. Where is all this talk of honorable intentions coming from?" His smile remained broad, but his gaze turned piercing. "What is this woman to you? Is she your lover?"

It was a hell of a question, and unexpected. "No." The honest truth, in the present tense, not that his body had accepted the new order well.

"Then perhaps you should let the lady draw her own conclusions about Whitmere. She looked sensible and mature. It is unlikely she will not perceive the truth of his intentions, whatever they might be."

Still angry, but not so inexplicably black-minded, Gareth forced his thoughts to other things. "Tell me about these meetings, so I can make arrangements for my dear guests to be occupied without me during those times."

CHAPTER 18

E va dropped the letter of introduction into her reticule, then made her way to Sarah's sitting room.
They would all be on their own today. Gareth had
business with Lord Ywain, so he would not escort
them around town.

A decision had been made to take the opportunity
to pursue their own interests. Wesley planned to visit
some men of business that he knew. Sarah wanted to
shop, and would take her maid as company. Rebecca
had chosen to tag along with Eva while she paid a call
on Mary Moser, the woman painter she had long
admired.

"You must take the carriage," Sarah said when Eva
arrived.

"You are the one likely to have packages. Rebecca

and I will ask a footman to bring a hired carriage around."

"I will agree, if you promise to be careful and to fight off any young men who start following our perfect gem." She beamed in Rebecca's direction. "Of course they all notice her, and some look at her too boldly, to my thinking."

"I will fight them off myself, Sarah," Rebecca said. "I do not see much in the young men roving the streets that would be appealing to any girl."

"They certainly do not look to have the substance of Mr. Mansfield," Sarah said while she tied on her bonnet.

"Nor the artistic soul of Mr. Trenton," Rebecca said.

Sarah shook her head in exasperation, then looked around for her reticule. "Where did I—"

A rap on the door interrupted. Her maid hurried over to see who had come. A white letter passed out of a footman's white glove. With an expression of surprise, the maid brought it to Eva.

Eva examined the letter. She had never seen anything quite like it. The paper must be the finest made. Thick, heavy, and rich, its finely laid surface might have been velvet under her fingers. An elaborately engraved escutcheon decorated its outside. With Rebecca and Sarah hovering near her shoulders, she opened it.

The finest hand had written a personal invitation for Miss Russell to attend a ball being held by the Earl and Countess DeVere next week.

"Well, I'll be—" Sarah muttered in a voice full of awe. "Do you think a mistake was made and it was intended for Rebecca?"

"Of course, no mistake was made," Rebecca said. "I think a countess knows that if one addresses a letter to Miss Russell, it will go to the eldest sister."

Eva was not so sure. A mistake made more sense than this coming to her.

"You must go," Rebecca said.

"I am not sure I must, or that I want to. It makes no sense that I received this. I do not know these people, nor do they know me."

"Someone arranged it, then," Sara said. "Mr. Fitzallen perhaps."

"If so, you really must go, Eva," Rebecca said. "It would be rude to refuse, after all his hospitality. And it is an earl's ball."

"But we will not even still be here next Tuesday."

"We will be now," Sarah said. "I've no idea what you will wear. I brought a ball gown, just on the chance that it would be needed. It will hardly do for such as this, however, no matter how hard we try to improve it."

A bit of pique penetrated Eva's astonishment. Surely Gareth knew she would be ill-equipped for such an invitation. She could hardly attend wearing her blue pelisse.

She stood, tweaked her bonnet's rim, and pulled on her gloves. "I will decide later what to do. I cannot think now. Come along, Rebecca."

"I'll be seeing if any dressmakers do fast orders," Sarah called after them as they walked to the stairs. "And I'll look in the warehouses for lace and such."

"What trouble and nonsense," Eva muttered.

The house on Upper Thornhaugh Street appeared handsome if modest. Eva handed her card and Miss Neville's letter of introduction to the servant who came to the door. She and Rebecca waited a good while before the woman returned.

"My lady will see you, but it cannot be for long."

Eva's excitement built with every step up the stairs. They were not taken to a drawing room or library. Instead the servant opened a door on a bedchamber. An elderly woman sat in a big chair beside the bed, covered in a blanket. Anyone who saw her would know she was ill, even without the scent of a sickroom that defied the spring breeze leaking in the window that had been set ajar a few inches.

The servant moved two chairs nearby. The elderly woman raised her gaze from Miss Neville's letter. A wry smile formed. "Welcome, Miss Russell. Who is your companion?"

Eva sat in her chair and introduced Rebecca to Mary Moser, one of only two women who had been made members of the Royal Academy of Arts thus far, and one of its founders. Although she had married years after she had established her reputation, everyone referred to her by her maiden name.

Mary's eyes narrowed as she examined Rebecca. "Lovely. Have you come to town for the Season, child, so men die from heartbreak over you?"

Rebecca shook her head. "We came to see the art and sights. I would not want anyone to die from heartbreak in any case, and I would hope my mind and character would be at least as much interest as my face to a man."

Mary chuckled, and waved the letter. "I think Jasmine has been influencing you. How is she faring up there in her rustic abode? Terrorizing the locals with her strong opinions?"

"She is quite the original still," Eva said. "We are both grateful for her generosity."

"She says you are an artist. With whom did you study?"

"Only a talented governess, but I work on my own. I think I have improved. I have done copies of fine pictures, and Miss Neville has offered me others from her own collection for further study."

A very polite smile grew on Mary's face while Eva talked. It was the kind given when a conversation had taken a boring turn.

"You will not remember me," she added quickly. "I wrote to you once. Eight years ago."

"Did I write back?"

"Yes. You gave me advice. You warned me how hard it was for a woman to be a painter. How marriage would compromise any such career. How the best training would not be available."

"I wrote all of that, did I? The last part is true. Life studies, for example, are not available. We are all too modest to draw the nude form from life, especially the male body, it is thought. Rubbish, of course. Yet without the rigor of such exercises, figures will always look a bit like cotton dolls. As for the first part—did you not think it odd advice, considering I had myself married?"

"I confess I was not aware of that at the time."

Her gray head rested back on the chair. Her eyes closed. "We both knew within weeks we had made an error. We took lovers and survived. However, I made that step late in life. I had already become all I would ever be as an artist by then." Her head straightened and she looked at Eva. "You are not married. Did you forgo it because of what I wrote to you? I do not think I want such a permanent decision on your part on my conscience during my last days."

"Be assured my marital state had nothing to do with you. In fact, I almost married. Since I did not, however, your words have influenced me to see my situation for its benefits. I do not seek fame like yours. I only hope to improve, so I can create on canvas or board what I see in my head."

She received a long look for that. Then Mary began coughing. The fit turned violent, affecting her whole body. The woman servant came over to calm her, and poured some potion from a little bottle into a glass that she held to her mistress's lips.

The medicine worked quickly. The body under the

blanket relaxed. The gray head lolled. The servant caught Eva's eye.

"We will leave you now," Eva said, standing. "You were very kind to agree to receive us."

Mary's eyes opened. "Will you be in town when the Exhibition opens?" Her voice came breathless and slurred.

"We will be gone by then, I am sorry to say."

"Pity. Do your copies of Jasmine's collection, and draw often. Hire a man to model for you, if you can find one willing to pose unclothed. With time you will improve, if you have talent like Jasmine thinks. It is a worthy goal."

"Thank you. We will see ourselves out."

Back on the street, she and Rebecca paused.

"I think she is dying," Rebecca said.

"I think so too."

They walked down the street, subdued. Slowly the sun and breeze lifted them out of their sad reveries.

"Eva," Rebecca said with an impish smile. "Which of the men in Landgon's End do you think will pose nude for you?"

As soon as Gareth entered the presence of the Duchess of Devonshire, he decided he did not mind at all that Ives walked beside him. He wondered if Ives felt the same way about him.

With difficulty he forced out of his thoughts the subject that had occupied him all morning and most of last night. He needed to charm answers out of the duchess, not address her with the surliness that colored his mood. Having left the house without seeing Eva had not helped. He was not accustomed to jealousy, and the effects of it sat badly on him.

To say the last duke's second wife knew her exalted status would be an understatement. She sat regally in a blue upholstered chair designed to complement her size and form. Her eyes regarded them much the way medieval queens must have looked at serfs. Considering that Ives was the legitimate son of a duke, and a lord in his own right, that took a good deal of boldness on her part. But then, this woman had made her way into that chair by playing a very long, calculated game.

Ives's manner as he greeted her struck just the right note of respect without descending into deference. Her thin smile suggested she would like the latter.

"We have come on a matter of personal interest to the Prince Regent," Ives said. "It is possible you can help us with an inquiry undertaken at his request."

"If you are going to use a preamble like that, I suppose I must help if I can."

"It involves some items stored in one of your late husband's properties. The house just north of Chatsworth. In the course of posing some questions to the servants there, my brother learned that you may have some knowledge of those items." Ives turned to him, cuing him to jump in.

Before he could, the duchess sliced down his body with a sharp gaze. "You must be the bastard."

"I am."

"Your father and my husband had a friendship of sorts, largely based on what they had in common in that regard. Have you met my first son? He chose a career in the Naval Service. As I hear it, your life took different turns." Her knowing smile insinuated much into the carefully enunciated last words.

"On occasion I occupy myself with less pleasurable pursuits. Such as this inquiry."

"Inquire, then."

He repeated what he had learned about her visit to the house after the death of the last duke. Despite his effort to suggest nothing untoward, she took insult. "I trust you are not so bold, or so stupid, as to accuse me of removing these items you seek."

"We only wonder if the men who served you had any cause to go up to the attics, and if so, whether they commented on its contents."

"They did go up. There was a lovely table from Italy that could not be found in its chamber, so I sent two men to search for it there. I do not remember any talk afterward. What might they have said?"

"Nothing alarming," Ives said. "Perhaps they mentioned it was hard to search, because of a great many crates there? Or alternately noted it was peculiar that one attic contained very little at all."

"If they had cause to move crates, comments pertaining to their weight, whether very heavy or oddly light—" Gareth prompted.

She appeared to give it honest thought. "It did take

them a long while to come down, and they never did find that table. One was not happy because he scraped his hand. I overheard him complain to the others about all those damned boxes. Could he have meant the crates you speak of?"

"Possibly," Ives said.

"Among the furnishings those men carried out for you, were any of them paintings?" It had to be asked, and Gareth decided to throw himself into the fire.

"Only an Angelica Kauffmann that I had long admired. The duke did not favor it, so had banished it there. He told me it was mine if I wanted it."

Ives bestowed his most amiable smile. "You have been more than generous with your time. We will leave you to your other callers."

Outside, Ives clapped a hand on Gareth's shoulder. "You did that very well. I was trying to find a way to ask which pictures she had taken, without using a word like *taken* itself."

"Was a Kauffmann on the list? You have gotten your hands on one by now, haven't you? It would be a hell of a thing if some of those pictures are hanging in plain sight in that house and we do not know it."

"I finally received a list. No Kauffmann. Let us get something to drink at the Black Horse. I will give it to you, and also prepare you for your next meeting."

The next meeting, tomorrow morning, was with Mr. Clifford, the first son of the lady they had just left. It sounded as if Ives had decided not to attend.

They sat with beer at the tavern. Ives passed a

vellum sheet across the table. Both sides showed three columns. The first had artists' names. The second held titles or descriptions of pictures. The last column showed the owners.

"Impressive," Gareth said.

"The artists?"

"The owners. I see the Prince Regent is not on the list. I thought you said it was partly his idea."

"He was convinced that it would look bad if it became known he stripped the walls of Brighton out of fear of an invasion. Since there never was one, some of his friends now see that as suspiciously shrewd."

"Men can be such asses." Gareth muttered that eternal truth while his attention shifted to the door. "Here comes Lance. You told him to meet us here, didn't you?"

"He was at loose ends this morning, which never bodes well."

"He of all men does not need a nursemaid. Stop being one."

Ives waved to catch Lance's attention. "I also thought that things ended badly yesterday. You have been piquish all day too."

"And you concluded I wanted to drink ale with him? So much for being the clever lawyer." He barely got the last of it out before Lance slid into a chair at their table.

"At least you bothered to shave today," Gareth said. "Since you do not appear to be a rustic just off a wagon from the Midlands, you can sit with us."

Ives tried a quelling glance, but Gareth was not in the mood to humor either one of them.

Lance felt his face. "I hate being shaved. I have thought of never bothering again, and growing a beard. Perhaps it would become fashionable. Not a long, curly one. A closely cropped one, like the Spaniards used to have."

"You are not, nor have you ever been, a fashion leader, so no one else would grow one and you would look eccentric at best. Even Ives here would not want to be seen with you."

Lance looked at Ives. "Is he right?"

"Do not grow a beard," Ives said. "Please."

Lance made a face. "If a duke can't grow a beard and others then grow them, too, what is the point in being one?"

"Shall I list the points of being one?" Gareth said. "We can start with the obscene income you will enjoy henceforth."

Lance smiled with chagrin. "I forget sometimes that you are a bastard brother, Gareth, and all that has meant to your life."

The anger building while listening to Lance's petulance eased on that note of fraternal warmth. Not that Gareth wanted it to.

Lance picked up the vellum sheet and read it. "Is someone planning a massive exhibition?"

Ives reminded him about the missing paintings. "Gareth and I are engaged in an inquiry about them."

"Oh, that." Lance narrowed his eyes on the list of lords. "What cowards."

"They only sought to protect their most prized possessions," Ives said.

"So the French could have their horses, their wives and daughters and servants, but not their pictures?"

"Presumably the wives, daughters, servants, and horses would be packed off as soon as the French landed," Gareth said. "Forgive me for changing the order. I am sure you put the horses first with no regard to relative importance, correct?"

"To hell with the order. It was ignoble to do this, when farmers and fishermen drilled in the fields, preparing to lay down their lives. Those men would not be able to send anything north, let alone their paintings."

Ives pushed Lance's tumbler closer to him, encouraging him to drink. Gareth's mind chewed over Lance's outburst.

"I wonder," Gareth said. "We have assumed the pictures were stolen for gain. Thieves, or at best a mad collector at work. What if instead they were taken as punishment? Perhaps someone who knew of the plan felt as Lance here does, and sought to ensure these lords regretted this move, one way or another."

"Considering the mood in the country back then, it is possible," Ives said. "I suppose we would first look at the lords who have estates near the coast who are not on this list."

"I will let you talk to them, if you don't mind," Gareth said. "I can think of no way to raise the matter without being insulting, and I'll be damned if I will die in your stead."

Lance tapped the vellum. "You are both so serious. First thievery is the reason, now patriotism. You are missing the most likely motive."

Ives raised his eyebrows and waited.

"It was a joke," Lance explained. "Don't you see how comical this is? All of that concern and care and secrecy about a group of damned pictures. There was a war going on, and the lords spent their mental faculties on this? I can imagine a band of bloods deciding it would be funny as hell to make those pictures disappear." He laughed and smacked his palm on the vellum. "Think of their expressions when they learned it was all gone. Um, no, Napoleon did not take your art, but someone did. Sorry, milords."

Ives looked at Gareth. Then at Lance, who remained lost in his merriment.

Gareth knew what Ives was thinking. Lance had always been a bit of a rogue.

"Lance," Ives said carefully. "Please tell me that you did not see the comical possibilities ten years ago, and . . ."

"If I did, I would be laughing now, seeing the two of you run all over England trying to find those pictures. Oh, wait—I *am* laughing now." And he did, heartily.

Ives's lids lowered. "This has now become not at all funny. I ask you again—"

"What do you think?" Lance's eyes came alive with devilish humor.

Gareth could tell Ives was losing his temper. "Damnation. If you know anything, tell Ives now. Stop being an ass."

Lance did not like that. What duke would? For that matter, what bad boy would? He did stop the taunting, however.

He picked up the vellum again, then let it drop dismissively. "It never entered my mind to teach these peers a good lesson. More's the pity."

"Do you swear it?" Ives asked.

"I have to swear it? That is insulting."

"Your humor has been odd of late."

Lance just glared. Then he shrugged. "Fine. I swear I had nothing to do with this, and know nothing about it."

Ives let out a solid exhale. He turned to Gareth. "Now, about tomorrow when you meet with Clifford. Broach the subject straight out. He was in the Service, and will not have a lot of patience with dissembling. The questions must be put to him eventually, so there is no reason to delay."

"Why is he questioning Clifford?" Lance asked.

"He is very good at speaking man-to-man, and that is what is needed."

"Bastard-to-bastard, I think you mean," Lance said. "Have you met him?"

"Several times, in passing," Gareth said.

"His situation is exquisitely hellish. Imagine that the Aylesbury estate was at least three times larger than it is. Then imagine that although a bastard, you had the exact same parents as Percy and me, and that the only reason those estates were not yours upon your father's death was because you had the misfortune to be born before your mother became his wife. As the second born, I tasted a small drop of what Clifford drinks every day, and a bitter brew it is."

"I am sure he has accommodated it," Ives said. "Gareth here would have too."

Gareth hoped he appeared agreeable to that belief. The truth was he knew something of that bitterness. Every bastard of a lord did. Normally one did not dwell on one's fate, but sometimes the foul bile of what had been swallowed soured one's mouth.

"Did Miss Russell agree to attend that ball?" Lance asked casually. "Ives here said you snared an invitation for her, and intend to escort her yourself."

Gareth glared at Ives, who made it a point not to notice. "I was not there when she received the invitation, so I do not know yet if she is agreeable."

"She will not go," Lance said. "She will want to. Any woman would. But she will not."

"You know that, do you?"

Lance nodded. "It struck me last night. No matter who the escort, or even if there is none at all, she will not go. She doesn't have a suitable gown and headdress. I'll lay odds on that."

Gareth just looked at him. Lance was right. She didn't. It would matter to her. To any woman.

One of Lance's eyebrows rose. "Of course, you could offer to buy her one. There is still time. Allowing it, however, carries certain implications. I doubt she is ignorant of that. So she will not accept the gift."

No, she wouldn't. She already hadn't, when he first broached the idea of this visit to London.

Lance showed smug pleasure in how he had cornered the entire question, but also some curiosity. "So, what is the vicar going to do?"

"He is not going to offer to buy her a gown, that is obvious," Ives said. "However, in an impulsive gesture of noblesse oblige, you will."

CHAPTER 19

"I am so enjoying this," Rebecca said while she and Eva strolled down a small lane in the City. All kinds of printer shops lined it, along with a few bookstores. "It is pleasant to spend an afternoon, just the two of us, taking whatever path we want."

"Very pleasant, although I have a confession to make about the path we have taken. We are not taking the path we want. We are lost."

Rebecca giggled, and they broke into peals of laughter. "Thoroughly lost, or just middling lost?" Rebecca asked after she caught her breath.

"Since I am perplexed as to the answer to that question, I suppose the answer must be thoroughly. The plan was to visit Mr. Christie's auction house. He is said to have frequent auctions, and often his gallery is full of works to be sold."

Rebecca looked to the sky. "The afternoon is get ting on. We should find it soon if we are going to visit."

Eva felt her reticule. A satisfying weight on the bottom moved, making tiny clinking sounds. The wonderful thing about money was one could solve problems like this. "I saw cabs on the last block. We will take another one. The coachman should know the way even if we do not."

A half hour later they walked into the auction house. A big, square room, its ceiling soared. In the center of the ceiling a large square section rose yet higher, with transom windows that permitted light to flow down on the pictures hung on the walls.

"Look at all the colors," Rebecca exclaimed. She peered at the pictures near the door. "Not all are great masters, are they? This one here is no better than your views. Not nearly as good, in my opinion."

Eva agreed, although neither she nor Rebecca were connoisseurs. She took heart that while her own efforts would never compete with the best on these walls, they also would not be laughable.

Other patrons toured the walls, strolling past the abundance of pictures. She and Rebecca stopped now and then at ones they especially liked. Eva scrutinized a few to see how some effect was achieved with the brush. She was doing that when Rebecca gripped her arm.

"Eva. Over there. Isn't that—"

Eva straightened and looked where her sister pointed. On the wall facing the door, right in the center, a still life hung at eye level. No one would miss it. Her gaze swept over the glass goblet depicted, and the blue porcelain dish, and the ripe fruit.

Her heart pounded so hard that her head throbbed too. She knew that composition very, very well. She had painted it four months ago in her library.

"It can't be," she whispered.

They scurried over to look more closely. Much like a signature—an artist knows her own hand at work. This was indeed hers.

Eva felt sick. "I do not understand."

"Don't you?" Frowning, Rebecca looked around the chamber, then marched over to a man standing in a corner. She spoke to him, and pointed at the still life. He in turn opened a pamphlet and pointed to a page in it.

Rebecca returned with the pamphlet. "It will not surprise you to learn that your name is not listed. According to the auction house, this is a work by the Dutch artist Cuyp, who lived two hundred years ago."

Eva examined the page in the pamphlet. "I must be a better copyist than I thought."

"Is that all you can think about? Eva, Mr. Stevenson is cheating you. I thought he acted most suspicious when he gave you all that money. But he is giving you ten shillings, then sending them here to be sold for many times that amount. That man said they expected this to get knocked down—I guess that means sold—for at least three hundred."

Three hundred pounds? Eva had trouble swallowing the idea. When she did, her stomach turned again.

"Rebecca, it will sell for that much because it is being sold as a picture by Cuyp. Not me."

"But you painted it. You should see more than ten shillings out of it."

Rebecca was missing the bigger quandary. The moral one. If they walked away without a word, someone would be cheated at the auction.

"Are there any others?" She turned to look at the wall they had not yet visited.

"None that I can see."

"Perhaps this was a mistake."

"Ha."

That *ha* echoed her own thoughts. *Dear Mary Moser, I write to thank you for your kind reception and advice. Unfortunately, I now find myself in Newgate while I await trial for theft through fraud after being implicated in a scheme to sell counterfeit pictures by the great masters . . .*

She walked over to the man in the corner. He greeted her nicely, but his gaze shifted at once to Rebecca when she came up alongside.

"I need to explain that a mistake has been made." Eva pointed to the picture, then to the pamphlet. "That is not by Cuyp."

"We are quite sure it is. A fine example of his art too."

"No, it is not. I am more sure it is not than you are sure it is, because I painted that picture."

He made a polite smile. Amusement sparkled in his eyes. "I'm sure you did, Miss."

That was it. Nothing more. He did not believe her, but he would not insult her by disagreeing, so he just smiled and smiled. Which left her standing there like the addled fool he thought she must be.

She took Rebecca's arm and strode into the middle of the chamber. *What to do?*

"He thinks you could not paint it because you are a woman," Rebecca said.

"No, he thinks I could not because he believes Cuyp did." She faced the painting. "It does look very good there, in that light. Far better than it ever did in our library." An inappropriate glow of pride flushed her.

"Perhaps if you told Mr. Fitzallen, he could convince them."

"What would I say to him? That the most amazing course of events has occurred? That I took a painting out of his property without permission, copied it, sold the copy in Birmingham, and now, lo and behold, it was for sale at a London auction as the original? Why should he believe I was not complicit and made the copies for this purpose in the first place?"

"Because you are his friend? And because you are telling him the truth?"

"The magistrate who is called will not be my friend. Don't you see how this looks? I made those copies in secret. No one knows about them except you. Even that will be suspicious now."

"Do you suppose the others that came to London

are likewise being sold as originals, elsewhere?" Rebecca asked.

The thought of that caused Eva's stomach to turn dangerously nauseated.

Rebecca gave her a little embrace and patted her shoulder. "It is just one painting that we know about for certain. Whoever buys it probably has a huge collection that includes other forgeries, and will never know. Especially if the original stays in that attic. You probably should never tell Mr. Fitzallen about the pictures up there, however."

They went to the door. Eva looked back at the painting. It glowed in the light, casting its own radiance. That goblet appeared so real one feared it might break.

Despite her concern over the painting's misuse, pride lifted her heart. Maybe Jasmine Neville was correct, and women were not taught to have sufficient ambition. Perhaps she, Eva Russell, possessed more talent than she gave herself credit for, and should aim not only to improve, but also to excel.

In the least, one thing could now be said. If Christie's listed her picture as a Cuyp, she was not only a middling copyist. She was a damned good one.

G areth made his way out of London, then kicked his horse to a gallop. The speed gave some release to the frustration building in him. He had endured yet another restless night, tempted beyond reason to wind his way through the house to where Eva's chamber lay.

He had not expected to mind so much how things now stood between them. She was of an age to be curious, aggressively so, and he had chosen to show her and teach her. If she had turned her back on pleasure sooner than he expected—or wanted, he admitted—it should not bother him the way it now did.

The truth was, he regretted arranging Eva's invitation to the DeVere ball. When he did so, he anticipated her delight at his gift, and a pleasant night watching her bedazzlement. It had never occurred to him that other men might compete for her attention. Not because she did not deserve such attention, but because, he had to admit now, in his head she still belonged with him. To him.

Whitmere's bald admiration of her made it clear just how bedazzled she might become. That ball would be full of lords and heirs. Gentlemen all, with strong lineage and extensive properties and titles. Oh, yes, it would not do to forget the titles. A title trumped everything, didn't it?

He pictured the sons of the nobility lining up, asking Eva for dances, seeking favor with her. In that ballroom, among those people, being a bastard would matter as it rarely did in his life. Nor could he warn them all off the way he had done with Whitmere.

He had never envied his brothers before. At least not much. Not with the surly edge he did now as he came close to cursing his birth. The guilt that provoked in

turn only fed his bad mood. All his life he had hoped
he might one day claim his half brothers as true family
in spirit if not in law. Today Lance had, without thinking twice, taken a big step toward that. *I sometimes forget you are a bastard.* Just remembering those words
now moved him to where he reined in his mount and
sat still with his thoughts.

Damnation, he could be an idiot at times. Only a
fool wasted his life angry over what might have been.
Nor had his circumstances left him impoverished or
obscure. He might be a bastard, but he was a recognized one. With Percy gone, already his brothers had
drawn closer. He turned his horse and rode back to
town at a slower pace. He handed off his horse and
entered Langley House. When he asked if Miss Russell had returned, the butler said she had, and was
currently in the garden.

At the back of the house, he looked out a window.
Eva sat on a terrace bench facing the back of the garden. It appeared she was sketching.

His mind saw her in her own garden. Forced to do
a servant's labor by necessity, the artist in her found
joy in it, not humiliation. He guessed the gentry
woman had too. In preserving that garden, she also
preserved the woman she had been born to be.

He opened the door and went out to sit with her.

Eva turned at the sound of steps approaching. When
she saw him, relief softened her expression. "Oh, it is
you."

"Did you expect someone else?" He sat beside her and angled his head to see what she drew.

"Mr. Geraldson. He sent up a note asking to speak with me here before dinner."

"Lance's secretary?"

"I know it sounds odd, but—" She set her sketchbook down on the bench between them. "This morning, an invitation came to Miss Russell. There is a ball next Tuesday. I think it was intended for my sister, but—"

"It was not. It was intended for you."

"Did you arrange this? So I would have a grand night?"

"I did. Also, so I could as well. I will escort you, if you are agreeable. I trust you accepted."

"I have not yet. I really did not come to town prepared for such a thing. Even Sarah's wardrobe cannot make me suitable. Anyway, when I returned to the house today, Mr. Geraldson sent up a note asking to meet me out here regarding the DeVere ball. Is the duke going too?"

"Neither brother will attend, due to being in mourning. I believe Mr. Geraldson is going to bestow a gift on you, of a new ball gown. My brother mentioned you might decline because you did not bring the necessary wardrobe."

"That is extremely generous of him, considering I have only seen him once in my life, and then for only a few minutes."

"He has a generous heart. I would not be surprised if Mr. Geraldson will propose that you have a gown made, and that you send him the bill."

"I am not sure that is proper."

"Being a stickler again, are you?"

She laughed, then nodded.

"Aylesbury is not even going to be present that night. He is not going to dance with you, and he certainly is not going to act like you owe him something in return for the dress. In a way it is not even a gift from him, Eva. Think of it as a gift from the House of Aylesbury."

She thought that over, half-convinced. "You do know how to tempt a woman, Gareth."

"I should hope so. However, it is your choice. I will be proud to have you on my arm no matter what you wear." A part of him, the part still carrying some of the annoyance that had led him to take that hard ride, hoped she would refuse the dress. If she appeared unfashionable, that should remove half the men from the line he imagined.

"I will think about it." She looked away, into the garden. "Gareth, do all dukes have men like Mr. Geraldson, who broach matters like this for them, so the dukes do not have to do it themselves? Matters that might be seen as somewhat inappropriate, or even very much so?"

"I expect so. However, this gown is a small thing, and considering the circumstances, it will not compromise you. Now, if a man offers you a carriage, a house, and carte blanche in spending on jewels, then you might well suspect that he is trying to buy you." He made a joke of it. Eva laughed, but her gaze turned serious.

"Is that how it was done with your mother? A Mr. Geraldson presented a proposal."

"It was. Better if my father had gone himself. His man was no match for my mother. She knew her worth, and drove a hard bargain." He imagined Eva tucking the information away in her head. Ever curious, she probably found the protocol fascinating.

"Did you have a nice day?" she asked, turning the subject. "I did. Well, part of it. I visited Mary Moser, the famous painter. Miss Neville gave me a letter of introduction. Can you believe she received me?"

"I was not aware she still lived in London."

"I regret to say she is very ill. She was able to hold a conversation, however. We talked about art. She gave me some advice, again. She had some years ago when I wrote to her. Sensible advice, I realize now."

"What sort? Work hard, draw daily, keep your brushes clean?"

She gave him a playful nudge with her elbow. "Not nearly that boring. She told me I needed to draw from life. Do you know what that means?" Her eyes glistened with naughty humor.

"I do indeed. Perhaps you can bribe your sister to—"

"Oh, that won't do. I must draw the *male* form from life. I can never fulfill my potential otherwise." She crossed her arms and tapped her chin thoughtfully. "I wonder who, and how could I convince him? Erasmus? A few coins should win him over."

"Or Mr. Trevor, the architect. I think he would be happy to do it and get in your good favor."

"Because of the property, you mean."

"Because of the scandalous possibilities."

"Mr. Trevor? What nonsense. Nor is there anything scandalous about it. It would be like looking at a statue. Or a fountain. Or a vase. An artist just studies the form and does not engage in sensual speculations when working from life."

"How do you know if you have never done it?" He did not believe for a minute that artists never were aroused by their models. That part of a man did not disappear when he picked up a brush.

"I just know. I have had the experience of drawing other things, and how the mind works while so engaged."

"What other advice did Mary Moser give you?"

"She reminded me that marriage and art do not go well together. She had written as much to me when I was a girl, and I did not believe her. I was sure it would be different for me. Then, when I had to care for my brother— I did less and less with my art, and eventually stopped. I was too busy. I had no time I felt was my own. It is the same when one marries. Duty crowds out all other ambition." She did not appear at all sad. "Whoever thought my singular state would be advantageous to my plans."

The way she embraced Mary Moser's decree did not sit well with him, for reasons he could not name. "Surely, it could be different, the way you thought when a girl. With the right man it could be."

"I hope you are not going to suggest Mr. Trevor again."

"Heaven forbid. He would probably give you ten children and no servants, and be jealous of your talent. It would have to be a man who knew your plan, and accepted it."

"You sound almost serious, Gareth, and quite sentimental for a man so cynical about marriage and its purpose."

He did sound sentimental.

"There are few men such as you describe. Moreover, if I chanced to meet one, he would have to be very wealthy in order to relieve me of the duties most wives know, except the rich ones." She raised her face to the lowering sun. "Even then— If you think about it, the women with the most freedom for art are women like your mother. She had no duty except making your father happy, and even that was not all the time."

Clever lady. She was correct, of course. For a woman looking for both security and independence, being the mistress of a wealthy man was an ideal situation. Not that he intended to agree with her. Not after the damned Earl of Whitmere spoke of needing *companionship* after meeting her.

"I do not think you would be happy in such a life,"

he said. "You are too much a stickler, and too afraid of the risks, which, I am sure you remember, include accidents such as me."

She gave his hand a squeeze. "I do not think any parent would regret an accident like you."

A quiet cough from behind interrupted them. He released Eva's hand, then turned and saw Mr. Gerald-son standing back near the house, discreetly positioned not to overhear.

Eva turned too. "Do you think he will talk down to me about this gown, or treat it as charity?"

"Neither. He will be correct in all ways, very formal, and respect will flow out with each of his words." Gareth stood.

"I am of two minds still. I am not sure what to do."

Left on her own, pride would make her refuse. That would spare him, but make the night poorer for her. "I will decide for you," he said. "Accept the gown and go to the ball in style, Eva."

CHAPTER 20

The week passed in a whirlwind. Eva barely had time to sketch, what with excursions into the City and visits to the dressmaker.

Madame Tissot, the fashionable modiste recommended by Mr. Geraldson, normally expected several weeks to complete a ball gown. For a duke, however, she made exceptions. Three of her seamstresses were put on the gown as soon as Eva chose the style and fabric. At the daily fittings she watched the ensemble come together.

Sarah and Rebecca insisted on accompanying her each time. Their excitement exceeded hers. She realized that they all would be attending that ball, she in person, but they in their imaginations.

She did not see Gareth very much. He escorted

them to the theater one night, and his brother Lord
Ywain joined them. He arranged for them to visit the
magnificent library of a marquess he knew, and the
art collection of an earl. One evening they all went to
Vauxhall Gardens and sat in a little box eating ham
before strolling the grounds and watching the entertainment and fireworks. Some days, though, they only
met at dinner.

Finally, the day before the ball, she found some
time for herself. After returning from Madame Tissot's and the final inspection of the gown, she begged
off further shopping with Sarah and Rebecca and
returned to the house. Up in her chamber she drew
the drapes back as far as possible so the cool northern
light would saturate the chamber.

She collected some objects into a still life that she
posed on a table near one of the windows so the light
hit the composition from the left. Settling down, she
began to draw.

Soon her observations absorbed her, and the smooth
movements of her crayon on the paper entranced her.

"Has it come?"

She looked up. Gareth stood near her shoulder.

"The gown? Is it here? I had hoped to see it."

"It will be delivered tomorrow morning."

"I will have to wait until tomorrow night now." He
stepped closer and angled his head to see her drawing.

"It is just that still life there. Not complicated, but
form is form, and there is no such thing as enough
practice."

"I expect that is true."

He hovered at her shoulder, watching her. She felt him there right behind her chair. His warmth, his energy—while he escorted her around town, there were others with them, diluting his effect somewhat, but at least distracting her from it. Now, in the silence she felt the air grow heavy with unspoken words and unacknowledged desire. She wondered if he felt it as well.

Perhaps it was different for him here in London where he was in his element. He had many friends here. They greeted him in the park and about town. Men stopped to chat and women smiled from a distance. His charm opened many doors, even for her. She doubted every visitor to London toured an earl's fine art collection, or paged through a marquess's priceless illuminated manuscripts.

She strove to concentrate on her drawing, but his proximity tormented her. "I do not think I thanked you for the gown."

"It is not from me."

"I only accepted it because of you. It was very exciting, having a gown made and being told not to count the cost. It was kind of you to do all of this for me."

"I will enjoy seeing you in it, Eva, and only regret the gift could not be mine."

Because that would imply things, even though they both knew there was nothing to imply now. What a muddle society's rules made of things.

She set down her crayon and closed her sketchbook.

She could not bear sitting here like this, with him so close.

He indeed stepped away from her.

"There is still time for a turn in the park, I think." He went to her chamber door. "Would you like to join me?"

"Don't." The words emerged without thought. "Please, don't leave."

He gazed down on his hand, gripping the door's latch. "You have me at a disadvantage, Eva."

"I know. But I do not want you to leave. Then I will be here alone, thinking, remembering . . ." She stood and put down her book and crayon on her chair.

"What do you want from me?" He sounded exasperated.

"I am not sure. But I do not want to walk with you with all those people about. I am always sharing you now. We have had little time together, the way we did in Langdon's End."

He faced her. "We were lovers then. This is how it is when you are friends. You often see each other in the company of other friends."

She went over to him. "Must it be that way? Can't we have time such as we did in the garden last week? My time is poorer when you are gone, and only half-joyous when there are others with us."

"Poorer? *Poorer?*" He strode into the chamber. "Eva, you demanded a promise from me, and I have kept it. However, I am a madman when I am with you. Can you even imagine what hell this has been? I do not just miss your company, damn it. I hunger for you. I walk around insane with lust while I play the visitor's guide and the good neighbor. So do not ask me to attend on you in private and provide amusement so your time is not *poorer*."

"I do not need amusement. I don't. I need—" She reached out and placed her palm on his chest. Warmth. She needed warmth. She closed her eyes and savored the connection under her hand.

"Eva, you are in grave danger of being ravished, and honor be damned. Remove your hand and step back."

She opened her eyes and looked at her hand. "I cannot remove it. It is stuck." She moved it across his chest, under his coat. "Oh, look. It can move. Not totally stuck. Just too heavy to lift, I suppose." She caressed up, over his shoulder, feeling all the bones and muscles that gave it such an appealing form.

He suffered it, showing more stoicism than she wanted. What happened to honor be damned? She stepped closer, so his scent filled her head. Her lips hovered an inch from his chin, tantalizing him. She smoothed her hand down between them lower yet. His stomach tensed when she passed over it. His erection brushed the back of her hand. She closed her fingers around it through his trousers.

"Damnation, Eva." His fingers stretched through her hair, holding her head against his chest. He turned her head so her face angled up. He claimed her with a kiss full of the hunger he spoke of. He throbbed in her hand, getting larger and harder. She embraced him with her other arm, and skimmed her fingertips down until they traced the hard swell of his bum.

Her arousal spun through her hotly, colored with the contentment of returning to a familiar place. *Once again. There can be little harm in that.*

Their bodies entwined, joined by reckless passion and desperate kisses and grasping embraces. She wanted more. More closeness. She pulled his coat down and he shrugged it off. Her own garments annoyed her. She wanted him totally touching her, his skin on hers and his body overwhelming her. She broke an arm free to try and reach back to unfasten her dress.

"There is no time." He pushed her so she fell onto the bed. He knelt beside it and lifted her skirt and chemise. "Come here. Closer."

She knew what he intended. "No."

"Yes."

"I will scream."

"Cover your mouth." He moved her himself, lifting her hips and shifting them to the bed's edge.

She did not resist. She did not want to. She parted her knees and waited breathlessly for the first kiss. All of her waited—urging, yearning, throbbing. When it came, she groaned with relief, then with astonishment at how the sensations destroyed all sense. Again she moaned. It turned into a begging cry. With her last bit of sanity she pressed her palm against her mouth.

She made no noises to be heard after that. They stayed inside her. Making her frantic. The pleasure built and built, and her eyes teared from the intensity. The scream of her release also remained inside her, multiplying its effect, lengthening the exquisite pitch of delirium.

She reclaimed the world and opened her eyes. Gareth stood in front of her, hot-eyed, aroused, overwhelming her with the power of his sex. She pushed herself up and reached to release his lower garments. When they dropped she caressed his phallus.

"Kiss me. Do you understand what I mean?"

For a moment she did not. Then she looked up at him.

He flipped her over. "I am too far gone, anyway." He made no more requests. He gave no instructions. He moved her as he pleased, until she knelt low with her hips high. He pushed up her garments again, until he exposed her bottom and legs.

He made her wait. He caressed her bottom. "It is hell that I want you so badly." He pressed his erection between her thighs, but not in her. It touched and pressed that most sensitive spot. She gritted her teeth to try and control the shudder of need that screamed through her. "When you are dancing at the ball, remember how you feel right now, Eva. Remember the bastard who can make you weep with desire."

He entered her, taunting her with his slowness. Again and again he tantalized her until she did weep, silencing the sounds with the bedclothes. Then gentleness disappeared and he took her harder than he ever had, until another release crashed through her in a cataclysm of howling sensations.

She collapsed on the bed. He did not. Sounds penetrated her stupor. She looked over to see him locking the door. He returned and sat on the bed.

"Damned boots," he muttered. He pulled them off. He shed his shirt and trousers, then turned and unbuttoned her dress.

When they were both naked and lying side by side, he began the passion again.

G areth rolled onto his back after the convulsive pleasure subsided. He took a deep breath and opened his eyes. Long shadows danced on the nearest wall. The light outside the windows showed dusk gathering to the east, but orange streaks enflamed the western sky. The window framed it all like a picture.

Beside him on her back, her head facing away, Eva watched too, as if she memorized it.

He turned onto his stomach and threw his arm over her. She turned her head to him. Their noses almost touched.

"You made me seduce you again," she said. "It doesn't seem fair. You are supposed to seduce me."

"I don't break my promises, unless forced to, like today."

"But you are supposed to be the bad one, not me. You are the one with the reputation."

"Not as a rake. Not as a scoundrel."

"No. As irresistible. I suppose I have proven that true once again."

"Do not blame me if you know that you should not have what you want, and you decide to take what you want anyway."

She turned her head, to look at the windows again. "It is pleasant lying like this. I suppose we cannot much longer."

He was too comfortable to move. "Dinner is not for several hours."

He began falling asleep, and dwelled on the cusp when she spoke again. "I am afraid a little about tomorrow night. I become more fretful with each passing hour. Even with that gown, I may not be suitable for such a fashionable assembly."

She worried that *she would not do*. That reminded him of Whitmere's assessment that indeed she would do.

"When you gaze in a looking glass, I do not know what you see, Eva. Not what I have seen since I almost knocked you down with my horse that day, that is obvious."

"What did you see that day, besides an angry spinster standing in a puddle?"

"I saw a woman who knew herself, and who had the self-possession to scold a stranger. A lovely woman with changeable eyes. A brave lady, who did not lie to herself about the unladylike notions entering her head during that argument."

"You were not supposed to notice the last part. I thought I was very good at hiding it."

"Were my own thoughts not following the same path, you might have succeeded. But when two people share a sexual attraction that powerful that quickly, it is impossible to hide."

She pressed her lips to his. "Also impossible to deny, it appears. It is very unfair that I must."

In his mind, he began piecing together reassurance that he would not expect her to lapse again, but delicious rest seduced him into silence. That and the fact that he would be lying.

The even northern light, gray now and deepening fast, showed Gareth's profile with heightened clarity. Subtle shadows formed, barely visible, that required the lightest touch with her chalk to imitate.

She sat in the chair she had moved to the side of the bed, down near its foot so she could challenge herself with a deeper perspective. Gareth lay on his stomach, his body uncovered, the arm that had embraced her still extended over the space where she had lain. Her sketchbook page showed his outline, and now she tried to make the figure real.

She studied his face long and hard, and with each moment she became less the artist and more the woman. She saw that face above her in her frenzy of pleasure, severe and sensual, not calm and almost soft like now. She saw it kind, with intimate humor in his eyes when he teased her.

She looked down and realized she had made no marks on the paper for some time. The light would fade soon, and she must wake him to leave. She finished the head, but not in detail. She drew efficiently so she had enough to call forth a memory of how beautiful he looked right now. Then she moved to his shoulders, trying hard to capture the complexity of anatomy there through highlights and shadows.

She had finished his shoulders and much of his back when the light became useless. She set her sketchbook and chalk on the table with the still life, and went to the bed. She touched his shoulder.

"You must go now. Dinner is in less than an hour."

He sat up, wiped his eyes, and reached for his garments. Ten minutes later he appeared the same as when he had entered this chamber. Elegant. Confident. Devastating.

He would look the same tomorrow night, only better. She would enter that ball on his arm. His gift to her was a night to remember forever, and one that few women ever knew.

Only the memory that would never die was that of this moment, while she watched him fix his cuffs in the chamber's shadows. She would never forget the emotion having its way with her.

Desire, he called it. Tempestuous and compelling, but still mere desire. Transitory. Not love the way the poets described. That was an illusion, invented to pretty up base lust.

Perhaps so. She lacked the experience to argue, or to contain and control it.

It was a cursed thing, the human heart. It knew no sense, no discipline. It led one to love what could destroy it, and did not know the difference between joy and pain.

The next morning, after learning nothing of interest in his conversation with Clifford, Gareth rode out to Ramsgate with Ives to talk to the owner of the transport company that had carried the pictures north. The man appeared honest enough, and Ives and he agreed that if something had gone wrong in transit, he was probably not involved.

Upon returning to the house in mid-afternoon, all was quiet. The preparations for the ball no doubt were under way. He doubted Eva would emerge from Sarah's chambers until it was time for the coach.

His own preparations had to wait. Lance had left a summons for him with the butler. He went above and found Lance being groomed for the day. Another man sat in the dressing room, sipping wine and looking impatient. Gareth knew him. Viscount Demmiwood had been friends with Lance until he had married and given up his more reckless, rakish habits.

The intervening years had not been kind to the viscount. While Lance looked to be on the older side of young, Demmiwood appeared more the younger side of old. A paunch of contentment stretched his waistcoat. The fair curls tousling forward over his forehead did not hide a receding hairline.

Right now that forehead showed the pink tint and

sheen of sweat that indicated the viscount experienced distress. He kept crossing and uncrossing his legs.

Lance interrupted his hated shave to greet Gareth. "You know Demmiwood. He has come to me with an extraordinary tale. I told him you and Ives should hear it, but the footman sent to Ives's apartment came back saying he was not home."

"We both went out of town. He should be back now. Send for him again."

"I've no time for this," Demmiwood said. "I have to prepare for the DeVere ball."

"As does Gareth," Lance said. "No time to waste, then. Tell him, Demmiwood."

The viscount set down his wine. Gareth gave his attention.

"Two days ago, a picture seller who has been known at times to get his hands on excellent pictures, wrote and asked to call on me. He had something very special, he said. Very choice. Secretive, he was, as if he dared not be specific because others might get in before me if the details were made known. From his excitement, I guessed it would be a Gainsborough. I, like my father before me, am well known as a collector of his work. Finding ones that are not portraits is difficult, of course."

"So you were interested."

"Certainly. I may not have my father's eye, but I am known as a connoisseur."

Actually, Demmiwood was known as an easy mark. His willingness to pay good money for weak work was infamous. He had amassed one of the finest collections of second-rate art in England. Gareth had been tempted to unload the less satisfactory remnants of one of his brokered collections on him, but did not out of respect for Demmiwood's old friendship with Lance.

"So I met with this man. He presented me with this." Demmiwood reached down beside the divan on which he sat and lifted a small picture with a gilt plaster frame. " 'Gainsborough,' he said. Normally I would have been delighted. However, with one look I knew all was not right."

"It is forgery, that is certain. A very good one, but still a forgery."

"I told you Gareth was good," Lance said. "He spotted a problem from fifteen paces."

"It is not only a forgery," Demmiwood said, his agitation growing. "It is a *copy*. The original used to hang in the gallery of my estate. That is my father." He pointed at one of the figures. "This is a portrait of him and his brothers when they were boys."

Gareth went over, took the painting, and retreated to a window to examine it in the light.

"Hell of a thing," Demmiwood said. "To be offered a forged copy of your own painting!"

"Did you accuse the picture seller of attempting fraud?"

"I did not. I swallowed my outrage, and asked him to leave it with me for a few days while I decided. I did not want to alert him that I knew his game and have him hop a packet."

"I am grateful you did not alert him. You said this used to hang in your gallery—"

"Demmiwood's county seat is in Sussex, of course," Lance said, meaningfully. "Gareth knows all about the missing pictures, Demmiwood."

"Then he may not be surprised that the original was among them. Packed up and shipped to safety, or so we all thought. Now, this." His hand flourished at the picture in Gareth's hands.

Gareth rubbed his thumb along the low corner. Still tacky. The painting had not been done long ago. More likely just months had passed.

Which meant whoever painted this had the original available very recently. It was the first mistake of whoever stole those pictures. With luck it would be all that was needed.

"When does this picture seller expect this back?"

"The painting or my money is expected tomorrow. I debated whether I could force him to tell me the whereabouts of the original, but after contemplating that, I doubted he would even admit to the crime, let along give information that might get him transported."

Gareth set the picture down next to the divan again. "Give me his name, please. And leave this here for now, in case it is needed."

Information in hand, Gareth went to his chamber and wrote a note to Ives informing him of the need to call on a picture seller in the morning. After that he read for two hours, until the manservant he was using at Langley House arrived to help him dress. At ten o'clock, he left his chamber, walked downstairs, and poured some sherry in a chamber that flanked the reception hall.

He did not have to wait long. Soon a genteel commotion hummed and echoed on the stairs. Feminine giggles and whispers, and one "Head high, now." He went to the reception hall and looked up the stairwell. He caught a glimpse of pale silk and flickering glints, of Sarah's red hair and Rebecca's young face.

They turned on the landing and descended. Eva looked resplendent in a blush silk gown dripping with tiny pearls and priceless lace. A matching headdress with two feathers decorated her curled brown hair and a downy shawl draped low on her arms. She all but floated down to meet him.

Beautiful. Poised. Regal. She knew it too. She glowed.

He took her arm. "You are stunningly beautiful, Eva."

As she entered the coach, he spotted something unexpected. Entwined amid her curls, almost hidden by the headdress, a spot of color offset all the whites and creams much the way a few violets caused a white night garden to appear all the richer. The artist had tucked a simple ribbon in her hair, to vary the palette just enough to avoid it being predictable. A lavender ribbon.

CHAPTER 21

Eva managed not to gawk and coo like a shopgirl, but the DeVere ball proved to be everything any woman ever dreamt a ball to be. The candles, the gowns, the musicians, the dinner room—she memorized all she saw, so she could tell Sarah and Rebecca.

Gareth claimed the first dance with her, as her escort. She enjoyed it so much she could not stop smiling. Then Gareth introduced her to other people. A great many people. Some of the gentlemen also asked to dance. After the fourth one, she looked for Gareth but could not see him.

She decided to find a chair near the wall. No sooner had she sat when another gentleman approached. She already knew him. It was the Earl of Whitmere, to whom she had been introduced her first day in London.

"Miss Russell! I thought that might be you." He bowed, then glanced around. "I don't suppose Aylesbury came after all."

"No. Mr. Fitzallen escorted me."

"Only to desert you? Well, what can one expect. He has many friends to attend upon, if you know what I mean." He smiled confidentially. Insinuatingly. "Aylesbury thought I should amuse him tonight, but I chose to amuse myself. I am so glad that I did." Another smile, full of meaningful flattery.

This earl was flirting with her.

For the Earl of Whitmere, flirting included talking about himself a great deal. She let him, wondering if there were some special etiquette involved in avoiding a peer's company.

"Are you rested? Shall we dance?" he finally asked.

"I would be most honored."

"Mr. Fitzallen—"

"Fitzallen must have fifty ex-paramours here, dear lady. For reasons unknown, they all remain his friends. I daresay you will not see him again until the night is over." He offered his hand. She took it and they joined the next dance.

She felt some obligation to be more vocal. As the country dance brought them together, she found a few questions to ask about his estate. He found a few to ask about her family. By the time it ended, he did not bore her as much.

To her surprise, one of the other men with an introduction asked for a dance. Lord Whitmere stood down, looking regretful. "Perhaps I will see you later, Miss Russell."

While she danced this time, she noticed that Gareth did as well. His partner never took her eyes off him. The lady was a very fair woman of incredible beauty; her gaze communicated too much for a public place. *She looks the way I feel sometimes.* That reminded her of Lord Whitmere's comment about Gareth's paramours and of Jasmine Neville describing how highborn ladies never wanted to give him up.

Rather suddenly she did not feel magnificent and beautiful, but very ordinary. Foolish too. What she had known with Gareth was not at all special *to him*. She was but one affair in a long line of them, enjoyed by a man who anticipated enjoying many more. How stupid of her to lose sight of that.

A nice young man, close to her in age and appearing very young, she thought, asked to accompany her to dinner. So she sat with him while he regaled her with talk of his horses.

Afterward, while she sat on a bench close to the musicians, listening to them play, Lord Whitmere again asked for a dance.

It was different this time. She could not name why or how, but his attention seemed more set on her. Their talk remained small, but she could not shake the sense that some assessment was under way, as if he were determining whether she measured up and had been worth the trouble. His gaze made her uncomfortable, even though he was as friendly and gracious as before.

When you are dancing at the ball, remember how you feel right now, Eva. Remember the bastard brother who can make you weep with desire.

She did remember, and a nostalgic simmer warmed her blood. Yet every time she saw Gareth, he conversed with another woman, making it clear that his blood warmed for many, not only her.

"Will you remain in London long?" Lord Whitmere asked as he led her away after the dance.

"Not much longer at all."

"Pity. With a little more time, I believe you and I could become great friends, Miss Russell." His smile, confident and condescending, said much more.

He meant friends the way she and Gareth were friends. The earl had dishonorable intentions.

She almost laughed at the phrase. And at her shock. Who was she to be insulted? She had boldly abandoned her virtue already, and did not even feel guilty about it. Had he guessed that? Did he consider spinsters of a certain age fair game?

"Surely life in that village you described does not compare with the excitements of town during the Season," he said. "Pray consider staying at least another week."

"I would not want to wear out my welcome as a guest."

"Ah. Yes, I see. A small problem, however, for

which there is always a solution. I shall put my mind to it." He bowed, kissed her hand, and walked away.

Whitmere stood near the musicians, eyeing Eva. Gareth eyed Whitmere.

He walked over. The earl's attention focused so completely that he did not notice Gareth until Gareth spoke.

"I told you I would thrash you, Whitmere. She is not for you."

"Then who is she for? You? Go dance with her three times and declare yourself if that is how it is."

Gareth looked at Eva. A young man to whom Gareth had introduced her sat by her side now, speaking earnestly. "She has plans that do not involve either one of us."

"I, at least, would not object to plans. I would be happy to help her with them, in fact."

There it was, of course. The real temptation that men like Whitmere presented. Money enough to relieve a woman, whether wife or mistress, of all duties so she could pursue her own interests. Eva had already figured that part out.

"You are wasting your time," he said anyway. "She is gentry through and through. If you make an overture, it will insult her. *That* is why I will thrash you."

Whitmere chuckled. "Then thrash away. Just tell me where and when. Because while the overture has not played, the strings have warmed up, and she did not appear insulted at all. Surprised and curious, but not insulted."

He walked away, too pleased with himself. Gareth walked over to Eva. He wanted to scold her. Warn her. But surely she had seen Whitmere's interest for what it was.

"Will you grant me the honor of a dance, Miss Russell?" he asked, interrupting the earnest young Mr. Pierpont. Pierpont took umbrage and frowned. Gareth stared him down. Eva took his hand, and he led her toward the musicians.

"That was a little rude," she said.

"He was boring you. I did the chivalric thing."

"How good of you to notice. That he was boring me, that is. Your arrival startled us both, however. I had almost forgotten you were here."

"Whenever I looked for you, you were well occupied."

She wore a false smile while they danced. When the music stopped, she hid a yawn behind her gloved hand. "I know these balls go on until morning at times, but I am ready to leave whenever you are."

"Then we will go now, if you like."

He was not sorry to depart. He escorted her to the reception hall, then went out to tell a servant to call for the coach. When he returned, he could not see Eva. Then he noticed a bit of her dress showing from behind a pedestal that held an antique statue.

Stepping to one side, he saw Eva deep in conversation with the Earl of Whitmere.

Eva looked up at the earl. The corner behind the statue was not entirely private. She doubted following him there would be thought scandalous.

The implications of his words would be, however.

"If you are agreeable, write to me, and I will put my secretary on it at once."

She did not know what to say. If etiquette existed for such a situation, no one had told her. Nor had he been explicit. He would leave that for his secretary, she supposed.

She smiled noncommittally and stepped around the pedestal. Ten feet away, Gareth stood, watching.

Lord Whitmere acted as if nothing at all were untoward. He bowed to her. He nodded to Gareth. He returned to the ball.

Gareth tucked her arm around his and escorted her out. "I trust he was not importuning you behind that statue."

"I am not sure that *importuning* is the right word."

"How so?"

They settled into the coach and it moved down the street. "He cajoled me to stay in town for at least another week, or fortnight. Or longer."

"In order to enjoy the pleasure of his company, I suppose?"

"Mostly to further my artistic studies, and meet important artists and other connections. To hear him speak of it, there is no other place for an artist to be."

"There is an advantage, that is true. Not an insurmountable one. Nor do men ask women to stay in town for altruistic reasons alone. I think you know that."

"Yes." Other than a crisp tightness in his tone, he did not sound angry or jealous.

Of course not. If she could have no expectations of him, he would not have any of her. Gareth would be very fair about that.

So why did she want to hit him?

"Behind the statue, he was proposing a solution to my exceeding my welcome in your brother's house. An alternative, so I could stay if I choose. One of his properties is vacant. A house just north of Cavandish Square. He is prepared to let it to me at a very good rent."

"How good?"

"A shilling a month. I am to write to his secretary, a Mr. Hoburn, about it."

Silence. No anger. No curses. Just Gareth sitting there, as if they discussed the weather.

After a moment, Gareth said, still in that cool, noncommittal tone, "An advantageous arrangement."

Her breath caught. Her heart felt sick and angry and horribly disappointed.

The coach pulled up in front of Langley House. Fighting her emotions, she found the poise to enter the house with him. In the reception hall, Gareth gestured for the night footman to leave.

"You were among the loveliest women there tonight, Eva." He moved to kiss her.

She stepped back. "You knew what he was considering about me, didn't you? You joked about a man trying to buy me with a carriage and servants and jewels, but it was not really a joke."

She felt tears brimming. For all the compliments, she felt insulted—but by Gareth, not Whitmere. "Did the two of you sit and plot it? Did you tell him about us, so he knew I was no innocent? Were you acting as his procurer?"

The anger that flared in his eyes made her cringe. "Is that what you think?"

"I don't know what to think."

His expression fell. He reached for her. She veered out of reach and stumbled away, blinded by tears. "Do not touch me. Do not."

She ran up the staircase. At the top of the third set, she composed herself and wiped her eyes. Then she entered Sarah's sitting room.

Sarah dozed in a chair. Rebecca had fallen asleep over a book in another one. With her entry, they both woke up.

"Was it wonderful?" Rebecca asked. "Did you hold your own? Did you meet other dukes? Was the Crown Prince there?"

Sarah moved to a divan and patted the cushion beside her. "You must share every detail, every moment, and every word."

Eva sat and removed her headdress. Then she told

them all about it. She shared her night with them, but not every detail, every moment, and every word.

"Hell of a thing," Ives said while he and Gareth tied their horses to posts on The Strand. "Someone got careless. Or impatient."

"Let us see if we can charm the information out of him."

"And if we can't?"

"Then you can threaten him in your best lawyerly ways, while I do the same in illegal ways."

Ives grinned. "I am shocked that you would insinuate violence to obtain information."

"Fine words coming from you. At least I only insinuate."

"Or so you say."

Today of all days he only said. If this man gave them the least trouble, he would probably thrash the fool gladly. He wanted to thrash someone for any reason at the moment. The argument with Eva, and her hurt and accusations, still rang in his head.

He thought he had been damned noble. He had tried not to stand in her way, and for his sacrifice she turned on him and accused him of all but selling her to Whitmere.

They entered the small picture gallery of Mr. Longinus Parala. A miniature version of an auction house or estate gallery, it bulged with art. Pictures crammed its walls, and bins held prints and watercolors. Gareth pretended to study the former, but actually his gaze quickly hopped from one picture to the next.

Ives sidled up to his side. "I do not see any of the others here. Do you?"

"Hard to say. This could be a copy of a Constable here. There was one on the list. When an inventory says only a landscape, however, it is hard to know which one."

A gentleman sitting at a fine inlaid-wood writing desk in the corner ignored them for a long while. Then, as if he suddenly realized he had company, he turned and lifted spectacles off his hawkish nose and set them atop his head on his dark hair. After he critically scanned their persons and garments, a smile broke on his thin, long face.

"My dear sirs. Can I be of service?" He stood and approached them. Dressed in gray from shoulders to hose, he broke the habit at his feet, where scarlet pumps formed startling bright spots.

"Are you the proprietor? Mr. Parala?" Ives asked.

"I am."

"Is that Italian? Parala? Your accent suggests as much, as does your name."

"It is. I was born in Genoa."

Ives smiled. Gareth could read his thoughts. This particular Parala might have ancestors from Genoa, but beneath the exaggerated accent one heard the unmistakable lilt of Scotland. Perhaps the picture seller believed the Demmiwoods would assume an Italian dealer knew his art, rather like French ladies' maids were assumed to dress hair better than English ones.

Ives walked to the door, and locked it. "I hope you do not mind. We would like a private conversation with you." For good measure he drew the curtains over the window. He came back and handed Parala his card.

Parala peered at the card in the sudden twilight of the gallery. He glanced sharply at Ives. Then at Gareth.

"He's the Duke of Aylesbury's full brother, and a barrister sworn to uphold the law," Gareth said, pointing to Ives. "I'm the bastard brother, born outside the law. He's the gentleman. I'm not. He's going to ask polite questions. If we do not like your answers, I will then ask them my way."

"Subtle," Ives murmured.

Longinus Parala's eyes bulged with alarm. "I'm sure I don't know—that is, I find this most irregular."

"Most irregular," Ives soothed. "My brother can be too impatient and rough. Well, what can you expect? Why don't you sit down. This will not take long."

Parala made the mistake of sitting in his chair again. That left him looking up while Gareth and Ives hovered above.

Ives asked him about the Gainsborough offered to Demmiwood.

"A fine piece," Parala said. "I thought of him at once. I find Gainsborough too sentimental, but there are those who still favor his style."

"Where did you get it?"

"I am not at liberty to say."

Ives looked at Gareth. "He is not at liberty to say."

"Damned inconvenient."

Ives menaced his size over the picture seller. "*Liberty*. An interesting word. If you do not tell us where you procured that painting, your own liberty will cease for many years. You may even swing. Demmiwood is prepared to swear information against you that you offered him a forgery."

"Forgery! How dare he accuse me of that?"

"Because it *is* a forgery," Gareth said.

Parala's mad gaze shifted from him to Ives and back again. "You sound very sure."

"We are completely sure."

"The paint isn't even totally dry," Gareth said.

"Oh, dear. Oh, my." Parala crossed his arms, tucked his scarlet shoes under the chair, and huddled in on himself. "I had no idea. You must believe me. There was no signature, but that is common. The style spoke for itself."

"Where did you get it?" Ives asked again.

Parala's face twisted with fury. He turned to his desk. He picked up his pen and jotted. "The blackguard. The rogue. To put me at such risk—I hope he hangs. Here is his name and place of business. Horace Zwilliger is his name. Tell him his old friend Longinus sent you."

"We must go at once," Ives said as soon as they left Parala's gallery. "We cannot risk this Zwilliger fellow bolting."

Gareth did not want to go at once. He wanted to return to Langley House, find Eva, and say all the things he would have said last night.

Ives rode off. Gareth grudgingly followed. They rode quickly to the address provided by Parala. It turned out to be a small house tucked next to a brothel in the St. Giles stews.

"It does not appear he has profited much from his crime," Gareth said.

"Do not let this fool you. I have prosecuted crime lords worth hundreds of thousands who hid amid this squalor. It makes an excellent camouflage. Do you have a pistol?" He reached down to his saddle and lifted a small one from a pouch there.

"Unlike you, I do not ride about town armed. But then I do not attract the attention you do, either." Gareth looked around pointedly. Several men had stopped on the street and now stared at Ives. "They know you."

Ives swung off his horse and tied it, making no effort to hide the pistol. "Have no fear. The fellow across the lane was spared the noose due to my efforts. When the cause is just, I do not always prosecute. Since he owes me his life, I think he will make sure these horses do not walk off."

Gareth led the way to the door of the house. Ives still carried the pistol. When the door opened, Ives handed his card with one hand, while he pointed the weapon with the other. It went without saying that they gained entrance.

Mr. Zwilliger looked to be late in his middle years. With his narrow eyes, big hearty build, and dark-haired head, he would make a good tavern owner. He listened to their introductions calmly enough, but he watched that pistol out of the corner of his eye.

Finally, he pointed to it. "Is this necessary, gentlemen? I am a peace-loving man. I know the neighborhood is not the best, but—"

"There is evidence you have committed a capital crime," Ives said. "I am always careful when meeting such men."

"I have committed no crime."

Gareth told him about the forged Gainsborough. "We assume there are others."

Zwilliger responded with shock. "This is terrible. I am undone. It is true that I handle art at times. I am no great expert, but my judgment is sound. Like most I depend on the honesty of those who sell to me. To learn I have been deceived and defrauded, and implicated in such a way—" He flushed and flustered and almost cried.

"Keep him here." Gareth pushed past him and strode into a dim sitting room. No art there, not even on the walls. He checked the whole first level, then went above. Stacks of paintings lined the wall of one of the chambers.

He called for Ives.

By the time Ives and Zwilliger arrived, Gareth had set out some of the paintings. Ives took one look and leveled his pistol again. "Are those—?"

"No. Forgeries. All of them. But like the Gainsborough, I think these are copies of what we seek." He glared at Zwilliger. "Where are the originals?"

"I swear I do not know what you are talking about. I bought those, and the Gainsborough, and several other fine works, from a well-respected man of business. If they are forgeries, I was robbed."

"How many?"

"Twenty in all were sold to me," Zwilliger said.

Not enough. Damnation. "These and the Gainsborough come to twelve. Where are the others?" He began flipping through another stack.

"Not here. Five were sold to a picture seller in Greenwich. Two to a gentleman. The last I placed at auction."

Ives gestured with the pistol. "You are not to sell or move these. I will send men for them in a few hours, and all had better be here. You had better be here too. It will be for the magistrate to decide if you are as innocent as you claim."

"I swear—"

"You will have time enough to swear. For now, tell us who sold you these pictures."

"A stationer in Birmingham. I was up there visiting my sister, and chanced upon his shop with all these pictures. Others, too, but not so fine or by such illustrious names. I bought them all, of course. London is a better marketplace for such things."

"Birmingham. How convenient," Ives said. "You will not even have to stay at an inn to finish this, Gareth."

Their missions for the day completed, Ives insisted on buying drinks and a dinner. Gareth ate quickly and spoke little. If Ives noticed, he did not mention it. They parted at nine o'clock, with Ives insisting that they meet early to track down the forgeries-at-large.

Gareth returned to Langley House. His intention of speaking with Eva was thwarted. When he asked after her, he learned the ladies had retired early in order to pack for their journey in the morning.

He consoled himself with some whiskey in the library. It was for the best, he supposed. Most of what he had intended to say to her should not be said. What little was left would be better heard in Langdon's End.

CHAPTER 22

E va opened the door to her house slowly. She peeked inside, half-expecting to see it ransacked again.

Rebecca pushed the door wide and walked past her. "Let us unpack quickly and go to the village. I want to see if any mail came while we were gone."

Rebecca went above, but Eva strolled through the house, letting its familiarity seep into her soul. They had not been gone long, but the spaces felt a little strange anyway. It was not the house. Nothing had changed here. She had, however, and not only because of the ball and other experiences. Her heart had changed.

She gazed out the window, to the spot where she and Gareth had sated their desire in the garden. That was supposed to have been the last time.

When she embarked on this affair, she assumed it would be brief. She thought he would make it so, being who he was and who she was. A dalliance for him and a chance to know a woman's carnality for her. That was all it was to be. Simple. So simple that she astonished herself with her own sophistication.

Now—not simple at all. She never guessed that the risk to her reputation would be the least of it. She never expected to love him, and to feel real pain because he would never love her. What sensible woman would?

She went down to the kitchen to see what provisions she needed to buy. She could hear Gareth saying that romantic love did not exist, that it was something made up to create an excuse for indulging in sensual desire that would itself pass. He did not use those words exactly, but he had given fair warning. She had understood him well enough.

Perhaps for him it already had passed, or was passing. He had not seduced her. There had been no honor be damned. She had had to seduce him in her chamber. And he had been willing to stand aside and allow another man offer to keep her as a mistress. What friend wouldn't defer to practicalities, should such an opportunity arise?

Rebecca waited upstairs, impatient to walk to town. They set off.

"I wonder if Mr. Fitzallen is back yet," Rebecca said. "Do you think he is?"

"How would I know? He may have journeyed somewhere else. We may not see him for weeks. What do we care if he is back or not?"

"I was just making conversation, Eva. You do not have to bite me for it." She pointed to Eva's arm. "You have your sketchbook. Are you planning to stop along the way to draw? Not on the way there, I hope."

"I thought that after we visit the post office, and before we do our shopping, we might call on the sisters Neville. You can read, and I can draw. They have some nice figurines, well made, that will keep me busy for an hour or so."

"That will be fun. I think I will enjoy my time there more if you are with me."

What a sweet thing to say. It touched her that Rebecca wanted to share more time with her.

"Jasmine can at times be too motherly," Rebecca continued. "If you are there, I do not think she will give advice that was not requested."

"She does that often, does she? And here I always found her so shy about her opinions."

"One cannot anticipate what her opinion will be. She can surprise one, and that can be vexing."

"What surprising opinion did she give you that you found vexing?"

Rebecca blushed. "I am not clever, am I? Not if you guessed there had been such an opinion recently. I wrote to them, and she wrote back two days ago."

"What did she say? Hopefully that you should never become a courtesan, no matter how much London had bedazzled you."

"I wrote to Ophelia while I was in town, and, along

with telling her of the sights we had seen, I also mentioned meeting Mr. Mansfield and Mr. Trenton while at Sarah's house, and how Mr. Mansfield then turned up in London. I mentioned how Mr. Trenton suited me far better, but cousin Sarah kept throwing me at Mr. Mansfield. Jasmine wrote back with a long lecture on the matter. I thought that bold, since I had not confided in *her*."

"I hope she did not lecture that you should not marry at all."

"She took no position on marriage, but she did take a position on Mr. Trenton and Mr. Mansfield. To my surprise, she favored the latter most decidedly. She warned me about entanglements with writers, and poets in particular. Her warnings were very . . . forceful."

"I would think Miss Neville looked kindly on writers."

"Wouldn't you? Her vehemence on the subject leads me to wonder about the soundness of all her advice now."

Eva would be happy to see Rebecca less influenced by the sisters Neville, but not out of rebellion against sensible advice.

No letters waited for Rebecca at the post office. Her spirits sank. She retreated into silence while they walked to the home of the sisters Neville.

The ladies in question received them. Eva discovered that they did not stand on ceremony with Rebecca. They did not sit for the obligatory fifteen-minute chat. Rather Ophelia waved them into the library after perfunctory greetings, and they went about their own business.

For two hours Rebecca read and Eva drew one of the figurines, a small bronze depicting Hercules fighting the Hydra. Although small in scale, the sculptor had modeled the forms as professionally as if it were ten feet high. The exercise challenged her, since both figures twisted in action.

A servant brought in lemonade and little cakes, set the tray on a table, and invited them to partake. Eva set aside her sketchbook and joined Rebecca at the table.

"They have the best cakes," Rebecca said, taking one. "Even if I did not love their library, I would probably visit just for these."

While they refreshed themselves, Rebecca told Eva about the book on mythology she was reading. As she did so, Miss Neville entered the library. She did not come to join them. Instead she strode to the bookcase in front of the table that held the Hercules bronze.

"I particularly find the story of Jupiter and Danaë peculiar," Rebecca said. "He often visited his lovers in different forms, to escape his wife Juno's detection. With Leda, for example, he became a swan."

"That does not bear contemplating too much," Eva said. At the bookshelf, Miss Neville pulled out a book, perused it, and returned it.

"No, but at least it makes some anatomical sense if one does, scandalous though it might be."

"Better if one does not, all the same." Eva wondered

just how much her sister knew about the anatomical sense of lovers' joining. It sounded like more than one might expect of a nineteen-year-old innocent.

Miss Neville had found her book. She turned to go. Then she stopped, angled her head with curiosity, and stepped closer to the Hercules.

"Yes. Well, with Danaë, Jupiter took the form of a shower of gold. How could a shower of gold impregnate a woman?"

Eva barely heard her. Instead her attention riveted on Jasmine Neville, who had bent toward the chair Eva had used for her sketching. She then straightened, holding Eva's sketchbook in her hand.

"I expect since he was a god, he would arrange for the gold to do whatever he chose it to do," Rebecca mused after a sip of lemonade.

Miss Neville began flipping the pages of the sketchbook much as she had done when Eva visited her last time. Eva trusted she would approve of the more recent drawings, the ones done in London.

The ones done in London.

Eva jumped up and rushed toward Jasmine, almost tripping over a stool on her way. She ran up to her hostess, hand outstretched, ready to grab the sketchbook before Jasmine reached one particular drawing.

Too late. She saw the page turn to reveal a drawing of a naked, sleeping man. She noticed Jasmine's reaction. Eyebrows up, eyes narrowing, head angling.

Then those eyes looked at her. Right at her. Right through her.

"I see you were busy with your studies while in town, Miss Russell."

"Yes. I did quite a few drawings. Of sculptures and such." She took the sketchbook, closed it, and tucked it under her arm.

"The *and such* appears to have inspired your best efforts."

Had Jasmine recognized the *and such*? Eva had not finished the head and face in any detail, and the angle of that face might make it unrecognizable in any case. She hoped so, but the frank expression in Jasmine's eyes suggested one person in Langdon's End now guessed the truth.

"I also called on Mary Moser. Thank you for your letter of introduction. She received us, and asked after you. She told me to find a way to draw from life." She hoped Jasmine would take that as a full explanation of the drawing.

A small, fleeting smile suggested Jasmine found the excuse amusing. "How did you find Mary's health?"

"Not well, I am sorry to say. I think she expects the end soon."

"Thank you for telling me that. I will write to her at once." One more open-eyed, direct look, one more glance at the sketchbook, and Miss Neville departed.

Eva returned to the table. "Are you done eating all the cakes? Let us go and finish our errands."

For the next hour, while they shopped for food and sundries, Eva tried to accommodate the idea that her reputation—her entire world—now rested in the hands of a woman known for outspoken opinions, radical ideas, and indifference to how society exacts high tolls on prohibited behavior.

Gareth returned north in one of Lance's carriages. He carried cargo that could never be transported on a horse.

He did not return to Albany Lodge right away, much as he wanted to. He intended to call on Eva as soon as possible. He had not been present when she left Langley House three days ago. He and Ives spent that day tracking down the paintings Zwilliger had put out for sale. Then they devoted a good deal of time forming a strategy that might bring this investigation to a close quickly and successfully.

It would be good to be done with it. It had become an intrusion and distraction. He would prefer to stay near Langdon's End and spend his days with Eva. Not in passion necessarily. That had perhaps come too soon. He wanted to explain his cruel practicality to her. He also wanted to ask her about her art, and her plans, and whether she might want to travel to distant lands. If she did not want him to continue as a lover, he could still be a true friend. She did not seem to have many of those. Neither did he.

The carriage wound its way through the city, past houses and shops, and into the center where businesses and banks hugged the streets. On the edge of that district, the shops became scarcer and the buildings larger and less distinguished. Chimneys abounded. Here were the factories where Birmingham's industry thrived.

The coachman took him to one of those structures. Gareth had two visits today. This one promised to be the more pleasant one.

Entering the factory was much like gaining entry to a good home. A man at the door inquired of his purpose for visiting. Gareth handed over a card and said Mr. Rockport expected him.

Much as with a morning call, he was escorted to the master of the house. Wesley Rockport greeted him in his office. Furnished in imitation of a gentleman's study, the office had bookshelves that held rows of neatly bound ledgers, and, Gareth could see with a glance, a few large tomes regarding the law. Of more interest was a long table set flush under a large window so the light could flood in. Row upon row of small metal objects lined the table's surface, displaying the products that paid for the room's moldings and furniture.

Rockport saw his interest and beckoned him to look closer. Together they viewed and touched the display. "These buckles are my pride and joy. Steel, they are. Expensive to make. I've twenty men who can forge them faster than most, and four who work the designs to their fancy. It is an indulgence of mine. The brass ones here go for much less, of course, but the volume is huge and the margin impressive."

The steel buckles' production harkened back to a generation ago, when artisans created almost everything made and bought in England. Like the mills replacing the home weavers, however, modern methods had changed Rockport's industry, altering design, quality, and even the need for skills. Lower cost, huge volume, and impressive margins were the hallmarks of successful manufacturing now.

Gareth listened to the rest of the tour, as Rockport pointed out the bits and bridles, the hinges and locks, the fittings, knives, and door handles. Small metal objects, all of them, each with a widely established purpose that fulfilled a necessity.

Rockport invited him to sit in a comfortable chair. He offered coffee and brandy, and sent for the former. He appeared pleased that Gareth had shown interest in his business.

Gareth liked Wesley Rockport. They had gotten on well while escorting the ladies around London. When Wesley had asked him to stop by this factory as soon as they returned north, he had agreed. He assumed there was a reason. He expected to learn what it was after the coffee came.

Sure enough, after drinking his cup, Wesley set it down and sent all of his attention in Gareth's direction. "Sarah has been speaking of nothing but your family's generosity. I fear that visits to London will become an expectation of hers now."

"My apologies, although you seemed to find much to occupy you too."

"I did indeed. I called on many of our patrons there. I learned some interesting things, regarding their future needs and present problems. I learned, for example, that our orders from the carriage makers have dwindled because the man I hired to call on them had not bothered to do so much, and was drunk most times he did."

"At least now you can rectify the situation."

"Already done. I mention it to explain that the most difficult part of this is having to rely on others. That is always a gamble. References and such only go so far."

Gareth nodded agreement. He wished he could see a clock. He did have that other stop to make, and he wanted to return to Albany Lodge by nightfall.

"I expect you know why I wanted to see you," Rockport said. "I am hoping that your coming means you are not averse to the notion and I have at least a small chance of convincing you."

Gareth had no idea what the man was talking about. "Not *averse*. Such a strong word. I am not averse to much at all, actually."

"I will be plain then. I need someone to represent this"—he gestured to the table—"and me, on the Continent. Not to carry around buckles to sell, as is done here. I can ship samples to those companies I know of. Not stores and such, but men who would distribute there."

"If you can ship samples, and have identified distributors—"

"A factor is what I need. A man to see to the contracts there, and arrange the receipt of shipments. A man to broker the arrangement in my behalf. I can't do it myself. I'm needed here, and I don't know the languages. There are ones I can hire, who present themselves for service such as this, but for all I know they, too, call on the patron drunk, if you see what I mean. You've a knowledge of those things. You gave me quite an education at that first dinner. I'm thinking you are the man to do it, if you can be persuaded."

Gareth did not know whether to be flattered or insulted. Despite the compliments about his vast knowledge of business and shipping, Rockport had just asked him to go into trade.

"I do not think I would care to live on the Continent."

"Nor would you have to. Such contracts are not signed every day or even every month. When one is ready to go, you could hop a packet, deal with it, and come back. At least hear me out before you decline."

Gareth agreed to hear him out. Rockport embarked on a fuller description of what this situation entailed. The more he talked, the more Gareth could not pretend that it did indeed sound remarkably like the way he brokered art collections. His knowledge of shipping and transport companies, of contracts and bills of lading, of international payments and credits, derived from that avocation, of course. Without those experiences, he could have never discussed Rockport's business affairs with him, let alone given him "an education."

"Now, I am sure you are curious about compensation," Rockport said.

"There is no need. I regret that I would not want to

be an employee, even of a firm as fine as yours. I am not accustomed to it, and would make a bad one."

Rockport grinned. "Well, now, that is fine with me if it is fine with you. I was prepared to pay you handsomely if necessary. If you prefer independence, so you can represent others in addition—I know of several men who would want to talk about that, in other industries, of course. I'd not want someone who competes with me— We can arrange it be for a percentage and expenses. Say two percent of the sale price?"

Just like the art collections.

Rockport stood and walked to his desk. After pawing through papers, he returned with a letter. "Let me see. This French fellow wants fifty." He closed his eyes and thought. "Fifty at two percent would be—"

"Hardly worth the journey, or your time, I would think."

Rockport looked at him, astonished. Then he burst out laughing. "You are quite the gentleman, aren't you? Do you think I do all of this for orders of fifty brass buckles or fifty iron hinges?" He leaned forward and held up the letter. "This Frenchie wants fifty *gross*. At ten shillings per piece. That's cheaper than he can get them made over there. He'll hand them off fast at eleven per, and the shops that in turn sell them will do so at thirteen and be happy."

Gareth did the math in his head. The commission on brokering that particular sale would be over eight hundred pounds. More money, and less trouble, than some of those art collections that took months to negotiate.

And there were others like Rockport who needed such a factor.

A gentleman would not be swayed, no matter what the profit, of course.

"I will think about it, and let you know within the week."

Rockport lifted his glass of brandy. "Here's to hoping you think rightly."

The stationer's shop was an odd place. Narrow and deep, it held a good position in the center of town. The proprietor had decided to make the most of that advantage by augmenting his papers with a motley assortment of other items. Gareth strolled past books and patterns, pins and threads, prints and combs. One shelf even held wooden toys, such as country carvers make.

Deep in the shop he spied Mr. Stevenson helping a woman choose stationery. Gareth waited until the customer had been served. After she left, Mr. Stevenson turned quizzical eyes on the only other potential patron in the shop.

Gareth asked to see some pens.

"Will you be wanting quills or the new ones? I like the latter myself, but some of the gentlemen prefer traditional writing implements." Stevenson slid a box with an array of new pens onto his counter.

Gareth toyed with them. "Mr. Zwilliger sent me. He said you have excellent items in your shop. He told me to ask if you have any more of those paintings. Good ones, like the ones he bought."

"So soon? Goodness, he visited a mere fortnight ago. The market in London must be flourishing."

"It is the Season. The whole ton is in town with money to spare, and spirits are high. That is the best time to sell art."

Stevenson peered at Gareth cautiously. "If I were to have a few more soon, would you be buying them for him?"

"I would, if they were of the same quality."

"I can guarantee the quality. What I cannot guarantee is whether more are available yet."

"When will you know?"

"Hard to say. I can send word and see, if you like."

Gareth debated whether to continue with the plan he and Ives had put in place. If this man told the truth, and it sounded as if he did since he spoke without dissembling, he was not the mind behind this fraud. The person who brought him the pictures was.

Gareth removed a card and placed it on the counter. He also placed one of Ives's cards beside it. "Stevenson, I have been deceiving you. I am not an agent for your London buyer. Nor will he be purchasing more from you. He is in Newgate awaiting his fate for selling forgeries. Forgeries he says he bought from you."

"Forgeries! No, you must be mistaken. I sold him simple pretty pictures."

"You sold him expert copies of works by major artists and old masters."

"Major—old masters—you are wrong, sir, and I'll not be impugned this way."

Gareth waited until Stevenson had collected himself. "Perhaps you were hoodwinked by he who gave you the pictures as well as by he who bought them."

"Indeed! I think so! If what you say is true, this is most shocking." He turned and reached up to a shelf behind his counter and fetched a paper fan.

"Give me the name of the man who supplied you with the paintings, and I will find out the truth, I am sure."

Stevenson flipped open the fan and beat the air near his red face. That pulled Gareth's attention away from the face, and to the fan. And to the wall behind the fan, the counter, and Mr. Stevenson.

His gaze drifted up to the shelf, then higher.

"Not a man," Stevenson said, struggling to speak normally. "A woman. Who would think a woman would do such a thing? What is the world coming to, I ask you? And what if she claims she was unaware and it is all my fault? Who is to believe me that I merely put some pictures in my shop to earn a few shillings? The magistrate? Not likely. This is—"

Gareth half-listened. His gaze had lit on a small painting hanging high on the wall like an afterthought. It showed a view of a field, with a large tree to one side and a ruin to the other. He narrowed his eyes on it.

Stevenson's exclamations turned into a buzz that barely penetrated his ears. Gareth thought he recognized the landscape, or rather the hand that had painted it. His eyes were almost sure, but his instincts were positive. He had seen the ghost of something similar on the floor of a ransacked house.

Surely not. And if so, it must be a thing apart from those forgeries.

"Her name," he snarled, interrupting Stevenson. "Give me her name, or join your accomplice in Newgate."

"Newgate! I'm a Birmingham man!"

"Give me the name, damn you, or you will be a dead man soon."

Stevenson appeared ready to faint. Gareth reached over the counter and gripped his coats so he did not go down before answering. *"Her name."*

"M . . . Miss Russell."

Holy Damnation. He barely swallowed the impulse to punch the stationer in the nose for daring to utter *that* name out of all the others in the world.

The man saw it. His eyes widened with alarm. "Eva, I think her name is." He spoke fast between short gasping breaths. "I believe she lives in— That is to say, I am sure she—" All that red drained from his face. He swooned and became a dead weight. He slid out of Gareth's grip and crumpled to the floor behind the counter.

Gareth strode to the back of the shop, found some water, and returned. He threw it on Stevenson's face, then left to the sounds of gasping and groaning as Stevenson came to.

CHAPTER 23

❧

Yes. Right here. This would do very well.

Eva threw down a small blanket on the little hill. She sat and made herself comfortable. The lake stretched out in front of her, and the sun had begun descending to her left, casting shadows that broke and formed as the water's surface moved. A line of houses marred the lake's shore close to her, where the village had begun to spill into the countryside, but she would leave them out.

She opened her sketchbook and paged to find a clean sheet. She would need a new book soon.

Her hand paused when a page turn revealed the drawing of Gareth. As she intended, her few lines indicating his face proved enough to revive the memory of looking at him in that beautiful light. Nostalgia squeezed her heart while she remembered that day. Sadder emotions hurt her when her thoughts turned to the night of the ball.

Had he returned to Albany Lodge? She had not seen Erasmus or Harold in the village when she walked there, so perhaps he had. Still, he had not called on her. After what she said the last time they saw each other, she could not blame him.

It was for the best. They never could be only friends. Not when her stomach did little flips at the sight of him. Not when she yearned for the intimacy and pleasure more than she worried about her reputation and future. If he still wanted her, she would succumb, gladly, perhaps even encouraging it as she had the last time. Then with time it would become known they were lovers, and she would be scorned, and Rebecca would never find a husband, and—

She found a clean page. She began drawing the view, with an eye to using her lines and notes to help her plan a painting.

The time passed quickly. Only the sun suddenly shining right in her eyes alerted her to how long she had been there. She emerged out of her reverie and eyed her page. The drawing captured the perspective well, and the shape and shadings of that stand of trees on the left shore. A closer tree, right down from where she sat, she had depicted in more detail, especially the way its branches framed part of her view.

"Impressive. Will it be a painting?"

She looked over her shoulder. Gareth stood behind

her, close enough to see the drawing. Her stomach flipped and flipped. Her heart filled with so much emotion it briefly made her dumb.

"Yes," she said. "That is why it is not very finished."

"Notes and reminders, you mean. Not a final draft."

"That is what I mean." She made to stand. He offered his hand to help. She tried not to allow the brief touch to affect her, but it did. "What are you doing here?"

"I called at your house. Your sister said you had come here. I decided you would need a ride home."

"I do not think it wise to ride through the village on your horse with you."

"Not a horse. Come with me. I will show you."

He brought her to the lane that ran along this side of the lake. A fine carriage with a matched pair stood there.

"I had some business that required a carriage," he explained. "Lance has at least four now, so I borrowed this one."

He stopped walking and faced her.

"Before we take another step, I want to explain something, Eva. My mother was a butler's daughter, and she herself would have gone into service if my father had not favored her. Not a bad life, and a respectable one. She did not even know him. He was the duke she glimpsed sometimes. But she took what he offered because it provided a security to her and her children better than anything she might otherwise know. So I do not see these arrangements as scandalous at all."

"Yes, you have explained that. I understand."

He looked away, his hands on his hips, exasperated with her. "I did not like it, if that is what you think. I did not encourage Whitmere. Quite the opposite. You had demanded that promise from me, however, so I had no right to interfere with your own decision."

"Of course. You do not have to explain. I should not have accused you as I did, or behaved so emotionally. I was tired and embarrassed. Let us not dwell on it."

He led her to the carriage and handed her in. She looked out the window as they rolled through the lanes of Langdon End. The village looked different from the seat of an expensive carriage.

When they reached the road that connected their properties, the carriage did not turn left toward hers. Rather it aimed toward his.

"Do not worry. I have no dishonorable intentions. I want to show you something."

Despite the way joy hummed inside her, she believed him about the intentions. Gareth could not be called cold today, but he remained distant in subtle but unmistakable ways.

"Have you made some amazing improvement? The roof is done?"

"I would not abduct you for that. This is far more interesting. While I was in London, I bought some art. The lodge's walls are too empty, don't you agree? I decided to purchase some pictures that are fitting to its heritage and the bloodline that runs through me. You will like them, and can come study them if you choose. If you are very nice to me, maybe I will let you copy them the way academy students copy old masters."

A breeze of misgiving made her nape prickle.

"That would mean spending a lot of time at Albany Lodge."

"It is a big house. You will not disturb me. If you are concerned that there would be talk, you can bring your sister or a friend."

She had not thought about there being talk. She had hoped to see a few wicked lights in his eyes to indicate he calculated having her in his house, vulnerable to his powers.

At the house, he handed her out. "The pictures are in the library. I will join you in a minute." He walked toward the coachman.

She entered the house and turned into the library. And froze.

Facing her, propped on chairs and mantel and against the wall, were the pictures Gareth had brought back from London.

Her pictures.

She strode from one to the other, hoping she was wrong, knowing she was not. She stood in their midst, unable to think. He knew. He must know. This could not be some coincidence. Unless he came upon the man who had bought them all from Mr. Stevenson—

"They are very fine, don't you think?"

She pivoted. Gareth stood at the doorway, leaning his shoulder against the jamb, watching her. Intently. Darkly.

She had never feared him before, but for a moment now she did.

"Most of them came from a Mr. Zwilliger in London. He said they were by masters like Gainsborough and Cuyp." He pointed at the three boys at the fountain, and the still life she had last seen at Christie's. "Or Carracci over here. He gave a good name to each of them. Quite an opportunity, it was."

"Did you pay the prices such artists would command?"

"That would have been stupid. After all, they are all forgeries." He walked toward her. "Aren't they, Eva?"

She wanted to die. Yes, he knew. He had guessed the truth, and suspected worse.

"They were not intended to be forgeries. I never expected anyone to be fooled. I am not that good."

"You are very good. Most people would be fooled."

"They were exercises, and a way to earn a few shillings. I would paint a copy and give it to a man in Birmingham, and he would try to sell it and give me half the money if he did. I never said they were by any masters. I do not think he did either. I said they were mine, and he sold them as in a master's style, but not by his hand. I see how it looks, however. If you think I was in league with this Mr. Zwilliger, I am not sure I can prove I was not."

He shed his topcoat, threw it on a chair, and sat on the divan. "Sit here with me, Eva. I want to make sure we hear each other clearly, and there are no misunderstandings."

She obeyed, sick to the depths of her being.

"Eva, are you saying you had no idea that your copies were being sold as originals? None at all? Did you never think they might be?"

"They were not good enough. I always saw them with the originals, and what they lacked was obvious." She hesitated, but forged on. "I did see that one in the auction house, given to Cuyp. I told them I had painted it, but the man ignored me like I was some addled fool. And, yes, I will admit that when that happened, it did occur to me that perhaps, after they were sold, there had been a misunderstanding about them."

"That is the wrong word. This was deliberate. In the chain between your handing off the pictures, and my finding them, someone chose to present them as originals knowing full well they were not."

She stared at her lap, too embarrassed to look at him. She did not want to see his thoughts in his eyes. The best excuse she had was stupidity and ignorance. So much for her fine character. Nor would this get better. More questions would come that would show her in even a worse light.

She wondered if Sarah would take Rebecca in if she were arrested. Probably so. Forgery was a serious crime. They might transport her. She wondered if forging paintings carried the same sentence as forging documents and such. Men had been hanged for that. The thought sent a shudder down her back.

"Eva, how these came to be sold in London as originals can wait to be sorted out. Right now I need you to tell me where the originals are."

She looked at him, surprised. "You do not know? I thought you did. Why else would you have bought these exact works?"

"Because I have been looking for the originals, and these copies might be a way to find them."

She wanted to laugh. His dark expression, totally without humor, stopped her.

"How did you come to copy these particular works, Eva?"

"Because they were all that were available to me. The originals are all right here, Gareth. They are up in your attic."

*S*hit.
       The pictures had been right under his nose all this time. He felt like an idiot.

And why not stick them here? It had been a dere-lict, unused manor. Who would know?

Gareth followed Eva up the stairs to the top level that housed servants' chambers. He had only come up here a few times before to inspect the damage done by the roof's disrepair. The newer wings had newer roofs, so no one had sought to find their attics.

She took him to the passage's end. To one side, in a nook tucked beside the final chamber's wall, she showed him a narrow door. She turned the latch. Behind that door lay a flight of stairs leading into an attic that stretched over one of the additions flanking the main part of the house.

Stacks of pictures lined the walls, the front ones shrouded in veils of canvas or burlap. Eva went over to one stack and raised the cloth. The Gainsborough boys cavorted around a fountain.

"These are the ones I copied." She pointed at the small works lined behind the first, then at a similar group of small pictures beside it.

He bent and flipped through them. The copies down below had their originals here. A few others had been made, however, not bought by Zwilliger.

"I only did small ones."

"I do not think a judge will care how big they were."

Her head bowed. "I was only going to explain I had chosen them because the larger ones were too clumsy to move."

He threw the canvas off a stack of larger works. He eased each one forward so he could see the subjects. Le Nain, Claude, Poussin, Vasari—the defined subject of each one allowed him to mentally check them off the list of missing art he had memorized.

He did not look at the rest. He counted, assuming all would be on the list. Thirty-one. Not enough.

Eva still stood silently, her arms huddling her body, her head hanging.

"Why did you not tell me these were here, Eva?"

"I took them, didn't I? I removed them without per-mission. I was carrying that one home the day we first met." She pointed at the Gainsborough.

"Yet you returned them."

"If I admitted to this, why should you not assume me capable of theft? Why should you think I returned all of them? Much went missing from this house."

He realized it was not what he thought, but what she thought, that weighed on her. Her own mind asso-ciated her use of the pictures with theft.

"Did you take something else? Did you keep one, for example, or—"

"Chairs. I took chairs. I sold them, the same way I sold our own furniture." She sounded miserable. "They were good ones too. Heavy. It took me an hour to get each one home, I had to stop so often to rest. Wooden and well crafted. Some had carving—"

"I forgive you for the chairs, Eva. Should there be questions about these paintings, we will not mention them to anyone."

She did not look at him. "Thank you. But you will forever know now that I am a thief, won't you?"

He pulled the canvas back over the paintings. "Not the one I am looking for, at least. These are not mine, Eva. They were taken years ago, and my brother and I have been investigating that theft these last weeks. I need to write to Ives and tell him that a third of them have turned up."

She finally raised her head. She gazed at the shrouded pictures. "Will no one think it odd that the paintings from this theft were found in your own home, Gareth?"

Odd hardly did justice to the possible reactions, he realized. All kinds of speculations could be made about this peculiar turn of events, and none of them would reflect well on him.

He remembered how everyone had been relieved he could prove he was out of the country when Percy died. He could not prove the same for when these pictures had gone missing.

The potential ramifications of this discovery crowded his thoughts.

Well, hell and damnation. He was about to discover just how much of a brother Ives really thought him to be.

"**D**o you believe me? That I copied with no intention of selling forgeries?"

Eva asked the question after they returned to the library.

"Of course."

"There is no 'of course' in this, Gareth. I cannot prove it."

She still appeared embarrassed, and very unhappy. He set his own concerns aside, and addressed hers. "Not all your copies went to Zwilliger. What happened to the others?"

"Mr. Stevenson sold some to people in Birmingham."

"If necessary, we will talk to those people and learn what they think they bought. However, it is obvious to me that you and Stevenson handled it honestly. It was Zwilliger who stumbled upon an opportunity when he opened Stevenson's shop door."

"Obvious?"

"Your distress is sincere, as was his. Zwilliger played a role on a stage."

A few sparks of humor glinted in her eyes. "Perhaps I play a role too."

What a charming, ignorant thing to say. "Eva, after what we have shared, there is not anything you can hide from me."

She smiled wryly. Almost sadly. "There are many things I hide from you very well, Gareth." She gave her copies a long look, then turned away from them. "I will leave now. Rebecca is probably wondering what became of me."

"The carriage waits. I told the man to keep it ready."

She did not talk on the short ride to her house. Her poise and her silence discouraged him from embracing her and offering comfort.

She did not allow him to help her down, but made do on her own, clumsily.

"I thank you for hearing me out, Gareth, and not just thinking the worst of me."

"I could never think the worst of you, Eva."

"You may not have, but you were not sure. Nor can you ever be again, can you?"

She turned and walked to her house.

He did not tell the coachman to move on right away. He debated whether he should follow her, and to hell with her composure. He had left London with things to say to her. Important things. After the day's revelations, it might be a long time now before he could speak them. He could still offer reassurance, though. Better than he had so far today.

He turned the latch and opened the door. He had no experience in really caring for a woman. It made him clumsy. She deserved better of him today than he had given her.

Suddenly, her voice broke the air, screaming his name. She appeared at her door, not at all composed. She called his name again, desperately, then disappeared.

He bolted out of the carriage and ran to her.

CHAPTER 24

He charged into the house. Hearing him brought back a little sanity.

She called to him from the library. She stood near the front window, holding the piece of paper. Her hands shook so badly that the paper fluttered like a sparrow wing. She heard his step and turned, frightened and furious.

"What am I to do? I do not know what she means. I do not know what they want." She wanted to sound calm. Instead she heard herself shrieking.

"She?"

"Rebecca. She is gone. She left this for me, but I cannot make sense of it." She began weeping, then stomped her foot hard, closed her eyes, and stopped the tears through sheer force of will.

He took the paper and embraced her. With her tucked against his body, he read the paper over her shoulder. His arms felt strong and good. His warmth bathed her in comfort. She allowed herself to be weak against him, and trusted strength would return as a result and she would not succumb to the chaos threatening her mind.

"It says that they told her to write that they want the treasure your brother took. What does she mean, Eva?"

"I do not know." She took a deep breath. "He had nothing. No treasure. Would we have lived like this if he did? It is nonsense. Some fools must have heard a stupid rumor, and now—" She looked up as a thought sliced through her worry. "Do you think these are the same men who tore this house to pieces when we were gone?"

"I think that they are. It appeared someone searched for something. Perhaps it was this treasure these men want." He pondered that. "It is an odd word. *Treasure.* Not money or another word for blunt. Treasure suggests something precious and valuable." He looked at the letter again, and read it aloud.

My dear sister,

I must write quickly, they say. I speak of the men who now stand around me and direct my pen. They arrived this afternoon, saying they came to take what our brother had left for them. When I expressed ignorance, they insisted on entering.

They are sure you know the whereabouts of what they speak. I hope so, because I am to go with them until you bring this treasure or its secure location to them. When you are ready to do either, you are to leave a letter with the proprietor of the Four Swans in Henley.

The one I think is the leader just said to write that you have his word that I will not be molested. Nor will I be harmed if you conclude our brother's business with him. He even promises you will have Nigel's fair share, as first agreed. If you go to the magistrate, however, you will get nothing, including me. I have explained that you are one woman alone in the world, and not given to bravery, and that you will do what you can, especially if you will get a share.

Do not worry too much for me, Eva. The leader seems somewhat intelligent, and fairly educated. As for my safety and virtue, I have my own ways of protecting myself.

Your loving sister.

"What does she mean, her own ways of protecting herself?" Gareth asked.

"Knowing Rebecca, she probably thinks the rightness and logic of her moral arguments will sway them." No sooner had she spoken than another possibility jumped to mind. No. Surely not.

She broke out of Gareth's embrace and ran up the stairs and into her bedchamber.

The trunk that held her winter wardrobe stood open. She dropped to her knees and pawed through it, hoping she was wrong. Gareth followed her in.

"It is gone," she said. "The pistol. They must have let her get some clothes, and she sneaked in and took that too. The powder, the balls—all of it is gone."

"Her kidnappers may have taken it, not her."

Perhaps, but Eva did not think so. "I hope she is not so stupid as to try and use it. She has never shot before, Gareth. She will probably load wrong and kill herself."

Strong, gentle hands lifted her to her feet. "She is not stupid, so she probably will not do anything more than tuck it under her mattress. If it makes her feel less vulnerable and frightened, it is good she has it. Now, come with me. We will go back to Albany Lodge. There we will eat something, and put our minds to solving this mystery of the treasure."

Eva allowed him to guide her down to the carriage. Once back at his house, she even let him find some food for them both. Left to her own devices, she would not have eaten, or bothered with the small talk that he used to distract her during their meal. She would have sat in her library, staring at Rebecca's letter, feeling helpless.

After dinner Gareth lit lamps in the library. He sat her down on the divan—there was no other way to describe how he drew her there, turned her, and pressed her into place. Then he collected all the pictures and stacked them away.

Finally, he poured out of a decanter and carried the glass to her.

She took it and he sat beside her.

"Brandy again?"

"You need it. Your coloring is ashen, and your eyes are like glass."

"The last time I put myself under your protection and drank your brandy, I woke in your bed. Am I in danger of that again?"

He lifted her hand so the glass pressed her lips. "Yes. Not now, not tonight, but yes."

She sipped. "I will say this for you, Gareth. You always give fair warning."

"Anything less would be dishonorable."

He waited for her to finish the brandy, then took the glass from her and set it aside. He submerged her in a warm embrace and held her while the spirits slowly untied the knots in her body.

"Tell me more about your brother."

"He was handsome. Like my sister, he took after our mother. It spoiled him, I think. He never had enough. There were arguments with my father about his debts. When he inherited, it got worse, as I told you."

"Did he have friends near here?"

She realized the questions had a purpose. "Yes. In this county and the neighboring ones. Other young men from families like ours, and better, would come by at times. Mostly he met them elsewhere. He would dress and ride out on a horse he had spent too much to buy, looking very fine. I imagine they spent their time doing what men do when alone together."

"Then he came home one night with a pistol ball in him, and he rode out no more. Were any of those friends loyal?"

She turned her memories back to the beginning of her brother's infirmity. "A few at first. Later, no. But he had changed then. He hated how that wound affected him. The ball had torn things in him, and the surgeon tore more. He was bent after that, and could not walk right, and his strength leaked away like water into sand. Finally, he did not move at all. A fever took him. He had no strength left to fight it."

She snuggled closer as she spoke. Thinking about her brother saddened her. There had been little love between them at the end. Their mutual resentments clashed silently in the icy atmosphere of his chamber.

She should have been kinder, and done better by him. She should have done better by Rebecca as well. Rebecca—

"What am I going to do, Gareth?"

"You are going to go to sleep, so you can think clearly tomorrow." He stood and raised her up and led her to the stairs.

He brought her to his bedchamber.

"I thought you said not tonight."

"I said no danger tonight. You will sleep better

here than in a strange bed. I will not wake you when I come in."

He gave her one sweet kiss before leaving.

G areth poured himself more brandy. It went without saying that he would not sleep much tonight.

He read Rebecca's letter again. No magistrates. That suited him fine. He did not want any magistrates getting in the way with their legal particulars when he found these men.

They were being bold. Rash. This treasure must have great value to them. Kidnapping was a hanging offense. The kidnapping of a gentry woman, an innocent—the entire country would want them drawn and quartered.

He had no plan, but he knew he would need help. He sat down and wrote Ives a letter, telling him about finding some of the pictures. He encouraged him to come north, for that and for another problem. He ended by saying Ives should leave his law books behind.

He threw himself on the divan, closed his eyes, and counted out the days. If this treasure or its location could not be found in three days, a crude and dangerous rescue would have to be mounted. Better to find it, in order to have some bait. Sly and calculated would far surpass violent and bloody, if there were a choice.

His mind drifted into a half sleep. Events and images from the last few days mixed and remixed at random. A line in Rebecca's letter loomed large. *I have explained that you are one woman alone in the world, and not given to bravery, and that you will do what you can, especially if you will get a share.* Clever girl, to insinuate an alliance to put them off guard. She knew Eva was brave enough but would not be alone in facing this.

He pictured Rebecca talking philosophy and radical politics until those men paid Eva to take her away. He smiled at the thought, but of course it would not be that simple.

Sleep did come then, but later, abruptly, he woke with a start. He sat and wiped his eyes. Disparate ideas in his head emerged, lined up, and forced themselves on him until he could not deny them.

A young man resentful of diminished fortune. A pack of friends riding the countryside. A treasure worth risking death for. A pistol wound, from an aim designed to kill. A painting washed with turpentine, so the underlying brushstrokes showed. Walls torn out and floor pried up and steps removed—

He looked up at the ceiling.

And a hidden cache of treasured pictures, right down the road from that young man's home.

The next night, Eva woke before dawn with the weight and warmth of Gareth behind her. His arm covered her in a sleeping embrace. He had never come the night before, so his presence surprised her.

She turned carefully, so as not to wake him. She

moved until she faced him, with her nose at his chest and her body against him and his breath in her hair. She laid her palm on his hip.

The intimacy relaxed her. Sleep the last two nights had been fitful, but now it descended like a soft cloud. When she woke again, light showed through the drapes. She lay there, not wanting to disturb the peace. The longer she did, the more time before the day brought back the sickening worry.

He nuzzled her head, making her scalp tingle. She wondered if he would do more than that. She would not mind.

"My brother will arrive today, I think," he said.

"I should return to my house."

"I do not want you there alone. Better if Ives stays at an inn in the village."

"If he knows I am staying here, there seems little point in that." Other than Ives, only Harold would know, however. Gareth had given Erasmus things to do elsewhere, so he would not be on the property.

"He will be more comfortable in the village. This house is too spare for him." He nuzzled again. "Eva, I think I know where the treasure is."

She looked up, angling her head so she could see his face. "You do?" She threw her arms around him and squeezed hard in her excitement. "Where? Can we get our hands on it quickly?"

"Eva, you are not going to like it. I put off telling you yesterday, but I am convinced I am right."

His tone, too kind, too gentle, made her joy disappear. "Tell me. I may not like it, but I pray you are correct."

He told her a peculiar story of lords packing up art and sending it north, and of that art disappearing at some time before they went to retrieve it after the war.

"The pictures in my attic are part of it. Perhaps a third."

"This was the art you searched for?"

"Yes. The question is how it got up there. For now, that is the only question, but of course another is— where is the rest?"

"Do you fear someone will think you took it? And put some of it here?"

"That is always a danger. I did not, of course. I think I know who did." He turned her on her back, and rose up on his arm to look down at her. "A treasure, Eva. Those pictures are worth thousands. When your house was invaded, they pulled out steps to see the space underneath. They pried off wallboards, to see if anything lay behind. Those men did not seek something small, like jewels. Or money. They went to the attics, your attics, because they did not guess that what they sought was in mine instead."

She followed his thinking. "You think the treasure that will save my sister is right above us now. It is the pictures."

"Yes."

"I wish you were right, but I do not think you are. If you are correct, that means my brother was involved and put them there. He was not a thief."

He caressed her face. "It may have been a prank gone awry. He may have disapproved, and gotten shot while trying to stop them, then could think of no way to return what he had without implicating himself."

She glared up at him. "You spent all of yesterday working out those excuses, didn't you? I don't think you believe any of that. Perhaps you should share what you do believe."

He fell on his back beside her. She was glad. She did not want to look at him now.

"I think your brother and some friends learned where the pictures were stored. I think they found a way in, and moved them to another place, to wait until the war ended and they could be sold abroad. I think your brother got impatient due to his financial state and took what is in the attic and put it here because no one lived here anymore. He took more than his fair share. Either then, or when they found out, I think he was shot, by either a guard or an accomplice. Probably the latter."

And because of his wound, he could not sell anything. The pictures just sat there, a half a mile away.

"Are you going to tell your brother this story?"

"Yes."

She sat up and turned so her back faced him. She reached for her garments. "You will impugn my brother's good name without any proof that the treasure they seek are these paintings. You will risk my sister to this bizarre theory."

She slid off the bed to go dress somewhere else. His grip on her arm stopped her. "Remember how your paintings were ruined, Eva? The views you had painted years ago? How they had been wiped with turpentine? Someone checked to make sure you had not painted over some of these pictures and hidden them in plain sight."

"That was just criminals being destructive."

"A lot of trouble for mere destruction. A knife would have been faster and more satisfying."

"Nigel died with nothing left but his good name. You are wrong about him. I pray your brother explains the error of your thinking to you, since you will not listen to me." She jerked her arm loose. Clutching her clothes, she strode out to find another chamber in which to be away from him.

As soon as Gareth heard the horses, he knew Ives had not come alone. He opened the door to see two stallions galloping up the lane. The riders reined in and dismounted.

"Lance insisted on coming," Ives said. "He decided an adventure was at hand, and town was boring him."

From the looks of things, Lance hoped for a violent adventure. Three pistols and a musket were tied to his saddle. After a nod of greeting, he set about removing them. One by one he threw the pistols to Gareth, then carried the musket to the door. "You told him to leave his law books behind. I know what that means, even if he pretends he does not." He passed into the house.

Harold took the pistols out of Gareth's hands. "I'll

be cleaning these, sir. But first I will ride to the village and inform the inn that two chambers are now needed, not one."

"Good man." He had confided the basics to Harold, whose reaction to the kidnapping had been fierce and dramatic. Such things did not occur in peaceful English villages.

"The lady will stay again tonight, sir?"

"Until her sister returns, she will remain here."

Gareth went to the library. Ives already lounged on the divan. Lance prowled the first level, peering through doorways, taking stock of the property. "It is better than I remember. As a boy I found this place old and musty, but now it seems comfortable enough," he said on joining them.

"You should have seen it two months ago," Gareth said. "Even the roof was not sound."

"It is only comfortable because Gareth has been making those improvements I told you about," Ives said.

"Better to spend the blunt that way than on bloodsucking lawyers," Lance said. "Nothing personal meant by that, Ives."

"Apologies accepted."

Lance threw himself into one of the chairs and gazed up at the ceiling moldings. "It is just as well that I never favored this lodge. Otherwise, what with the good hunting land attached, I might be tempted to—"

"Which you will not be, however, having already told the solicitor to drop the matter," Ives said.

It was the first Gareth had heard of that. Under different circumstances, he would have celebrated. Today, with Eva remaining invisible and with Rebecca in danger, he only reacted with allowing a corner of his soul to know some contentment that he was officially a man of property.

Gareth brought out port and brandy and told them to help themselves. "Before you ask, there is only one servant, and he is taking care of your guns and horses."

"I'm not above doing for myself." Lance poured himself a good measure of port. "So, whom are we going to kill?"

Ives closed his eyes and shook his head. "No one, I am sure."

"Hopefully, no one," Gareth corrected. That got their attention.

First he explained the discovery of the paintings, and Eva's unwitting involvement in the production of the forgeries. A long silence greeted the end of that half of the tale.

"If that stationer Stevenson sold some to families in Birmingham, we must get the names, and contact them for the particulars of those sales," Ives said. "That will prove neither he nor Miss Russell attempted to pass off her works as originals."

"My thinking exactly," Gareth said.

"No one has asked my opinion," Lance began. "However—"

"We knew we could count on you to give it anyway," Ives said.

"As I will. Not that either of you needs me to point out that it is essential to find the rest of the stolen works now. Otherwise, Gareth here becomes a convenient target of accusations. We have enough of that already, so it would be best all around if any revelation he has been in possession of a third of those works comes at the same time my fellow lords are celebrating the return of all of them."

"Not that we have any doubts about you, of course," Ives said to Gareth.

"None at all," Lance said. "Of course."

"The lady, however—" Ives's eyebrows rose.

"She is telling the truth. I know her and she was ignorant from beginning to end," Gareth said.

"Again, finding all of the pictures will make that question a moot point," Lance said.

"It is already moot. I am saying it is. Her brother, now deceased, may not have been ignorant, however." He described the invasion of her house two times now, and let them read Rebecca's letter.

"As you can see," he concluded. "We now have a line that leads to the men who executed the theft. Find them, and we will find the rest of the pictures."

Silence. Lance and Ives sipped their drinks.

"My plan is simple. First we need to get the girl back. I will leave a letter at the Four Swans to arrange that, and bring the pictures. You two will lay in wait at the inn, and follow whoever comes for the letter back to their lair. Once the girl is safe, we will pay a call on them, and retrieve the rest of the collection."

Ives set his glass down, rose, and strolled to the window, deep in thought. "Where is the lady now?"

"Right here. In the garden, I think."

"It is best if we know for certain where she is from now on. It was wise to confine her here."

"I did not confine her. I brought her here to protect her."

"Whatever your reasons, the move was prudent."

Gareth did not care for the expression on Ives's face. Normally one saw that scowl beneath a white wig in a courtroom when he served as the Crown's prosecutor.

"He thinks you may have interpreted your evidence incorrectly, Gareth," Lance said, his gaze also on Ives. "I confess that I wonder too. The lady may not be so innocent. She is at the heart of everything you have told us. Do not pretend you have not seen that."

"It may appear so at first telling, but her role has been unintentional on all points. You can trust my judgment on that, or you can ride back to London. I do not need to spend my time protecting her from the two of you as well as the others."

"If the rest of the pictures are not found—"

"Then you are to keep her name out of it entirely, Ives. Let suspicion fall on me, if that is how it must be."

Ives and Lance exchanged long looks.

Ives did not press the point further. "Let us say we learn where the rest of the art is hidden. Do you think to ride up to the door and ask for it?"

"Why not?"

"We should ignore what that letter said, and bring the magistrate."

"If we inform him, he will want to bring fifty men with him. Word of that will travel ahead of us, and we may end up with nothing."

Ives rubbed his brow. "We do not want fifty, but it might be wise to have more than three." He looked to Lance for agreement.

Lance shrugged. "I've five pistols with me. I am expecting immediate surrender if we are well armed."

Ives sighed. "Let us have the lady join us so she can write the letter."

Gareth found Eva in the garden. She sat on an old bench near the rebuilt section of wall. Her sketchbook lay on her lap, unopened.

"They have arrived?" she asked, not shifting her gaze from where she stared down the garden to a small orchard at its back. Blossoms had formed on the fruit trees. A few more warm days, and there would be a haze of white and pink back there.

"They are waiting in the library. We need you to write the letter to be left at the inn."

She did not respond, or look at him. He waited.

"Did neither one of them question those copies I made?" she asked.

"No. They know your character as I do."

"You are lying. You seek to protect me by serving up my brother instead."

He sat beside her on the bench. "Do you want me to make you the criminal, Eva? Do you want to spare your brother's name enough for that?" He took her hand between his. "I will do what I can to keep his role from being well known, but they name him as their partner with this bold move they have made. I will not pretend they did not, because it would be convenient or might end your coldness toward me."

Her lashes fluttered. Her gaze lowered to the shrubbery and flowers, then to nothing. "I am angry with you, for forcing the truth on me."

"I tried alternatives. I had good excuses to offer last night."

"It appears we know each other too well for me to believe them. I am so embarrassed, Gareth. For him, and for me. To now face the duke, and Lord Ywain—"

"They have nothing but sympathy and concern for you, Eva. And relief, that we can settle this quickly and your sister will be back home." He stood, still holding her hand. "Come and write this letter." He picked up her sketchbook and tucked it under his arm.

She finally looked at him. As they walked to the house, she favored him with a small, rueful smile. "Whoever would have guessed that in seeking a few moments of wicked pleasure, I would find such a good friend."

He gave her hand a reassuring kiss. *Whoever would have guessed.*

CHAPTER 25

Eva sat in her library, trying to read. Three lamps burned, so anyone looking inside could see she was alone. They could also see ten paintings propped against the walls, their colors glowing like melted jewels.

The plan was simple and, she hoped, not at all dangerous. She had carried her letter into the tavern all alone, and left it for the proprietor, with nothing untoward occurring. In it she acknowledged she had the treasure, expressed relief someone had finally come for it, and declared she would, of course, trade it for her sister. They were to come tonight and take the pictures that exceeded her brother's share. If they did not bring Rebecca with them, she had threatened to raise the hue and cry.

She tried to contain her fears, but they chewed away her confidence as time passed. No matter how often she reminded herself she was in no danger, that three armed men roamed outside and would watch everything, she could not remain calm. If Rebecca were not in the middle of this, it might be different. If Rebecca had not taken the pistol, having it nearby might have helped too.

There was no telling how long she would have to wait. She tried reading again.

She had turned ten pages when she heard a gentle commotion outside. Soft voices and quiet footsteps approached the house. She bent forward so she could see the reception hall. The door opened and Rebecca's yellow dress appeared. Three sets of boots followed her in.

She stood, and Rebecca ran to her. While they embraced, Rebecca whispered, "I've the pistol right here in my shawl. They don't. Have pistols, that is."

Eva looked past her to the three men. One might be thought a gentleman on a good day, but drink had turned his skin ruddy and eyes shallow, even though he was probably only thirty years old. The other two were working men. She recognized the biggest one as one of the strangers she had noticed in the area the last couple of months. The other, smaller one's presence shocked her.

"Erasmus? How are you involved in this?" she demanded.

He gave her one of his grins. "Just making sure no one gets hurt, Miss Russell, least of all you or Miss Rebecca. Some of these sort forget their manners at times."

"You can picture my surprise to see him upon being removed from the carriage that took me away," Rebecca said. "I am very disappointed in you, Erasmus."

"Life has a way of doing that, Miss. Disappointing one, that is," he said.

The gentleman ignored them all while he peered at the pictures.

"They call him Crawley," Rebecca whispered. "Appropriate, since he makes my skin crawl when he looks at me."

Right now Mr. Crawley examined the pictures like someone who knew what he was about. These were originals, not her copies, in the event the thieves had very good eyes for art.

"Where are the others," he asked. "There should be more. Twenty or so."

"The others are my brother's share. I was told I could keep them."

"The shares are not a matter of number, but value. These here are the smallest, and not one third the value, so the rest is not all yours. Not that offering that was agreed to by me to start. I will need the others too."

"My brother insisted the rest were ours. He was very clear on that when he told me the location of the art while on his deathbed. Therefore, I arranged for their sale."

Crawley's expression hardened. "You sold them? That was most unwise."

"I said I arranged for their sale. This was recent, and they are not yet sold as I understand it."

"Then I ask again, Miss Russell. Where are they?"

"I expect they are still in the possession of the agent who will facilitate the sale. Mr. Gareth Fitzallen."

Crawley's colorless eyes reflected astonishment, then humor. "Fitzallen! Aylesbury's mongrel? Now that is delicious. I expect it is back to town for me to speak with him. I regret your sister must accompany me until the share you keep is indeed fair."

He gestured to the large, rustic man who had stood silently through the entire exchange, and at Erasmus.

"Best if you come, Miss Rebecca," Erasmus said.

"I do not think so. I will stay here."

Crawley sighed with exasperation, and gestured toward her while glancing to the big man. Those heavy boots took two steps.

Eva dug into the bundled shawl and brought out the pistol. "Neither my sister nor I will be kept as a hostage in this misunderstanding. Go and speak with Mr. Fitzallen if you must. You do not need to travel to London since he lives right up the road. The rest of my brother's share is there, awaiting transport to the coast."

The pistol stopped the big man, who appeared confused at seeing the weapon. He scowled at Crawley, as if the rules in some game had unexpectedly changed without warning. Crawley eyed Eva then the pistol. "I've yet to see a woman hit her aim with one of those. Hell, women don't even know how to load them."

"I practiced until I could, after your men tore my property to pieces. I can overlook that if our business is completed with fair dealing, sir, but I will not allow my sister to be at a stranger's mercy, especially if I have concluded that stranger's honor is dubious."

An ugly aura poured off Crawley. One malevolent

and dangerous. Eva pushed Rebecca behind herself and held the pistol as steady as she could.

"Fitzallen has a buyer on the Continent?" Crawley asked.

"He does. It took some time to arrange, but all is settled, he told me."

He appeared to think that over. It was hard to tell. His slack face and vacant eyes made his thoughts and considerations impossible to know.

"Just up the road, you said he was."

"Barely a half mile. You cannot miss it. Erasmus will take you there. He knows the house well."

"You had better not be lying to me. I find that house empty or those pictures gone, I'll not be worrying about anyone's honor then, least of all mine."

"You disappoint me, Mr. Crawley," Rebecca said. "After all our conversations about moral philosophy, for you to make such a crude threat is most disheartening."

Crawley rolled his eyes, then pointed at Eva. "You come with me, and leave her and her reforming notions here. I'll be needing you to tell Fitzallen that you agree to what I want." He turned to the big man. "You stay here with her, Wiggins."

"Hell, I don't want to listen to her either!"

"Then don't listen. Just don't let her or these pictures leave."

Eva handed Rebecca the pistol. Rebecca smiled at the big man, and sat down. He sat down also, overwhelming the chair. He did not look happy.

As Eva left, she heard Rebecca speak. "Good and

bad all come down to whether we have souls, Mr. Wiggins. Unless we do, the question of our goodness has no meaning. When I asked your opinion of that yesterday, you never answered. Allow me to elucidate what various philosophers have argued on that point."

"She changed the damned plan," Ives said as he and Gareth mounted their horses.

They had heard her conversation with Crawley while pressed against the house below a window. "Hers is better," Gareth said. "Brilliant. He will come right to us now. If I play the cards well, we will learn where the other pictures are. He is sure to want me to include them in this foreign sale if I can."

Ives reached over and grabbed the bridle so he could not ride. "Let us have a right understanding. Neither Crawley nor that scrawny one leaves. Lance will take that big one as soon as the way is clear, but I don't trust the big fellow to know what we need. Whatever game you play, it does not include any of them walking away tonight."

Gareth agreed, although it would limit his options. Left to his own choice, he would dangle a quick foreign sale of the entire cache of pictures in order to get hold of the rest. Ives, however, feared Crawley bolting. He assumed Ives believed that, if necessary, Crawley could be made to talk.

He was sure Erasmus could be.

He thanked the sound instincts that had kept Erasmus

ignorant of this business and away from Albany Lodge
most of the last fortnight.

They tore up the road at a gallop, knowing a carriage would follow soon. Crawley had left it at the end
of the lane and walked up to the house. As he rode,
Gareth paced out Eva's way back to that carriage. He
and Ives turned the bend just around the time he
expected the equipage to roll.

"I'll take the horses," Ives said when they reined in
at the lodge. "I'll come in through the garden and
make my way up so I am not far from the library.
Leave the door open so I can hear."

Gareth entered the library, lit two lamps, pulled
out a book, and shed his frock coat. He placed his
pistol in the drawer of a nearby table. He had just settled in to read when he heard the carriage arrive.

Hurried steps sounded on the stairs from below. Not
Ives. Harold appeared, pulling on his coats and comb-
ing his hair with his fingers. He stuck his head in the
library. "Your brothers, sir? Or visitors?"

Gareth cursed. He had clear forgotten that Harold
had stayed tonight, the better to serve the duke and
lord visiting by day. "Visitors, I believe." He had to
decide fast whether to trust Harold, or send him back
down, to be dealt with by Ives. "I need you to show no
surprise when you open that door. Just bring them
here, then go below. Lord Ywain will be there. Do
whatever he says."

Good soldier that he was, Harold did not even

express surprise at the odd command. He straightened and disappeared.

The door opened. Muffled sounds of conversation. Erasmus laughed. Footsteps, and Eva entered the library, followed by Erasmus and another man.

Eva introduced the stranger as Mr. Crawley.

"Crawley," Gareth repeated. "Aren't you the cousin of Viscount Demmiwood?"

"I am. I likewise know who you are. The lady says you are holding some art of hers. By an unfortunate misunderstanding a few of my own pictures got mixed in with them."

"The hell you say." He scowled at Eva. "This is most irregular, Miss Russell. Had Mr. Crawley become aware of this a fortnight hence, retrieving his property would have been difficult and expensive."

"I cannot blame you for being vexed, Mr. Fitzallen. I also am relieved this was discovered in good time."

Gareth smiled at Crawley. "The pictures are all crated for shipment, but if you tell me which ones are yours, I will—"

"Well, now, not so fast. You've a buyer for all of them, it sounds like. No need to change plans. Just when you receive payment, you can split off mine."

"That would certainly simplify matters." Gareth invited Eva and Crawley to sit, then returned to his chair. "Now, which ones are yours?"

Crawley's gaze drifted to the decanters on one bookcase. He pulled his attention back. "The Annibale

Carracci is one. Then the Claude landscape, and the Titian Danaë."

Gareth swallowed the urge to throttle the man. He had just identified three of the most valuable pictures. Along with the ten he already thought Eva was returning, he was probably not leaving her with anything resembling a fair share.

"Are you sure you agree to this, Miss Russell?" he asked.

"Of course. Mr. Crawley is better familiar with how the collection was divided than I am." She looked over. Her eyes all but said, *It doesn't matter. Remember?* Which it didn't, he reminded himself.

"Then that is how it will be."

Crawley chewed his upper lip for a moment. "Would this collector be interested in others? I've more, you see. Important works."

"I am sure he would be. However, if you have other pictures of this quality, you can do better selling here in England. It was only the lack of sufficient provenance for her pictures, and the need for a fast conclusion, that led me to advise a foreign sale to Miss Russell."

"I, too, would prefer a fast sale, all at once, much as she is doing."

Gareth pretended to ponder that. "I had intended to transport these soon. There will not be time to write and confirm that he also wants yours. I think he will, but—"

"If you are going with them, I would send mine as well, and travel along. If this collector does not want them, another might."

"Oh, certainly. If they are all you say, I am sure another would."

"Mr. Fitzallen does not broker anything but the best," Eva said. "He came highly recommended. Why, he would not even talk particulars with me until he had seen the pictures."

"What Miss Russell says is true. I would have to see what you have. Is the collection nearby?" Gareth hoped Ives was listening carefully and appreciated how damned close they were to being led to the rest of the art.

"A day's ride. Maybe two." Crawley's eyes narrowed rather longingly on the decanters again. "It would be better for me to bring several of the works here."

Not close enough. Damn. "You do own all of them free and clear? No estate encumbrances, for example? I once wasted almost a year on a collection that it turned out required the death of the man's father before it could be sold."

"As it happens, all the required deaths have taken place." Crawley found that very amusing.

Eva glared with dangerous eyes. "Are you speaking of my brother?"

Crawley's mirth died. "No, dear lady, I am not."

Eva did not believe him. Neither did Gareth. Crawley twitched nervously. He stood. "I will remain in touch, Fitzallen. I expect you to as well. Once the pictures are sold, we can settle up. If all goes well, we can see about the others."

"I trust my household will be spared any more intrusions," Eva said.

Crawley faced her fully and made a bow. "You have my word." He turned to go, and froze. The way out was blocked. Ives stood there, pistol at the ready.

Crawley pivoted, his gaze desperately searching for another exit. Gareth shook his head, and brandished his own pistol.

Ives walked over, placed a firm hold on Crawley's shoulder, and pressed him down into his chair. "There are many more questions about those pictures before you go anywhere."

Through the doorway, Harold could be seen marching to the entrance with his own pistol in hand and an uncompromising look on his face.

"Gareth," Eva said. "Erasmus remained in the carriage."

Gareth reached the door just as Harold raised his aim at a figure darting into the dark.

"Don't kill him, Harold."

"If you so command, sir."

The crack of a shot sounded, then a cry of shock and pain. Gareth and Harold walked the short distance to where Erasmus writhed on the ground, holding his leg. "You damned broke it," he screamed.

"Be glad you have the life left to complain," Harold said. "In the army we dealt with turncoats better. Why Mr. Fitzallen here wanted you spared is beyond me."

Gareth reached down and dragged Erasmus up by his arm. "I wanted him alive because he likes to talk. Don't you, Erasmus?"

CHAPTER 26

Talk Erasmus did. All the time that Harold cleaned, bound, and braced his leg in the kitchen, he poured out what he knew to Eva and Gareth.

He had come late to the scheme, unfortunately, and did not know the names of all involved. Eva assumed that Lord Ywain was persuading Mr. Crawley to fill in those details upstairs.

She listened instead to how Nigel had recruited Erasmus to help retrieve some property stored some distance away, and how they drove a wagon there over almost three days and moved many flat crates onto it. She heard how another man arrived as they drove away, and exchanged pistol fire with Nigel, who took that ball in his side.

"Cursing he was," Erasmus said while he watched

Harold handle him none too gently. Sweat dampened his hair, the result of terror and pain. "Cursing those who first expected him to wait forever to turn the goods into blunt, then lied to him and said it had all gone up in flames so there'd be nothing to sell after all. He guessed it was a lie, he said, and he needed money."

Eva wanted to accuse him of lying, only right now Erasmus was too frightened to lie. Her heart sickened. Nigel had helped in the theft of the pictures, just as Mr. Crawley had implied.

"Did you help him store the crates once you returned to Langdon's End?" Gareth asked,

Erasmus shook his head. "He left me off on the other side of town. I told him I should help, that with that wound he would only kill himself dragging the big ones off the cart and around. He wouldn't hear me."

Dragging those crates up to that attic probably had made the wound worse, Eva thought. It possibly did kill him, eventually.

"How did you come to be with this man tonight?" Gareth asked.

Erasmus flushed red. "Came upon them the first time they went into Miss Russell's house. She asked me to check on things every morning, and that morning these two men were there. Wiggins, that big one, and another one. Tearing it apart, they were. They flipped me five shillings and just continued on. I'd no idea it had to do with those crates from that night. I told them there was nothing to steal, but they didn't listen, and I couldn't stop them. Then, the other day, Mr. Crawley was in the village with Wiggins, who pointed me out, and there was another five shillings in my hand."

"Did you recognize Crawley from that night you helped Nigel Russell?" Gareth asked.

"I didn't see him there. He may have been, though. I was in a wagon with the cattle under Mr. Russell's whip, wasn't I?"

Just then Harold pulled the rope to tie the splint in place. Erasmus screamed in pain. "Hell, you don't have to try and kill me! We're friends, for mercy's sake."

"Friends? For years you've been smirking about some big secret, and I go to find it was this. You're no friend of mine if you deal in with such as that blackguard above us." Harold gave the rope another pull for good measure. "That should fix you fine until the surgeon cuts out the ball. You'll be fit as a fiddle for the gallows."

"Gallows!"

"What do you think becomes of them that kidnap girls from their homes, you fool?"

"I didn't. I insisted I go so she wouldn't be scared. I thought that Wiggins fellow might get ideas, and I could keep her safe."

"You tell that to the court, and maybe they'll believe you better'n I do." Harold walked out in disgust.

Gareth offered Erasmus his arm. "You will have to stand now, and come outside. There will be other questions."

Eva helped Erasmus too. Together she and Gareth got him out to the garden. Mr. Crawley already sat there, firm-jawed and resolute. Harold stood nearby, weapon at the ready. Lord Ywain sat twenty paces away, his pistol on the bench beside him. When he saw them emerge, he walked over.

"He is not speaking. Not a word. Moreover, he finds something about this very amusing."

"It does him no good to cooperate," Gareth said. "To give you the location of the other pictures would only prove he had taken them, after all."

"We need that information, however."

Gareth examined Crawley's self-satisfied expression. "He waits to hear that you will let him go once the pictures are retrieved. Their location is his only card, but it is an ace."

Lord Ywain's face turned to stone. "Are you suggesting that I—"

"Do not pretend you never have before, if it were the only way to learn what you needed."

Lord Ywain looked at Eva. "I apologize that you are hearing us bargain with justice, especially since it is your family's justice that will be denied if we do this. Say the word and we will settle for a partial loaf regarding those missing paintings."

Eva looked at Crawley. He had decided it would be a game to the end. She wondered if it had been a ball from his pistol that condemned her to five years of penurious drudgery with a bitter, melancholy Nigel.

Did it matter? She wanted this over. Finished. She wanted Crawley and the paintings gone. She wanted her life back, so she could look to the future, not the past.

"If you can make him leave England, I do not care

what bargain you strike. But if he goes free, so do Erasmus and the others."

"See if you can find out who the other gentlemen were," Gareth added. "I doubt he will tell you, but try."

Lord Ywain paced over to Mr. Crawley.

"You do not have to agree to this," Gareth said to her. "We could try to beat it out of him."

"Your brother would never agree to that."

"You do not know my brother very well."

She had to smile. "My generosity is not pure, I am ashamed to say. I am hoping that if Mr. Crawley is shown mercy, I will be as well. I am trusting that in light of so much bald thievery, your brother will not care much whether I copied those pictures with innocent intentions, or deliberately forged them."

"I think he has forgotten about that entirely."

"For now, perhaps. But he will remember it soon."

"He will not care about that. It is not part of this mission." Gareth took her hand and drew her farther from the others. "They will leave soon. When they do, stay here."

"My sister—"

"Have them take her to the Neville sisters. She should do normal things today, not turn the remaining hours into a monument to her ordeal." He raised her hand and kissed it. "Stay here with me."

She closed her eyes so nothing distracted her from how that kiss touched her like the stroke of a velvet brush. Happy pleasure moved in her, reminding her that her own normal had been wonderful recently.

"I fear that if I agree, I will be in danger again," she said.

"Stay anyway."

His slow smile and warm gaze promised the best danger.

"I will go in now," she said. "Make what excuses you will for me."

"Hell of a thing," Ives said. He did not appear happy with his conversation with Crawley. "He only thinks he knows where the rest of the pictures are, and even then in a general way. According to him, after the paintings were stolen and stored, the leader informed them that a fire destroyed all of it. Crawley was suspicious, but indeed the location was reduced to cinders when he went to check."

"How did he know Nigel had some of them?"

"He only discovered some of the paintings survived when he also stumbled across one of Miss Russell's copies three months ago in a Birmingham house he visited, and realized Nigel must have taken some before the fire. Or after, if the fire was a ruse. As for that general location where he suspects the rest of the paintings are now stored, he will not give it to me. Unless he is paid a handsome sum along with going free."

"That won't do."

"No. Nor will he give the names of the other gentlemen involved, although he says that leader is dead now. He will gladly hand over the Wiggins and such, of course. It did start out as a joke, by the way. He learned about the movement of the art from overhearing Demmiwood talk of it. He and some friends from these parts, a few years after the last Duke of Devonshire died, drew away the butler on a ruse and marched it all out again."

"I expect eventually it stopped being a joke. Probably when one of them learned the value of certain old pictures."

"They fell out over it. Some, like Russell and Crawley, wanted desperately to sell. Both were young and in debt at the time. Others, including an unnamed gentleman who held considerable sway over the others, this leader Crawley speaks of, did not. That is why Crawley thinks that fire was a ruse. That other gentleman ensured he got his way by telling them there was nothing to sell due to it, but Nigel accused him of lying. When Crawley recently chanced upon one of Miss Russell's copies, that proved the paintings still existed somewhere, and he assumed that copy meant she knew where they were."

That unnamed gentleman probably knew a large sale of art was easier said than done, Gareth guessed. Crawley would have learned that quickly enough. Had Ives not been given this mission and drawn his bastard brother into it, would one day Crawley have approached Mr. Fitzallen to obtain help with that sale?

"What are you smiling at?" Ives asked.

"A bit of potential irony. So, all is as set as it will be, it appears."

"In exchange for his freedom, he will take me to

where it was stored before the fire. The mere notion of doing so had him laughing for some reason."

"Why not see if that big fellow Wiggins knows too? Then you won't have to bargain. Lance may have terrified Wiggins enough he told everything he knows."

"That is a good idea. We should go find out. Erasmus can ride atop the carriage, the lady inside, Crawley can walk, and you and I will take our horses."

Ives began walking away.

"I think I will leave the rest to you," Gareth said, stopping him. "And the lady is resting, I believe. She is tired, being of a delicate nature."

Ives turned and walked back. "Feeling faint, was she?"

"Completely undone by the drama."

"And you intend to stay behind and watch over her health?"

"Someone has to."

"She has a sister. What are we to do about her?"

"Take her to her friends in the village. The Neville sisters. She will like that."

Ives laughed lightly. "For the ladies' sake, and their reputations, my intention is the village learn nothing of this kidnapping. I trust they also will be discreet?"

"Miss Russell is the soul of discretion. I am sure her sister will see the rightness of it too."

Once more Ives walked away. "I will come when all is finished and tell you where we found what pictures could be retrieved, if we find any at all."

"Better yet, write me a letter."

CHAPTER 27

✇

The spring breeze drifted over Eva, stirring her anticipation. She lay immobile and listened to the sounds also entering through the window she had set ajar.

Voices and boots moved around the house to the front. Horses grunted and stomped, and a carriage door opened. Erasmus exclaimed in pain, and Harold cursed him. Then the carriage rolled, its sounds diminishing with each moment.

She listened, waiting. Finally, bootsteps on the boards below paced slowly into the library. A pause, then more steps coming to the stairs. She imagined Gareth noticing her bonnet on the chair in the reception hall.

Up the stairs those boots came. The sound of each footfall aroused her more. She cast aside the sheet

that covered her, so he would know at once that she
wanted all the danger he could provide.

He did not enter the bedchamber. Instead he went
into the dressing room. She heard him in there, moving
around. He made her wait a long time. All the while her
desire tightened until she was hot enough that the breeze
tantalized her body with its cool, feathery caresses.

Finally he entered the chamber, his hair damp from
washing, his eyes full of passion's depths. He was naked,
too, just like her. Naked and beautiful and aroused.

He came over and stood beside the bed. "You are
impatient."

"Yes."

"I think I will make you wait, anyway." He caressed
two fingertips down the side of her face. The slow
stroke continued along her jaw, then her neck. Her
breath quickened as he touched lower yet, up the swell
of her breast. When he grazed her tight nipple, her
back arched in reaction to the exquisite sensation. He
dallied there until she writhed and moaned and gave
up trying to contain the pleasure.

"No more demands that I not touch you, Eva, or
that we retreat into friendship. No more being good
and careful."

She was beyond arguing. She would agree to anything. Yet not only her body accepted the command.
Her heart nodded as well, secure and sure that love
left her no alternative. No more denial of what now
centered her world.

His fingertips meandered again, down her body.

Despite how her whole consciousness licked at the pleasure, she likewise wanted him to know such sweet torture. She reached over and used her own light caress on his erection, running her fingers up the shaft.

She had imagined making love to him many times since their last encounter in London. She saw herself doing it properly with great sophistication. She had not pictured it like this, so passive, almost languid. She had been a goddess of Venus in those dreams.

She swung her legs around and sat on the side of the bed. She took him in her hands more purposefully. She circled the shaft with one hand and used the other to caress the tip. "Like this?"

"Yes." His voice came ragged and low. "Damn, yes."

She liked that note in his voice. Loved that he stood in front of her, feet widely placed as he sought not to sway. Loved how he let her learn on her own what made his teeth grit and affirmations come out like muttered curses.

He stepped closer yet and reached below her arms to tease her breasts. The power and impatience claimed her again. Control trembled out of her. She kissed his stomach while she caressed him. Kissed him in gratitude for the pleasure and so much else. And it seemed very natural to move the kisses to the tip of his erection.

His reaction told her how much he wanted that. His quiet moans guided her explorations. Tension coiled tighter in him until she suddenly found herself falling back on the bed. He spread her thighs wide and lifted both her hips until they angled off the bed. He thrust

into her three times. Each time his head went back
and his eyes closed as if he felt the same as she did,
that this joining relieved an unbearable hunger. Then
he hitched her legs around his hips and took her,
watching while she cried out, and begged for more.

"I should go home. Rebecca will be alone."

"She is visiting the sisters. Harold will bring
her back, and wait. There is no need to go yet."

"You worked that out neatly."

"I thought so."

She sat up and scooted to the edge of the bed. "I
am hungry at least. I will go find us some food." She
reached for her chemise and pulled it on.

"I'll come. The day is fair. We will dine out in the
sun." He went to the dressing room and pulled on
some clothes.

When he returned, she looked down on her half-
naked self, then at him in nothing but trousers again.
"There will be no one to see us out in the sun, but it
still seems a wicked thing to do."

"You like wicked, so that should please you."

Down the stairs they went. He spied her bonnet
and sketchbook in the reception hall and picked them
up on the way. He set the bonnet on her head. "That
will spare your complexion."

She felt the bonnet, looked again at her dishabille,
and laughed.

In the kitchen Eva set about making up a tray to take

outside. Gareth idly paged through her sketchbook, flipping back and forth. He found a drawing she had done of him while he slept. She must have done it that afternoon in London. It was very good. Like her copies, it showed a keen eye and steady hand. If given half a chance she would probably become a very good artist.

He flipped more, and the pages opened at a most peculiar drawing. "What is this?"

Eva looked over. "Oh, that. Nigel did that. There are a few others there. While first recovering, he proved too restless to handle. He did not even sleep well, but he could not walk far or rest enough to read. I suggested he try sketching. That was the sorry result. Still, it occupied him for several days at least." She reached up for plates.

Gareth tucked the sketchbook under his arm, took the tray, and followed Eva out to the garden. They made their luncheon at a rustic table under a budding tree. He puzzled over Nigel's odd drawings while he munched on ham and hard eggs.

"I think it is a view," he said. "A primitive one. Old maps were done this way."

She stretched to look. "Perhaps. He had no training. That is how a child would draw, mixing up perspectives like that. However, now that you mention it, I think that is the view out our back window. That would be the far garden wall there, and these must be the trees."

He turned the page to see more of the same, only much more elaborate. This view had buildings. A memory, perhaps.

He paged on, to Eva's recent work. She had been busy. While he studied her drawings, however, something about Nigel's kept prodding at him. Suddenly he knew what it was. He went back to the second one.

He knew this place. He identified the house and walls and ponds and hills. The outbuildings lined up exactly as they should. Crude little horses even stood in their correct pasture up near the edge of the page.

"Eva, did your brother know someone connected to my father's family?"

"I don't think so." She came and peered over his shoulder. "Why do you think he did?"

"Because this looks like Merrywood. Even the drawing of the house is a childlike rendering of it, with the hipped roof and rusticated basement level."

"If you say so. I always assumed he was trying to replicate my views, with poor results."

It was not the main house that had attracted Nigel's best attention. Rather the rendering of the outbuildings showed great care in details and placement. He had included a few tenant cottages to the east as well, and had even drawn the roads leading to them. He had mapped the estate fairly well. One of the cottages showed no wagons or chickens near it. Vacant, then. Nigel had graced this cottage with a thick dark line beneath it. To the left of it on the same road another little cottage appeared, only with half a roof and darkened walls, as if a fire had destroyed it.

He stared at that cottage.

One of the gentlemen involved in the theft had died

recently. The one who held great sway over the others. The one who had probably faked a fire to convince his comrades the paintings were gone and unavailable for sale.

The one who had a burned tenant cottage in view of his main house, that he had neglected to rebuild or repair for over five years? Gareth remembered noting just such an eyesore as he approached Merrywood.

Percy, you thieving blackguard.

No wonder Crawley thought it so amusing that he and Ives were the ones to be tracking down those pictures. How he would laugh when, after buying all he could by dangling the promise of more information, he finally took Ives to Ives's own family home as the most likely place to find the rest of the collection.

Eva rose and strolled over to some shrubbery. Early bulbs had sent up flowers in front of the greenery. She bent over to pluck a few. Her chemise rose in back as she did, revealing the lower swells of her bottom. Gareth closed the sketchbook, far more interested now in his lover's charming eroticism.

He would write to Ives and tell him to search Merrywood and its cottages for any pictures the family should not have. He would not have to tell Ives anything else. With a few inquiries it would probably be learned that Nigel and Crawley at times rode out to drink in country taverns with Percy, Duke of Aylesbury, a man known to cause pain and grief to others for no other reason than his own perverse amusement.

CHAPTER 28

"You are very subdued, Eva. This journey is supposed to be fun for you, but you have been lost in your thoughts for long stretches, and are now again."

Eva pulled herself out of her thoughts. She squeezed the hand of the man riding beside her in the coach. "I am sorry. I received a letter from Sarah right before you came by to get me."

"Bad news?"

"Not really bad, although Sarah is beside herself. It appears Mr. Trenton has been calling frequently now that Rebecca is staying in Birmingham again."

"The poet."

"Yes. Worse, however, is that Mr. Mansfield has not been calling at all. Sarah is sure that Rebecca has ruined her chances there."

"If she did not favor the man, you would not want her to marry him, would you? Life is long to be in a marriage one does not want."

Very true. Eva could not fault that response. Besides, she would never want Rebecca to be one of those girls who finds herself merely tolerating the marriage bed. Not when she knew herself how wonderful that could be.

"But *Mr. Trenton*?" She sighed. "Am I too horrible for hoping my sister marries a man with at least a modest fortune and decent prospects?"

"She is young still. Eventually she will talk philosophy with Mr. Trenton, too, and that should end that flirtation."

She laughed. The duke had told Gareth that upon his arrival in her home, he had found Wiggins close to tears, holding his head, while Rebecca lectured him. Wiggins had told Lance he would rather be sent to the hulls than spend one more minute listening to her.

"We are entering the town," Gareth said, pointing out the window.

"Are you going to tell me which town it is now? Your secrecy has been peculiar."

"It is Coventry. When we pass through the oldest section, you can imagine Lady Godiva riding slowly on her horse. Out of respect, everyone went inside and shuttered their windows, so her gesture on their behalf would not carry the humiliation her husband intended."

The carriage took them to those lanes, then turned off onto another one with fine houses lining it. It stopped in front of one that looked to be the sort that would house a prosperous merchant. Three stories high and built of cleanly dressed white stone, it had a small garden in front surrounded by an iron fence and gate.

Gareth opened the carriage door and stepped out. "I want you to meet someone."

She accepted his hand and joined him on the pavement. "Who?"

"My mother."

She instinctively dug in her heels. "You might have warned me."

"I might have, but I didn't."

She felt her hair, to make sure it had not been too ruined by an indiscretion that took place in the carriage an hour ago. "Under the circumstances, you should not have been wicked. She is sure to know just looking at us." She gave him an examination and found no evidence at all. "Fine. By looking at *me*."

"Do not worry. A mother knows her son. If she guesses, she will blame me, not think badly of you." He took her hand. "Come now. You will like her."

They entered the house through a door held by a manservant. A footman escorted them to a drawing room. Upon their arrival, a woman looked up. No one had to say this was Gareth's mother. They looked much alike. She was not a pretty woman. Perhaps not even beautiful in the usual way. But her dark eyes and hair, and wide mouth and chiseled face created a memorable, striking visage that might make more predictable beauty appear shallow and boring.

Her eyebrows rose when she saw Eva. This visit was equally a surprise for her, it appeared.

"Mother, I would like you to meet Miss Russell, a neighbor of mine. Miss Russell, this is my mother, Mrs. Johnson."

"She is not only a neighbor." His mother stated that as soon as Eva left the drawing room. On hearing the house had a good garden, she had asked to see it, after suffering through a pointed interview in which his mother asked about her family, her life, her education, and a number of other motherly questions.

"No."

"You have never brought one of your lovers to meet me before."

"No."

His mother sipped the remnants of her tea. He waited.

"She has almost no fortune. Her family lands are much diminished, and what there is must be shared with that sister. She has been on the shelf for some years already, and while she is attractive, she is not a great beauty like some of the women you have known."

Had the list of deficiencies come from anyone else, he would have responded harshly. She was only being a mother, however. He was just lucky that Eva did not have one who could point out what he lacked.

"She suits me."

She laughed. "They have all suited you, for a while."

"I think she will suit me for a long while. A very long while."

She appeared a little dismayed.

"I came to tell you that the property is mine now. Lance withdrew the petition. The house is mine, and the property, as my father wanted."

Her face lit with joy. "I never thought I would see this day. I am happy for you, and glad that Allen's wishes have been respected."

"It should be habitable by summer's end. I would like you to visit Albany Lodge in the autumn, and see what I have made of it."

She stilled. Her expression became unfathomable. "Albany Lodge?"

"I suppose I never told you. That is the name I gave it."

"Your brothers do not mind?"

"It is not for them to mind or not. However, neither seemed shocked or unhappy about it."

Her proud expression trembled. Her eyes filmed. He went over and sat beside her and took her hands in his.

She sniffed, and dabbed her eyes with her delicate handkerchief. "Thank you. I am honored, Gareth." She composed herself, and gripped his hands. "That young woman. If you get her with child, you must do the right thing."

"Yes, Mother."

"You will have no excuse, and it will not do to have a whole line of bastards in the family."

He laughed. "Yes, Mother."

She smacked his shoulder. "Oh, stop that. I am glad you care about her. You would have never brought her here otherwise. Go to her now, and be on your way."

He stood, then bent and kissed her head. "I will see you again soon."

He was almost at the door when she spoke again. "Gareth, do you think there is any chance that you may in fact someday get her with child? That I may someday have a grandchild?"

He smiled, and went out to the garden.

"I think we should get married, Eva."

Eva blinked, and looked down her body to where Gareth's dark head nestled between her thighs. He did something that made her groan fill her garden.

"I— This is most—" She tried to speak through her astonishment and madness.

He did it again. She almost fainted. When her head cleared, she was clutching at grass, gasping for breath. "Stop that! We need to talk."

"One moment. It would be rude to leave you like this."

He didn't, of course. He never did. With alarming efficiency he sent her crashing into a climax, then moved up to lie with her.

She took several minutes to collect herself, then held his head and looked in his eyes. "That may be the most unusual proposal a woman has ever received."

"Thank you. I thought it inventive."

"It will be hard to describe when friends ask for the particulars, however. Did he kneel, Eva? Did he wait for a glorious sunset? Actually, no, Sarah. He proposed while his tongue was making shocking explorations of my private parts."

He pecked a kiss on her cheek. "At least you will never forget it."

No. Never.

"I thought you did not believe in marriage except in the most practical ways. There is nothing about marrying me that will enhance your fortune, so this makes no sense."

He ran the side of his finger along her jaw. "I have discovered that my views on the matter were ill considered. About marriage, and about love."

"They were? About love too?"

"Definitely about love. As you might imagine, I am astonished to learn how wrong I was."

"Just how wrong were you?"

He laughed. "You are not going to make this easy, are you?"

"After all your fine talk about it in the past, I want to hear a full recanting."

"Not a recanting. A codicil. An addition."

She waited.

"All that I said that day still is true, usually. However, if a person is very lucky, it is possible for him to feel a very special love for a woman. One that affects the pleasure in the best ways, and is bigger than it, or anything else centered on himself."

Her throat burned. She pressed a kiss to his lips.

"And if that man is truly lucky," he said. "That woman has the same love for him. Do you, Eva?"

She nodded. "Oh, yes. Yes, I do."

"Then I want to know that you will be mine forever. I want us to marry."

She did not know what to say. She had prepared no answer, since she had never expected to hear the question. "Were this only about love, I would agree with all my heart, Gareth. I have fallen desperately in love with you, despite my better judgment and even expecting it to cause me heartache."

"There will be no heartache. I promise you that. I cannot blame you if you do not believe me, but I will never hurt you in any way."

"After being bad for so long, do you really think you can stop?"

"I swear I will. I'll still get to be bad with you, of course. You would not want me if I were too good."

"If we are married, what we do would not be truly wicked anymore."

He laughed, and tapped her nose with his fingertip. "You are adorable, and still at least half-ignorant. There is much we will do that you will still find very wicked, even if we are married."

"There is?"

"We have barely begun to tap the variety of the pleasures you will know."

She laughed, and kissed him. "I think you are trying to bribe me."

"Think of it as negotiating the settlement."

She climbed on top of him so she could embrace him closely, with her ear to his chest and her body molded to his.

"We are agreed then?" He held her closely. "I want you to know that I have found a way to allow you to still see your own plans through."

She had been too happy to think about her plans and how marriage did not fit them. "I expect I will have to alter them a bit."

"Not much. Rockport proposed I broker sales for him on the Continent, much as I have at times brokered art collections. If even half of what he said comes to pass, we will have all the servants you need. We can spend some time in London each year, so you can study your art too. Or you can have a house in Birmingham, and study with a master there."

She rose up so she looked down on him. "You are going to take employment with Wesley?"

"Not really. I will be doing what I have always done for years now, however."

"You do know that you do not have to marry me to have me, don't you?"

He reached up and cupped her face with his hands. "Have you already forgotten the most important part? I love you, Eva. I do not want you as a mistress. I want us to live together so I can have you whenever I like, and so we both have a place in the world and it is together." He pressed her head down and kissed her. "Say you will marry me, Eva. You have not yet. Not properly."

She wiped the brimming tears from her eyes. "Yes, I will. Yes."

He worked the buttons of his trousers. "Then open to me now, before I die from wanting you."

She helped to free him from his garments, then rose up and lowered herself, taking him inside her. They neither moved for a while, but remained still in this first union of their life together. She savored each instant, so she would remember forever how she felt.

Then Gareth caressed down her back, and lower still until his fingers explored in a most shocking way. His eyes flashed naughty lights at her reaction.

She reached back and smacked his hand away, then rode him with joyful pleasure.

Read on for a special preview of the next
historical romance from Madeline Hunter

TALL, DARK, AND WICKED

Coming soon from Jove Books

Loyal.
Good-humored.
Clean.
Intelligent.
Uninhibited.
Passionate.
Accommodating.

Lord Ywain Hemingford—Ives to his family and closest friends—read the list of the qualities he required in a mistress. He had jotted them down, in no particular order, during an idle moment the day before. Only the first one deserved its ranking without question. In fact, it should be underlined. There were other qualities that attracted him, too, but these

seven, he had learned through experience, were para-
mount.

He tucked the paper behind some pages, to be later
returned to its current duty as a marker in his book.
He settled into his favorite chair, propped his legs on
a footstool with his feet aimed toward the low fire,
and again turned his attention to a novel he had been
meaning to read for four months now.

Vickers, his manservant, set a glass and two
decanters—one of port and the other of water—on a
table next to the chair, then stepped back out of view.

"If your brother the duke should come by this evening, sir, should—"

"Deny him entrance. Bar the door. I am not home
to him. If God had any mercy he would have inspired
Lance to remain at Merrywood, not allowed him to
venture back up to town where he will be a nuisance
to all whom he encounters. I am done with being his
playmate, or his nursemaid." At least for a while, he
added to himself. After a recent, renewed week of
barking, the hounds had again retreated, but they had
not given up the hunt.

Ives did not mind being his brother's keeper. He
resented very much playing the role for a brother who
treated his advice like it came from an old aunt. One
would think that a man under suspicion of murder
would be more circumspect in his speech and actions,
and want to create favorable impressions, not stick out
his tongue at society whenever he could.

"Very good, sir."

Padding steps. A door closing. Peace. Ives closed his eyes and savored for a moment that rarity in his life—freedom to do whatever he damned well pleased, whenever he chose, with nary a claim on his time or attention.

Several developments allowed this respite besides the dwindling interest in Lance by magistrates out for blood. No cases awaited his eloquence in court for at least a fortnight. By coincidence, his mistress had a week ago been most disloyal, giving him the excuse he had sought for some time to part with her.

That left him free of her too. Of attending on her. Of purchasing gifts. Of feeding her vanity. Of joining in little parties that she liked to hold that bored him more than he ever let her know.

It did, of course, also leave him free of a sexual companion. That was not a situation that he by nature welcomed, but he did not mind too much. Contemplating with whom to end his abstinence would give his forays out on the town an enlivening distraction.

He anticipated a glorious stretch of pointless activity. Several long rides in the country beckoned, following whim more than roads or maps. A stack of books like this one waited, too long unread. He could indulge in regular practice with sword and fists, to improve his prowess at fighting with both. And he looked forward to at least one good long debauch of drunkenness with old friends too long neglected.

"Sir."

Vickers's voice, right at his shoulder, surprised him. He had not heard Vickers return.

"Sir, there is a visitor."

"Throw him out, I told you."

"It is not your brother. It is a woman. She says she has come on business. She says you were recommended to her."

Exhaling a sigh, Ives held out his palm.

"She gave me no card, sir. I would have sent her on her way, but she would not indicate just who had recommended you, and the last time such an unnamed recommendation came your way it was from—"

"Yes, quite right." Damnation. If someone, or even Someone, thought to interfere with the next fortnight by having him running around England on some mission or investigation, Someone was very much mistaken. Still, he should at least meet this woman and hear her out, so he could construct a good reason why he could not help her.

He stood, and looked down at himself. He wore a long banyan over his shirt and trousers. The notion of dressing again raised the devil in him. Hell, it was long past time to call at a lawyer's office, even if Someone recommended him. He would be too informal for a stranger, or for business, but he was hardly in a nightshirt. This woman would just have to forgive him his dishabille. With luck she would realize she had interfered with his evening, which she rudely had, and make quick work of whatever she wanted.

He walked to the office. She was probably a petitioner for some reform cause, or the relative of a friend looking for his advice on which solicitor to hire. Her mission this evening no doubt could have been completed more humanely by writing a letter.

He opened the door to his office, and immediately knew that his visitor had not been recommended by anyone significant, let alone Someone really important. Her plain gray dress marked her as a servant. He could not see one bit of adornment on either it or the dull green spencer buttoned high on her chest. The simplest bonnet he had seen in months covered her black hair and framed her face.

Eyes lowered, lost in her thoughts, she had not heard him. He considered stepping out just as silently, and telling Vickers to send her away. He placed one foot back to do so.

Just then she lifted a handkerchief to her eyes—nice eyes, he could not help but notice, with thick, black lashes that contrasted starkly with her pale skin. Radiant skin, as it happened, giving her face a notable presence, if he did say so, even if she was not a beautiful woman. Handsome, however, even if somewhat sharp featured.

She dabbed at tears. Her reserved expression crumbled under emotion.

He hated seeing women cry. Hated it. His easy sympathy had caused him nothing but trouble in the past too. Still—

Hell.

He waited until she composed herself, then walked forward.

Padua sniffed, and not only to hold back the tears that the day tried to force on her. She also checked for the tenth time to discover if her garments still smelled.

They did. In fact, they stunk.

Newgate Prison reeked. The stench that London gave off seemed to concentrate in the Old City, but Newgate smelled like the source of it all. She had never experienced anything like it. It remained in her nose, and apparently it had permeated her clothing.

She sat rigidly on the chair the servant had pointed out, and debated whether to open one of the windows to the autumn breeze. Her surroundings caused a good deal of worry to spike. She had perhaps been rash in following the advice to seek out this lawyer. Probably so, considering the person who had given the advice had been a bawd incarcerated in the prison.

Normally, she would not take advice from a prostitute or a criminal. Yet when that woman called her over as she found her way out of the prison, and showed sympathy, she had not been herself. Just talking to someone eased her distress. After hearing her tale of woe, that woman advised she get a lawyer, and even provided the name of one who had aided a relative who was wrongly accused. Suddenly the prostitute appeared as an angel sent by Providence to offer guidance out of the Valley of Despair.

Now she awaited that lawyer's attendance. Not only a lawyer, but also a lord. She thought it odd that a lord was a lawyer. She would assume the bawd erred on that, except the servant here did not blink when she used the title in requesting an audience.

Now that she was here, she could believe the lord part. Although she sat in his chambers, this was no apartment, nor merely a set of offices. Rather, she sat on the entry level of what appeared to be a new house facing Lincoln's Inn Fields. There had been nothing to indicate that others lived or worked above. This lawyer had a good deal of money if this whole building was his home.

The mahogany furniture and expensive bookbindings said as much. Her feet rested half submerged in the dense pile of the carpet on the floor. Her rump perched on a chair that must have cost many pounds. Real paintings decorated the walls, not engravings done after famous works of art.

His fees were probably very high. She doubted she could afford them. The bawd had guessed as much. *If you've not the coin to pay him, he'll probably take other payment, dear. Them that works our side of the Old Bailey almost all do.*

Could she agree to that? It would disgust her. She recoiled from the idea. Only in the most desperate of circumstances would she stoop so low.

She closed her eyes, and immediately was back in the prison, peering into a cell full of men. The stench, the dirt, the ugly sounds all assaulted her senses again. Hopelessness and death reigned in Newgate Prison. No one would leave a loved one inside it if she had the means to get him out.

These were indeed desperate circumstances.

Tears pooled in her eyes. She dabbed them away with her handkerchief and fought for composure. She never cried, but this was not a normal day in so many ways.

"You asked to see me."

The voice jolted her out of her reverie and drew her attention to the man suddenly standing ten feet in front of her.

His appearance startled her in other ways too. He was not what she expected. Not at all.

She had pictured a man of middle years with gray hair and spectacles and a face wizened with experience. He would wear dark coats and a crisp cravat and be accompanied by a clerk or two.

Instead the man assessing her—there was no other word for the way his gaze took her in—could be no older than thirty or so. He possessed classically handsome features and a fashionable mane of dark brown hair of an enviable hue. He wore a long banyan that could pass for a greatcoat if not made of midnight brocade instead of wool.

An impressive man. His green eyes captivated

one's attention. Right now they reflected aloof displeasure. Very attractive eyes, however. Intelligent. Expressive.

She found her wits. "Are you Lord Ywain Hemingford?" She had no idea how to pronounce Ywain. Surely not Ya-wane, as the bawd had. She tried EE-wane instead. His subtle wince said she got it wrong.

"I am. You have me at a disadvantage, however." Those eyes flashed a spark of impatience.

"My apologies. My name is Padua Belvoir." She took in his informal dress. "I have intruded at the wrong time. I am sorry about that too. I have been so distraught I have not paid proper mind to the hour, and I could not rest until I sought the help I need anyway."

"You told my man you were recommended to find me. May I ask by whom?"

By a prostitute in Newgate Prison. "I do not think she wants me to tell you her name."

He strolled across the chamber. "I assume you are here regarding a criminal matter."

"How did you know?"

"Because that is the only reason she would not want her name used, and because from the smell of you, you have recently been in Newgate." Ever so calmly, he opened one of the windows. A crisp breeze poured in.

She felt her face burning.

"Please, do not be embarrassed. The prison is a fetid place," he said. "I had a coat that had to be burned after I wore it there one summer day."

"It is not only fetid, but horrible in every way. The conditions are disgraceful. The inmates are wretched."

He settled his tall body into a chair near hers. He sat in it like a king might sit on a throne. His arms rested along the tops of its sides and his hands hung in front of its carving. "I thought you had come to request a donation, perhaps in order to attempt to improve those conditions. Just as well you did not. It would be a noble but futile quest. People tend not to worry overmuch if criminals are not comfortable."

"I am not here to ask for a charitable donation, although someday I hope to have the time to devote to such good causes. And not everyone in that prison is a criminal."

"I assure you that most are." He offered a half smile, no more. "Since you do not want money, perhaps you will explain what you do want."

"I want your eloquence and skill to help my father, who has been so affected by prison that he is too weak to help himself. He has been wrongly accused of a crime."

"How long has he been there?"

"At least two weeks, but perhaps a month. I only learned about it yesterday. I received a letter, from whom I do not know, telling me. Normally I receive news from him at least once a month. It has been some six weeks since I last received a letter, so I had become concerned."

"Why did you not visit him, and see what was wrong, if the letter did not come?"

"We are somewhat estranged. There was no argument between us. He is just not by nature a warm man, and is much engaged in his own pursuits. I could not visit, because I do not know where he lives in London."

More than somewhat estranged if you did not know where he lived. He did not say it, but she could see the reaction in his eyes.

"I went to Newgate to inquire after him. I was allowed to see him. He is in a large cell with many rough fellows. He is unwashed and unshaved and frightened. I fear he will get ill there. So many others are sick."

"Why was he put there?"

"He would not tell me. I wonder if he even knows. If he does, he did not admit it, nor accept my offer of help. He told me to leave and not come back."

"Miss Belvoir, I am sure you were dismayed to find your father in a cell with men unsuitable for polite society. However, if you do not know the crime with which he is accused, how can you know that he is wrongly accused? His refusal to speak of it even with you suggests the opposite."

"My father is no criminal, sir. He is a scholar. He has taught at universities throughout the Continent and had a position as a teacher at Oxford until he married my mother. He spends all his time on his research and his books, and is more apt to argue over some debatable mathematical proof than politics. There can be no justifiable reason for him to be imprisoned, unless being an intellectual has now become a crime. A serious miscarriage of justice is about to occur."

It poured out nonstop, the way her excitement often betrayed her. Lord Ywain just sat there, listening, exerting a presence that crowded her despite his sitting six feet away. He did not appear especially interested.

"You are sure of this?" he said.

"Positive."

"And yet you do not even know where he lives in London." His words did not dismiss her outright, but his expression almost did. His eyes had narrowed over his smile in a way that suggested he had heard petitions like hers from relatives many times in the past.

She felt her best chance to help her father slipping away.

"I beg you not to think his silence is an admission of guilt. He is a proud man, and I think he is too embarrassed to let me know the details and hoped I would remain ignorant and think if he disappeared he had fallen in the river, which, with his tendency to distraction, would not be unthinkable."

"Miss Belvoir, I have known innocent people who initially took that stance with relatives. It never lasts three days in Newgate, let alone two weeks or more. The guilty, on the other hand—"

"I told him that his silence was foolhardy. That is why I am here. I was told that some people have lawyers at their trials now. I was told that you at times speak for those accused." *Slow down. Stop gushing words*. "My father is incapable of defending himself, and may even be unwilling to do so. The accusations are insulting, and he is the sort to refuse to engage in the insult by refuting it."

Lord Ywain had not moved. Those hands still rested at the end of the chair's arms. Nice hands, as handsome as his face. His gaze had not left her, and the shifts regarding what he looked at had been subtle but unmistakable. Not only her face had been measured. She did not think she had been as closely examined in her life, let alone by a man like this one.

In a different circumstance she might be flattered, but the bawd's words made the attention dangerous. He did not appear of a predatory nature, and a man like this hardly needed to take advantage of an accused man's female relatives if he wanted to satisfy carnal needs. However, she was not accustomed to attracting the less despicable version of that kind of attention, so it raised some alarm and a good deal of confusion.

"You do not know the accusations, so you cannot say they are insulting," he said.

"Any accusation of a crime would be insulting to a man like my father. If you met him you would understand what I mean. Hadrian Belvoir is the least likely criminal in the world. Truly."

The smallest frown flexed on his brow. His attention shifted again, to the inside of his head. She ceased to exist for a long moment. He stood abruptly. "Excuse me, please. I will return momentarily."

Then he was gone, his midnight banyan billowing
behind him.

H adrian Belvoir.
　　Ever since his visitor introduced herself, an
indefinable something had nudged at Ives. The pokes
implied he should know her, yet nothing about her
was familiar.

Hadrian Belvoir. That name did more than poke.

He strode up to his private chambers, to a writing
desk there where he dealt with personal letters. He
pawed through a thick stack of old mail, discarding it
piece by piece, frowning while he sought the letter he
wanted. Finally he found it.

He flipped it open and held it near the lamp. There
that name was, buried amidst a casual communica-
tion. *You can expect to be asked to be Prosecutor for
a Hadrian Belvoir, once his case is brought forward.*

He checked the date. This had been written a month
ago. No wonder the name had not been in the front of
his memory. If Mr. Belvoir resided in Newgate Prison,
why had this informal approach not turned into a
formal one by now? It was possible his victims had
hired their own prosecutor, of course, but if that were
likely, this sentence would never have been written.

Whatever the situation, it was time to inform Miss
Belvoir that she must look elsewhere.

He returned to the office and the bright-eyed Miss

Belvoir. He had realized, while she talked and talked, that her eyes sparkled even when she did not cry. He had also calculated that if she stood she would be very tall. An idle curiosity had crossed his mind, about what it was like to take a very tall woman. His mind had pictured it, making the necessary adjustments . . .

Probably just as well if she looked elsewhere.

No sooner had he walked into the chamber than she started again. "I think you can see that a great injustice will occur if my father does not receive your help, sir. I beg you to consider accepting his case. I am prepared to pay you whatever fees you require."

Not likely, from the looks of that dress and spencer. "Miss Belvoir, allow me to explain that I will be accepting no financial remuneration from you or anyone else for defending in this matter."

She went still. Her lips parted in surprise. He felt bad that she was shocked at his refusal, but there was nothing else for it.

"I see." She stroked her hands nervously over her lap. "I was told that with the Old Bailey, things are often done differently. When it comes to lawyers, that is."

The least he could do, since his evening was already ruined, was give her some guidance in seeking another. "It does not work the way it does in the other courts, like Chancery, that is true. The hiring of lawyers for criminal cases is admittedly crude in comparison."

"I understand completely. I was told what to expect, and that it is customary for those who argue in the

Old Bailey to anticipate payment coming to them another way."

"That is certainly true for barristers like myself."

"My only concern is the extent and timing of such payment. Paying up front might make sense to you, since you will then know you have been paid, but I, on the other hand, will not know you in fact defended until you are committed by the trial being under way. Would the end of the first day of the trial be equitable?"

He had thought she understood how barristers were not paid directly, but apparently not. "Miss Belvoir—"

She held up a hand. "Please, allow me to find out what I face, before I lose my nerve." She stood and began pacing nervously. "Since we are strangers, I would appreciate if this payment were of the most basic sort. Would that be agreeable to you? I am worried I will be grievously shocked or repulsed if more adventure is sought under these circumstances. Oh, dear, you appear taken aback by that. Have I made a blunder in attempting to make that demand? I suppose, if it is absolutely necessary, I might consider a small range of alternatives of the milder variety. If you insist, that is."

Taken aback did not do justice to his reaction. Her assumptions, now clear, stunned him. He was torn between being very amused and highly insulted.

"I suppose I should also make sure I understand what is expected, as to the amount of time involved, so I do not—"

"Miss Belvoir, I must insist you stop. As a gentleman I must, although I confess a profound curiosity as to the time involved." He went to her, took her hand, and led her back to her chair. "When I said I would not accept financial remuneration, I did not mean I wanted other payment. Certainly not the kind I believe you have alluded to."

"But I was told—"

"So you said. In my case, you were told wrong." Not in every lawyer's case, however. He pictured her trying to hire a solicitor without much money. There were those who would strike the bargain she outlined.

She looked up at him, confused. "Are you saying you will do it for free?"

"I am saying that barristers do not get paid by clients, they are engaged by solicitors who take care of such things. Barristers will be insulted if you offer to pay them like they are tradesmen."

"So I must first find a solicitor and have him ask you. Instead of one lawyer I must hire two."

"You must find a solicitor to investigate, but I will not be the barrister he engages to argue the case in the courtroom. I cannot be the defending lawyer. When you mentioned your father's name, I realized I have already been approached to serve on the other side."

"Other side?"

"Prosecutor."

She looked away. She remained immobile and silent for a long count, while her pale face took on a very rosy hue. She shot him an accusing glance. "You might have stopped me sooner."

"I would have if you had made your meaning clear at the outset."

"I think you did not because in your mind you were laughing at me."

"Miss Belvoir, laughing is the last reaction a man has when a woman offers herself with such specific and lengthy detail."

Those lashes lowered. "You do understand I would have never said any of that if I did not believe it to be required in order to help my father."

"Your devotion to him is laudable."

He expected more reaction. Anger, perhaps even tears. Certainly more umbrage that he allowed her to get in so deep in describing her alternate payment.

Her forthrightness about it all fascinated him, as did her clear and passionate articulation of the terms. She had said enough, euphemistically, to suggest she was no innocent and not averse to adventure given a different circumstance.

. . . Intelligent
Uninhibited
Passionate
Accommodating . . .

No, that would never do. Pity.

She turned those eyes on him fully. She gave him a good look. He saw her mind working at something. Hesitation flickered, then resolve. "I wonder, sir. Are prosecutors ever persuaded to put forth something other than their best efforts?"

Considering the currency under discussion, it was

probably the most enticing bribe he had ever been offered. "Not this one."

"Forgive me for asking, and for insulting you, but I had to try." She stood, which brought her close to him. Her crown reached his nose. "I am sorry to have taken your time, and at an unsuitable hour at that."

She walked toward the door.

"I will find out about the charges," he said. "That way you will know what you face, at least. Leave your address with my man, and I will make sure you are informed."

She turned. "Thank you. That is very kind, coming from someone I must now see as an adversary."

"It is the least I can do, considering all you were willing to sacrifice."

She blushed deeply, turned on her heel, and strode out.

From *New York Times* bestselling author
MADELINE HUNTER

The Accidental Duchess

When Lady Lydia Alfreton is blackmailed over the shocking contents of a manuscript she wrote, she must go to the most desperate of measures to raise the money to buy back the ill-considered prose: agreeing to an old wager posed by the arrogant, dangerous Duke of Penthurst, a man determined to tame her rebellious ways...

madelinehunter.com
facebook.com/MadelineHunter
facebook.com/LoveAlwaysBooks
penguin.com